STITCHES

A MÈNAGE ROMANCE

SAM MARIANO

D1698386

ISBN: 9781983795718

Stitches © 2018 by Sam Mariano

Cover by: K+A Designs

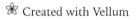 Created with Vellum

Author's Note:

Since I don't normally write ménage romance and I don't want to throw my regular readership, I wanted to include a brief note. This is specified in the blurb (and Amazon subtitle) but for those who may have missed it, this is a *ménage romance*. MFM ménage romance, which means two men with a romantic interest in the same woman. It is not a love triangle. This is simply a less traditional love story; there are two heroes and one heroine.

If you're open to all that, I hope you enjoy the story of Sebastian, Griff, and Moira! :)

1

SEBASTIAN

THIS IS NOT HOW I WANTED TO END MY WORK DAY.

This is not how I want to end *any* day.

I drag the little bar at the bottom of my computer screen backward and hit play one more time, filled to the brim with irritation and dread. I know I wasn't mistaken. I know what I'm going to see; I just don't know what the hell to do about it.

The grainy footage shows an attractive blonde woman standing in a hall, a random man pressed right up against her. She fists her hands in the fabric of his T-shirt and looks up at him, her eyes swimming with manufactured conflict—anything to raise the stakes and make the stolen moment more exciting. She wavers, grabs the back of his neck, and pulls him in for a kiss. The man wastes no time, palming her breast over the material of her slinky dress, then hiking her thigh up and pushing between her legs. She moans and tilts her head back, as if in ecstasy.

"We can't," she says. It's so flimsy. It's not an objection, really, it's an invitation for him to show her how much he wants her, how nothing could possibly stop him from having her, even if only for a fleeting encounter.

Not even the $27,000 worth of commitment jewelry on her left hand.

Not even her husband.

Luckily, *I* am not that husband.

Unluckily, my best friend *is*.

I watch the screen for a another minute, just to verify my mind isn't playing tricks on me—Ashley *did*, in fact, let another man fuck her in the hallway of the club her husband and I co-own together, knowing full-well we have security cameras on the place.

This is a fucking disaster.

This is going to crush him into a million tiny pieces that *I'm* going to have to sweep up.

Five years together and she pulls this shit. Cuckolds my best friend like an asshole. Personally, I never thought this bitch was right for him, but she could at least have the decency to appreciate her good fortune. Griff has gone out of his way for Ashley from the moment he met her—love at first sight, if such a thing ever existed—and she never seems to give anything back.

This isn't even the first time I've had to deal with this shit. The first time was two years ago. She hooked up with a drunken customer after the place closed. I confronted her the next morning and she sobbed, told me it had been a mistake. Me, I don't believe in that kind of mistake. In the five years I've been with Moira, I've had more than a few women try tempting me to fuck around on her. I've never considered it for a single second.

Ashley has now fucked around on Griff *at least* twice.

I never told him the first time. The knowledge would have crushed him, and if it was really a mistake—even if I don't believe in that shit—I didn't want to wreck his life over it. I also didn't want to be the messenger who delivered that kind of news. I didn't want to deal with the inevitable fallout.

But now here I sit, reliving the same fucking bullshit. If she's put me here twice, she'll put me here a third time; I'm gonna have to tell him.

The office door swings open, and Griff peeks his head inside. Sympathy hits me right in the gut. I hastily stop the video, then close the feed altogether and sit forward. "You need something?"

Griff shoots me a funny look since I just acted a little like he walked in on me watching porn. "You done yet? We're supposed to pick up the girls in less than an hour."

Of course. Motherfucking date night. Our wives didn't always get along—Ashley is jealous, hilariously enough, and my stunning wife attracts the gaze of any man in the room, married or not. Griff would never cheat, has never admitted to having any kind of attraction to Moira, but I know he does. It's harmless, but it's there. It's not just the long raven locks that cascade down her creamy shoulders, drawing the eye to her magnificent breasts. It's not her narrow waist and flared hips, or the magnificent ass on that woman. Moira's got a good heart. She'd give you the shirt off her back, the shoes off her feet. She would open our front door to the sketchiest fucking vagrant and ask them in for a nice, hot shower and a warm meal. She loves and she loves, and she never asks for anything in return.

I shower her with everything, though. She deserves everything.

I'm the luckiest bastard in this city, maybe in the world.

And then there's Griff, stuck with Ashley—this skank who can't keep her legs closed despite being married to a man who would do literally anything for her.

Since Griff doesn't know any of this, he cocks a golden brow and awaits my response.

"Yeah, just give me a minute."

I watch until he backs out into the hall, closing the door behind him. Then I sigh, my head lolling back, and massage the bridge of my nose.

I can't tell him right now. Ashley needs to be dealt with—I told her last time I wouldn't cover her ass again—but right now all I can do is go home to *my* wife and endure what may be the last couples night she's gonna get.

———

TWO WILLOWY ARMS reach for me, locking around my neck and drawing me close. I look into my wife's beautiful face, her big blue eyes so full of fondness at the sight of me. I know a lot of men, some of them married, but I don't know any who are lucky enough to come home to their wife of five years and still have her look at them like this. Like because I came home, there is happiness in her life. Because I am hers, she always has a reason to smile.

Interrupting my happiness is the idea of Griff having to see this tomorrow, or the next day, or the day after that. Normally he rolls his eyes at us. Calls us newlyweds. We still act like it, I guess. I just thought this was what a happy marriage looked like, but he and Ashley have never had this.

Ashley and Moira are mirror opposites. Where Moira is sweet, Ashley has a bitchiness I've never found appealing. Griff didn't see it at first. It didn't come out until she got comfortable with him. The high of a new relationship makes her soft and excites her, but once she settles into it, she gets bored. She starts looking around at everyone else, wondering why she doesn't have what they have.

The day I met Moira, everything changed for me and Griff. Me, I don't believe in any kind of love at first sight, but I can't deny *connection* at first sight.

When I met Moira she was a waitress at a little coffee house, serving up specialty drinks, bringing out plates full of scones and shit. Frankly, there's no reason we should've met. I wasn't in the habit of wasting my time in places like that, or my hard-earned money on pricey frozen coffees. I just had to piss, and the establishment she worked at had the "customers only" rule for their bathroom. I bought a muffin, and as I dug some cash out of my wallet, I caught sight of a petite woman with shoulder-length hair, so dark it was nearly black. She knocked an iced coffee off the counter and looked horrified as it fell to the floor and splashed all over the fitted black pants clinging to her shapely legs. Flushing, she bent to pick it up, darting a look up at me.

Something lodged in my gut. I'd been with pretty girls all my adult life, but it wasn't just her looks. I wasn't even sure what it was. She quickly stood and shoved the stuff off to the side, shooting me an apologetic smile. "Sorry about your wait; just give me two seconds." She turned around and washed up at the sink, then came back to fill my muffin order. As she handed it to me, she flashed me a sweet smile. It was the first time I'd ever looked into someone's eyes and seen pure kindness.

I knew she had a well of it, and to be honest, I am not a particularly kind man. Over the years, I've stepped on people and taken advantage, walked right over men and right out on women to build something for myself.

Well, myself and Griff. We'd been a team since we were kids, and that'll never change. There's no blood between us, but he's the closest thing I've ever had to a brother.

I went back to that little coffee shop four times after that. Moira was only there three of those times, but at the end of that last transaction, as she slid my coffee across the counter and smiled at me, I told her, "I want to take you out."

Her blue eyes widened with surprise, her kind smile slipping. "Out?"

I nodded once, like I couldn't afford to waste them. "I'm gonna take you out," I stated. "What time do you get off tonight?"

She flushed with pleasure and looked down at the counter, nibbling on her bottom lip. It could have agitated her the way I *told* her we were going out instead of asking, the way I didn't bother asking if I had any competition, if there might be some poor sap waiting at home for her. I didn't care if there was. I wanted what I wanted, and if there was anything in my way, it needed to move. I didn't even ask if she was free tonight, just claimed her time as my own. Plenty of women might take issue with that, but not Moira. She mulled it over for a few seconds, then looked back up at me and finally answered, "I get off at seven."

Right then I had the slightest hunch she might be made for me. "Then I'll see you at seven," I told her, taking my coffee, winking, and walking out.

By the time our first date ended, she had me. She was still dressed from work when I picked her up since I didn't give her time to change, but she didn't complain. I took her somewhere simple—I don't like to take women on fancy first dates; I like to see how they respond when I just take them to a deli or something, only buy them a sandwich that costs a few dollars. Call me paranoid, but there are plenty of money-grabbers out there and I like to filter 'em out.

Moira didn't care that I took her to a $12 dinner for the first date I demanded she go on with me. It was my company she enjoyed, my personality she was drawn to, and that was exactly what I wanted.

Moira went on plenty of expensive dates after that. When I asked her to marry me, I spared no expense on the ring. I'm no cheapskate; I just don't like materialistic user assholes like Ashley Halliwell.

Once Moira and I got together, though, she sort of took over my life. I loved having her around and never wanted to be without her. Griff and I used to hang out every night before Moira, but once I had her, that left Griff alone a lot. Moira didn't want him to feel excluded, so she'd ask me to invite him over from time to time—she'd make us both dinner, we'd all watch a movie or play a board game. We'd drink together sometimes, and Moira would tell us dirty stories that made Griff get all bashful, since he didn't think he should be listening to dirty stories my girlfriend made up.

Then he met Ashley, and all of a sudden, he was in love. Part of me honestly thinks he was just jealous of what Moira and I had, feeling left out, in need of attention. Ashley filled the void I left in Griff's life when Moira crept into my heart and took it over.

Now his heart's going to be broken. Now I have this shit to deal with.

Moira's forehead creases, her blue eyes clouding over with concern as she looks up at me. "What's wrong, honey?"

I shake my head. I do want to tell her, but not when we're about to go out with them. Moira's a shitty liar. She's too open, can't keep a secret to save her life.

I kiss her forehead, tugging her closer and hugging her. "We'll talk about it later."

She still looks concerned, but I turn away and head to the closet for a dinner jacket. Moira follows me in, coming up behind me, her hands sliding up my muscular chest. "Tell your wife what's wrong?"

I smile faintly. "Your tricks won't work on me, little minx."

"My tricks always work on you," she states, letting one of her hands slide down until she's rubbing my cock.

I catch her wrist in a firm grasp to stop her. "I told you, we'll talk about it later."

"But I want to lighten your load *now*," she tells me.

"Then why don't you get on your knees—I'll give you a load."

I'm mostly teasing her, but I should know better. Moira sinks to the floor in front of me, unbuttoning my slacks and dragging them down. She looks up at me playfully, then frees my cock and takes it into her mouth, eager to please me.

Luckiest bastard in the city, I'm telling you.

Once my wife finishes sucking my cock, I *am* feeling a lot better. Griff's problems are still big, but I don't have to think about them for a few hours. Right now I want to take my wife out and let her have a nice night—she can't do that if she's worrying about me the whole time.

It's easy to let go of my cares when it's just me and Moira. It gets a little harder when we get to Griff's house and I see Ashley stroll out in front of him, draped in some expensive fucking designer dress she spent his money on. I'm not a greedy bastard; I worked my ass off to build something for myself so I could enjoy it, and I spare no expense to please *my* little minx, but *she* deserves it. She's loyal and loving, not going behind my back doing things to hurt me.

Meanwhile, Ashley cheats on Griff and treats him like an afterthought. She stops outside the car and fiddles around in her purse, waiting until he comes to open the door for her. He offers her a tepid smile, but she doesn't return it; she just drops into the car, beaming a fake smile at Moira as she slides in beside her.

"Hey, girl."

"Hey. Ooh, I love your dress," Moira enthuses, not knowing we're supposed to be mad at Ashley tonight. I couldn't muster up a compliment for her right now if my life depended on it, but Moira doesn't know any better.

I shake my head at her in the rearview mirror. Griff offers a fond smile at Moira, and at least *she* offers a warm smile back. "Hey, Griff. You look handsome tonight."

There's gruff affection in his tone as he greets her back. "Hey, Moira." Since his wife is less cool about things than I am, he does not offer a compliment back. Moira knows the drill and doesn't expect one.

"Took you long enough," Griff tells me, shutting the passenger side door and shifting around in his seat. "You're slow as fuck today, man. What's your deal?"

"Sorry. My wife was giving me head," I say bluntly.

Moira shoots me a look of disbelief, covering her face with her hands. "Oh, my God, Sebastian."

I grin at her unabashedly in the rearview mirror. "What? It's a good reason."

"That is a good reason," Griff admits, glancing out the window instead of at me.

"You little slut," Ashley jokes.

The fucking gall. She just took a stranger's cock last night, and she's teasing my wife for pleasing her husband.

I can't fucking help myself.

"Well, maybe you and Griff would be in better moods tonight if you'd have sucked *his* before we picked you guys up."

Griff looks over at me and scowls. "Relax. It was a fucking joke. Obviously she doesn't *really* think Moira is a slut."

"Jesus," Ashley huffs. "What's your problem today?"

You're my fucking problem, I want to tell her.

I don't. I turn my attention to the road, avoiding Moira's look of confusion. She wasn't really offended. I'm sure she just took it as Ashley joking around. Even if she knew it was more than that, she would shrug it off. Moira hates conflict.

It's a rough ride to the restaurant. Ashley is in a snit now; Moira is uncomfortable, and Griff seems to think if he looks at me hard enough, he'll be able to see into my head and figure out what the hell is wrong with me.

It was a mistake to come out tonight. I thought we could have one last night out, but I'm too pissed off at Ashley. I'm pissed off for Griff. I'm pissed off for selfish reasons—this is going to be a fucking mess that I don't want to deal with. When I tell him, it's going to break his heart, but I have to. This is the second time I've caught her; that doesn't mean she hasn't done shit like this other times and just been smarter about it. I keep searching her for some sign she feels guilty, but there's nothing.

I've known for years Ashley needed a lot of attention. She's insecure about herself—tries to hide it behind bravado and layers of make-up, but she's missing something inside her. Even though she doesn't have to, she likes to put on slinky clothes or tight tank tops and sop up the male attention she gets working at the club.

Attention is one thing. Fucking the assholes is another.

Maybe it's not her fault one man isn't enough for her, I don't know. All I know is, if she wanted to fuck someone over, I wish she hadn't picked my best friend.

Griff doesn't fall in love easily, but when he does, he really sinks into it. I've always known he's a lifer, since he attached to me and never left my side. It was the same when he fell in love. The first time he'd been young, only 18. Eva, the best friend of a girl I was seeing. He got really attached to her, but she didn't attach the same way. Cracked his heart wide open, then continued to fuck with him on and off for the next year.

After that, he was strictly casual. Me, I've always been pretty casual. I've had exactly three serious relationships—Moira is the third, and obviously the last. Other than that, I liked to keep it light. A few months, tops. Once I started feeling bored, I moved on.

Griff and I were busy anyway. We worked our asses off, pooled our money, built everything together. Accountants told us it wasn't smart, that we should keep our shit more separate than we do, but we knew what we were doing. Griff and I were partners. We were brothers. Whatever we built together, we would enjoy together.

I steal a look over at him now, trying to imagine how I'd feel in his place. I can't even put myself there, though. Moira would never do something like this. She puts the needs of others ahead of her own, and we're happy, anyway.

I wish I could just clone her and give one to Griff; she could fix him right up after Ashley's betrayal slices his heart open.

2

GRIFF

Sebastian is pissed off tonight, and I don't know why.

He's not a short-tempered man to begin with and he usually enjoys when we all go out like this together.

Not tonight. Every time Ashley speaks, he looks at her like her voice offends him. He's not even trying to hide it. When he wants to, he can execute a pretty good poker face. I mean, I know him too well, so I normally see through it, but even Moira can tell he's pissy tonight. Her demeanor is dimmer. Ordinarily, Moira sparkles like a diamond, but tonight she's more subdued, her troubled gaze drifting to Sebastian every few minutes.

They couldn't possibly be having problems, could they? Problems are for mere mortals; they're the golden couple. Ashley and I have problems; Moira and Sebastian still run late to date nights because she wants to worship his cock before they leave for dinner.

Lucky fucking bastard.

I can't remember the last time my cock went anywhere near

Ashley's mouth. We've only had sex once in the last six fucking weeks. I know, because I bought a fresh pack of condoms and there's only one missing. Every time I look at the box in my bedside stand, it aggravates me. Other married guys say shit like that is normal, but then there's Sebastian with the wife who still lusts for him and the relationship that disgusts the rest of us with how fucking perfect it is.

Not that I don't want Seb to be happy. Of course I do. He's had a shit life, and I'm glad he found what he has with Moira.

It would just be kinda nice if I had it, too.

Thinking about it makes *me* glum. My gaze drifts to Moira and I feel myself needing alcohol. Our waiter seems to have disappeared.

I push back my chair, pulling the cloth napkin from my lap and dropping it on the table. "I'm gonna go see if I can get us some more drinks."

Ashley doesn't look up from her phone.

Moira's look of concern drifts to me, then her lips thin with determination and she pushes back her own chair. Seb looks up at her, but she leaves him there and follows me.

Aw, Christ.

"What is up with you two tonight?" she demands, speeding up to match my strides. I ignore her, so she places a hand on my arm, trying to win my attention.

Of course it fucking works. She's hard enough to ignore when she's not touching you.

God, I need whiskey. "Nothing's up," I tell her, cutting in front of her and heading for the bar.

She leans on the bar top right next to me and raises her dark eyebrows. "You are so full of shit. You both are. Sebastian was off earlier too, but no one wants to tell me anything."

"Maybe that's because it's none of your business," I offer, lightly. "You ever think of that?"

"If it involves my husband, it is most certainly my business."

That shouldn't drain the last ray of lightness out of me, but it does. I wish Ashley cared enough to ask me what's wrong when I'm in a shitty mood, let alone fish around and try to drag it out of my best friend.

"Are you and Ashley fighting again?" she asks, suddenly. "You guys seem a little off tonight, too."

"We're not fighting, she's just pouting."

"Why is she pouting?"

"She didn't want to come," I mutter.

The bartender comes over, looking at me expectantly.

"We need drinks," I tell him. "One vodka martini, two whiskeys—no, you know what? Make that three whiskeys. Moira, what do you want?"

She glances back toward our table. "I still have some of that watermelon martini left."

"Get her another watermelon martini," I say, drawing out my wallet.

Moira leans in and nudges my arm playfully. "You don't have to buy me a drink."

My stomach tangles up, old feelings wrapping around my gut like a mess of fucking vines.

I know she's not flirting with me. I know that because I've known Moira for years, I've seen that sparkle in her blue eyes and that playful nudge, the touch of her hand on my arm—I've seen her do all that before, and it's always innocent. I know she doesn't mean anything by it. I know my innards are only responding like she is because my life is a fucking mess right now. Because I'm so fucking unhappy. Ashley's eyes wander all over the place when she's unhappy—she looks for something new. I don't think she'd act on it at this point, but she likes attention, so she'll flirt. It pisses me off, but at least when she pisses me off I can take it out on her in the bedroom. Then we both have a little fucking fun. It fizzles fast, though. One night of good, angry sex does not a marriage make.

My eyes wander sometimes, too, but they never wander far. They wander to the same place they wandered five years ago, when I was terrified I would lose the closest friend I'd ever had.

One sure way to fuck up a friendship? Falling in love with your best friend's girlfriend.

I felt it happening so I pulled back. Not like I would ever act on it, not like I would try to take her away from Seb, but spending so much time with them together had me all twisted up. She'd make us dinner and drinks like some 50's housewife, then she'd tell us naughty stories with her innocent blue eyes sparkling mischievously. Don't know how she managed to look innocent, tossing around the words that tumbled out of that pretty little mouth when she got drunk, but she did.

Then she would lie down on top of Seb right there on the couch and gaze at him like he'd hung the moon. She would kiss him, his hands would roam her body, and I'd feel lonelier than I ever had before, even before I met Seb.

Then I met Ashley. Then I had a girl of my own, and I could save my relationship with Seb. I could even spend time with him and Moira without thinking about what she looked like naked. I got them both back—and a girlfriend, to boot. It was perfect.

It was perfect, but it didn't last. Our relationship moved fast, from dating to married in a little over a year. Seb and Moira weren't even married yet, but they were engaged. Moira had a thing about not getting married until they'd been together for two years. She wanted to make sure when she got married, it was going to last.

That was smart. If I'd have done that, I probably wouldn't be married now.

Ashley cheated on me before our first wedding anniversary, after all.

No one knows, not even Seb. It was just a mistake. Actually, it was the night of their fucking wedding. I tried to do better that night, I tried not to watch Moira so much, but I failed. I counted the dances until I thought it would be appropriate to ask if I could cut in. Then I gave myself a hit of my own temptation. I'd never cheat on Ashley, even if I wasn't happy—I just wouldn't do that to someone. I couldn't deny the rush I felt holding her in my arms, though. I'd been the best man at her wedding. I watched her walk down the aisle in her big white gown, all soft smiles and loving eyes for Seb. I was happy for him, happy for her, but I couldn't shake the whisper at the back of my mind. The one that wondered, could that have been me? If I'd found her first? If things hadn't worked out between them and I could've scooped her up?

It didn't matter, though. I didn't have Moira the way I daydreamed about before Ashley, but this way, I could have them both. I wouldn't lose my best friend, but I could still have a relationship with his wife. A harmless relationship.

I told myself it was harmless to enjoy holding her more than I enjoyed holding my wife. That it was harmless to breathe in her scent and memorize the happy look on her face as I whisked her across the ballroom.

Ashley didn't agree. That was what pushed her to go to the bar and drink too many drinks, what chased her into the arms of someone else.

I left the dance floor feeling good, and I left that wedding feeling fucking crushed. I went home with my wife, visions of another man's hands pushing up her bridesmaid dress and fucking her.

I couldn't touch her for two months.

I tried to forgive her, but I don't know if I ever did. I don't know if she ever forgave me, either. If we ever forgave one another, you certainly can't tell.

Moira nudges me again, but this time she keeps her arm pressed against mine. I'm not sure if she knows quite how capable she is of torturing me, but she must have a little idea or she'd move her damn arm.

"What's wrong?" she asks more solemnly.

I look over at her now. She's so concerned, so eager to listen, so eager to help. She's happy to let me bend her ear.

I could tell her I'm not happy, but it would hurt her heart to know that. She and Seb live in this blissful fucking bubble, and I'm left out in the cold like I always was. Only now I'm out in the cold with another person, and we both sit at the table not even wanting to look at each other while they sit there gazing at one another like two people in love.

Go figure.

"Sometimes…" I shake my head, trying to figure out how to tell her that sometimes being around them shows me all I'm missing out on. That sitting there and seeing them so interested in one another, touching like newlyweds, makes me feel so lonely I wish the floor would open up and swallow me.

Before I can find the words, Seb walks up behind Moira. He snakes his arms around her tiny waist and leans in, kissing the ball of her bare shoulder. "What are you two over here talking about?"

Moira smiles slyly. "Griff here is about to buy me a drink. Are you jealous?"

"So jealous," he says dryly, his hand sliding down and running over her ass. I can't help watching. I may be able to buy her a drink, but I sure as fuck can't do that.

Seb quirks an eyebrow at me and I realize he just watched me watch him touching his wife. That was probably a little… eh, whatever. I need a fucking drink.

The bartender *finally* brings them over. I slam back the first whiskey and push the empty glass back across the counter, then I give Moira and Seb their drinks, picking up mine and Ashley's so we can head back to the table.

Seb hangs back while Moira walks ahead. "Hey, everything okay?"

"Yep, all good."

"Just thirsty?" he asks.

"Yeah," I mutter, "just thirsty."

"WHAT A LONG FUCKING NIGHT."

I already feel tired of this conversation, and Ashley has just started talking. She sits at the vanity I bought her, taking off the pearls I gave her for our second anniversary.

I peel off my suit, feeling a decade older than I am. I'm only 31 fucking years old; I shouldn't feel so drained. I shouldn't feel like any joy life once had to offer is gone and I'm coasting down-hill from here.

My life shouldn't feel like it's over.

I need to do something. I need to jumpstart my marriage again. I'm not sure you can resuscitate something that's been dead so long, but I should try. We made promises to one another, after all. I can't stand the idea of spending time alone together without work or friends to interrupt, but that's wrong. This is my wife, for fuck's sake. I loved her once, didn't I?

"Why don't we go away for a few days?" I suggest, stepping out of my trousers.

She glances at me in the mirror of her vanity, interest flashing in her eyes. Not because I'm undressing, but because I'm suggesting a vacation. "Yeah? Where do you want to go?"

"I don't know. I'll have to talk to Seb and make sure he can cover for me, but I'm sure we can get away for a few days. We'll go somewhere and have fun, just the two of us."

"All right," she says, easily enough. "I would say we could go into the city, but it's too cold. Why don't we fly to Palm Springs instead?"

I unclasp my watch and set it down gently on the bedside table. "Palm Springs it is."

Ashley flashes me a faint smile, then goes back to her nightly routine. I finish undressing and climb into bed. A blanket of dread feels much heavier than the comforter I pull up over myself. Sometimes it feels so awkward, lying here side by side, not touching. My mind wanders to Moira and Seb. I bet they're cuddling already. I can picture them lying side by side, holding hands, just so they don't have to stop touching, even in sleep.

Meanwhile, Ashley sits on the edge of the bed and puts her glasses on the end table. She wears contacts during the day, but she can't see for shit. She turns off the lamp on her side of the bed and wiggles around in her spot until she's comfortable. Her back is to me. I scoot closer and wrap an arm around her waist and pull her against me.

"You looked beautiful tonight," I tell her.

"Thanks," she says, but I get the feeling my compliment makes her uncomfortable. Funny, since she loves when random men compliment her, but coming from her husband it doesn't seem to mean much.

I think about trying to escalate things, but it feels so exhausting. I don't know if I can handle more rejection tonight. I can feel anger beneath the surface and I don't feel like an angry fuck, either.

I feel sad, and no one likes a sad fuck.

After a couple minutes enduring the cuddle I initiated, I roll over on my back. If she missed the contact, she could easily roll over and snuggle up against my bare chest, but she doesn't.

To be honest, I don't want her to.

What a fucking life.

3

SEBASTIAN

"Can you cover me for a few days?"

I glance up from my ledger, looking up at Griff as he stands in front of my desk and makes this request. He seems tense today. His request comes off as urgent, but he almost looks like he's hoping I'll say no.

"For what?" I ask.

"I'm gonna take Ashley to Palm Springs."

My gaze deadens. He notices and looks vaguely annoyed with me, but he doesn't say anything about it.

Well, shit.

I can't let him take the little slut to Palm Springs, thinking everything is just fine. He shouldn't waste another dime on that dumb bitch, let alone give her a vacation. He should divorce her ass and let her work at the club in earnest.

Well, no, not our club. But let her make her own way in the world and stop sponging off him.

I glance at the door. He left it open when he came inside. "Can you shut that? We need to talk."

Griff frowns, but he falls back a few steps and closes the door to my office. He crosses the room and takes a seat on the other side of my desk, regarding me seriously. "What's wrong?"

"There's something I need to... I was reviewing the security footage last night and I saw something I shouldn't have."

"What do you mean? Someone skimming again?"

I shake my head. "Nah, nothing like that." I don't know how to tell my best friend I saw his wife fucking someone else. I don't know how you hear something like that. Not when you're not expecting it, at least. If he at least had suspicions, that would be one thing, but he hasn't told me about it if he does. Maybe I can give him a hint. Call "timber!" before I chop down a tree and crush his fucking marriage.

"Then what?" he asks.

I lean back in my chair. "How are things with you and Ashley lately?"

He frowns—confused, like he doesn't see what that has to do with what we were just talking about. "Things are... fine, I guess. You know, a little stale. That happens to normal folks," he adds, rolling his eyes at me. "I thought a few days away from everything might be nice."

"Yeah, she leads such a stressful life," I say, rolling my eyes.

"What is your problem with her lately?" he demands, scowling at me. "Moira stays home and you take care of the finances; you don't have a problem with that."

"Of course I don't."

"So, why are you being snide about me spending money on *my* wife?"

"She fucked someone else."

He blinks, then looks surprised. Not crushed, just surprised. "How the hell did you find out about that?"

Now I'm the one scowling. "What? You *knew*? Why the fuck didn't you say anything?"

"What do you mean, why didn't I say anything? Why would I say anything? It was a long fucking time ago. You went off on your honeymoon. You want me to call you up in Rome to cry on your shoulder because my wife got drunk and let someone else fuck her?"

"Rome? My—" I halt, trying to keep up. He's not talking about right now. He's not talking about the other time I know about, either.

She cheated a third time.

At least. If she cheated three times, I bet she cheated more than that. She's not a weak bitch who makes mistakes; she's a serial offender.

"Aw, fuck," I mutter, rubbing my temples and closing my eyes. "Griff, no. I don't mean... I didn't know about that. Friday night. At the club."

His face sort of freezes. His expression doesn't change, he just stares at me, like if he stares long enough, this moment will expire and we can pretend it never happened.

We can't do that, though. Maybe he's willing to forgive the stupid whore, but I'm not. He's not wasting his life on this cheating parasite. Fuck that.

"I'm sorry," I tell him, leaning forward and holding his gaze. "It was tactless, the way I told you. I can do better than that. I just can't stand seeing you waste another minute on this bitch."

"Watch it," he says, but it's an old instinct to defend her. I assume he's just used to it, not that he means it. Why would he defend her?

"Just calling a spade a spade," I inform him.

"No, you're calling my wife a bitch," he says distinctly.

My eyebrows rise. "Yeah, your wife who cheated on you.

More than once, apparently. Would you like me to bring up the footage? You can see for yourself."

"Don't be a fucking asshole," he says.

"I'm not trying to be an asshole."

"Just comes naturally to you, doesn't it?" he mutters, standing.

I frown and watch him turn his back and head for the door. "Where are you going?"

"I don't know."

"Griff... come on."

"You're the last person I want to talk to about this," he states.

That's cold. He's angry, though. I should have known. No one likes the asshole who has to play messenger in a situation like this. I should've made someone else tell him. I just didn't want to embarrass him. I figured the fewer people who knew, the better.

He'll come around. He just needs some time to process.

I DON'T SEE Griff for the rest of the day. I texted Moira after he stormed out to let her know he might be stopping by the house, but I guess he never did. I didn't explain why, even though she asked. I figured that was his story to tell, not mine.

Moira's a good listener, so it's where he should have gone.

He probably went home to talk to Ashley. Hopefully to burn all her fucking clothes and toss her out on her ass. Poor guy. He has a lot to deal with.

When I walk in the front door tonight, I'm even more grateful than usual that I have Moira to come home to. I have a great wife, and I wish Griff did, too.

"So, why did you think Griff might stop by?" she asks me, cutting up her grilled chicken as we sit together at the dinner table.

I tried to get in touch with him all day, but he ignored every text, declined every phone call. "He and Ashley are having problems," I say, as vaguely as I can.

"Oh no, again?"

I glance up at her, surprised.

She shrugs one shoulder. "Well, Ashley said they were a few months ago, but then she didn't say much else; I figured it got better." She pauses, taking a sip of her water. "She seems difficult. I wouldn't want to be married to her. I feel sorry for him, to be honest."

"Yeah, so do I," I murmur.

Moira goes on. "She just seems so mean to him sometimes. Griff is such a sweetheart. I don't get it."

"She's a stupid whore."

"Whoa." Moira frowns at me. "That's a little—no, a *lot* harsh. What did she do?"

I stab a piece of broccoli. "*Who* did she do, you mean. And I don't know his name."

Her face falls, like I've just devastated her. "She didn't."

I nod, her dread making my own grow.

Her fork clatters as it hits the plate. "Oh, my God, how could she? Poor Griff." Heaving a sigh, she throws her napkin, like she can't even enjoy her meal now. "I can't believe this. How is he? Is he with her? Are they... trying to work through it?"

"I fucking hope not. If they are, I'll kick his ass."

"Well... Sebastian, they're married. Maybe that means something."

"If it meant something, she shouldn't make a hobby of

fucking other men and making him look like an asshole. This wasn't the first time she did it. Apparently, she cheated at least two other times."

Moira stands, shaking her head and walking over to the counter. She grabs her phone and starts scrolling.

"What are you doing?"

"I'm calling him. We need to make sure he isn't alone, and if he is, he knows he doesn't have to be. He should come over and spend the evening with us."

I push back my chair and stand, sighing. "That won't help, Moira."

"Why not?" she flings back, ignoring me and tapping her screen before bringing the phone to her ear.

"Because his marriage just fell apart; he doesn't want to see us enjoying ours."

"So I'll ignore you and pay attention to him," she says. "You get my attention all the time. Griff needs us now."

I walk up behind my loving wife and wrap my arms snugly around her waist. "I love you."

Caressing my hand, she tells me, "I love you, too."

I wait there, holding her. I can hear the phone ringing and ringing, then it clicks and goes to voice mail.

He ignored her call.

She waits for his voice mail message, then says brightly, "Hey Griff, it's Moira. Sebastian and I were just bumming around at home tonight and we wanted to see if you were busy. If not, you should come over and hang out with us this evening. We already had dinner, but there are lots of leftovers. I could make us some drinks and we'll all watch a movie together like old times. If you're interested, we will be waiting. Hope to see you soon. Bye!"

I smile as she ends the call, then I grab her jaw and turn her face toward me so I can kiss her. "You're a good friend."

"Griff is family," she states.

I caress her face approvingly. "Agreed."

"I hate that he's alone and sad right now. It just breaks my heart. I think it might be even worse if he's *not* alone and sad. I'm so mad at Ashley right now; I can't believe she did this to him. I know she has her bad habits, but I never thought she'd take it this far."

I'm obviously pissed at Ashley, but I'm also worried I embarrassed Griff. It's thoughtful that Moira wanted to reach out—natural, given their friendship—but it was also transparent. When he gets that message, he'll know I told her. I probably shouldn't have, but I couldn't keep it from her, either. We don't have that kind of relationship. Moira and I don't have secrets.

It takes about three minutes for him to text me. One word: Asshole.

I text right back, "Just stop sulking and come over."

He doesn't answer.

"There's no reason to feel bad. It isn't your fault Ashley's a faithless slut. It doesn't make YOU look bad, it makes HER look bad."

"Would you stop with the fucking name-calling?"

My eyes widen with surprise. "No. Slut, tramp, cocksucking daughter of a fucking whore. I'll keep going. Do not defend her. Fuck that bitch. If you haven't already, call Carrie tomorrow and set up an appointment. Get rid of her ass."

"So I can sit in the shadows and watch you live your perfect life with your perfect fucking love and your perfect wife? I'll pass."

"Don't be like that," I text back. "We both love you and neither of us wants you to be alone right now."

"I'm always alone," he sends back.

I stare at that one for a minute before sending back, "You don't have to be."

"Seems like I do," he answers.

"Come over," I say again.

He doesn't respond that time.

He doesn't respond for the rest of the night.

4

GRIFF

I'm entirely too drunk to drive home.

The bar is closing, so that's bad.

I should call for a ride. Uber or some shit. I squint at my phone, then blink, stumbling over my own feet as I make my way outside. Fuck, I am drunk. I can't see clearly.

I don't have the app I need, so I open up the app store, but it seems like a lot of steps. I have to touch the tiny fucking buttons to type in the name, then I'll have to wait for it to download. I'll probably need to sign up for an account or some shit.

Too much work. Fuck it.

I swipe away from all that and touch the green contacts icon. I scroll down toward Seb's name, but I stop at the sight of Moira's.

I'm drunk enough to tap it.

My head feels so heavy. It lolls back as I wait for the rings to stop. Finally, she answers, her tone raspy from sleep. "Hello?"

"Hey, friend," I say, grinning.

"Griff." She clears her throat, trying not to sound sleepy. "Hey, what's up?"

"Can you come pick me up?"

"Of course. Where are you?" Now she sounds urgent, like she's afraid I beat the shit out of whatever asshole put his dick in my wife and got myself arrested. Not like she can't bring the bail money considering who she's married to, but it would still distress her.

"Callahan's," I slur, leaning back against the brick storefront. "I can't drive. Way too drunk."

"No, don't get behind the wheel," she says, and I hear the rustling of fabric. I close my eyes, imagining her pulling on clothes to come get me. That shouldn't turn me on, but it's probably the alcohol. I'm an ornery drunk. I should tell her to bring Seb so I don't say or do anything idiotic when she gets here.

Instead I tell her, "Come alone."

"Of course," she answers, like that was a given.

It wasn't though. I expected her to hesitate, and it almost makes me irrationally annoyed that she didn't. It makes me feel like she pities me. Oh, poor fucking Griff, couldn't even keep his wife satisfied so she had to surf a sea of other cocks to get off.

Fuck, that hurts.

And it's insulting.

And I don't want Moira to think I can't please a woman.

"I don't know why Ashley—It wasn't because of me," I tell her.

"Of *course* it wasn't," she agrees, vehemently. "Ashley has her own issues. It's terrible that she betrayed you and hurt you this way. I want to kick her in the face."

That makes me grin. "Yeah?"

"Oh yeah," she says, gaining enthusiasm. "Nair in her sham-poo, cut the butt cheeks out of her favorite pants. If it's petty and mean, I want to do it to her."

My grin widens. "You're adorable."

"I'm not adorable," she mutters.

"You are. The meanest thing you can think of is cutting the butt cheeks out of her favorite pants. That's fucking adorable."

"I opened with kicking her in the face," she states. "That was mean. And Nair in her shampoo? That's super mean. Ashley would be ugly without hair. She even looks weird when she pulls her hair back in a pony tail. All of this is purely vicious —totally not adorable."

"Yeah, with all this badassery, we better lock you up and throw away the key."

"Damn straight," she agrees. "Lock up your sons and daugh-ters; I'll corrupt them all and cut the butt cheeks out of their pants if they piss me off."

I can't stop smiling. That's a nice change from earlier. We sit here for a few minutes in companionable silence. I don't know how silence can be companionable over the phone, but I just listen as she gathers her things and gets in her BMW. I'm feeling the alcohol hard, but thankfully I have this building here to hold me up.

"Tell me something nice," I tell her.

"Something nice?" she asks gently. "Like what?"

"I don't know."

That's not helpful, so she has to think about it for a minute. "My sister finally had her baby. It was a girl. They named her Layla. I'll show you a picture when I pick you up; she's so adorable. Looking at it gives me just a touch of baby fever."

My face screws up with displeasure. "That's not nice."

She sounds surprised. "Why isn't it?"

"Because you're going to have babies with Seb."

Laughing lightly, she says, "Well, yeah, he's my husband, so I should hope he's the one I'm having babies with."

"Like I said," I mutter.

She falls silent. After a moment, she wrongly interprets why this bothers me. "I'm sorry, that probably made you think of—I meant to distract you with something nice, not rub your nose in... I mean, I don't even know if you and Ashley were planning to have... Sorry. I'm just snowballing. Let's pick a new topic." She misses a beat, then she says, "You're going to spend the night at our place tonight, and I won't hear otherwise. I have the guest room already made up. Then tomorrow morning I'm going to make you and Sebastian both breakfast—and cookies," she adds, inspired. "Because cookies make everything better."

"You're not his housekeeper, you know."

"No, I'm his wife."

Just hearing that clear fact makes me surly as hell. "You do everything for him."

She doesn't reiterate what she already said, but she probably wants to.

"Ashley never made me cookies," I mutter.

Displeasure seeps into her tone. "Ashley's probably too stupid to read a recipe. Clearly she couldn't read her marriage vows."

Her words cause me to visualize Ashley with some nameless fuck. That image has played through my head about a thousand times today. I never saw it before—never saw the guy from the wedding, never even knew his name. I didn't want to, after the fact. When I decided to stick it out with her, the best thing to do seemed to be to learn as little as I could about it so I had less to relive.

But Seb had to go and tell me there was footage this time, so once he left, I just had to go back and watch it. That was a mistake. Now I'm haunted by her enthusiasm—enthusiasm she hasn't had for me in a long-ass time.

"I can't get it out of my head," I finally say.

Her tone is soft and understanding. "I can imagine."

"Why am I not allowed to be happy? I tried so fucking hard."

"Oh, Griff." She says this like I'm breaking her heart.

"It's just... impossible. Maybe it's me. Maybe I'm the problem."

"You are *not* the problem," she states. "You are amazing and Ashley is an idiot."

"Your name-calling is much less aggressive than your husband's," I inform her.

"Well, yeah," she says, and I can picture her rolling her eyes. "Want me to step it up a notch? I can be meaner."

I shake my head, completely fucking enamored. She's made me feel better in the space of a few minutes than I've felt in... I don't even know, months? "Sometimes I can't get you out of my head."

She falls silent again, but this time I doubt it's companionable. For her, anyhow. I'm drunk as fuck; it's just fine for me.

Instead of responding, she pulls in a moment later. I shield my eyes with my hand and look at her car as she navigates into a spot in front of me, then I walk around to the passenger side and open up the door. I practically fall inside, yanking the door shut and narrowly missing my foot.

"Fuck, I am drunk."

"I figured," she says, lightly, reaching over and absently patting my thigh. "You okay? If you're going to be sick, please do it outside the car. I know Sebastian loves you and all, but he will kill you if you vomit in my car."

I lean my head back and smile at her. "I'm good."

"Okay," she says, laughing a little. "Put your seatbelt on."

"Thank you for coming to get me," I say.

"Anytime, Griff."

I force myself to sit upright and buckle the belt around me. Moira waits, then puts the car in reverse and drives me back to her house.

Their house.

The house where Seb lives with his perfect wife who would never cheat on him.

Fucking Seb.

I love the guy to death, so I hate being jealous of him, but I am. The ache I felt years ago feels so much worse tonight. I was wrong about her getting dressed—the rustling must have been the sound of the bedclothes, because right now she's dressed in a satin nightie—baby blue, like her eyes. God, she looks good. I want to forget she's married to my best friend. I want to push her up against the wall, hike up that nightie, and fuck her until she's crying out my name instead of his.

She shoves her key into the lock and opens the front door for me to come inside while she pushes buttons on the alarm. I follow her inside the darkened entryway, but fuck, I can't keep my eyes off her. She offers me a little smile and takes her jacket off, hanging it on the coat rack. Then she moves up behind me and peels off my overcoat, hanging it up beside hers and Seb's.

"Come on," she says quietly, taking my hand and guiding me to the staircase. It's not a far walk, but I'm so drunk she must not trust me to get there on my own. She lets go so she can walk ahead of me, but she glances back to make sure I don't miss the first step.

If she looks back at me again, I miss it. My gaze starts at her bare legs, then drifts up to the short little nightie she's wearing.

She should not have walked in front of me. I can see practically all the way up...

Fuck me. She isn't wearing panties. I'm at least 90% sure she is not wearing panties.

Seriously? She couldn't pause long enough to pull on *panties* before coming to get me? Now I'm just thinking about the whole time she was driving me home, when she was sitting there with her exposed thighs and her panty-free ass and I was too drunk to notice.

Of course, not noticing is the right reaction. I should definitely not be noticing that my best friend's wife has a bare pussy and a nightie so short it barely skims her ass.

Unaware of my thoughts, Moira opens the door to the guest bedroom and walks in ahead of me. "I made it up earlier in case you came over for the movie," she tells me, glancing back over her shoulder. "So everything is nice and fresh for you. You have your own bathroom right through here," she adds, pointing to the door. Her gaze wanders over my chest. "If you need a fresh suit in the morning, you might be able to wear one of Sebastian's. You're a little bit bulkier than he is, but it might work."

"Nah." I shake my head. "I'll go home and get clothes. Thanks, though."

Moira nods, but she looks reluctant to leave. "Do you need anything?"

Since I'm feeling ornery, I can't stop a very bad idea from tumbling out of my mouth. "You could help me get undressed."

Her eyebrows rise and her mouth opens just a couple inches, but then she catches herself and steps forward. "Sure, no problem."

This is a mistake. This is a terrible idea. I look down at her as she stops right in front of me. When she looks up at me, uncertainty is written all across her pretty face. She hesitates before finally reaching for my jacket and pushing it down over my muscular shoulders. She swallows audibly and shakes the wrinkles out of it with impressive focus. She takes a step back, sets it aside, then comes back to stand in front of me. She looks up at me again, and I can't help reading into those little glances. What is she thinking?

I don't mean to ask, but my brain overrides my hesitation. "What's on your mind, Moira?"

Her gaze drops to my chest pointedly, but I can see from the rise and fall of her chest, she's breathing a little less evenly than usual. She adopts what I think she intends to be a stern look, but Moira's like a kindergarten teacher who can't even control the little people in her classroom. Sternness is not her thing. She can't pull it off. She's gentle and sweet. Still, since I'm her husband's best friend, she tries for stern. She stares at the button hole as she undoes the top buttons of my shirt.

"I'm thinking that I feel sorry for your liver right now. You haven't treated it very well tonight."

God, she's so close. I could reach out and touch her right now if I wanted to. Instead, I watch her fingers move down my chest, pushing little plastic buttons through the neatly sewn holes. I'm a head taller than she is, so looking down at her like this, I can see right down her top. I can see the tops of her high, rounded, perfect fucking breasts, not even restrained by a bra. I force my eyes away, but then I'm just thinking about the curve of her ass, her long, strong legs. She's a runner, I think. I know she used to be, not sure if she still is. It certainly looks like she still is.

I want to touch her ass. I want to grab it and yank her against me right here in the guest room. I envision it, imagine her gasp as she falls against me, her hands moving to my chest to instinctively push me away. Maybe she would hesitate.

Maybe I would see just a split second of longing in her pretty blue eyes before she did the decent thing and pushed me away.

I keep my hands to myself and my fantasies in my head, but fuck, I don't want to.

Is it cheating if Ashley cheated first? Wait, no, Ashley isn't the problem. Seb is. That bastard has never cheated, and he probably wouldn't take too kindly to my pinning his wife against this wall and kissing the fuck out of her, my hands roaming down to squeeze that incredible ass.

Nope, he wouldn't like that at all. I'm pretty fucking sure of it.

She probably wouldn't, either. Unlike Ashley, Moira is actually happy with her marriage.

That brings me back down. Fucking reality is a real asshole.

What a shitty fucking day. I woke up this morning with at least a little enthusiasm for Palm Springs, now here I am, drunk and lost while Moira undresses me—and not because she wants to fuck me, but because I'm too fucking drunk to do it myself.

Suddenly I push her hands off my chest and scowl. I can unbutton my own damn dress shirt. She takes an uncertain step back, but waits for me to peel my shirt off and drop it on the floor.

Sighing, she bends down to pick it up.

I look down the front of her nightie again.

Dammit, Griff, quit that shit.

She drags her ass out of bed in the middle of the night to come pick you up; you stop acting like an asshole and pay her a little respect.

I have the best of intentions until she pops back up, tossing my shirt on the chair, and gets distracted by the sight of my bare chest. She looks vaguely surprised, and I'm not sure whether to feel insulted or flattered. She clearly likes what she sees—and why wouldn't she? I log the gym time and I was born with a good arrangement of muscles to begin with—but still, that she sees Seb naked every day and still pauses at the sight of me makes me feel kinda good about myself. Seb and I look absolutely nothing alike. His appearance is more refined—dark hair, deep blue eyes, a touch of elegance to cover up all his rough edges. If Hollywood approached him tomorrow and asked him to be the new Bond, exactly zero people would be surprised.

Me, I could never pull that off. No one expects me to pull up in an Aston Martin with a Bond girl in the passenger seat and a tumbler full of expensive liquor in my hand, ready to take care of business in time for us to make our dinner reservations.

I vaguely look like the questionable man in all black that you would meet at a dive bar and slide an envelope full of cash to kill your spouse so you can collect the insurance money. It's always worked for us in business. Seb is slick, he's got the charisma and he's a good wheeler and dealer. I'm good at playing bad cop, coming down hard on people and making them wiggle when they're positive there's no wiggle room.

Just not good at keeping my wife from fucking around on me, apparently.

Fuck, my mind had to go back there.

Moira has recovered from ogling my muscular chest and now she nervously plucks pillows off the bed and pulls back the blanket. She has to lean over the bed to do it though, and I cannot help looking at her ass again.

I just want to move closer. I'm not going to touch her. That's my intention, but I'm too fucking drunk and I bump into her, knocking her on the bed.

I hear Moira gasp as she catches herself on the soft surface beneath her.

"Aw, shit," I mutter.

Moira looks back, startled, then she laughs when I trip and catch myself on the bed.

"Oh, my God, you are so—"

I'm fairly certain she's about to tell me how drunk I am, like I don't already know, but the words die on her tongue. Instead of letting her up, I shove her little ass to the center of the bed and lie down beside her.

When I initially move so close to her scantily clad body, Moira looks understandably hesitant. I can only imagine what's going through her mind as her eyes follow my every movement, then cautiously dart to my face. I settle in beside her, but I don't make a move to touch her, so she tries to pretend this is a normal thing for me to do.

"You didn't finish getting undressed," she remarks, since apparently that's all she can think to say.

"So finish undressing me," I murmur, watching her.

"Um, I..." She hesitates, but loses whatever argument she has with herself in her head. Rolling her eyes, she finally says, "Fine."

My heart kicks up a couple speeds as her hands move toward my belt. I watch her fingers as she pulls back the leather and pulls the prong from the hole. She's careful—too careful—not to touch me as she slides the leather through the buckle, then drags it through the loops of my slacks. She leans over me and tosses the belt near the chair where the rest of my clothes are.

"Missed," she remarks with forced lightness.

"Zero points."

She cracks a smile, then it drops as she looks down at my pants. "I'm not sure I should take these off. Your drunken brain might get the wrong idea."

I scoff, amused. "Probably. Don't be offended if you encounter a hard-on."

Moira blushes, but at least she doesn't seem uncomfortable. "Like I said, probably shouldn't take those off. If you want to, feel free. I can go grab a pair of Sebastian's pajama pants for you, if you'd like. That would be much more comfortable to sleep in. You both have slim hips, so I think those would fit you just fine."

My drunken brain tells me an okay thing to do right now is to reach for *her* hips and draw them closer. I've resisted the bad ideas up until now, but somehow this one travels through me before I can stop it, and before I know it... I do.

She lets me pull her closer to my body, but she looks understandably uncertain about it. "Griff, what are you doing?"

I know the right thing to do here is tell her to go back to Seb's room, but that leaves me alone, and alone is the last thing I want to be right now.

I shouldn't take advantage of her sympathy—and that's exactly what I'm doing—but I can't keep the words from tumbling out of my mouth. "Stay with me."

I see resistance in her eyes. I see the very reasonable argument that she can't stay with me because she needs to go back to her husband, my best friend, and while she feels terrible for me that *my* wife is a faithless cheater, she isn't, so she isn't going to lie here and cuddle with me while her husband sleeps alone in the next room.

Since I see that argument in her turbulent blue eyes, I add, "Please."

It pokes a hole right in her perfectly good argument, exactly as I intend it.

Fuck, drunk me is an asshole.

But he's a smart enough asshole, because Moira nods and stays put.

I don't want to make her uncomfortable, but Drunk Asshole Griff isn't as worried about it. I find myself reaching over and touching her face, running the back of my hand along her smooth cheek. I can't help being drawn to her. I've never been able to help it. I was drawn to her at first sight, but that's nothing new. Moira is an incredibly beautiful woman, so it's commonplace for men to be physically attracted to her.

I tell myself it's normal to think about her breasts and her ass, to imagine yanking up that pale blue nightie and pinning her body beneath mine. It's normal to imagine kissing her, to think about how soft her lips would be, what she would sound like. Is she a loud fuck, whimpering and crying out? Or is she more soft sighs and low moans? She seems like she would be soft sighs and low moans, but then I think about the naughty stories she used to tell us. Maybe she's dirtier than I give her credit for. It's always the quiet ones, after all. When Seb says she was busy sucking his cock before dinner, I imagine him as the aggressor, but maybe she's hungry for it.

Fuck, now I'm hard.

Now I'm picturing Moira opening her pretty little mouth for my cock, looking up at me with those big blue eyes as I slide into her throat.

"Fuck."

"What's wrong?" she asks.

I shake my head, tempted to roll on my back so I don't have to keep looking at her, but that might draw attention to the tent currently erected in my pants.

I gotta get my head right before I end up doing something I'll regret.

"What movie were we going to watch tonight?" I ask to distract myself.

Her expression lightens, since this is a safe subject. "*Sabrina.* It was a Hepburn night."

"Oh, well, I'm despondent that I missed that."

She smiles and pokes me in the arm. "Whatever, you love it. Remember when we all watched *Breakfast at Tiffany's* together?"

"I've tried to block it out. I lost street cred that night."

She grins up at me. "You still have all your street cred. I kept your secret, so no one knows."

"Mm-hmm. They can smell it on me."

"Remember when you guys made me watch *Boondock Saints*?" she asks, raising a pointed eyebrow. "You got me back."

"Please. You thought the one guy was hot."

She nods. "Got me there. He was hot. I can't deny that. Still, not my favorite movie. I also watched *Scarface* with you guys. Nobody in that movie was hot."

"And *we* watched—what was the one with the cheerleaders?"

Moira rolls her eyes. "Yeah, I'm sure it was a real hardship watching a league of hot girls jump around in skimpy skirts with exposed midriffs. I feel enormously sorry for the emotional trauma I must have inflicted upon you."

"You should," I mutter.

She smiles and shakes her head at me. "Just for that, we're doing a Hepburn double feature next time. You should come over tomorrow after work. I'll make you guys dinner—whatever you want—and then we'll watch movies all night long."

"I don't like being your third wheel," I tell her.

Her smile falls. "You are *not* our third wheel. We both love having you here. You're our best friend. What's third wheel-like about that?"

"You just described being a third wheel," I inform her. "You two are a couple and I'm the friend that tags along. I'm not going back to that. I can't."

Her brow is creased and she looks a little sad. "You don't like hanging out with us? I loved all those nights with you guys. You were just enduring them?"

"It was fucking torture."

Not for the first time tonight, Moira looks completely disillusioned. "But why? We never tried to make you feel that way."

"We, we, we." I roll my eyes, rolling onto my back and bending one arm to rest a hand behind my head. "That's why I had to stop coming around, Moira. It was too hard."

"I don't understand."

I cut her a look. "Yes, you do."

"I just said I don't."

"Girls like you always know. You used to torture me."

Her jaw drops open. "Girls like me? What is that supposed to mean? And please elaborate on this torture, because I always remember being nice to you."

"You're too fucking nice, that's the problem. You're lying here in bed with me, both of us half-naked, you without any panties, because you're *nice*."

That leaves her speechless. There are a lot of things she could say, a lot of things she probably should say, but she knows I'm hurting, so she chooses not to. She keeps her mouth shut, simply rolling over and climbing off the bed.

I don't ask her to stay this time.

It's best she goes.

5

MOIRA

I CAN'T SLEEP, SO I FINALLY GIVE UP AND GO FOR MY morning run a couple hours early. It works out, anyway. I'm feeling the need to run a little longer than my usual two miles. I go for three, then walk for another half hour before returning home to shower.

Sebastian is awake. I feel relieved when I get back to the bedroom and he's up. Griff is still in bed—poor guy's probably going to have a hell of a headache. I took a bottle of water in and left it on the end table before I went for my run, just in case he woke up and needed it.

I don't know exactly what to make of last night, so I do my best to shrug it off. My handsome husband swallows up my attention, joining me in the shower and getting me off while he soaps me up. I'm weak from my orgasm and he bends me over, shoving his glorious cock inside me and fucking me like a ragdoll.

God, I love him.

I'm weak and fully under his spell when we step out. It's

hard to let him leave in the morning sometimes. I miss him terribly when he's gone. I think about him on and off all day. I've never been so in love in all my life, and I didn't know this feeling could last. He's just the most incredible man I've ever met. Sexy and generous and elegant. Any given day, he's dressed so well he might've just stepped out of GQ. He turns me to mush.

He knows it, too. Right now, as he straightens his tie and looks at me draped naked and exhausted across our bed, he's so damn smug.

"Shut up, you handsome devil," I tell him.

"I said nothing," he says with ridiculous innocence. There's not an innocent bone in this man's magnificent body.

"You wore me out and now I have to go make cookies."

His dark eyebrows rise with surprise. "Cookies? For breakfast?"

I manage a nod. "I promised Griff cookies. I'm not sure he'll even remember, but on the off chance he does, I don't want to disappoint him."

Sebastian walks over and smacks my ass. "You couldn't disappoint a man if you tried."

"Yes, well, you probably feel that way because we just had shower sex. Given Griff did not just get a morning orgasm, he probably doesn't feel the same way. I have to give him cookies."

"If they're supposed to make up for lack of orgasms, you better be making one hell of a batch of cookies."

I crack a tired smile, then drag my butt out of bed so I can get dressed.

As it happens, I have an incredible recipe for ginger cookies that *may* be as good as sex. Not sex with Sebastian, but probably sex with stupid Ashley. What a jerk. Griff is such a wonderful, attractive man; I honestly can't believe she would do this to him.

I bake them some fresh cookies while I prepare their breakfast. I go for a classic mix—some fruit for starters, scrambled eggs and sausage to go with it, and a slice of toast with a thin layer of grape jelly.

I also make them coffee and get out the orange juice, just in case.

Griff comes in behind Sebastian, but he is not as ready for the day. He did pull his dress shirt back on, but the brightness of the kitchen lights make him squint so I go over and turn them off. I light a candle on the table instead.

"Thanks," Griff mutters.

"Of course," I say, brightly. "How did you sleep?"

"Like shit," he answers, appearing confused that I already made him a plate and put it on the table for him. Nonetheless, he drops into the chair and stares at it for another moment.

"How do you take your coffee?" I ask, pouring a cup for him and stopping with enough room for cream and sugar.

"Black," he answers.

I nod and top it off, then carry it over and slide it up next to his plate, flashing him a smile. "Want some orange juice, too?"

"No, thanks." He frowns at me, like I'm some sort of oddity. "Man, your house is full-service, isn't it?"

I smile faintly. "I waited tables for years; can't break the habit."

Never had a reason to. Sebastian has a traditional streak. He enjoys having me wait on him, and I take pleasure in doing it; it all works out.

I pour Sebastian some coffee—he takes it black, too—and take it over. It's only natural for me to bend down and give him a kiss afterward, but as I straighten, rest my hands on his shoulders, and give them a gentle squeeze, I can't help noticing Griff watching, his gaze narrowed, almost like he's annoyed by it. His words from last night come back, but they bring dread with them.

Griff and Sebastian aren't merely friends—they're family. When I met them Sebastian told me that, how Griff is really the only family he has. My husband is an orphan, and Griff was half an orphan. He had a mom out there somewhere, but he ended up in foster care alongside Sebastian, and that's how they met. They didn't stay in the same house for the duration, but they did stay at the same school until Sebastian aged out of the system. He's older by a year, so Griff ditched his foster family and went to stay with Sebastian until he aged out, too.

For half their lives, they've been inseparable. Their loyalty to one another is the only thing in the world they never question. I hate to think Griff is going to drift again because of me. I can't be the thing that comes between them.

I don't even know how I could be. You wouldn't know it by his drunken behavior last night, but Griff has never had feelings like that for me.

It has to be because of everything that's going on with Ashley. It has him off-kilter and lonely. He knows how happy I make Sebastian, and he feels like it's me, like I'm the harbinger of happiness. I'm not, though. Sebastian and I are just really lucky to have found one another. We're cut from complementary panels, like fabric cut haphazardly that somehow, sewn together, creates something perfect.

I'm not perfect and he's not, either; it's just that our flaws fit together seamlessly and give off the impression of perfection.

Griff doesn't have that, though. I've never felt like he and Ashley had that kind of connection, and now that I know she's been sleeping around behind his back, I'm quite sure of it. I would never do that to Sebastian, not for anything in the world. If I ever felt unhappy, I would talk to Sebastian about it and we would fix it.

It's incredible to have that, and I'm so sad Griff doesn't.

I think about him implying he felt left out last night, so as I walk past, I try to throw him a bone, letting my hand drift across his shoulders and giving him a one-handed gentle squeeze.

Then I feel ridiculous for thinking "throw him a bone," like Griff is someone who needs pity attention. Not by a long shot. He may be in pain right now from Ashley's bullshit, but Griff is impressive in his own right. Sebastian and Griff are both incredible specimens—not just physically, but their unrelenting drive. These two men know what they want, and they'll do whatever it takes to get it.

They began their journey in life as castoffs with nothing. They sacrificed and saved and worked their *asses* off—five jobs between them, at one point—living in squalor so they could make something of themselves. They purchased their first business at the tender ages of 22 and 23. They continued to work their asses off, and now they both have so much. Half a dozen businesses, beautiful homes, loving wives....

Well, no, I guess Griff doesn't have that anymore.

Dammit, Ashley.

He can do so much better, though. If she doesn't appreciate what she has in Griff, she doesn't deserve him. It kills me that he's in so much pain now—even if he won't properly show it, I know he is. Last night wouldn't have happened otherwise. Last time Griff called me drunk to come pick him up in the middle of the night was right before he met Ashley. He had stopped hanging out with us, then one night he called me out of the blue. He told me he was walking around and couldn't find his house. I told him to stay put and I went to find him so I could get him home safely.

Now, he's a grown ass man. Sebastian is 8 years older than me, so Griff is 7—that makes him 31. He should be settling down, not going through his first divorce.

I wanna give Griff a hug, but given last night, I decide not to. I felt like I should mention it to Sebastian this morning, but I also didn't know what to say. Nothing untoward actually *happened*. He joked that if I took off his pants he might get an erection, but that wasn't a big deal. Sure, he pulled my body close in bed, but he's lonely and hurting; he probably just needed some affection. I'm sure in his vulnerability last night, he probably said things he didn't mean.

"So, what should I make you gentlemen for dinner tonight?" I ask casually, grabbing my own plate and taking a seat at the table.

Griff raises a dark golden brow at me. "Us gentlemen? I don't live here."

"You don't remember last night?" I ask.

His blue eyes dull a little and his gaze drops to the table.

I guess that answers that.

I skip that part, though, and say, "I invited you to stay tonight. You owe me a Hepburn double feature. I'll make dinner, and we'll stay in and be lazy asses."

Griff shakes his head. "Gonna have to pass."

"Why?" Sebastian asks.

Griff glances over at him, but he seems a little uneasy, and I hate it. "Got shit to do."

"What kind of shit? Packing up Ashley's clothes and tossing it on the lawn shit?"

Griff just rolls his eyes.

"If that's what you have to do, I'm happy to help," Sebastian volunteers. "We'll get it done fast, then we can come spend the rest of the night with Moira and Audrey."

Shaking his head, he spears a forkful of scrambled eggs. "You're relentless," he states, before taking a bite.

"You are leaving her, right?" Sebastian pushes, watching his best friend.

"Stop," Griff says, cutting Sebastian an unfriendly look as he reaches for his coffee. "I don't want to talk about this."

"Then tell me you're calling a divorce lawyer this afternoon and I'll gladly drop it," Sebastian states. "Otherwise, I'm going to keep talking about it."

"Then I'm going to leave," Griff says.

Sebastian feigns a grimace. "Your car's at Callahan's."

"I'll walk," Griff shoots back. "I'm not going to sit here and discuss this shit with you, Seb. It's my life, not yours."

"She makes you miserable. She cheats on you. You put up a good fight, Griff, but there's nothing left to fight for."

Pointedly ignoring my husband, Griff eats his food in silence.

I'm not nearly as pushy as Sebastian, but I'm uncomfortable with the fact that it does seem like Griff *isn't* planning to leave Ashley.

If I thought it was because he loved her too much or they had more good times than bad, that would make sense. It breaks my heart right in half even imagining it, but if Sebastian cheated on me, I don't know how I could leave him. I'd want to, I'd be completely miserable, but we've had all these happy years and I'm sure we have more ahead of us.

It doesn't seem like the same can be said for Griff and Ashley. They had a good year, followed by a couple of tepid years, and then a couple of shitty years. What's the point? Marriage means something to me, but my relationship is wonderful. Griff seems to have married the wrong woman, and I hate that he's settling for unhappiness.

He forgot his phone in the bedroom, so while I won't ask in front of Sebastian, who has already been quite vocal in his opinion of what Griff needs to do next, I follow my friend down the hall to retrieve his phone.

Checking behind me to make sure Sebastian isn't in hearing range, I step inside. Griff pauses when he turns back and finds me standing in the doorway.

"Why are you staying with her?" I ask him.

He doesn't get as annoyed when I press him about this as Sebastian, but he's not quick to answer, either.

"Is it because you love her too much to let go? Because your life feels empty when you think of it without her? Is it because you know you'll get past this and have many beautiful years together? Or is it because you don't want to be alone? Because if it's the last one, I think you're making a huge mistake. Ashley doesn't deserve you. I think you deserve a woman who looks at you and *sees* you. Who values you. Who knows your worth. You deserve much better than 'not as lonely,' Griff. You deserve to be loved, and I don't think Ashley loves you."

A sad smile tugs at the corners of his mouth. "No one does, Moira."

"That is *not* true," I tell him, firmly. "*We do.* We love you. And someone else will, too. Someone who deserves you—not someone who uses you and treats you like shit."

"Stop with the 'we' shit, please," he says, brushing past me on his way out of the bedroom.

I grab his shoulder. I shouldn't—I should let him go, but I feel like I'd be letting him go to make the biggest mistake of his life. My stomach twists, because the alternative might be making the biggest mistake of mine.

I mean this, but not the way he might take it.

"*I* do," I tell him, halting his departure. "I love you. And I want more for you than you can have with her."

He stands there for a moment like I stole his ability to walk. He finally looks at me over his shoulder—no, *glares*. "That's fucking mean."

My heart sinks clear down to my stomach. "I'm not trying to be mean."

He laughs a little before walking away, but there's no humor in it. "Yeah, you never are."

6

SEBASTIAN

It's been three weeks since Griff has come around on a social visit.

It's impossible for him to avoid me altogether at work, but he has rearranged his schedule so we see less and less of each other.

Today he has asked for a meeting.

I can already sense the distance in him when he walks into my office. I can see it in the way he doesn't look at me as he takes a seat. He's not here for anything pleasant. He's not here to tell me he'll finally take Moira up on one of the ten invitation texts she has sent him in the past three weeks, all but begging him to come over for dinner.

"How are things?" I ask him, since I'm not up-to-date on his life.

"Fucking fantastic," he answers, dryly.

This whole situation is fucking garbage. I can't help thinking he blames me for the fallout—like if I'd just kept my mouth shut, or if I hadn't reviewed that particular piece of footage, everything would be fine.

But how many other nights might there have been? How many nights had Ashley done the same damn thing, and she just lucked out that no one checked the tapes?

Whatever is going on between them, Ashley no longer works at the club. Griff handled all the termination paperwork himself—citing the incident in the hallway as the reason we let her go. Given they share a last name, it's awkward, but having sex on our property definitely crossed lines; we have every right to fire her, whether or not they're married.

Thankfully, he was smart enough to get a prenup, but I don't even know whether or not he's divorcing the lying little slut.

"How's Ashley?" I ask, since it's as subtle as I can be.

He cuts me a look to let me know he's not amused and, for whatever reason, I no longer have the right to ask about that.

I feel it in my gut. Griff's the only person—outside of Moira, of course—I can't stomach losing, and right now, our friendship feels more tenuous than it ever has.

I'm losing him.

I don't know why, but I know I am.

"Come to dinner tonight," I say, when he doesn't answer.

"No," he snaps.

"We don't have to stay in. We'll all go out. Dinner, drinks— whatever you want."

Griff shakes his head, then ducks it and stares down at the ground. "Just let me get this out, would you?"

I lean back in my chair, nodding for him to go ahead.

"I want you to buy out my half of the club. I don't want this partnership anymore. I'll give you a better than fair price, I really just... I just want out. I don't care about the money. All the money we've made may have worked magic for you, but it's done nothing but make me fucking miserable. Attracted a fucking gold digger that I couldn't see through, bought a big, beautiful prison that I can't stand to spend the night in... I'm more alone than I've ever been in my life, Seb, and I want out."

I feel like he just kicked me between the fucking legs. "You want *out*? Of our partnership? Of our *friendship*?"

"I can't *do* this anymore, Seb. I can't. I don't want to. I'm at a point in my life where I have a choice; I can choose to be unhappy, or I can try something new and maybe get a different result."

I scowl, sitting forward and irritably shoving papers across my desk. "No. Fuck that. You're making an emotional decision because Ashley fucked you over. This is not... no. You can't just *quit* on me."

"Yes, I fucking can," he says, causing my stomach to sink.

"So, you're just like everybody else now, huh?" I demand, gesturing toward the door. "Every other fucking person who just leaves. Does our friendship mean this little to you? Do *I* mean this little to you?"

He places a hand on either side of his head, as if that's the only way he can keep it from exploding. Like I'm so fucking infuriating that he can't even wrap his head around it. "This isn't about *you*. I can't make every decision in my life to fit *you*, Sebastian. You have *everything*. I have *nothing*. You've got the perfect fucking life—you are *not* alone anymore. You *have* a person who will never abandon you. You have Moira. What do I have?"

"You have me. You have both of us," I state, feeling walls erecting around my heart. There have never been walls between me and Griff. He's the one person in the world I knew had my back, the one person in the world I didn't hesitate to trust.

Now he wants to fucking walk away.

I guess I was wrong. Over half my fucking life, and I was wrong.

I want to know why. I want to rage at him and demand he explain to me why our friendship went from the most important thing in his life to something so meaningless, he'll toss it out and move on like it never happened. Like we haven't been partners, building our lives together for *more than half our lives.*

But there's no answer that could make me understand. In his place, there's nothing that would have made me walk away from him.

Nodding my head, I clip, "Fine. If that's what you want."

He sighs, the weight on his shoulders appearing heavier instead of lighter. "I have to talk to my lawyer this afternoon. I'll schedule an appointment with the accountant afterward. I'll let you know when I have a fair price for you."

I nod mechanically, but I couldn't give a fuck less about the price. I don't want his half of the business; I want him to stop this shit and stay on.

Instead of taking any of it back, he stands. He heads for the door, pausing just before opening it to leave.

"I'm sorry," he says quietly.

"Of all people, you should know how worthless those words are," I tell him, coldly.

He nods slowly. "You're right. I do."

So, without another word, he leaves my office and begins the official steps of dissolving our friendship.

MOIRA SNUGGLES UP beside me on the couch, absently running her hand up and down my arm. All night she's been trying to settle me down, but she doesn't know what's wrong. I haven't been able to bring myself to tell her.

I keep feeling like if I don't tell anyone, then it won't happen.

That's never worked before, so I'm not sure why it would now. When I was a child, standing at the double funeral of both my parents, it didn't make me feel any better that I didn't cry.

When I was first dumped into the home of strangers with four other children, not showing that I was scared didn't make me feel any braver.

As I was dumped from house to house, forever without a family or a home to call my own, I could feel myself growing cold and hard, could feel my world getting smaller and smaller until I was the only one left. There may have been a whole world out there, a whole house full of people I lived with, but my personal microcosm shrunk and shrunk until there was only room for me.

If there was only room for me, it felt better. It wasn't that no one else wanted to be a part of my world; it was that there was no room for them, anyway. It was *my* choice.

Then I met Griff. Someone else as cold as winter, as angry and lonely as I was. For a while, we were just lonely together. Two separate planets sharing the same immense space, convinced we were worlds unto ourselves. We were islands, both of us. We learned not to need anyone—and that was true. That wasn't a front. We truly learned to be self-reliant, impenetrable fortresses of solitude.

But then, over time, we got the idea that maybe since we were so alike, we could trust each other the way we trusted ourselves. Our worlds were so small, so exclusive, that "they" couldn't get in.

But maybe *we* could. Maybe we were safe, because we were

alike in the way that mattered. We knew what the world was. We saw the same things when we looked out the air holes of our tiny, self-imposed prisons of loneliness.

It was like that forever, until Moira. Until I let someone else in my world—not like the other girls I had dated. It had been different with Moira from the start.

Maybe he felt I abandoned him a long time ago.

Maybe he felt this years ago, and it's only hitting me now.

"What's wrong, honey?"

I look down at Moira, peering up at me with concern. For the first time since I met her, the thought crosses my mind that maybe she's the intruder. I kill it instantly and feel shitty for even thinking it.

Moira is my other half. Moira makes me happy in a way no one ever has. She loves and accepts every piece of my soul, even the darkest, loneliest corner. I don't *need* to be safe from Moira; she loves me unconditionally.

I'm the luckiest bastard in the city.

It just doesn't feel like it right now.

There's never going to be a better time to tell her, so I meet her gaze and break the news. "Griff wants out."

Her expression clears and she brightens. "Of his shitty marriage? He's finally leaving Ashley? Well, I think that's great news."

"No, sweetheart, not..." I pause, sigh, then say, "Of our partnership. Of our... friendship, I think. He hasn't been talking to me and I don't get the impression he will again, but I think he wants to leave Ashley and then... maybe leave town. Maybe start over somewhere else, with no ties."

The horrified look on Moira's face mirrors exactly what I've been feeling all day long. I feel shitty, because somehow this all feels like my fault. I'm not sure exactly what I did—or what

I could have done differently—but it must have been something.

"Did he say why?" she asks, lowly.

I shake my head. "Not really. Some vague shit, but... He's not happy. He thinks this is the way to fix that."

Moira sighs, burying her face in her hands. I wrap an arm around her shoulders and tug her close, kissing the top of her head.

"But what about us?" she asks, sadly. "Why doesn't...?" She trails off, shaking her head. "This is all my fault."

"Don't be absurd. This is not your fault," I state.

Her gaze meets mine, dread swimming in the blue depths.

Alarm runs down my spine and I straighten. "What is it? What haven't you told me?"

"I don't know. I don't know if it's anything. I don't know if it even has anything to do with this. I feel horrible even mentioning it, it feels so... so arrogant and inconsequential, and I don't want to... I don't even want to say anything about this."

Alarm trickles through me. "About what?"

"When he stayed the night... the night I went to pick him up. I know he was drunk and lonely, so I didn't take anything seriously." She pauses, licking her lips and swallowing, as if buying time.

I don't like where this is going.

I almost want to ask her to stop, not to say anymore, but I can't.

The last thing I need is for my wife, the person I love the most, to tell me the person I love most after her tried some shit I'm going to have to punch him for while he was drunk.

"Sebastian, I think he might have... feelings for me. Or he thinks he does," she adds, quickly. "I just chalked it up to him being drunk—you know how *I* get when I'm drunk, but he kept saying things. He said we made him feel left out. We made him feel lonelier. I thought maybe he just meant more aware that he was single, that he didn't have what we have, but... I'm not sure if it was just that, or maybe a little more." She watches for a wary moment before continuing. "He... he said some other things that night, but I know he would never hurt you, and you know *I* would never hurt you, so I told myself it didn't matter. But..."

"He wants you," I say slowly.

She looks so tense she might explode. "I can't be *sure*, but... I got that impression. It may have just been the alcohol," she says, quickly, like she hopes that's the case. "I'm sure he didn't mean it. It's not like he wished you any harm, he didn't want to steal me. I think he feels left out because all those years it was just you two, and then suddenly I was there, but I was only yours. I think maybe it feels unfair to him, and he feels..."

She trails off, not quite sure how to finish that sentence.

To be honest, I'm not sure either.

How the fuck did this sneak up on me?

Griff and I *have* always shared the things that mattered to us —we shared our shelter, pooled our funds, built businesses; we built an entire future with one another. Nothing was *his* or *mine*, everything was ours.

Until Moira.

I kept Moira for myself, of course. That's what people do.

But keeping our businesses and our finances separate is another thing people do—it isn't what *we* did. We trusted each other in a way other people didn't trust one another—in a way *we* didn't trust anyone else.

Until Moira. I trusted Moira, and even though they had a friendship, I still kept the most fun parts of her to myself.

It all makes sense. Suddenly I feel like an idiot for not seeing it sooner.

He's not the one reneging on our partnership; I did, when I formed one with someone else and left him out.

So, how the fuck do I fix that?

Well, I suppose there's one glaringly obvious way; I could let him fuck her. I could tell my gentle, loving wife to spread her legs for Griff.

My little wife enjoys a certain level of subservience, in the bedroom and in our lifestyle, but I'm not sure it extends that far. I'm not sure what that would do to *us*. I'm not stingy with the people I love—they're the only ones I'm openly generous with. The rest of the world, they can all go fuck themselves. They never gave a rat's ass about me.

Griff did, though.

Moira does, always.

But that would be a big fucking risk. Moira is the most important person in the world to me. If we tried something crazy and it fucked up our relationship, I don't even know how I would get past that. I don't know what I would do if something broke us.

If I don't try, though, I will lose Griff. *We* will lose Griff. He's important to Moira, too. She loves both of us, but I don't think she loves Griff in that way. She doesn't think she's allowed to, though. Moira is faithful, so she would never open that door at the cost of hurting me.

What if I let her? What if I opened it for her?

Could we share her?

Griff and I have never struggled with sharing any of our resources, but could we share a woman? I'm not sure how I feel about it. I'm not sure what it would be like to know another man—even Griff—had his hands on my wife.

She wouldn't just be mine anymore; she would be *ours*.

I keep one arm around Moira, but reach into my pocket with the other and draw out my phone. I open the last chain of texts that exists between me and Griff. I try to envision it first—Moira naked on our bed, but Griff is the one between her legs instead of me. He'd need to have her body to himself sometimes.

Could Moira pull that off? Could she love enough to fill both of us up? She is full of love, so maybe.

But maybe not.

Fuck, I hate the stakes here. Either I bet everything and try to keep them both, or I let one of them go and just keep the other. I don't have to open this door. I can buy out Griff's side of our businesses and send him out into the world with money and no ties. Maybe he can find his own Moira.

Would it even hold the same appeal, though? I think a large part of why he wants Moira is because she belongs to me. It's the sharing that he feels entitled to, that he wants to be a part of. Griff and I were always a family, and now Moira is my family—he just wants to be included.

I think I could do it. For Griff, I think I could do it.

I'm no prude, beside the fucking point. Maybe it would be hot to watch Griff with Moira. Two people I love giving one another pleasure. Maybe it won't be painful. Just because Moira is sharing her love with him doesn't necessarily mean she'd have any less to give me.

Before I can change my mind, I open up the text and tap out, "I want you to come over. Moira told me some things about last time you spent the night and I think I understand what's bothering you."

It takes a minute for him to type back, "It's not what you think."

"I know," I assure him. "No one's mad. We just want to talk to you. Moira wants to talk to you."

"I don't want to talk to her," he states.

"You will when you hear what she has to say."

There we go, that'll whet his appetite.

Surely enough, it does. He sends back, "Why? What does she have to say?"

"Come over and you'll find out."

"When?" he asks.

"Now," I send back.

He'll come. He'll be too curious not to.

I close the text and put my phone away. Now comes the hard part. I'm not sure what Moira will think about all this, so I can't give her the opportunity to say no. If she has it, she will—out of loyalty to me. She'll think she's required to say no.

"I need you to do something for me, sweetheart. I want you to go upstairs to our bedroom and take off all your clothes."

A saucy smile creeps across Moira's pretty face. "Oh yeah? I can do that."

I smile at her, leaning in to kiss the shell of her ear. "Then I want you to climb into bed and wait."

"What are you doing in the meantime? How long will I have to wait?"

"Griff's going to come over," I tell her, and her smile falls. Not because she understands where I'm going with this yet, but simply because the mention of Griff makes her sad, given what I just said.

"To sign papers?" she asks somberly.

"No, not to sign papers. He's going to talk to me, then he's going to come up and talk to you."

"Oh." She frowns, confused. "So... I'm *waiting* to take my clothes off."

"No," I say, holding her gaze. "You're going to wait in bed, like I just said. I'm going to send Griff up to talk to you about his problems, and you're going to listen. You're going to give him what he needs."

It's starting to hit her, what I'm saying, but she looks a little scared. "You mean, an ear? I'm going to listen to him… naked?"

"You're going to give him *whatever* he needs." So there's no confusion, I grab her between the legs and she gasps. "If he needs this, you give it to him."

"Sebastian…" Her voice shakes a little, then her head shakes. Here comes the obligatory denial.

"The alternative is he leaves, Moira. He doesn't think he can have happiness here because he thinks I won't share mine." I let a finger move up under the scant fabric of her panties and run it between the folds of her pussy. "We love Griff, don't we?" She nods her head tentatively and I push a finger inside her. I can see how tempted she is for her head to drift back, but she's focused on me, on my directions for her to go up to our bedroom and wait for another man to come fuck her.

I circle her clit lazily, making her feel good, but not *too* good.

"So we're going to show him," I tell her, pressing my lips against the side of her face to soothe her. "Only you can fix this, sweetheart. I'd fix it if I could, but my hands are tied. What he needs, he needs from you."

"I don't think this is a good idea," she tells me, her tone soft. "He'll only feel teased if you do this. If he has me once, that doesn't make me his, it only gives him something else to think about when he's feeling left out. And I don't *want* to be with anyone but you. Only you're supposed to touch me. I belong to *you*. We're married. We spoke vows to one another— and I meant them."

"So did I," I assure her, calmly. "But you're not doing

anything wrong. I'm the one suggesting it. You aren't hurting me. You love Griff, don't you?"

Her eyes dart away from mine. "Well, yes, but..."

"And you don't want him to leave? You don't want him to dissolve our partnership and disappear from our life?"

"Of course not."

"Then do as I say." I withdraw my finger from her body, pulling her dress back down and leaning in to kiss her lips. "You're a smart woman with good instincts. You'll be able to figure out what to do with him. Do whatever you need to do. Show him he doesn't have to feel left out."

Frowning, Moira stands. "I'm not a toy, Sebastian. I may follow your orders when it's fun, but this is too far. You can't just rent me out to your friend. Did you already tell him to come?"

"I did."

"So, what if I don't *want* to have sex with Griff? What then?"

There's not much I can say to that. "Well, sweetheart, then I sign the papers and let him out. You don't have to do anything you don't want to do, obviously, but don't say you don't want to for me. I don't want Griff to leave. I don't want that to happen. If you can't do it, you can't do it." I shrug. "If you can, I want you to. I love Griff and I don't want to lose him, but I don't want him to be miserable, either."

That seems to knock some of the wind out of her sails. She crosses her arms protectively, rubbing her elbow and looking off at nothing. I think she just doesn't want to look at me. "It doesn't bother you? To think of... of someone else *being with* me?"

"Someone else, yes. Griff, not so much. Not if he needs it."

"It would bother me," she says softly.

I smile at her. "Well, I should hope so. I don't want anyone but you."

"Exactly." She sits on the edge of the couch and rests a hand on my thigh, her big blue eyes imploring. "And I only want you."

"All right." I nod, but I know I don't look pleased. I probably should be. All I can feel is the loss, though. It's not even fair to expect Moira to fix this for me, but that's what Moira does. She fixes things—if a button pops off my shirt, she sews it back on; if something weighs on my mind, she listens and shares the burden.

Maybe this is too much. What Griff wants isn't simple, I know that. I'm willing to try it, I'm willing to share, but if she's not, the idea pretty much dies.

Finally, looking at my knee instead of my face, she says, "Tell me again why I should do this."

"It's gonna hurt to lose him," I say honestly.

"Hurt you," she says, to verify.

"Of course. And you, I imagine."

She nods her head, pensive.

"But if you're not attracted to him, this is a moot point."

"I didn't say *that*. It's... I'm not... You're my husband, so I only feed my attraction to you. You know I love you both, but not the same way. This is not something I ever thought... I don't know how this works." She looks up at me. "What if I do this and you're wrong? What if you're not okay with it?"

"This is *my* idea. I accept full responsibility for it."

"What good will that do if you can't even look at me tomorrow?"

"That's not going to happen," I assure her, placing my hand over hers. "I love you. I'm secure in our love, in our relation-ship, in your attraction to me. It doesn't make me feel threatened if you're attracted to Griff, too. I love Griff; I want good things for him. You're the best thing I have."

She rolls her eyes. "It's just more complicated than loaning him your favorite dinner jacket, Sebastian. This could harm our relationship."

"We won't let it," I assure her, even though I had the same thought.

After a brief pause, she asks, "You *really* want to do this?"

"It's worth a try. If we don't, we lose him anyway. If we try and it doesn't work out, if there's no spark or he's worked it all up to something in his head that can't stack up… well, then we had an adventurous experience and it's over. We move on with our lives. It's you and me forever, sweetheart, for better or worse. I wouldn't tell you to do this if I didn't believe in my ability to handle it."

She stands quickly, like she has to or she'll change her mind. "I'm going upstairs. I'm going to take off my clothes and get in bed. Whatever happens after that is up to you. If you want to send Griff up, send him up. If you change your mind, come up yourself. I don't know how I feel about this, but I don't want Griff to leave us, either. I don't know."

7

MOIRA

I DON'T KNOW IF IT'S THE CHILLY WEATHER OR FEAR that makes me shiver as I step out of my panties and reach behind my back to unclasp my bra. I feel vaguely nauseous.

I can't shake the feeling that this is a terrible idea, but it may just be because this is outside my comfort zone. I have always been a firmly monogamous person. I've never even *dated* casually, so when Sebastian slipped the platinum band on my finger, that was it for me. I don't struggle with attractions to other men. I don't spend a moment of time wondering what else is out there. I am overwhelmingly happy with the amazing man I married. There's nothing missing from our relationship or my life. We don't *need* this.

We don't, but *Sebastian* might.

I worry that if Griff leaves, something important *will* go missing from Sebastian's life. If Griff leaves now, maybe Sebastian blames me. Even if not intentionally—he may still feel it's because of me he lost his best friend, his only family. He won't even be wrong. It *is* because of me. Not because of anything I've *done*, but because of me, nonetheless.

This is a unique predicament I'm in.

Then there's Griff himself. I don't want him to be unhappy either, but I don't know if I can *make* him happy. I've only ever thought of Griff as a friend. Sure, he's a wonderful, handsome man—as I saw a few weeks ago when I helped him out of his shirt, a *very* handsome man—and I enjoy his company, but having a sexual relationship with him is another matter entirely. Plus, I know Griff; it won't just be sexual. He'll need an emotional connection, too. He'll need a full-blown relationship.

I'll have *two* relationships with two different men. I did not sign up for that.

I pace around the room and debate locking the door.

Finally, I follow my husband's directions and slide into the king-sized bed where Sebastian made love to me just this morning. Flashes of this morning come to mind, Sebastian's kisses on my neck, his hands roaming my body. It makes my stomach sink. Only Sebastian should be in this bed with me. Only Sebastian should have my body. I don't want my husband to lose his best friend, but I shouldn't have to do this to keep him here. Sebastian told me to, though.

I go over the same confusing thoughts and feelings while I wait. I talk it to death inside my own head.

Perhaps I should have stayed downstairs and taken part in this conversation. This is about me too, after all. Sometimes Sebastian gets a little heavy-handed in matters like these. I don't mind overly much, but it annoys Griff. Ordinarily, I defend Sebastian's more domineering impulses, but ordinarily it's something insignificant—what we should have for dinner, what color of lingerie he wants me to order. Not the parameters for my sexual relationship with another man.

I'm playing in another league tonight, and I never even went to a try-out.

The sound of knuckles rapping lightly on the door draws me out of my thoughts and kills my last hope that Sebastian might come up and save me from all this. Sebastian would never knock on our bedroom door—he would stroll right in.

So, of course, when the door eases open, it's Griff. He looks confused. I am, too. I have no idea what he and Sebastian discussed. Does he even know he's here to potentially fuck me? I say potentially, but I'm naked in this bed—how many other ways can this go?

Oh my God.

Another man's dick is going to be inside me. A man who isn't my husband.

Griff eases inside the room like he thinks he might be in the wrong place. "Uh… Seb said you wanted to talk."

My heart thumps loudly in my chest. I swallow, tightening my grip on the sheet around my breasts, and nod my head. His gaze drops to my bare shoulders, to the way I have the sheet wrapped around me. I can see by the way his face freezes that he's realizing I'm naked underneath.

He clears his throat. "Am I interrupting? I can… this can wait."

My stomach feels all fluttery, but I shake my head. If Sebastian wants me to do this, then… well, I'll try. "Come over here," I tell him, patting the empty space on the bed next to me. Not Sebastian's spot—my side of the bed, if we kept to sides. We don't. Sebastian and I sleep snuggled up against one another, but I can't think of that right now. I'll never be able to go through with this if I do.

Maybe that means I shouldn't.

As I grasp for a way out of this situation, Griff looks reluctant to even enter it. He looks anywhere but at me, like he's invading my privacy. We don't speak. He eventually takes a seat on the edge of the bed, but I pat it again and he moves full on it next to me, stretching out his long legs. He stares straight ahead.

"What did Sebastian tell you?" I ask, watching him closely.

"Not that you would be naked," he states. "He said you wanted to talk to me. This part he left out."

"He told me you're leaving," I begin, softly.

His broad, muscular shoulders rise and fall in a shrug far too casual. "It just feels like time."

"Because of me," I say.

"No, not because of you."

"Because of Ashley?"

He drags his gaze to mine, making a visible effort not to let it drop below my face. "It's for me, all right? There are things I want out of life that I can't get here, and I may not be able to get them anywhere else either, but at least somewhere else, no one's rubbing it in my face."

I think it's unfair that our relationship's existence, our happiness, feels like rubbing it in his face. We don't go out of our way to express it in front of him, that's just how we are with one another.

But maybe he understands that, and that's why he wants to leave. This isn't an instance where anyone has done anything wrong; we've simply outgrown one another. Maybe the right thing to do is to let him go. I would miss him all the time, and I know Sebastian would miss him even worse, but maybe that is the right thing for Griff.

Sebastian won't agree with that, though. I adore my husband, every corner of him, but he has a rigid side when it comes to his loved ones. It works for me; I'm flexible and happy to go along with most things. Letting Griff go is not something he will accept, even if it is better for Griff in the long run, because it will hurt. Because Sebastian thinks he can control the situation; he thinks he can use me to stop Griff from leaving. I understand, though. I feel for him. Sebastian has lost enough in his life, and he won't volunteer to lose anything more—especially a relationship so crucial to him.

I can't make Griff stay if it will make him miserable, but I can't let him go because that will make Sebastian miserable.

These two men that I love are breaking apart, and maybe I am the only thing that can stitch them back together.

I try to visualize where to go from here. I imagine sliding up against Griff's hard body, running a hand up under the black T-shirt he's wearing tonight. I can explore the muscular chest that I got a good look at a few weeks ago. I can dip my head and kiss him, swirl my tongue around his nipples, run my hands down his chiseled abdomen.

It all makes me feel... I don't even know. Too many things. There is attraction mixed in there somewhere. Curiosity. What would he do? What would it feel like to have his rough hands skimming the planes of my body? What does he taste like? What does his cock look like? Is he a tender lover, or more aggressive?

I shouldn't know any of this about Griff.

"You okay?" he asks, watching me go through this weird range of emotions.

I meet his gaze. "I don't want you to go. *We* don't—" I cut myself off, since he rolls his eyes. He's already told me to quit the "we bullshit," but...

"Sometimes you have to do the hard thing, Moira."

"What if you didn't?" I ask.

"I do. I've thought this over. Sebastian already—"

Instead of waiting for him to finish telling me how he needs to leave for reasons I already know, I give him something new. I scoot closer, tentatively looking up at him. His blue eyes are wide and wary. They drop to my sheet-covered body again, drifting down like he's imagining what's underneath.

"Would you still need to go... if you didn't just have to watch?" I ask, feeling my whole body flush at my brazenness.

It's heady, the way he looks at me. Like I'm the most valuable thing he can ever imagine looking at. Like he'd give everything to be able to see beneath the sheet.

I can see his struggle when he meets my gaze again. I wonder how I haven't seen it before. Was it always there, just beneath the surface, or did this just start with Ashley's betrayal?

"Did you leave Ashley?" I ask.

He nods slowly.

I heave a sigh of relief. "Good. She didn't deserve you."

"I don't understand what's going on," he tells me.

I don't know how to explain it with words—or I guess I do, but I don't have the nerve left. I don't have it in me to tell him my husband is willing to let him fuck me, if that's what it takes to make him stay. He wouldn't like that, anyway. Even if Griff literally dreams about what it's like to be inside me, he wouldn't like Sebastian using me that way.

Sometimes I like being used. Not like this, but... well, we've never tried it before.

In the most direct way possible, I explain—by dropping the sheet and revealing my naked breasts. For the briefest moment, he stares. Then he forces his gaze away, demanding, "What the hell are you doing?"

I swallow down the lump of nerves in my throat. "Do you

want me, Griff? Is that what this is all about? Can you stay if you have me?"

"Moira..."

I feel vulnerable, sitting here half-exposed to him and him not even looking. I know he's just confused and doesn't know what the fuck is happening, but it still doesn't feel good.

So, I throw the sheet off me completely.

He can't resist that temptation. He turns his head, his hungry gaze roving over my bare breasts. Like a magnet, his eyes are drawn between my legs and he groans.

In a split second, he's on top of me. I scoot down on the bed and he braces his weight on top of me, looking at my breasts again, then dragging his gaze to my face. "What are you doing, Moira?"

My heart hammers so loud, I'm worried he can hear it. "Sebastian said... he said he'll share me, if that's what you need."

He holds my gaze for a moment, but I can't interpret the turbulence in his gaze. Then he palms my left breast and I gasp, taken off-guard by the contact.

"You think I'm some charity fuck, Moira?" he demands, his tone low and gravelly. I think he's offended.

"No," I say on a gasp, as he squeezes my nipple between his thumb and forefinger. "Of course not, Griff. That's not what this is."

He dips his head and catches my hardened nipple between his teeth. My stomach sinks, but falls straight into a pit of arousal. I throw my head back against the pillow as his mouth fastens over my nipple, sucking and then circling, his tongue flicking the sensitive bud.

I grab at the sheets beneath me, fisting my hands in the soft fabric. He releases my nipple, kissing my breast, then turns the same attention on the other one. The rough pad of his thumb moves back and forth over the other one to keep them both stimulated. I can't keep my head straight. There's probably more talking to do, but I can't think with his mouth leaving my breast and moving down my abdomen.

I'm supposed to be the one pleasing him, I'm certain of it, but he drags his hands down my body like I'm something precious, then positions himself with his face between my legs.

"Oh, God, Griff."

He gives me a searing look that unleashes a whole new swarm of butterflies in my tummy, then he buries his face between my thighs and tastes me.

This is a mistake, it has to be. My stomach pitches with nerves and excitement as Griff's tongue moves up and strokes my clit. Jolts of pleasure shoot through me and I twist, trying to turn away from it. He grabs my hips hard and holds them in place so he can explore my pussy without interruption.

Oh, God, he feels so good. He's so tender, while at the same time pushing his will. His will is to please me, to taste me, to make me feel good. He hasn't thought of his pleasure once yet.

It makes me desperate to give it to him. I want him... I want him inside me. I want to know what Griff is like as a lover. I want to know if he holds me down and drives his cock inside me, if he watches my face for every sign of pleasure so he can learn just what I like.

I already feel the climb toward intense pleasure. He's relentless with his tongue and he won't let me move away. It turns me on more. I'm used to Sebastian's dominance—it's so much different from this. Griff holds me here to please me; Sebastian holds me here to please himself.

Turns out, I can see myself liking both.

I cry out as pleasure erupts within me, arching up off the

bed and reaching down to tangle my hands in Griff's hair. He comes up and I fall back against the bed.

I'm sated for the moment, but it feels intensely erotic the way he's still fully dressed, while my body is completely bare beneath him. The fabric dragging across my sensitive breasts, the roughness of his jeans on my smooth legs. I want him nearer. I wrap my arms around him and pull him close. He leans his head on my shoulder briefly, then begins kissing his way across my shoulder, toward my neck.

My mind drifts to Sebastian's kisses, to his lips on my neck. It's like ice water being dumped over my prone body. I try to push it away, but now my husband's face is in my head. I imagine how he would feel watching this. It was his idea to begin with, but I didn't expect my body to fall so easily into wanting it.

I just had another man's mouth all over me. Lavishing attention on my breasts, kissing his way down my body, putting his mouth on my pussy, making me come.

Griff's rough hand brushes my hair back off my forehead and I realize he's looking down at me, watching my face. "You okay?"

I manage a bright smile and nod. "Yes. Thank you."

At that, he laughs a little. "You don't have to thank me."

He remains above me, but he doesn't seem to be in a hurry. He doesn't drag his shirt over his head or free his cock, at the very least, so he can push it inside me and take his pleasure now. He runs his fingers across my abdomen, just touching me. Tenderness swims in his eyes, like he's dreamed of being able to do this forever.

"Tell me what you're thinking," he requests.

I swallow, knowing I can't say what I was *really* thinking. Or maybe I can. I don't know where his head is at in all this, either. "Have you two ever shared a woman before?"

"Not intentionally."

I blink. "What does that mean?"

Vague amusement enters his intense blue eyes. "I'm not sure I should tell you."

I narrow my eyes at him, but lightly. "Well, now you *have* to."

"There was this one girl we both knew. A casual, just-for-fun kind of girl."

I roll my eyes. I don't savor thinking of Sebastian ever being with another woman. Of course I know he was, probably plenty, but it's still annoying to hear about.

"Anyhow, we were really young, early twenties."

I bite my bottom lip to keep my smile small. "My age," I point out.

"Well, we were much less… domesticated."

"I bet you were."

He continues to caress my skin while he tells me his story. It feels nice, the casual tenderness. "Her name was Stella. She was one a few people who would crash at our place every now and then. Seb and I were both really busy, we both worked two jobs, so we were almost never home at the same time. I started getting to know her when she would stay over. To be honest, I didn't even know where she slept. It's not like she lived there, so I figured she crashed wherever she fell. One night I was home and she was there. One thing led to the next, I took her to my room."

I screw my nose up again.

Griff smirks. "Then a couple days later Seb and I *were* home at the same time. He came out in just a pair of sweats, she came out wearing his T-shirt. Didn't take a detective to figure it out, but in case I wondered, he grabbed her ass and kissed her while he waited for the coffee to brew."

My eyes widen. "No."

He nods. "Yep. It wasn't a big deal, like I said. Neither of us were *involved* with her, but... yeah, turns out we did both fuck her at the same time."

"She could have told you," I point out.

"Could've," he agrees. "Didn't."

That's not the same situation at all, but it's the closest thing I have for reference. "And that didn't cause any sort of trouble for you guys? It wasn't weird?"

He shrugs one shoulder, considering. "More funny than weird. There were no feelings involved; we just thought she was a tricky little ho."

I can't help smiling. "She does sound a bit like a tricky little ho."

"At least she had good taste," he jokes.

I nod my head, raising an eyebrow. "I can't argue that." It still doesn't answer my question, though, so I meet his gaze more seriously. "Can *you* share? Even if he's able to make it work... can you?"

"Do I not strike you as good at sharing?"

"Not especially," I say honestly.

A grin claims his lips. "All right, I guess that's fair. You're his, though. His first, at least. That makes it easier. I shouldn't have you at all, but if there's a way we can *both* have you... that's appealing. Is it good with you?"

I still haven't entirely decided, but the only response I can muster is a positive one. He's still running his fingers across my skin like he can't believe I'm here. I went from nauseated to wanting him in the space of about ten minutes, so it seems like

I can bring myself around to it. I just need them to be okay with it. I'm already happy; I'm doing this to make *them* happy.

It seems like it's working for Griff so far, so I nod my head. I only hope it's working for Sebastian, and that it continues working. "Yeah, I want to try it. I just want everyone to be happy. I don't want anyone to get hurt."

"I don't, either. You know how it is with me and Seb."

"I know how it *was*," I state. "But you tried to leave him today. *You* know he doesn't deal well with that."

"Well, I didn't think this was an option," he states.

"But since it is…" I look up at him, waiting on him to assure me he'll stay.

He does. "I'm not going anywhere just yet."

That brings a genuine smile to my lips. "Good."

He smiles, another smile that feels so much lighter than is typical.

I never thought of Griff as being guarded around me, but the unguarded tenderness he's shown me in just the last few minutes is so much different than how he's been with me in the years we've known one another. It's too drastic a change to have occurred in a few minutes, so I have to believe he held all these feelings behind some kind of floodgate. It fortifies my belief that I'm what came between them, that I'm the reason he had to leave.

I just didn't know.

I never knew.

It should be impossible for someone to have these feelings and manage to keep them all separate. This must have been so hard on Griff.

Overcome with tenderness, I reach up to run a hand along his scruffy jawline. I smile softly, then work my fingers through his hair, around the back of his head. I pull him down for a kiss. He hasn't even kissed me yet—well, on the mouth, at least.

His lips brush mine softly, like he's afraid to be too demanding. Like he, too, still feels I'm not his to kiss.

I don't think about that. I close my eyes and give him access when he deepens the kiss just a little. I still want him. Arousal pools between my legs, even though he satisfied me. I run a hand down his muscular torso and unhook the button of his pants. Next, I unzip them and shove my hand down the front, rubbing his cock through the fabric. Boxer briefs? I go for the waistband to shove my hand inside those, too, but he catches my wrist and tugs it out of his pants.

I break away from his lips to shoot him a look of confusion. "That has to come out if you're going to fuck me."

Laughing lightly, he says, "It does? Well, I guess I've been doing sex wrong."

I frown. Despite his lightness, he isn't looking me in the eye. "What's wrong?" I ask. "Don't you want to…?"

His gaze jumps to mine, startled. "I do. Of course I do."

"Then what's the problem? Is it Sebastian? He told me to do this—he swears he's fine with it."

Griff shakes his head, but breaks my gaze again briefly. "No, it's not that. There's nothing *wrong*, I just…" He meets my gaze. "I want to take you out first."

I blink at him. "Take me out? Like, on a date?"

"Yeah. You're not some hooker I hired for the night; you're Moira. If we're going to do this, we should do it right. Not because Seb *told* you to. We should go out just the two of us. I should take you on a proper date."

I grin up at him. That's such a Griff thing to insist on. He already has me naked in bed, he's already given *me* an orgasm, but he doesn't want to have sex with me until he feels he's fulfilled his gentlemanly duty by taking me out first. "All right, if you say so."

"I'd kinda like to stay a little longer, though," he tells me. His gaze drops to my breasts, but unapologetically this time. "I'd like to spend a little more time looking at these, too."

"Look your fill," I tell him. "Look, touch, taste—I don't have anything else to do right now."

So he does. It's unspeakably tender, lying here in bed with Griff. We talk a little more, kiss a lot more, and he touches me all over. It's so much different from what I'm used to.

Sebastian loves me intensely, of course, and he pleases me so much, but I feel more like an extension of Sebastian than Griff. Sebastian treats me like something that belongs to him— that's a given. Griff treats my body like a coveted treasure that he can't believe he's allowed to have. He savors the feel of my skin, the brush of my lips. He kisses me slowly, like he's memorizing the taste.

It's lovely.

When the door opens, I'm snuggled up on Griff's chest, my head resting on his bicep, our hands twined together between us. I immediately let go and sit up, fear traveling down my spine. I still feel like I've done something irrevocably wrong, and when I see Sebastian walk through the door, all the justifying and insistence that he said he was okay with it flies right out the window.

The sight of my husband shouldn't hurt, but I feel guilt weighing down on every part of me, threatening to crush me. It replays the sounds I made just a little bit ago when Griff had his face buried between my legs, the tenderness I felt for him while we snuggled and talked. The guilt is so heavy I can't breathe properly.

This man is the only one I'm supposed to be doing these things with.

Sebastian walks in, by all appearances relaxed. My husband is the most capable man I've ever met. It takes a lot to shake him. He's at ease in any given situation—and if he's not, you'll never know.

Now he's stripped off his suit jacket and left it behind somewhere, probably in the living room. He's wearing his white dress shirt unbuttoned at the top. The tie he wore to work is long gone, but he's still neatly tucked into his black slacks. The sleeves of his shirt have been pushed up to his elbow and he's holding a glass with a couple fingers of amber liquid in the bottom.

I don't look at his face until he pauses at the foot of the bed and raises the glass to his lips. I can feel his eyes on me, so even though it makes me sick to my stomach, I meet his gaze.

I feel changed, and I wonder if he can see it. I wonder if it's real, or if I'm just worried his vision of me will be forever tarnished by this.

I tell myself it was his idea, but that doesn't necessarily matter. If this was his idea and he can't handle it, that won't change the damage that's been done. It will be worse, too, because I'll hurt Griff trying to make it all up to Sebastian—and this was *his* damn idea in the first place.

I'm starting to get mad at Sebastian, but I'm more terrified than mad, so that emotion wins. That's the one that consumes me. That's the one I'm sure he sees swimming in my guilty eyes when I look up at him.

He swallows the liquor, then walks around to his side of the bed and puts his drink down. I get up on my knees and crawl closer, needing to be near him. I need him to look at me the same way he did this morning. I need him to touch me, to kiss me. I need to know nothing is broken between us, nothing is damaged.

He has to know all this, he has to see it, but I'm not the one he checks in with first. That makes me think he's definitely mad at me. I should be the one he takes care of first, but he glances right past me to Griff.

"Have fun?"

Griff doesn't seem to know how to respond to that, either.

Sebastian smirks, shaking his head as he unbuttons the rest of his shirt. "You're a couple of fucking puritans, you know that?" Instead of finishing his drink, he grabs it and passes it to me.

I shoot him a questioning glance as I take it.

"Drink up," he says. "Seems like you need that more than I do."

8

SEBASTIAN

My wife is completely terrified.

I wasn't entirely sure how I would feel walking into this, despite my earlier reassurances that everything would be fine. It was what had to happen and I'm a man who does what needs doing, but it's one thing to decide logically that this is the course of action, and quite another to walk into my bedroom where my wife lies naked in our bed, the smell of sex in the air, her hair mussed from someone else's hands running through her dark locks, both of them with faintly guilty looks on their faces.

They're bad at this already.

I'm sure they'll adjust, though. This is uncharted territory and they're not sure how it works. That's understandable. I'm not either; I'm just much better at taking the lead even if I have no fucking idea where we're heading.

So, that's what I do. Moira looks up at me with all her feelings in her big blue eyes. I think she'd burst into tears if I so much as frowned at her. That makes me feel bad. I don't want

Moira to be so fragile about this, but I get it. The idea of fucking up our relationship scares me, too, I'm just not going to bleed my fucking feelings all over the place like she does.

Someone's gotta be the strong one. I should've known it would have to be me. Griff usually handles his shit a lot better, but he doesn't look much more comfortable than Moira right now.

Well, in my opinion there's one sure way to blow past this kind of discomfort, to stop this sort of tiptoeing and show everyone once and for all how I want things.

Moira finishes the whiskey, grimacing like she just swallowed poison. I can't help smirking. She hates hard liquor, but it'll help her nerves. I take the glass from her and put it down on the end table, peeling off my shirt and starting on my belt.

Moira's gaze drops to my belt, then darts back to my face, a bit uncertainly.

Griff clears his throat. "Should I go?"

I shake my head, meeting his gaze. "No."

He eases back on the pillow, but he looks no more certain than Moira.

"Did you come inside her or did you use a condom?" I ask.

Moira wilts—visibly wilts, like she wants to sink into the floor and disappear. No, no, no, that's not what I want.

Seeing the way Moira reacts, Griff's gaze shifts from her to me, picking up some hostility on the journey. "I didn't—" He shakes his head, his jaw locking. He makes a visible effort to unlock it, then continues, "It didn't go that far."

Now I frown, cocking my head in confusion. "What didn't go that far? What are you talking about? You didn't get off? You stopped? What the hell were you two doing up here?"

Moira buries her face in her hands.

Griff looks worried about it. He can barely keep from glaring at me, since I'm the one making her so damn uncomfortable. "Do we have to tell you that? Do all of our activities have to pass inspection?"

I shuck my pants and shake my head, eyebrows rising. "I guess not. I just figured I send you upstairs to fuck my wife, stands to reason that my wife would get fucked. I'm not sure where in there my intent got lost—I was pretty clear with Moira."

"Yeah, well, I don't fuck at your behest," Griff states.

I meet his gaze, and he raises a challenging eyebrow.

I shrug. "All right. If you don't want to fuck my wife, then don't. I don't know what all this is about then."

"Don't worry about it," Griff says.

"So, you *don't* want to share Moira?"

"No, I do."

I frown. "But you don't want to fuck her?"

"No, I… Yeah, I do. Not like this, though."

I shake my head at him and walk over to turn out the light.

"What are you doing?" Griff asks, as soon as the room goes dark. "Am I staying the night? Shouldn't I at least go to the guest room?"

"We have a king bed. There's plenty of room for you to stay here."

I pull back the blanket on my side and slide in. Moira immediately comes to my side, needing reassurance. I can see the fear in her eyes even now, so I cradle the back of her neck in my hand and draw her in for a soft, slow kiss. She melts against me, wrapping her arms around me, clinging to me. Her fear ignites desire within me. I don't make Moira worry about losing me on a regular basis—that would be cruel—but I like knowing the thought of losing me terrifies her. It's reassurance that her little ass isn't going anywhere.

Right now she's desperate to make it up to me, and I like that, too. There's nothing more intoxicating than the repentant trail of Moira's lips along my jawline, down my neck, across my chest. Without words, she expresses her love. With the kind of raw need most healthy people can't feel in a vacuum like this, she makes me feel like the most important man in her world.

Of course, Griff being right here on the bed with us, that's probably not feeling so good for him. Feels great to me, though. I need to give a little back.

"It's Griff's turn," I tell Moira.

She tears her lips away from my chest and looks up at me, confused. "What?"

I cock my head toward Griff.

Moira sits back on her heels and hesitates. "You want me to...? In front of you?"

I nod my head.

Moira swallows audibly, looking none too confident, but she turns and crawls over to Griff. His mouth opens to object, but as Moira straddles his lap with her naked ass, he can't summon the willpower. She sits there for a second just looking at him, then she runs her hands up his chest before leaning in and kissing him. There's no deepening of the kiss—just soft little pecks. There's tenderness, but no desperation. She doesn't kiss him like she needs him, the way she kisses me, but he doesn't seem to be in a position to complain.

No, the tables have turned now. His hands go to her waist like he can't help touching her. He follows the pace she sets, but he's the one who needs her. Moira needs me, Griff needs Moira, and I... well, I guess I need Griff, because there's really no alternative I can envision where I'd be sitting here watching another man fondle my wife.

Watching him need her turns me on. I have power over him

now, because I have total power over Moira. That motherfucker isn't going anywhere as long as Moira has him by the balls.

Relief spreads through me. I'm feeling better about life, about this decision. I'm feeling grateful for my dutiful little wife, even as she straddles someone else's cock, as his big hands palm her breasts and trace the curve of her back.

I push up and prowl across the bed, grabbing Moira's hips and dragging her off his lap. A startled gasp slips out of her and Griff looks immediately bereft when her mouth leaves his, but since she's mine, he doesn't dare object.

Oh yes, I like this already.

Moira looks back at me over her shoulder. She's on her hands and knees. I put a hand on her back and pet her, partly to reassure her, partly to push her into the position I want her in. I grip her hips a little tighter and pull her ass up in the air. She's accustomed to this, so she lowers her upper body toward the bed and her legs spread for me naturally. I can't resist pushing a finger inside her sweet pussy to see how wet Griff made her. I close my eyes as my finger sinks inside her. Oh, she's fucking drenched. Too drenched. Did he really make her this wet?

My gaze drifts to Griff and I see him watching me, watching my finger as I move it in and out of my wife. His gaze drifts to Moira, in position like a good girl. The way I have her, she's looking right at him while I finger her.

After a few more seconds—and a strained moan from Moira—Griff clears his throat. "I'm gonna go in the guest room."

"Stay or go," I say casually, pushing a second finger into my wife's pussy. "If you stay, we can fuck her together."

Moira shudders, pushing against my fingers.

Griff's eyebrows rise. "Excuse me?"

"Did you eat her pussy, Griff?" I ask casually, as Moira lets out another soft moan. "Did she come for you? I hope you made her come hard. Moira's a good little wife." I withdraw my fingers and then shove them into her up to the knuckle. "She deserves to come hard."

I can see part of him still wants to leave, but now he's looking at Moira again, at her struggling against her arousal already. She loves my mouth, so when I talk about Griff eating her pussy like that, it has to make her crazy. Judging by the hooded look on Griff's face as he watches her, by the simple fact that he's still sitting here, she's turning him on, too.

He looks up at me. "Is this how we're doing this? We're supposed to fuck her together?"

"Tonight," I say, pulling my fingers from Moira's pussy and running my hand over her perfect ass. She makes a faint noise of disappointment and I smirk. "What better way to seal the deal?"

Since I'm not going to wait for him to decide, and because there's probably a better chance he stays if I do, I stop wasting time, stroke my cock a couple of times and guide it to Moira's pussy. I rub the crown against her. She's so fucking wet, it eases right inside. I slide home, burying myself balls deep in my eager-to-please little wife.

"Take her mouth," I tell Griff.

He tears his eyes away from Moira's face, his gaze lingering briefly on the visual of me pulling out and impaling her again, but then he meets my eyes, his brow furrowed in consternation. "What?"

"Fuck her mouth," I say slowly, rocking my hips and drawing a low moan out of her.

"This isn't right," Griff says, shaking his head. "This isn't right. This is Moira. We shouldn't be treating her like some whore."

I grin at him as I shove inside my wife again. "Trust me,

Griff, Moira wants to be treated like your little whore. Don't believe me? Get on the bed and see how loud she moans when we're fucking her tight little pussy and her sweet little mouth at the same time."

"Oh, God," Moira murmurs, pressing her forehead to the bed.

"Tell Griff you want his cock, Moira."

"I do," she tells him, gasping again as I piston my hips and fill her pussy. "Griff, it's okay. I want to."

That's all the encouragement he needs. He's made of stern fucking stuff to be able to resist this long, but now he pushes his jeans down and kicks them off, pushing off his boxer briefs. His cock springs free—he's already hard, which shouldn't surprise me. If he could watch Moira get fucked, listen to all her little sounds and *not* get turned on, I would be more concerned.

He gets up on his knees and grasps his cock in one hand, but he looks like he still doesn't want to put it near Moira. He's probably got some sort of Madonna complex—thinks of her as untouchable, so he shouldn't put his dirty hands on her. He'll have to get over that. I guess Moira's needs can be met by me alone and she can just manage him, but I'd like for him to learn how to please her. Otherwise he'll probably start to notice I can do things for her he can't and we'll be right back at square one.

"Put your cock in her fucking mouth, Griff."

He glares at me, not appreciating my direction. Then, like he actually wants to annoy me, he fists a hand in my wife's hair and holds her still while he eases his cock into the warm, wet cavern of her mouth. Moira moans around his cock as she takes him, and fuck if it doesn't turn me on even more.

Yes, this is fucking beautiful. I pump my hips harder and Moira's body jerks forward, but now Griff is on the other side. She keeps her weight braced on the bed with one hand, but she grabs Griff's hip with the other to anchor herself to him so she has *some* control over how deep he goes into her throat while I fuck her.

My little beauty is a natural. Griff's head falls back as Moira takes every inch of his cock. I reach under her and stroke her clit, wanting to reward her even more for the excellent job she's doing. This is fucking perfect. My cock in her pussy, Griff filling her mouth, and she's loving every second of it.

God, I love her little sounds. They're muffled around Griff now, but that makes them even sexier. I could fuck her a little slower or change positions so this lasts a little longer, but this doesn't need to be a marathon. As hot as Griff is for her—and if she didn't already get the poor fucker off—he's not going to last long with Moira working his dick the way she is. I'm more turned on than I thought I would be by Griff taking Moira's mouth, and of course, my wife's pussy is as hot and tight as it always is. Fuck, I love her.

Nah, no marathon, we're just sealing a deal. I grab her hips and fuck her hard. I circle her clit hard and fast until she comes the first time, still impaled at both ends with me and Griff so she has nowhere to go. I know the sound my wife makes when she's coming, though. I know the way her pussy squeezes my dick. I let up off her clit and assault the fuck out of her G-spot.

"Fuck, Seb," Griff says, fisting both hands in her hair and fucking her face. "I'm gonna come."

"Spill it all down her throat," I tell him, as Moira's desperate moans fill the space between us. "You swallow every fucking drop he gives you, you hear me, sweetheart?"

She's too full of Griff's cock to nod, but I know she hears me. I thrust into her hard and fast a few more times and she cries out, a broken glorious sound as her pussy convulses around me. I push deep and groan with my own release.

"Oh, fuck," Griff says, before practically growling as he pours his own cum down my wife's throat. "Fuck, fuck, fuck," he chants, before easing back.

"Mm." Moira moans softly and I can imagine her sealing her lips around his cock as he leaves her, making sure she gets every last drop and leaves him clean. She always does for me.

I pull out of her pussy at the same time. Moira collapses in a heap on the bed. I'm fucking spent, so I drag my ass back to my spot and wait for Moira to collect herself.

Griff doesn't. He's gotta be as drained as I am right now, but he gathers Moira up and pulls her against him. She nestles right into his side and he keeps a protective arm wrapped around her, pressing a kiss to her forehead and murmuring, "Are you okay?"

Moira sighs, nodding her head. "Mm-hmm. I'm good."

"I got a little rough with you there," he says, holding her like she's something precious. She is, but it's weird to see someone holding *my* something special that way.

"I won't break," she assures him, fondly running a hand across his muscled chest.

I let them have their little moment—he's more considerate than I am, I pick that up right away. I know what Moira's body can handle, though; this is all still new to him. I wonder if Moira likes the dynamic with him. I wonder if she likes how exalted she is in his eyes. Moira's my greatest treasure and she knows it, but I don't fawn over her like this. That's not our way.

I'm tempted to take her back. A well-placed command, probably even just speaking to her would draw her back my way.

Griff needs it more than I do tonight, though. He needs to know she has affection for him; he needs to know he can use her body and not hurt her; he needs to know what it feels like to fall asleep with Moira in his arms.

9

GRIFF

WHEN I WAKE UP, I'M ALONE IN A STRANGE BED. THE pillow next to me smells of lavender, like Moira. She slept beside me most of the night. I felt her roll away and heard her snuggle up next to Seb at one point.

I stretch, looking around, a little confused. I know where I am, but I don't know where everyone else is or why they didn't come get me. I don't even know what woke me until I hear a reminder vibration from my phone. Where is my phone? I think it was still in the pocket of my jeans, so it's probably in the tangled mess on the floor.

Or, it should be, but there's no longer a tangled mess of clothing on the floor. My jeans have been picked up and folded neatly, placed on a chair in the corner with my phone on top.

I drag my ass out of Seb's bed—*that's* weird—and go over to grab my clothes. Flashes of last night run through my mind— the feel of Moira's mouth around my cock, her soft hand planted on my hip, the way her body lurched forward and she took my cock down her throat while Seb fucked her.

Damn, that was a hotter sight than I was prepared for.

My blood starts to stir so I push the thoughts away. I don't even know what time it is. I grab my phone to check and see a text message from Moira. "Wake up, sleepyhead. Breakfast will be done soon."

Breakfast? This comes with breakfast?

I try to remember the last time Ashley and I had breakfast together. We didn't have our house yet. I was staying in an apartment. So it's been years—I wanna say that was the first few months of our relationship.

I wanna take a shower, but I guess if Moira's making breakfast I should go downstairs. That means Seb is probably down there, too. I wonder if the morning after will be weird?

Once I pull my clothes on, I head downstairs. Seb is seated at the table, poring over his morning paper and drinking coffee. He looks relaxed and civilized as ever in a crisp gray suit, not at all a man who just last night coaxed me into fucking his wife's mouth while he buried his cock inside her at the same time. He looks up as I walk in and smiles pleasantly. "Morning, Griff."

"Morning," I murmur back, but my gaze goes to Moira. Upon hearing Seb acknowledge me, she turns her head and looks at me. She already looks lovely, in a soft-looking black sweater with little white fabric posies all over the front. Her long dark hair is pulled back in a low pony tail, and she has a tight black skirt on. She's wearing kitten heels, even though she's in the house. I'm not sure what the rules are for interaction like this when we're all together, but I just follow my instincts. A woman is making me breakfast, a woman I just spent the night with last night, so I go over and wrap my arms around her tiny waist from behind. She's in the middle of flipping sausage patties so she pauses to look back and flash me a smile over her shoulder.

"Sleep well?" she asks me.

I nuzzle my face into her neck and leave a little kiss there. "Very well. Did you?"

"Oh, yes," she says, placing her free hand on my arm. "I hope you're hungry."

"Everything smells delicious," I tell her.

"Thank you."

I let her go and head over to the table, flicking a glance at Seb to see how he feels about all this. He doesn't appear to be concerned, folding up his paper and setting it aside now that I'm here.

"Now that all this is settled," he begins, "are you taking the meeting with Donovan today or am I?"

"*Is* this all settled?" I ask him. "We never actually talked about it."

"We fucked about it," Seb says, smirking. "That was more enjoyable."

"I still have questions."

"Then ask them," he says simply.

"I want to take Moira out tonight after work."

That's not really a question, but it is a request. It rankles a bit, feeling like I need to ask his permission to take her out, but I can tell by the way his blue eyes dance with pleasure that Seb enjoys it. Bastard. Of course he does. I can't be too mad, given he is sharing his wife with me, but leave it to him to be a real pain in the ass about it.

"Okay," Seb says, nodding once. "We don't have any plans. I'll be at work anyway. That's fine."

"So, do I bring her back here, or take her to my house?"

"This is our home. Bring her back here."

"What if I want to stay the night with her?"

He quirks an eyebrow at me. "You just did, didn't you? So stay the night."

"It's not going to bother you to come home to us in your bed?"

"Only if you're in my spot," he quips.

I give him a dead look, but Moira interrupts, bringing over a plate full of toast and putting it on the table between us. There's green stuff smeared on top.

"Do you like avocado toast?" she asks, placing a hand on my shoulder and squeezing.

"Sure."

She returns to the stove and comes back a minute later with two plates. She gives me mine first, then goes over and puts Seb's down in front of him. Before she can move away, he catches her around the waist and pulls her onto his knee. She goes easily into his arms and he leans in to give her a kiss.

"Thank you, sweetheart," he murmurs.

She sighs against his mouth, wrapping an arm around his neck to hold onto his kisses, like she needs more of them. I want that. I probably shouldn't compare, though. It's not like they developed that level of intimacy overnight. They've built their relationship together over *years*. Of course we're not on their level on day one.

It's not important that we mimic their relationship; we can build our own.

I'm not Seb and I don't want to be. I've always had my own relationship with Moira and I still do. It's just different now. It won't have the limitations we had before. I'm no longer an observer—I just had my arms around her a few minutes ago. I get to take her out tonight and spend some time with her. Then, after we come back alone, I can peel those clothes off her and make love to her.

Right now his hand is the one on her breast, his lips tugging up in a helpless grin as she greedily steals more kisses, but later it will be me.

God, she's beautiful. Her blue eyes dance with amusement and pleasure as she peppers his face with kisses and I can't help smiling. This is kinda nice. This used to feel like torture, but now the jealousy is gone. It's nice to see Seb so happy. It's always been nice to see him happy; it was just tempered with the shitty covetous feeling of not having it for myself.

I don't feel like I'm on the outside now. Even if it's not my lap she's on, not my face she's peppering with kisses, I don't feel excluded.

She finally stands so she can go get herself a plate, but she winks at me and lets her hand skate across my shoulders as she passes.

"WHAT ARE YOU DOING IN HERE?"

I look up from the desktop monitor at Seb. We had been talking to the club manager out on the floor, but my lawyer called and I came to the office so I could take the call in private. Of course Ashley isn't letting the divorce go through easily— why would she? As I listened to the lawyer yammer on and run up my bill, I decided to start looking at restaurants to take Moira out to tonight.

It crosses my mind it might be weird for her that I'm not divorced yet, but then she's married—this is far from a typical courtship.

Since I didn't answer, Seb walks around the desk and takes a look for himself.

"I'm trying to decide where to take Moira tonight."

After briefly surveying the restaurants on the screen, he squeezes my shoulder and tells me, "You want to know a secret?"

"What's that?" I ask.

"She's gonna fuck you at the end of the date. You don't have to try this hard."

I roll my eyes and shrug his hand off. "Don't be an asshole."

"You give me that advice a lot," he says, straightening.

"You should heed it one of these times."

"But then what would we talk about?" he asks lightly.

"Business? Baseball? The woman we're sharing?"

Seb rolls his eyes. "You know I don't give a fuck about baseball. I'll just keep being an asshole so we always have that to fall back on."

I nod once, eyes on the monitor. "Great, you do that, I'll plan my own date; everybody wins."

"What'd the lawyer say?" he asks, dropping into the chair on the other side of the desk.

That bullshit is the last thing I want to think about right now. "Ashley's stalling, trying to put off the inevitable. Nothing to worry about."

"I don't want to rain on your parade, but you know the terms of your prenup better than I do. Do you think it's a good idea to go out with Moira right now? Might be smarter to stay in just until you get the papers signed."

A scowl transforms my face. "What do you mean by that?"

He lifts his eyebrows. "I mean, if Ashley is looking for ways to bleed you for more money, could she fuck you over with the infidelity clause? You're still legally married until she signs the papers."

I look up at him, my eyes widening with fucking indignation. "The *infidelity* clause? I wasn't unfaithful. She was. She's the one who fucked three other men while we were married. Now we're separated."

"But separated isn't divorced. You know I'm on your side here; I'm just trying to look out for our best interest, that's all. I'm obviously not saying you're *actually* doing anything wrong, I'm just saying if she's looking for dirt on you, maybe don't take Moira out tonight to some swanky place that Ashley's friends go to."

"It's public knowledge Moira and I are friends. We've been seen together plenty."

"You have, but usually not without me and at the kind of restaurant you only take a woman you want to fuck. Let's be real here, as good as it might be, you're not going for the chocolate soufflé."

I dismiss his concern. "We've been places without you."

"Not like this," he states. "You have plenty of time to take Moira out after the ink is dry on your divorce papers. Why don't you stay in until then, just to be safe? I won't be home tonight. Moira can make you dinner; you'll still have a night to yourself. Or get takeout, but something you would've done when you were just friends—get tacos or Chinese. Don't go the whole nine yards until it can't be used against you. When the divorce goes through, you can take Moira out and pay $70 for a dessert if that's what makes you happy, but wait. What's the rush?"

"Nah, fuck that. I'm not going to let Ashley dictate how I do this."

Naturally, Seb does not back down. "Why don't you talk to your lawyer about it first? For me. It'll set my mind at ease. You do own half of everything I own, after all. If your whore ex-wife gets the ammunition to take you to the cleaners, it's going to be inconvenient for me, too."

I shake my head, tapping the link to make a reservation.

"Never should have fucking married her. Why didn't you talk me out of that?"

Seb shrugs and crosses his arms. "Thought you were happy. Didn't have all the information. You should've just told me you wanted Moira back then, could've saved us a lot of time and trouble."

"Well, I kinda figured that would be the end of our friendship," I point out. "I still don't know how you're so cool with this."

"It's all in how you look at it," he assures me. "What I'm getting out of it is worth what I have to invest."

"This isn't a business deal."

"Everything's a business deal, Griff." He pushes up off the chair, nodding his head at me. "Including your divorce. You need to call your lawyer and make sure you're not going to get fucked if Ashley finds out about you and Moira."

"You know how you said you weren't trying to rain on my parade?" I ask.

He smiles faintly, heading for the door. "Next time I'll bring an umbrella."

10

GRIFF

WHEN I PULL UP INTO SEB'S DRIVEWAY TONIGHT, I feel good. Better than good. I can't wait to see Moira. I kill the engine and slide out of the car, pocketing my keys and heading for the door.

I still remember the first time I met her. It wasn't unusual to see Seb with a pretty girl. Between his looks, charm, and money, he made his way through his fair share of them. He started to resent the ones who only came with the money, though. One of the girls he dated even had money herself—*old* money, which apparently means something to people. Personally, I don't understand how there's more prestige in inheriting a fortune from some dead grandpa who made a fortune in publishing back in the day than guys like me and Seb who busted our asses to make every dime we have, but "society people" are ass backward about that shit. This one girl, Evelyn Curtis, was the worst of them. Even with Seb's financial situation being what it is, she never felt he was good enough to introduce to her family.

He dumped her ass, then suddenly she came around to his

new money. Tried to explain the unique pressure she was under, being so special.

God, she sucked. I was glad when he dumped her.

Especially because he met Moira shortly after, and I liked Moira on sight. It wasn't just her looks. Moira is a looker, no question, but she exudes a sweetness that a lot of ladies these days don't. There's a spark of gentleness in her. It's not hidden. It's there in the sweet sound of her voice, the kindness in her eyes. The night I met her, I joined them for dinner at a restaurant; Moira went out of her way to talk to me and make sure I felt welcome. She didn't have to. I felt welcome the first time she smiled at me.

It took a while before I started to feel jealous, though. I liked her too much, enjoyed being around her. I had always more or less had Seb to myself, even when he was seeing someone, but with Moira it was different. I kind of figured she'd be the one he married right from the get-go. You could just tell.

Now I stand outside the door of their house and I don't know whether I should knock or let myself in. Formality wins out and I press the illuminated round button. I hear the doorbell ring out inside the house and a minute later I can see the outline of Moira's figure approaching through the frosted glass of the door.

The door opens and she greets me with a smile, putting an earring in her left earlobe. "Hey, Griff. Come on in. I just need five more minutes."

She changed clothes. I don't know why I'm so pleased to see that; she looked lovely in what she wore earlier, but she changed into a sexy-as-hell black cocktail dress that hugs her curves just right. She's dressing up to go out with me, like she's excited. I can't tear my eyes away from her as I step inside. She leans behind me to close the door, and I can't help catching her around the waist and pulling her close for a kiss.

She stops fiddling with her earring and wraps her arms around my neck, drawing closer, slanting her mouth over mine and closing her eyes as she kisses me back. Blood rushes through my veins, heading straight for my cock. Fuck, I'm not supposed to be turned on already.

After a minute, she breaks the kiss and smiles at me mischievously. "I guess I don't have to ask if you like the dress."

"I'm a big fan of this dress, but an even bigger fan of the body it's covering up."

She grins, playfully swatting my arm and turning away to head for the bathroom. "You better stop that or we'll never get out of here."

That Chinese takeout is starting to sound damn good. The restaurant I made reservations at is great, but the chef is a real high-maintenance pain in the ass. Dinner and dessert will take every bit of two hours, maybe two and a half.

I adjust my slacks, watching her ass as she walks away. I guess a few hours having to look at her in this dress isn't *so* bad when I consider what I get to do to her as soon as we leave.

Seb is the best fucking friend in the world. I know I give him hell sometimes, but damn.

Moira comes back a few minutes later with a fitted black coat over her dress and a pearl-encrusted clip in her hair. She styled her hair up tonight with a few loose locks hanging down. She's so pretty I could die just looking at her.

Her blue eyes shine with affection as she takes my arm. "You look very handsome tonight."

I tear my gaze from her to look down at myself. I wore a blue suit with a white shirt and matching navy tie. I'm not really all about suits, but Seb has been since we could afford them. He wanted us to look the part when we first had the money but didn't feel like we fit the part yet. We could wrap ourselves up in as many $4,000 suits as we wanted, but I still felt like the kid who wore hoodies 'cause no one bought him a winter coat and he was too surly to ask for one.

I'm a long way from that now, though. Moira's looking at me like she can't see a trace of that kid, and if she could, she'd have bought him a fucking coat herself.

I take her out to the car and open the door for her. She gives me a smile and a thank-you as she slides in the passenger seat.

Honest to God, I can't believe this is happening. Seb's the kind of guy who gets the girl like Moira; I'm the guy who only dreams about her from afar. Only here she is in my car, all dolled up to go out with me.

Once we get out of the driveway, I ask, "So, how are you doing with all this?"

"The sharing?" she questions. "Well, I certainly have no cause to complain so far."

That draws a smile out of me. "Glad to hear it."

"How about you? Are you feeling good about it today?"

Is she kidding me? "I don't see how I could feel any other way, to be honest."

"I know Sebastian has a sort of... transactional view of things sometimes. He sees something that needs to be done and then he does it. I didn't think that would extend to this, but... well, here we are."

I nod my head in understanding. "I just wanted to make sure *you* feel good about it. I know Seb can steamroll over people sometimes when he gets an idea in his head, and I know you tend to be pretty submissive to him. I don't want you to be here because you feel like you have to be."

She reaches her hand over and places it on my thigh, giving it a reassuring squeeze. "I want to be here, Griff."

"Was last night okay?" I ask, daring a glance in her direction.

"If I said no after four orgasms, someone would need to show up and punch me in the face," she informs me.

That surprises a shot of laughter out of me. "Four? I counted three."

"You miscounted," she says, slyly.

"Damn, we do some good tag team work, don't we?"

Moira grins. "You sure do."

The restaurant I picked out for us has valet parking, so we stop out front and give the attendant my keys. I feel a little like a king, placing my hand at the small of Moira's back and escorting her inside. A couple of men turn their heads to watch as she walks by. If she notices, she doesn't show it. Of course, she's probably used to it. When she and Seb are out, they get looks from both sexes, ogling the pair of them as if resenting their monopoly on good looks. If people stick around long enough to notice how in love they are, they just have to hate them. No one should look the way they do and be so goddamn happy, to boot.

Tonight it's me, though.

Tonight *I* get to be the luckiest bastard in the city.

The waiter brings us cocktails while we look over the menu. I don't even like half the shit on it, honestly, but I like the atmosphere of this place. It feels private and intimate, even though you're in a room full of people.

I brought Ashley here twice. The first time was all right, but the second time she ran into someone whose name she could drop later, so she invited them to join us. I had to spend the whole dinner sitting there, listening to them talk about dumb shit I couldn't give a fuck less about. Ashley regularly talked about shit I couldn't give a fuck less about, and I listened like any good husband, but when it's three against one and they won't shut up? I wanted to offer to pay for them to eat and slip out by myself.

After that, I was too worried we would run into someone again, so I didn't want to come back. Ashley came without me a few times, with friends—though now I wonder if they were friends at all. I never really worried about her spending time with other men, but I guess I should have.

"Do you have a lot of male friends?"

Moira glances up as she takes a sip of her martini, then shakes her head. "No, not really. I have a few male acquaintances, but no one I really consider a friend." She gives me a funny little smile. "That's an odd question to lead with."

I frown a little, nodding my agreement. "Yeah, it was. Sorry. I was thinking about—" I stop, my frown deepening. Talking about the wife I'm not quite divorced from yet and how she probably cheated on me with all her male *friends* probably isn't the right foot to lead with.

She seems to understand exactly what I'm thinking about, though. Her smile sobers and she glances at the table. "You know, before I met Seb I dated this real asshat. I don't remember if I ever mentioned him—probably not. But we dated off and on for about a year. I was miserable after six months, I just couldn't figure out how to get out of it. I thought maybe it was just a rough patch, but it was the strangest thing—I'm really not an insecure person, I don't worry about other women, but I started to feel like I couldn't trust him. His behavior got really sketchy. He'd keep his phone tilted and turned so I couldn't see it, he'd cancel or change plans at the last minute, all that kind of stuff. My sister insisted he was cheating on me. I didn't believe her, but I couldn't bring myself to shake the insecurity anyway. So one night he pulled his 'plans changed last minute' shit when he was supposedly hanging out with a friend. My sister got fed up; she dragged me to her car and went to the place he said he would be hanging out with his friends. He wasn't there. So my sister—who, I should warn you, is a raging lunatic—loads me back in the car and hauls me around to all his usual haunts, looking for his car. This could have been a profound waste of time, but we got ice cream sundaes while we did all this, and when are ice cream sundaes ever a waste of time?"

I'm baffled that there exists a man idiotic enough to step out on her, but I offer a smile and shake my head. "Never."

She nods. "So, Gwen finally found his car. We went inside to see who he was with, and he was there with some brunette chick. We didn't confront him, Gwen just hauled me back out to his car, handed me her sundae, and got out a tube of lipstick. She wrote 'cheating whore' on his windshield, 'tiny dick' on the driver's side window, and 'minute man' on the passenger side window."

I want to be pissed off on her behalf over this cheating asshole, but Moira's laughing at the memory, so it must not hurt too much.

"Anyway," she says, shaking her head and smiling as she looks down at the menu. "I digressed a bit, but the moral of the story is, I have been cheated on, and I know how shitty it feels. Obviously, we weren't married, and it's far worse that Ashley did this to you after making that kind of commitment, but I understand that it can mess with your ability to trust. That's what I was getting at. And also, I would never do that to someone."

"Neither would I," I assure her.

"I know," she says, smiling softly. "And if you do, my sister will vandalize your vehicle, so you've been warned."

"I like your sister," I tell her. "I need to meet this woman. I wanna shake her hand."

"You met her. Remember at the wedding? Gwen was my maid of honor."

"That's right. I didn't know this story then, though. I wasn't appropriately impressed."

Moira smiles. "Long story short, you don't have to worry about me having male friends. If you *did* have to worry about that, I wouldn't be worth holding onto."

I shake my head, glancing up at her. "You're far more sensible than I was at your age."

She shrugs, perusing the menu. "Honestly, I'm glad he cheated now. Imagine how much longer I might've stayed with him. I would've never met Sebastian. If he had asked me out that day, I wouldn't have been able to go. It all worked out. Change isn't always such a bad thing."

"My relationship with change has been a little rockier. When I was younger, I hated it. I hated the instability of everything. I just wanted something solid and reliable."

"Then you met Sebastian?" she inquires.

I nod my head. "Mr. Solid and Reliable."

Her smile warms with love. "He is. Sebastian is wonderful."

"Agreed."

"I wish I had known you back then," she tells me. "You guys needed a friend."

I can't help smirking. "We had Stella."

"Ugh," she mutters, rolling her eyes. "I said friend, not tricky little ho."

"We had each other. That was all we needed. Besides, you would've been a kid back then. When I was 18, you were only, what, 11?"

Moira rolls her eyes at me. "That's not such an enormous age difference."

"Not now that it makes you 24, but back then it would've been a little unsettling."

I see the server headed our way, so I ask her, "Do you know what you want to order?"

"I'm so much more interested in the dessert. There's chocolate soufflé *and* crème brûlée. How's a girl to choose?"

"Well, we have three courses to get through before we come to that life-altering decision."

"Why don't you pick for me?" she suggests. "No oysters or escargot. Otherwise whatever you want."

Whatever *I* want? I'm not the one eating it. I have no idea what her tastes are. She's already decided the matter though, putting the menu down and turning her attention to her drink.

The nice thing about restaurants like this is the chefs don't like giving you too many options. Each course only has four choices and she told me what she didn't want, so I make sure to order us both different things; if she doesn't like what I ordered for her, we can swap plates and she can have mine.

I bet Seb orders for her all the time. He's a bossy motherfucker. Always had to be, so he learned to love the role.

"Do you and Seb ever come here?"

Moira shakes her head, gently placing her cocktail back down. "We came once to see what all the fuss was about, but we didn't like it so much that we went out of our way to come back." Probably realizing she's telling me she's not too fond of the place I picked, she flashes me a smile and adds, "It was a different menu then, though. I'm excited to try what you ordered tonight. And I *do* remember the crème brûlée was delicious."

"We'll get one of each and we can share, if you'd like," I offer.

"I would like that very much, thank you."

"You don't have to keep thanking me for things," I tell her.

Smiling faintly, she says, "I don't remember how to do first dates. It's been a long time. I never thought I'd go on one again, so I threw out the manual."

My eye is drawn to the sight of her left hand, decked out with a sizeable engagement ring and a platinum wedding band. I look at my own hand, suddenly missing the wedding band I've worn for years. I actually didn't take it off until this morning. Didn't feel right to wear it after last night. You can still see a faint indent on my finger where it used to be.

"Do you miss her?" Moira asks gingerly.

"No," I answer, quickly.

"It's okay if you do," she assures me, empathetically. "She was part of your life for years. That would be completely natural."

"It's not that I miss her," I say, shaking my head. "Honestly, I wish now I'd never married her. She's being a pain in the ass about the divorce."

"Do you think she's still in love with you?"

My eyebrows rise and I look up at her. "No, I think by the time she took the third or fourth dick that wasn't mine, she was pretty firmly not in love with me."

Moira darts a look to our left, then our right, subtly making sure no one overheard.

"Sorry," I mutter, grabbing my drink and taking a long sip.

"No worries. I just don't want gossips to hear your business. Sometimes the people who come here are real busybodies, you know?"

"Yeah, I know that." I lower my glass to the table with a

thud and look across the table at her. "I don't want to talk about Ashley."

"We don't have to," she assures me. "Just know that we can, if you ever feel like it. Just because we're lovers now doesn't mean we can't still be friends."

Lovers. That's sure an odd thing to hear coming from her mouth.

By the time the first course arrives, Moira is tipsy. Cocktails seemed like a good idea to calm our nerves, but they made them strong and I didn't consider what a lightweight Moira is.

When Moira gets tipsy, her sexuality comes out to play. Ordinarily she's a lady in public—even if she enjoys being fucked from both ends by two men, apparently—but the alcohol melts away her inhibitions in grand fashion.

Smiling at me across the table as the server clears away her barely touched second course, she asks, "What's the first sexual thought you ever had about me?"

The server pauses and stares down at her, and I can guess he's having *his* first sexual thought about her right now. I stare at him until he catches my eye, then he flushes and hastens away from the table.

I look at Moira, the little minx, still sultry and playful. "I honestly can't remember. There have been too many over the years."

"Have you ever had a sex dream about me?"

"Oh, yeah. Many times."

She grins, pleased by this information as she sips what's left of her drink, just barely enough to cover the ice cubes. "I had some pretty dirty thoughts about you the night you spent in the guest room. When you asked me to help undress you."

"Oh yeah?"

"Mm-hmm." She nods. "I shouldn't have at that point. That was naughty of me."

The playful way she says it gives me cause to shift in my seat. Now I'm thinking about the blue satin negligee she wore that night, how she didn't have on any panties underneath. "You wouldn't happen to be wearing anything like you wore that night underneath that dress, now, would you?"

Moira doesn't blink. "I'm wearing a black lacy thong under this dress. Nothing else." She plucks the cocktail pick out of her martini glass and holds my gaze as she drags the olive off with her teeth. "Figured I'd save you a little time when you take it off me tonight."

My cock jumps to life, hearing her say that—knowing it's real. I really get to do that as soon as we get out of here.

Fuck, where is that waiter with the third course? She's talking like this, and I already promised her dessert.

Seb was right; we should've kept it simple tonight. I should've just taken her for a simple dinner and drinks—I do like the tempting shit that comes out of her mouth when she drinks.

"You know what? I think I just remembered the first time I had a dirty thought about you," I tell her.

Her eyes dance with merriment and she clasps her hands together with exaggerated glee. "Tell me."

"We were all hanging out and you had too much to drink. You were sitting on Seb's lap and getting way too handsy. I was starting to get antsy so I went to the bathroom, mostly just to get away from you. When I came out, you were waiting in the hall to go in. You beamed a smile up at me and went to squeeze past me, but you tripped over my boot and fell right up against me. I swear to God, I felt my heart fall right out of my body. You just smiled up at me, went 'whoops' and sauntered right into the bathroom. You didn't even shut the door—I had to do it real quick before you dropped those snug jeans you were wearing and really ruined my life."

Moira laughs a little, shaking her head. "I'm such a slutty drunk."

"You're not slutty, you're just relaxed... and okay, sure, a little more sexual, but there's nothing wrong with that. I was worried that night, though. I was one part turned on, but also worried you might end up in a bad situation, doing shit like that."

"I could've," she says, but not with nearly enough soberness. Instead, her big blue eyes widen theatrically and she leans across the table. "You know what could've happened?"

Oh no, I can feel one of her dirty stories coming on.

I search the vicinity for the waiter.

Come on, asshole, bring out the duck so we can get the fuck out of here.

"You could have been a real asshole," she says. "Maybe you liked the feeling of my body pushed up against yours. Maybe you liked it so much that instead of shutting the door and leaving me to my privacy, you followed me inside. Locked the door, so no one could walk in on us."

I can't help visualizing her story, even if I would've never done that. The guy in her story is a creep, and I may not be perfect, but I wouldn't corner my friend's drunk girlfriend in a bathroom and come onto her. Still, I'm probably gonna like her depraved story. I always liked these fucking things, even if I couldn't understand how they came out of a sweet girl like Moira.

Then again, if she came four times between the two of us last night, I'm probably still underestimating her sexual appetite just because I keep pigeon-holing her into this sweet category. Moira's gotta have a little bit of kinkiness in her to enjoy what she enjoys—maybe even to be with Seb in the first place.

"Now we're all alone in the bathroom," she continues. "Me, I'm a little drunk, a little vulnerable. I don't immediately understand why you locked the door. I don't really care."

Fuck, fuck, fuck. It's already depraved, and my cock is already rising at her enjoyment of her own story.

"Then you walk me back up against the wall, pin my arms above me at the wrist while you slide your hand down the front of my jeans." She covers her mouth with one hand, feigning shock. "I'm not wearing any panties."

Where is the fucking duck? I'm ready to cancel the rest of the damn order and just haul her ass out of here. At this rate, she might attack me in the car, and the whole point of this night was to do this right. I want to get her home first.

"You sure are happy now. You cover me with your hand and slide a finger inside me." She lets out a little noise, half sigh, half moan. "I'm already wet for you, Griff."

"Fuck me," I mutter. I finally catch sight of the waiter, so I wave him over.

Moira grins. "I didn't get to finish my story. What are you doing?"

"I'm very interested in this story, but we need to get you that dessert."

The waiter approaches, appearing confused. "Did you need something, sir?"

"Yes, I need you to box up the chicken and the duck. Can you just bring out the dessert? We're sort of... in a hurry."

He fails to bite back a smile. "I bet you are. I'll see what I can do."

I sigh, raking a hand through my hair as he walks away.

Moira looks quite pleased with herself. She tilts her glass back and drains the last drops of liquid, then she sets it down and tells me, "I can't wait to have your cock inside me, Griff."

"You are the devil," I inform her.

She grins at me across the table. "There's a reason Sebastian calls me his little minx."

"How do you go from housewife to sex kitten on a dime like that?" I ask, shaking my head.

Moira smirks. "Lots of practice. Little bit of alcohol doesn't hurt."

THROUGH SHEER FORCE OF WILL, we finish dessert. We make it back to the house and stumble through the front door. Moira already has her arms looped around my neck, her lips attached to mine.

I taste the faintest trace of dessert on her lips. Her kisses are like crème brûlée—molten sweetness that I want more of as soon as it's gone.

Now her lips are gone, and I feel bereft. She only broke away to shove her coat off though, then she's back, pulling herself even closer, her sweet lips brushing mine. I can't shake the idea that this can't be real. I can't shake the feeling of being an imposter here, of stealing a spot in a life that doesn't belong to me with a woman who isn't mine to kiss.

It's only night one, I remind myself.

Well, night two if last night counts. I guess it has to.

Moira breaks away with a little smile and takes my hand so she can lead me up the stairs. It reminds me of that night a few weeks ago when she picked me up and brought me back here.

I remember she's wearing a black lacy thong and nothing else beneath that dress. I can't wait to see that.

Turns out, I don't have to wait long. As soon as we're in the bedroom, Moira turns her back to me. "Unzip me, please."

I've always liked this part. It's so intimate, being in the bedroom with a woman, helping her undress. Moira's bare shoulders are too tempting to pass up; I bend to kiss my way across them, running my fingers lightly down her arms. Her soft sigh of pleasure is like a salve to my battered ego. Moira's used to *Seb*, and here she is reveling in *my* touch.

Once I'm done kissing her, I grab the zipper and pull it down, revealing inch after inch of exposed skin. Moira tugs the dress down past her hips and shimmies right out of it. She tosses me a saucy smile over her shoulder, then bends at the waist to grab the dress. She lingers, giving me a painfully good view of her ass in that black lacy thong she told me about.

I grab her hips and yank her back against me, making her feel how hard I am. Her blue eyes look darker as she turns back to face me, lust written all across her pretty features.

"You want me, Griff?" she teases.

My hungry gaze rakes across her perfect breasts, down her flat abdomen and settles on the black triangle of fabric between her legs. "You have no idea."

She leans in and kisses me, murmuring against my lips, "Then take me."

I don't have to be told twice.

I grab her ass and lift her. She wraps her legs around my waist and I carry her over to the bed. I love the way she smiles at me, the way her blue eyes sparkle, the way she rests her hands on my shoulders.

I can't believe I get to do this.

I can't shake it. I try, I tell myself I'm allowed to be here, but it keeps washing over me. I put her down on the bed and she scoots back, making room for me. I crawl over her, trapping her beneath me and gathering her arms at the wrist, pinning them over her head, just like in the fragment of story she told me.

Moira's eyes close and she sighs with pleasure. "Oh, yes."

"Yeah?" I murmur, leaning down to kiss along her jawline. I keep her arms pinned with one hand, but I drop down to kiss her breasts, taking a nipple into my mouth and licking the already-pebbled tip until she's moaning and writhing beneath me. I turn my attention to the other one. My free hand drifts down her abdomen and I rub her through the lacy fabric.

"Griff," she says, on a moan. Her legs spread for me, welcoming me—and only me—to touch her. My finger moves beneath the fabric and I feel how slick she is already. It goes straight to my cock. That's for me. She wants *me*.

I release her wrists and pull my hand from her panties before I even get to play with her. I'm wearing far too many items of clothing. I shrug my jacket off and toss it, then start to unhook my belt, but Moira puts her hands on mine and stops me.

For a second, my heart stalls. Is she having second thoughts? I'll die of blue balls here and now if she changes her mind.

Her smile turns sly, like she knows she just gave me half a heart attack, then she begins unbuckling my belt herself. "I want to open my present," she tells me, winking as she feeds the leather through the buckle.

I can't help smiling even as she torments me, unbuckling my belt and dragging it off as slowly as she fucking can. "Your present, huh?"

She nods eagerly. "I want to taste it. It's been almost a whole day since I had your cock in my mouth, Griff. That's far too long."

Fuck me. "You're something else, you know that?"

With exaggerated innocence, she runs her hand over my cock through the fabric of my slacks. "That's a good thing, right?"

Christ.

My voice is strained when I tell her, "A great thing."

She smiles and unbuttons my pants, then she unzips them and tugs them down. I ease back off the bed so I can shove them down the rest of the way, then I make quick work of peeling off my shirt, and join her back on the bed.

"Lie down," she tells me, climbing up on her knees. "I want to taste you before you fuck me."

I damn sure don't argue. I watch Moira's breasts until she sits on top of me, her back to me. I groan as she leans down, giving me a perfect view of that thong-covered ass. She grips the base of my cock and gives it a couple gentle strokes. This is a view to fucking die for. She knows it, too. She wiggles her ass as she bends her head and guides my cock into the hot paradise of her mouth.

It's basically an out of body experience, Moira sitting on top of me, laboring over my cock. I can't keep my hands off her. I run a hand over that beautiful ass of hers, then slide my hand beneath her so I can play with her pussy while she blows me. Her moan reverberates around my cock and I thrust my head back against the bedding. Her mouth doesn't let up. She's like a fucking Hoover. Holy shit. Now that I'm fingering her and toying with her clit, she keeps moaning around my cock.

This is the pinnacle of fucking pleasure, but I need to be inside her and she's doing good work. I pull her off my dick and toss her on her back, climbing on top of her.

"That is a beautiful fucking mouth you've got there," I tell her.

"Glad you like it," she says, smiling as I yank the lacy fabric down her legs and toss it behind me.

I want to be inside her, but I want her to come on my face first, so I pin down her hips—*she likes to try to squirm away*—and bend down, latching onto her pussy. She lets out a moan and reaches down to tangle her fingers in my hair. I savor her little whimpers and moans as I lick along her pussy, drawing her clit into my mouth and sucking.

"Oh, God, Griff," she cries, her fingers curling in my hair and tugging.

I keep stimulating her clit, but I slide a finger inside her tight entrance while I do and she gasps. I work my finger in and out of her, but all I can think about is how fucking tight her cunt is going to feel around my cock.

She cries out my name again and bucks her hips. I push a second finger inside her, pumping my fingers fast, zeroing in on her clit until she gets there.

"Griff!" She screams my name and my cock jumps as she groans. Fuck, I already love to make her come. I barely let her recover from her orgasm. Her body is limp as I move to my knees, lifting her legs and hooking them over my shoulders. She's trying to come back around, but I don't wait—I grasp my cock and push it up against her tight little hole. Fuck, it feels good as I push inside her. She moans as I fill her, then moans more as I pull out and shove back inside her.

"Your pussy feels like heaven, you know that?"

"Having you inside me is heaven," she tells me. "Fuck me harder, Griff. Take everything you want from me."

It's hard to let loose with Moira—she's petite and delicate-looking, while I'm nearly 240 lbs of muscle. I don't feel like she can handle me at full capacity. She's used to Seb's roughness, but he isn't as bulky as I am. I saw he wasn't afraid to fuck her full-force last night, but I'm a little worried I'll hurt her.

She must be able to see it. "I can take it," she assures me. "Give me all you've got, Griff. Fuck me like this is the only time you'll get to, and you never want me to forget."

Her words send a specific wave of fear lancing through me. *Like this is the only time?* I only just got her. I need more than once. Nonetheless, her words fill me with a sense of urgency. I give it to her a little harder. When she takes it in stride, I pull out, turn her over so she's face-down in the pillow, and drive my cock into her from behind.

"Oh, God, yes," she cries, reaching above her for something to hold onto.

I grab a fistful of her hair and pull her back like a bow as I piston my hips inside her even harder. "Like that?" I ask roughly.

Her body moves with the violence of my thrusts, but she manages an enthusiastic, "Yes."

I can tell she does. She fucking loves it.

I shake my head, taken off guard. This isn't what I imagined Moira like in bed, but I like it. I like it a lot.

She pushes against the bed so she can meet my hips thrust for thrust. She really gets into it, moaning, crying out, telling me, "Fuck me, Griff. Give it to me. Oh, God, yes."

She's magnificent. When she's close again, I want her to come more than I can remember wanting anything. I want her pussy squeezing my cock, her beautiful sounds emanating from her throat as pleasure I provided courses through her sweet little body.

Satisfaction surges through me when she does. I summon the willpower to last through her clenching—I want to make sure she gets every second of pleasure, so I fuck her like a ragdoll even as she cries out, pleasure erupting inside her.

When her body sags, I turn her over on her back and bury myself inside her so I can watch her face. It only takes a couple thrusts until I join her, emptying myself, pouring the last of my strength for the moment into her pussy. I come down on top of her and Moira wraps her arms around me, holding me close, pressing her lips against my shoulder.

Moira sighs contentedly and the sound goes straight to my heart. Contentment rolls over me too, like it's contagious. I don't want to crush her, so I pull out of her body and roll over beside her. I'm closer to Seb's side than the side I slept on last night, but I don't intend on staying here, I just want to get my weight off her.

Moira snuggles up close and drapes her arm across my waist. I must not be close enough, because next she hooks her legs over mine and uses it to drag herself even closer.

I laugh lightly, snaking an arm beneath her and pulling her on top of me.

"Great, now I'm gonna crush you," she tells me.

"Yes, all ten pounds of you," I shoot back.

She runs her fingers through my hair and waits for me to catch my breath, then she scoots off me and heads to the bathroom. A moment later she returns and climbs in bed beside me. She rests her face on my chest and looks up at me. "Thanks for taking me out tonight."

"Of course," I reply, running my finger along her arm. "Thanks for letting me."

She smiles and pecks me on the mouth before settling back into my embrace and closing her eyes. Her head gets heavier after a few minutes, her breathing even. She fell asleep in my arms.

I try to fall asleep with her, but I can't. I keep running over the events of the night, the memories she stirred, thoughts of last night. I sure didn't expect to fall asleep with another woman this soon after leaving Ashley. That it's Moira naked and sated in my arms is un-fucking-believable.

I don't really think about the fact that I'm on the wrong side of the bed until I hear Seb's car pull into the driveway. It's late and I still haven't slept, I've just been enjoying holding Moira, but Seb wastes little time coming upstairs. The bedroom door swings open and he steps inside. His gaze sweeps across Moira in my arms, then me, then his spot.

"Remember how I said you could fuck my wife, just stay out of my spot?" he asks idly. "Was that not generous enough for you?"

I crack a smile. "I'm not in your spot. If anything, I'm in Moira's spot."

"Don't take this the wrong way, Griff, but you're not the one I want to cuddle with."

"The feeling is mutual," I assure him.

He lifts his eyebrows, his blue eyes twinkling with devious intent. "We could wake her up."

"She's tired."

He rolls his eyes. "Yeah, I'm sure you wore her out. Moira's an all-star fuck. She could still go another round."

"You just fucked her last night. Seems like tonight should be mine."

This seems to amuse him. He smirks at me as he sheds his jacket and starts to unbutton his dress shirt. "Is that a joke? We fuck every night. We're not 80. I'm willing to share; I'm *not* willing to go to bed every other night without my wife."

"So, is that how this goes? I'm the guest? I don't get her to myself any nights?"

"Maybe once in a while. Not every other night. Is your masculinity threatened by sharing a bed with me and the woman we both fuck now?"

I roll my eyes. "No, my masculinity is just fucking fine. I don't live here, though. If I'm going to spend the night from time to time, I need to leave a couple outfits here. This morning after run-around is going to get old fast."

Seb steps out of his slacks and drapes them over the chair on his side of the bed. "That's fine. You can fill the closet in the guest room, the bathroom—put whatever you want in there. Make it yours. I like having you here. It's like old times."

I smile faintly. "Yeah, it is. A little more spacious, though."

"Plus we have someone to keep us fed now," he points out.

"And our balls empty."

Seb laughs shortly. "Yeah, Moira's a pretty good deal all the way around."

I'm taken off guard by the peaceful little minx snuggled up against me suddenly whacking me in the stomach.

Sebastian's gaze jumps across the bed. He's faintly amused instead of alarmed that she overheard us being assholes. "Evening, sweetheart."

She narrows her eyes at him, then me. "You're both terrible. I'm not just a personal chef or a warm body to stick your dicks into. I thought you were gentlemen. I hope you both enjoy blue balls, because these legs are closed for the next few nights."

I go conciliatory, rubbing her arm. "We were just joking around. You know we don't really think of you as—" I can't even repeat what we just said, so I probably shouldn't have said it in the first place. "I'm sorry."

She appears slightly mollified, but her expectant gaze drifts to Seb.

"I'm not." He shakes his head, his expression dry as hell.

"Nice try, sweetheart."

"Blue balls forever," she tells him.

"Never make a threat you can't follow through with. Then people won't take you seriously," he advises her.

"Then I guess I can never have sex with you or cook for you again," she states, primly.

He climbs on the bed and heads in my direction aggressively enough that I almost move, but I feel absurdly like I should keep myself between him and Moira.

He grabs her and drags her over my body, back into her spot. I scoot back over where I belong, and Seb cradles the back of Moira's neck in his hand, drawing her in for a tender kiss. Her hand drifts to his side and she leans closer, despite her announcement that he was in for a week's worth of blue balls. He kisses her a little longer and she sinks against him, sighing softly in defeat.

Then, because he has a point to prove, he pushes her down to suck his dick. She goes without complaint. I can't really complain either; I get a damn good view of her ass as she labors over his cock the way she labored over mine earlier. My arousal stirs watching her go down on him, listening to her faint moans of pleasure. They're not as frequent or as desperate as when we both fucked her, but every last one of her moans turn me on.

Thankfully, she finishes him off before I can get too revved up.

Seb smacks her ass when she's done, then drags her against his side and kisses the crown of her head. "See what I mean, sweetheart? No follow through."

"I'm going to make you weak-ass coffee in the morning," she mutters. "Like a teaspoon of coffee grounds and that's it."

Seb grins. I shake my head. It isn't news that he has Moira wrapped around his dick, so I shouldn't even be surprised.

11

MOIRA

I HUM TO MYSELF AS I PUSH MY CART THROUGH THE grocery store. I'm making prime rib for dinner tonight, but I've been so distracted this past week, I haven't followed my usual schedule. It's different, having two men around the house. Griff doesn't live with us, but he's over all the time now. He generally spends the night, and though I'm used to sex every night, I'm not used to being fucked by two men every night, and more often than not, that's been happening.

I certainly don't mind, but it's making me extra tired. When I should be getting up to go for my morning run, I'm still in bed, lazing in someone's embrace. By the time I drag my butt out of bed, it's time to get myself dressed and start breakfast.

I sail right past the cases of meat and approach the butcher. Sebastian is particular about his prime rib—he wants the better cut, so I order it special.

The butcher smiles when he sees me. "There you are. I thought you were coming in yesterday."

"I know, I'm sorry. I've been so busy this week; I lost all track of time."

"Oh, I'm sure." There's condescension in his tone—like he wants to appease silly little ol' me, but what could a housewife possibly be busy doing? He's not the first boob I've encountered and he won't be the last.

I paste on a fake smile and he goes to the back to retrieve my prime rib.

"Moira?"

I don't have the most common name in the world, so I turn my head when I hear it. It's Claire Randall from my weekly barre class. I don't consider her a friend, but we do see each other once a week. "Hey, Claire."

"I didn't see you at class this week. Hope everything's okay," she says.

Obviously, I can't tell her I'm a little tender between the legs due to the two men who fuck me every night, so I offer up a pleasant smile and say, "Yep, everything is fine. Sebastian's been keeping me busy."

"If I had a husband that looked like him, I'd let him keep me busy, too," she says, winking at me.

"I'm a lucky woman," I agree, vaguely.

Now her smile shrinks and she moves closer. "Did you hear about Ashley and Griffin? Well, he and Sebastian are close, I'm sure you have."

Memories of Griff kissing my breasts last night while Sebastian went down on me flash through my mind. A pang of arousal stirs within me, but I ignore it. "Yes, I did hear about that." I'm not sure what she knows or what's actually being said, so I don't offer anything further. If no one knows she cheated, I'm certainly not going to say so and bring Griff further embarrassment. At the same time though, I don't want people thinking he's the bad guy for filing for divorce from the faithless hussy.

"To be honest, I never liked her," Claire tells me. "She had no class. May have married into money, but the way she behaves, working at that bar."

Given the distaste on her face, I remind her, "Yes, my husband owns that *club*."

"Oh, of course, I know. But he owns it. It's an investment. Ashley only hung around to get attention from lowlife men. Everyone saw that. Everyone *talked* about it," she adds, raising her eyebrows like this should matter. "I'm glad Griffin finally came to his senses. He can do much better than her."

I'm not at all comfortable with this conversation, but the butcher is taking his time in the back so I can't even get away.

"You know, we should set him up with Laura from class," she tells me.

"I really don't think he's looking to date just yet."

"Oh, but Laura's so pretty."

I blink at her, but finally I just nod my agreement. Of course Laura is pretty, but Griff isn't interested. I can't tell her that, though. She's a bit of a busybody, clearly, and I haven't actually talked to Sebastian about public perception of our arrangement. It hasn't come up yet, but if people are finding out about Griff's divorce, it's bound to now.

We'll have to discuss it during dinner. Does he want to keep it secret? Does he care if people know? I know I'll get judged hard if any of the more conservative ladies learn that I'm letting two men have sex with me—sometimes at the same time!—but I'm not that worried about it. If I spent my whole life worrying over what people thought of me, I'd never do anything.

I don't want Sebastian to look bad, though. We understand it was entirely his decision, that he has no reason to be embarrassed—he's the one in control of this situation, after all. Griff and I follow Sebastian's lead—but the rich and the bored live for scandal, and our arrangement would surely fit the bill.

It will hurt me if people are mean to Griff or Sebastian about it. Jealous, tiny-hearted men who don't understand having Sebastian's loyalty, having the capacity to love another man the way Sebastian loves Griff, who could never fathom being secure enough to let Griff have me, too. They'll say horrible, wrong things about Sebastian not being able to satisfy his harlot wife, about Griff settling for his best friend's leftovers. Bitter, jaded women whose husbands are "gone" or busy all the time will crucify me if they find out I don't just get one sexy, desirable man... I get two of them.

Meanwhile, Claire just had to go on a spa weekend to recover from her husband's latest mistress having a pregnancy scare—and the old bastard still won't dump her.

I get it. I'm lucky. It's no reason to be vicious, but they will anyway. Jealousy is an ugly monster.

Probably best to keep this quiet.

Not sure how well that will work out long-term, though. I don't want Griff to feel shortchanged, and he might if our relationship is so obviously in the backseat.

The men and I will have to have a discussion about this arrangement. We've spent this first week just enjoying it, living in our little bubble where no one had to know and we didn't have to worry about any practical complications, but I have a feeling that bubble is about to pop.

I'M LYING on my yoga mat, eyes closed, focusing on my breathing as I stretch my body out. This is the greatest relaxation there is. Peace flows through my body as I reach my arms as far as I can over my head, reaching my toes as far as I can in the opposite direction. I could lie here stretched out like this forever.

I might. I've finished my routine and this is my last stretch, so I think I'll remain here in my peace bubble for a while.

At least, I think that until a pair of hands skate up my legs and I feel a decidedly masculine presence looming above me. I don't know which one it is. He hasn't spoken yet and he's down by my legs, so I don't catch his scent.

I smile and keep my eyes closed. I kind of like the mystery, but I ask anyway, "Who goes there?"

"You could open your eyes and solve the mystery yourself."

Griff.

"Why are you lying here on the floor?" he asks.

"It's comfortable. You should try it sometime."

"Lying on the floor isn't comfortable. I've done it plenty in my time."

I open my eyes, but keep my arms overhead. "You probably didn't try it with a mat. It feels nice at the end of a yoga routine."

"Don't you run? Why do you have to do yoga, too?"

"Improves my flexibility," I tell him. "You know all those positions you guys like to put me in when we're in bed? Thank yoga for my abilities."

Griff smiles, lowering his body until he's on top of me. "In that case, I appreciate yoga very much."

"You better," I murmur, before his lips brush mine. I'm reluctant to move, but I finally lower my arms so I can wrap them around his neck and kiss him back. Mm, he's in a tender mood this afternoon, tasting me, running his tongue along my lower lip before softly invading my mouth. Our tongues tangle and I wrap my legs around him, pulling him closer. My fingers move through his hair while we kiss. After a minute, he breaks away and pulls back to look down at me, an appreciative smile on his face.

I smile up at him, running my fingers through his hair one more time. "This is a nice surprise. What are you doing home so early?"

This appears to amuse him. "Home?"

"You know what I mean," I tell him.

He shrugs, his eyes roving over my face. His eyes are warm with tenderness and I can't resist leaning up and stealing another kiss. He cracks a smile when I do. "I was just wondering what you were up to. Thought I'd swing by and check."

Even though I'm glad to see him, I can't resist teasing him a bit. "You know, they have these nifty things called phones. You can just type out a message and send it. Within a minute or two, I could've told you what I was doing."

"Eh, I was between places anyhow. Thought I'd take my lunch."

"You want me to make you something?" I offer. "I was just about to have a snack; I could throw something together for you."

"You don't have to feed me all the time, you know," he tells me.

"I like taking care of my guys," I tell him.

That makes him smile again. I'm hitting all the right notes today.

I shove lightly against his broad chest. "Let me up, I'll make you some lunch."

"If you insist," he says.

I push up off the ground and head for the kitchen. "You're in luck, I just bought groceries. Are you in a hurry? I can make a sandwich if you are. Otherwise I can cook."

He wraps his arms around my waist and hugs me from behind as soon as I approach the counter. I smile and lean my head back against his shoulder. "No hurry. Whatever you feel like making is fine with me."

I let him hold me for a minute, then I head for the fridge and gather up some ingredients to make a couple of salads. His gaze follows me as I put hard-boiled eggs, grape tomatoes and cheese on the counter.

"What can I do?" he asks.

"You want to help?" I ask, lifting an eyebrow.

"Sure, why not?"

I shrug, watching him open the container of grape tomatoes. "No reason, I suppose, just not used to it. Sebastian doesn't cook. I'm not sure he can."

Griff shakes his head. "Seb's an ass. He *can* cook, but he exaggerates how bad he is at it so no one ever asks him to." Griff grabs a knife out of the block and points to the cabinets. "You got a cutting board somewhere?"

I eye him up with interest as I walk past. "A man who can cook, huh? I like it."

"Most of us are capable. You found yourself a fifties throwback, I swear to God."

I grin as I reach into the cabinet for the cutting board. "When I first met him, he sort of reminded me—now, don't ever tell him I told you this," I add, realizing Sebastian probably wouldn't find it as amusing as I do.

"Of course," Griff says, taking the cutting board and grabbing a handful of grape tomatoes. "Quarter these?"

I nod my head. "That'll be perfect. Okay, so, when I first met him and realized how... helpless is the wrong word."

Griff snickers. "If you're talking about household chores, helpless is exactly the word. He used to make his hook-ups do the laundry if I wasn't around."

"That does not shock me at all."

"Sometimes I think he brought girls home specifically because the basket was full."

Laughing a little, I admit, "That wouldn't surprise me either."

Griff shakes his head. "Anyhow, go on with whatever you were saying."

"Okay, so, you never met him because he died a year or so before I met you guys, but I had a grandfather who had married three times. His first wife died and he was living with someone else within a month or so. His second wife died and he got together with someone else just as quickly. Then his third wife died, and he got married *three weeks* later. It was appalling."

"Was he a serial killer? Why are all these women dying?"

"Well, they were old. Not his first wife, that was just bad luck—she had an aneurism—but the other two… just health issues due to old age, I guess. No, he wasn't a murderer. But my mom thought it was so tasteless the way he would just get remarried like it was nothing, how he could *not* live alone."

"Seb's not like that, though. He's good at being alone."

"Well, that's the thing," I tell him. "We always assumed Granddad was just bad at being alone, but when my mom finally asked him about it, you know what he said?"

"I'm afraid to ask."

"He couldn't cook. Didn't know how to do laundry. If he walked into a grocery store, he didn't know where to find anything. He *needed* a wife to survive. He and his first wife got married in a different time; they got married at 18, he went to work, she stayed home and took care of the house and their family. Obviously, Sebastian and I do things this way because that's what we like and it works for us, but back then... it was just what they did. So, from the time he moved out of his mother's house, Granddad always had someone to take care of him. When Grandma died, he literally didn't know how to take care of himself. So he just got remarried."

Griff shakes his head. "That's crazy. Seb knows how to do this shit, though, don't ever let him tell you he doesn't. He's just an ass who thinks his time is too valuable to waste on shit like this. He's not *much* of a cook, but he could chop up some fucking tomatoes."

I shrug. "It doesn't bother me. I enjoy serving him. I know it's not for everybody, but I get a little charge out of it."

He quirks an eyebrow and looks over at me. "Out of serving people?"

"Out of serving Sebastian, not people. It suits our dynamic." So he doesn't feel left out, I add, "And you, too. I like this, but I'm happy to do the work myself. It makes me feel good to take care of my loved ones."

"Needed?"

"Yeah, I guess so."

"It doesn't bother you that it's something anyone could do?" I frown at him, so he clarifies, "Like, your grandfather needed your grandma. But when she died, he just brought in a replacement."

"Well, sure, if literally my only use here was doing chores, I could be replaced. Hell, I could be replaced with a *housekeeper*. That's not all it is, though." I recall their boorish conversation that woke me up the other night and I narrow my eyes at him with mocking reproach. "I don't just cook food and drain balls."

He has the good grace to grimace. "I said I was sorry for that."

"Sebastian has specific needs, and I'm good at taking care of them. It took time for us to learn one another and to be as good together as we are. Now his needs have shifted." When I took on my need-specific, sometimes rigid husband, I certainly never expected his needs would extend to me having a romantic relationship with another man to keep him in Sebastian's life. That was a bit of a surprise. I shrug, picking up where I left off. "But I adapt well to his shifting needs, that's why I work so well with Sebastian."

Griff nods, but he appears introspective as he uses the blade of the knife to move the quartered tomatoes and heads over to the sink to rinse it off. "So, can I ask a question?"

"Of course."

"His needs have shifted to include me now, right? So, what if they shift again? What if he realizes he doesn't want to share you anymore?"

"I don't think we need to worry about that now," I tell him, partly because this is new and Sebastian really seems to like it, partly because I have *no idea* what happens if he changes his mind about this. I don't want to be put into a hypothetical scenario like that. "Obviously, Sebastian is fine with this arrangement. It was his idea to begin with and given our bedroom activities most nights this week, it clearly does *not* bother him to see us together. He loves both of us. He wants both of us to be happy. If we've found a way for all three of us to be happy together, why would he change his mind?"

Griff nods, considering what I've said. "You see a future in this, then? You don't think this is just... an experiment he'll lose interest in?"

"I don't think he would play with you that way, Griff. Obviously, if he had reacted differently, if he would have let you have me that first night and then realized he couldn't deal, that would be a different thing. But he's fine with it. We've talked about it just the two of us, too. He's really not bothered by it. All of our needs are being met; he's happy with the way things are. I don't see why that would change."

Griff cracks and peels the hard-boiled eggs while I grab plates and get the rest of our salads ready. Once they're finished and topped with all the fixings, Griff takes a seat at the table and I grab a pitcher from the fridge, pouring us both glasses of ice water.

As I take a seat, Griff looks over at me. "I like being with you."

I smile softly, placing my hand over his on the table. "I like being with you, too."

"I don't want it to only be because of Seb," he adds.

I lose my smile, my eyebrow furrowing. I don't think I make him feel that way, but maybe we talk about my husband more than we should. I've obviously never dated Griff, so I'm not sure how sensitive he is to that. "It's not just because of him," I tell him. "If I didn't want to be with you, I wouldn't. I adore my husband, Griff, but I'm not an escort. I don't go where I'm assigned if I don't want to be there." Drawing my hand away, I ask, "I mean, do you think I've been faking all along? We've been friends for years; obviously I care about you and enjoy your company. I admitted to having had not-so-pure thoughts about you even *before* the sharing was a reasonable possibility. I wouldn't have acted on it because I'm not a shitty person, but I'm also not a sex doll."

"I know that," he says, searching my face for something. "I didn't mean it that way."

I push back from the table and stand. Griff's gaze jumps to mine, concern in his blue eyes. He probably thinks he's offended me. He pushes his chair back too, but before he can stand, I place a hand on his shoulder, step over his legs, and sit on his lap, straddling him. The concern is gone, replaced with surprise. He's not sure how he just went from having possibly offended me to having me on his lap.

I smile at his confusion and wrap my arms around his neck, leaning in and giving him a kiss. "I told you before, Griff. You're a wonderful man. You're a sweetheart." I lean in and kiss his neck. "You're sexy as hell." I kiss his neck again. "You have a big, beautiful cock and you know just how to use it." Another kiss, but now I can feel his arousal straining against the fabric of his pants. "I could keep telling you all the wonderful things I like about you, if you want." I let my hand slide not-so-innocently down his muscular torso and caress him through the fabric of his slacks. "Or I could just show you how much I like you. I can sink to my knees right here beneath the table, free your cock, and worship it with my mouth until you come down my throat."

"Fuck, Moira."

I nip at his earlobe. "Or you can come on my tits, if you want. Then we can shower together and wash it all off." I drag my lips down his neck, then lean back and offer him a little smile. "Whatever you want, baby."

Griff shakes his head, looking at me like he can't quite believe me—still. "You are a filthy little angel, aren't you?"

I grin at him. "I like that."

"I like you."

I smile, leaning my forehead against his. "I like you, too."

12

GRIFF

I KNOW AS SOON AS ASHLEY SITS DOWN ACROSS FROM me and her boobs practically spill out of her shirt that my lawyer was right—I should not be here.

Not because I'll fall for her bullshit, obviously. But because this is going to be annoying, and it's unlikely to go the way I hoped when I agreed to meet her.

My hope was that I could make her see that stalling is pointless. When we fought, Ashley always knew she could wear me down. Obviously, she thought she could get out of cheating on me just as easily. It's not a thing I like about myself, but I have a weakness for beautiful women. Not like I can't keep my shit together around any given beautiful woman, but when I give one the keys to my castle, I don't like to take 'em back. Doesn't matter if they shit all over everything, doesn't matter if they throw everything I invested in them back in my face. If they come crawling back, some sick shit inside of me tells me I should take it. Tells me it's all I deserve—more than I deserve, really. I should be glad they even *want* to crawl back to me.

Right now, the sadistic side of my brain that spits out poisonous shit like that doesn't have a leg to stand on, though. Because I have Moira, and Moira is everything I've always wanted. Everything Ashley could never be—that Ashley has no interest in being. I remember keenly the loneliness I felt last time I tried to hold Ashley. Whereas now, sitting here at this table, I can recall the warmth of Moira snuggled in my arms this morning, her soft lips moving tenderly along my jawline. What a way to wake up.

No, I'm not worried about getting sucked back in to Ashley's shit; I just want her to go away, and frankly, if I can throw a little money at her and make that happen faster, I'd like to.

My lawyer told me I'm abso-fucking-lutely not allowed, though. Her words. She swears if Ashley smells money in the water, she'll latch on and suck me dry.

The cut of her shirt tells me I probably should have listened. Ashley isn't here to let me go; she's here to try to draw me back in.

"It's so good seeing you, Griff. You look so good," she tells me, reaching across the table and patting my arm. I draw my arm away as soon as her hand makes contact. Her mouth forms a little pout. "Don't be like that. Please? I want us to have a nice lunch. I've missed you."

I shoot her a look to let her know I'm not impressed. "Don't do that."

"What?" she asks, innocently. "Tell the truth? I really do, Griff. I miss you so much."

"Please stop." I look around for the waiter, partly because I'm embarrassed, partly because I want him to come take our order so we can get out of here faster.

"You have no idea how happy I was when you agreed to meet me."

I stop looking for the waiter and turn my gaze on Ashley, meeting hers so she can see I'm serious when I tell her, "That is not why we're here. This is not a reunion. I agreed to meet you because I wanted to tell you, face to face, to stop your bullshit."

Her eyes dim and she sits back in her chair. She has the fucking nerve to look wounded. "My bullshit?"

"You're stalling. You're using every trick in the book to try to drag this shit out. It's a waste of time and money, not to mention energy. You and I don't have kids or intertwined family; there's nothing to untangle. There's no reason for this to be a whole thing. We had a relationship that didn't work out. That's it. Keep your rings, keep your clothes, keep all your fucking shoes and purses—just sign the goddamn papers and let me out of this godforsaken marriage."

Ashley shakes her head, looking at me like my words disgust her. "You think this is about *stuff*? Fuck you, Griff. Fuck you for saying that."

"Fine, fuck me. I don't care anymore. Just sign the papers."

"Stop saying that," she snaps. "This isn't a *relationship* that didn't work out, it's our marriage. We got married. We made promises to each other."

I sit back, laughing a little at her gall. "Wow. Really? *You* want to talk to *me* about promises? You weren't too worried about those promises when some other asshole was balls deep inside you in *my* fucking club, now, were you?"

Her eyes well up with practiced tears. "I made a mistake, Griff. A horrible, stupid, selfish mistake. I was feeling... I was just feeling so neglected. You hadn't even touched me in weeks; you didn't look at me like you wanted me. Then suddenly this stranger did, and it was stupid, I know that. It was cruel and the wrong thing to do. I should have resisted. I should have gone home and tried talking to you about how I was feeling."

If she thinks that little speech is going to gain her sympathy, she's sadly mistaken. "You always blame me, don't you? You did the same shit after Seb's wedding."

Her eyes flash with anger. "That *was* your fault. You were mooning over Moira the whole fucking time. You watched him dance with her and then—" She holds a hand up, as if to stop herself. "This isn't productive. This isn't what I want. It's not about blame. It doesn't matter who was at fault. We don't have to dredge up the past. It doesn't have to matter, that's what I'm saying. We've both made mistakes. Let's start fresh."

"You've made mistakes," I state. "You. Not me. I never fucked anyone else. That was only you. Even when I was miserable, I kept my fucking dick in my pants."

"But you didn't *tell me* you were miserable! I didn't *know*."

My eyebrows shoot up. "You couldn't *tell?*"

Ashley sighs. "I'm not a mind reader, Griff. Sometimes marriages get hard."

I shake my head. "That is *not* what happened between us. That's not what it was. We were not two people in a good marriage who went through a rough patch. I wanted to believe that too, but it wasn't true. It was bullshit, Ashley, just like our relationship. I never should have married you in the first place and I think you know that. We moved too fast, we made a mistake. That doesn't mean we should be miserable for the rest of our lives."

"I think it's a little much to say I made you miserable," she informs me.

"Yeah, well, you weren't in the room when my best friend

with his fucking fantasy marriage had to tell me he saw my wife fucking someone else. Maybe then you'd have a different perspective."

Ashley points at me, like I just proved her point. "That right there is the problem, Griff. You always compared our marriage to theirs. *Always.*"

I stare at the water in front of me, at the condensation on the outside of the glass. We haven't even touched our water and I already want to leave. The waiter hasn't approached yet, and I'm already so fucking annoyed that I want to crawl out of my skin. I don't know how I thought I could sit through a whole fucking meal with her.

"You know what?" she says, still ranting. "Their marriage isn't as perfect as you think it is. They're full of shit, Griff, that's what they are. No one is that happy all the time. No couple still looks at each other like that after being married for years."

"You're wrong," I state. "Just because we didn't doesn't mean no one does. They take care of their marriage. They go out of their way to make one another happy. They're happier than we were because they're good together, Ashley. Because they care enough to never stop nurturing their relationship." My eyebrows rise. "We never did. That should tell us something."

"That we didn't try hard enough," she states, following the same logic, but coming up with a much different result.

"Maybe," I say, shrugging. "But it doesn't matter now. You've done things I can't get past, and I've already moved on. All I need is your ink on the paper and we're history. We don't have a marriage anymore, Ashley. We don't *have* a relationship. If you wanted to work on things, if you wanted to start taking care of our relationship, you came to that conclusion too late.

Literally anytime *before* you fucked some other asshole wouldn't have been too late, but now? Your window hasn't just slammed shut, I took a wrecking ball to the whole fucking wall—the window doesn't even exist anymore. I have no romantic feelings left for you, Ashley. None."

She pales a bit. For once, she's unable to come up with anything to say.

"I'm sorry if that sounds harsh," I add, to soften the blow. "Honestly, I don't even have any resentment about it at this point, I just want it over. I don't want to play games. I don't want to fuck around with expensive lawyers. I just want this marriage ended legally, since as far as I'm concerned, it's over in every other way."

"Are you seeing someone?" she demands, eyes narrowed with suspicion.

My eyes widen and I stare at her. "That's what you took away from what I just said?"

"Yes," she says, digging in. "This isn't like you. You don't give up on people like this. You're not the guy who walks away. I call bullshit. You said you've already moved on. Who is she?"

I shake my head, staring at the table. "You are fucking unbelievable. Forget it. Forget this." I push my chair back and stand.

"What are you doing?" she demands, her voice rising. "We haven't even ordered."

"We're not going to. I thought I could do this, but I was wrong. I'm done here. If you have anything else to say to me, say it through your lawyer."

Ashley stands and grabs my arm to try to keep me from leaving. "Griff, come on. Please." When I don't stop, she follows after me. I shake her arm off, but she just grabs my shoulder. "Stop. Dammit, stop and talk to me."

I pry her hand off me and keep walking.

"Griffin!"

I ignore her and head out the door. We only ordered waters so there's no bill, just an annoyed waiter. Probably should've left a tip. Oh well, too late to go back now.

By the time I get to my car, I'm so fucking agitated I can't think straight. I need to calm down, and all I can think about is Moira.

I check my watch. I'm not even sure if Seb's home or not. If he is, I probably shouldn't show up. I'll be by later for dinner, as it is.

When I start the car, though, it practically drives there without me. Relief pours through me when I pull in and Seb's car isn't there.

I go to the door and bang on it, then remember there's a doorbell. Before I have to ring it though, I see the shape of Moira coming toward the frosted glass window.

She smiles as she opens the door to greet me. "Hey, what are you doing here in the middle of the day?" Her expression turns teasing. "You want lunch again, don't you?"

She's so fucking pretty. She's standing there in this soft white sweater with a tight black skirt, mauve flowers printed all over it. Her hair is pulled back like the night I took her out, with dark strands hanging down around her ears and neck. Her blue eyes sparkle with warmth at the sight of me, like she's happy to see me.

I swoop forward and cradle her face in my hand, drawing her in for an unexpected kiss.

"Oh," she murmurs before our lips crash together.

Her right arm drifts to my side and she tugs me close, her left arm going around my neck. I walk her backward, kicking the door shut behind me. I don't let go, don't break away from her lips, until I have her backed up against a wall.

I finally have to let her go because I'm wearing all these bulky fucking clothes. I yank off my coat and toss it on the floor behind me. I need to touch her again, so I advance on her, grabbing her and pulling her in for another kiss.

She kisses me back, but my hunger makes her hesitant. She breaks away as soon as I let her and searches my face. "Griff, is everything okay?"

I nod, then bury my face in her neck. I leave a trail of kisses, then when I get near her ear, I murmur, "I need you."

Moira melts against me, pulling back to look in my eyes. Hers have a tender gleam in them now, but there's something vulnerable there, too. I don't have time to think about it, then she's running her fingers through my hair and yanking me back in for a hard kiss. One hand drops to my belt so she can unbuckle it. I grab her delicate-looking shirt and yank it off. She's wearing a white bra today.

"Can we go upstairs?" she asks.

My raging hard-on says no, I need to pin her to this wall and fuck her right here, but I manage a nod anyhow.

Moira takes my hand and hauls me up the stairs, leaving our discarded clothing in the entry way. By the time we get to the bedroom, I toss my belt and shuck my pants. She reaches behind her and unzips her pretty skirt, pushing it down and revealing a pair of white panties with delicate little roses on them. She looks so fucking pretty. I just want to freeze this mental image of her and keep it forever.

She looks down, then back up at me, my little sex kitten acting all innocent. "See anything you like?"

I keep my eyes on her as I stalk closer. "I see *everything* I like," I tell her, honestly.

She flushes with pleasure, her gaze dropping to my groin. I'm completely naked while she still has her bra and panties on. We need to fix that.

"On the bed," I tell her.

She eagerly obeys and I follow, yanking off her delicate panties and tossing them on the floor. I want her so much, I'm tempted to leave the bra on, but the idea of not seeing her bare breasts gives me enough patience to reach behind her and unhook it. I take just enough time to peel it off before burying myself inside her.

It's after we've both finished that I get what I need, though. The sight of her excites me and I wanted to fuck her until she came as hard for me as she does for Seb, but she's so affectionate afterward, lying in my embrace, fitted snugly against my chest with her head resting on my bicep. This is what I craved when I was driving over here. Her fingertip traces little shapes on my chest. Her leg is hooked over my thigh to keep me close. Her hair's a fucking mess.

"What are you smirking at?" she asks, poking me in the chest.

"I fucked up your hair," I tell her.

"Worth it," she assures me with a playful wink. When I don't say anything back, she lets the moment pass, but keeps her watchful blue eyes on me. "You wanna tell me what's wrong? It seemed like something had you upset."

I really don't want to bring up my not-quite ex-wife, especially right now, but I don't want to lie to her, either. "I had to meet with Ashley today. Well, I didn't *have* to. My lawyer actually told me not to. But she's still pulling all kinds of shit to try to stall the divorce and I thought maybe if I talked to her face to face she'd stop it."

The corner of Moira's mouth tugs up with little humor. "Didn't go as planned?"

I shake my head, tracing the curve of her shoulder. "Not quite."

"I'm sorry."

"It's all right. It'll get done, I just... I just wish it wasn't taking so long. I want that part of my life over. I want that mistake filed away and dealt with."

Moira nods her understanding. "What did she say that upset you so much?"

"I wasn't upset," I say defensively. "I was annoyed."

"Fine. That annoyed you so much, then."

"Just bullshit. How she's sorry for what she did—still blames me, though, of course—and it was a mistake. How she wants to start fresh. Just a bunch of shit to try to buy fucking time so she can talk me out of it."

I hate everything Ashley said today—especially the nice stuff. She makes me feel like an asshole for not wanting to try, but I *did* want to try. I *did* try. I tried for years with that woman, and all it got me was cheated on and made a fucking fool of.

I'm lost in my own thoughts so it takes me a minute to realize Moira has gone silent. I wouldn't be too worried about it, except her brow is furrowed, her finger has stopped tracing shapes on my skin, and she's staring vacantly at the wall of my chest in front of her.

"What's going on up there?" I ask, lightly tapping her temple.

She looks regretful, but she attempts a smile. "I was just thinking."

"About what?"

Her big eyes meet mine. "Is there any part of you that wants to?"

I can't believe she'd even ask that after I fled Ashley's presence to come see her. A little doubt in my mind whispers that she's thinking about that because she wants it to be true. After all, if this was just some fantasy I had to fuck Seb's untouchable wife, I've more than sated it. I've fucked her myself, fucked her with him—I've fucked every hole, fucked her a dozen times now. If I only needed to get her out of my system, if I only needed to possess her because she was some ideal to me, I've already done that.

If that's all it is, maybe I could go back to my unfaithful wife with my pride avenged, having fucked my dream girl every which way. Maybe when memories of Ashley's infidelity crossed my mind, memories of Moira desperately gripping Seb's bed sheets and coming for me would be enough to soothe me. Maybe now I could get on with my life, be with someone without constantly comparing them to Moira, our relationship to hers.

Is that what Moira hopes? Is she waiting for me to get her out of my system so she can have her life back? Is she just trying to fuck me until I get bored with her?

"Do you like being with both of us better than just being with Seb?" I ask her.

Moira frowns, since that's not an answer to the question she just asked at all. "In some ways, yes. I don't like to compare, though. You're evading my question."

"I'm not evading your question."

"It's okay if you do," she assures me. "I think that would be natural, to have doubts. Especially after seeing her today. You were married to her for years, and you haven't seen her in person recently. Is that what happened? You can tell me, I won't be offended."

"I don't want to be with Ashley," I snap.

Moira's eyes widen, surprised at the sharpness of my tone. "Okay," she says. "I was just asking. For the record, I don't think you should either. I was just trying to be an unbiased ear in case you needed one."

"I don't *want* you to be unbiased, Moira. We're sleeping together, for fuck's sake. We're in a relationship—maybe a weird one, but a fucking relationship, nonetheless. You should definitely have a preference in this scenario."

She can see that I'm getting agitated, so she curls closer and runs her fingers tenderly through my hair, her features softening. It's exactly the right thing to do. I can't attack her if she's being soft; I'll feel like a fucking monster.

Ashley always rose to the occasion. The more agitated I got, the more agitated she got until we combusted.

Moira leans in and kisses her way along my jawline. "I *do*, Griff. My preference is your happiness. If that's with me and Sebastian, wonderful. If it isn't, I would never guide you away from it just because I want you. That wouldn't be fair. I would understand if you wanted a person all to yourself. I wouldn't *like* it," she adds, holding my gaze. "But I would get it. That's a natural thing to want."

"I don't, though. I want you."

She smiles softly. "You *have* me."

I probably shouldn't tell her this, but it spills out of my mouth anyhow. "I can't help feeling like you're gonna slip away from me. Like Seb's gonna take you back."

"He won't," she assures me. "I love having both of you. He loves sharing me with you. We are *all* happy, Griff. Stop looking for reasons not to be."

"I'm afraid of losing you, Moira. I can't help it."

She sighs, her blue eyes clouding over. I can see that she's not sure how to reassure me, and to be honest, I'm not sure either. I don't think she can. I think it's something that'll only go away in time.

I *hope* it goes away in time.

"You're not going to lose me, Griff," she promises, grabbing my hand and twining our fingers together. "We're in this thing now. All three of us."

That doesn't make me feel any better. Maybe it should.

Moira's tone softens, and I get the feeling she's unsure about what she's going to say. "I think maybe with your personal history, with your childhood and the fact that you've sort of been abandoned before, maybe that's why you worry about this. I'm glad we're talking about it, but I'm not sure you feel this way for any external reason. I don't think we've given you any reason to worry about this. Sebastian is clearly trying to give you what you need. I certainly am. I'm sorry you can't trust it yet. You should know by now that I'm reliable. It's one of the things Sebastian loves about me. I'm no quitter. He's not always easy, either. He has some rough edges and personal issues, too."

Yeah, maybe he does, but he'd never bleed them all over her this way. Seb likes to come off strong at all times, and this shit here... this is not that.

I'm gonna scare her off with my irrational bullshit. It won't even be Seb's fault, it'll be mine.

"Maybe it's because all of this is new," she suggests. "Maybe you just need some time to get used to it. Then you'll feel stable."

"Maybe," I murmur.

Moira brings her other hand up and clasps both of them around mine. "I'm yours, Griff. You wanted me and you got me. Stop waiting for the sky to fall. It's not going to. Let yourself enjoy this—not because it's going anywhere, but because that's a nice way to live life. Don't worry about it so much, okay? There's nothing to worry about."

I nod, but I'm not completely convinced.

She must be able to see that. Her expression drifts toward the contemplative and she says, "You need to spend some time with Sebastian. He'll straighten you out."

At that, I have to smile. "That's your answer for everything, isn't it?"

She grins like I've caught her. "Hey, if I'm stumped, I turn to him. You two made it through life together for years without me, so he must have figured out some way to convince you *he* wasn't going anywhere."

I'm about to respond when we're interrupted by the sound of the doorbell. I frown and Moira's eyes widen.

"Are you expecting someone?" I ask.

She's frowns, yanking back the blanket and climbing out of bed. "No."

I gather up my clothes and get them back on before she can. She's flustered, running around looking for her shirt.

"It's downstairs," I remind her, putting a reassuring hand at the small of her back.

She looks up at me just as the doorbell rings again.

"Dammit," she mutters, raking her fingers through her hair. "Where's my clip?" She asks, but then before I can even answer, she makes her way out of the bedroom.

I go over and grab the clip I tossed—I should probably be more careful about throwing all her shit when I'm undressing her—then follow her downstairs. When I get down there, she's tugging her shirt down. She may have clothes on, but her hair is still all mussed, her clothing askew—far from the composed appearance she had when I got here.

She slides her hands down her hips one more hopeless time

as she approaches the door. She knows she's still not put together, but she opens it anyhow.

My coat is still in a heap on the floor, so I pick it up and hang it on the coat tree before walking over to see who is at the door.

13

MOIRA

I HAVE NO IDEA WHAT TO SAY OR DO AS I STAND IN the open front door. I know I look just like what I am—someone who had afternoon sex, then had to sloppily pull on clothes and run downstairs to open the door.

"Oh, hi," I say a bit haltingly.

My sister Gwen looks back at me, eyebrows rising. She bites back a smirk, looking away from me to the baby girl she's lightly bouncing on her hip. "I take it Sebastian came home for lunch today."

Before I can summon a single word, Griff must come into view behind me because Gwen's gaze catches and then her face loses color. All amusement has fled and her gaze jumps back to me.

I hold up a steady hand, as if that can stop her from jumping to conclusions. "It's not what you're thinking."

She mouths 'holy fucking shit,' shaking her head and refusing to look at me. "I can't even... Are you *nuts*?"

"Come inside," I tell her, taking a step back. "It's cold out."

She looks past me at Griff to give him a dirty look, but she steps inside anyway. As soon as I shut the door behind her, I turn around to explain, but I'm not entirely sure how. Sebastian said he didn't want people to know about this until Griff's divorce was official, but Gwen isn't really *people*, she's my sister. Besides, given what she just walked in on, it's either explain, or it looks like I'm cheating on Sebastian.

"Okay," I say, glancing from Griff to Gwen. "Um, Griff, this is my sister Gwen. Remember I told you about her?"

Gwen gapes at me and ignores Griff. "You *told* him about me? What the hell is going on here? What happened to Sebastian?"

"Nothing," I tell her. "This is Sebastian's best friend, Griff."

Her eyes widen. "His best friend? Seriously?"

Griff smirks to himself, raking a hand through his hair. "The pleasure's all mine," he remarks, dryly.

"You're damn right it is," she snaps. "I would tell you she's married, but you clearly already know that, you son of a bitch. You're both horrible."

"Whoa, whoa, whoa," I say. "Gwen, relax. We're not having an affair."

Gwen rolls her eyes. "Oh, sure. You guys were just moving furniture, right?"

"No, we were doing what you think we were doing," I say vaguely, glancing at the baby. She can't talk yet so it's not like she can repeat anything, but I still can't say sex in front of a baby. "But it's not an affair. Sebastian and I are still together, nothing happened. We've just... started doing something different. I'm seeing Griff, too. Sebastian knows. It was his idea."

Now her face goes blank. "What?"

"It's hard to explain," I tell her. "The gist of it is, everything is above board. There's no reason to hate us. No one is getting hurt."

Gwen looks back at Griff, but with less hostility and more curiosity. Now that she doesn't want to kill him for being a cheating bastard, I'm sure she's a little more impressed by the sexy, muscular, well-dressed man before her. Even if he is a little mussed, he's more put together than I am.

"We can start over," he offers, along with his hand. "Griffin Halliwell, Sebastian's best friend and business partner. Please don't vandalize my car."

"Not gonna shake your hand since you were just feeling up my sister, but pending Sebastian's confirmation on all this, I will not vandalize your car." Her gaze swings back to me. "Also, you told him about that? How long has this been going on? How could you not tell me? How is Sebastian okay with this? I am so confused."

I nod my head sympathetically. "It's a lot to take in. Come sit down, I'll make some tea or hot cocoa. I haven't even had a chance to say hello to my adorable niece."

"I was going to ask if you could watch her while I run a few errands, but I didn't expect you to have naked company."

"He's fully dressed," I say dismissively.

"Wasn't ten minutes ago," Griff remarks.

I bite back a smile and Gwen points toward the bathroom. "Please go wash your giant hands. All I can think about is them all over my sister."

I nod my agreement. "And you need to meet Layla."

Griff shakes his head but goes to wash his hands anyway. Gwen grabs my arm and widens her eyes at me. "I'm going to need explicit details about all this. I'm one part horrified and one part... I'm not sure. You get two hot guys? Where's mine?"

"You're married," I remind her.

"So are you! To a dreamboat! And you get a bonus hunk. That's not fair. Our husbands need to talk. Sebastian needs to sell Carl on the value of having a second man around the house —particularly one that looks like that. Does he live here? Do you guys just have a giant love nest?" Her eyes widen and she gasps in sudden realization. "Oh, my God. Do he and Sebastian...?"

I shake my head. "No. I mean, sometimes they take me at the same time, but they don't do anything to one another."

"At the same time?" she echoes, like I've just given voice to a sacred, unspoken legend.

"We'll talk later," I assure her.

"How does that even work?"

"Really, really well," I tell her.

Gwen and I migrate to the kitchen. I wash my hands at the sink to set my germophobe sister's mind at ease, then I set about making everyone some tea. I'm not sure tea is an adequate beverage to go alongside today's news, but I need to do something to busy myself.

While the water is boiling, I text Sebastian to let him know that while I tried to keep it quiet, Gwen knows about our arrangement. He tells me I need to swear her to secrecy, at least until Griff's divorce goes through. Gwen doesn't run in the same circles, so it shouldn't be an issue. She and her husband are comfortably lower middle class, so they don't even know most of our snobbier friends.

"Listen, I didn't tell you about Griff because we're not really advertising it at this point. Griff is going through a divorce, and his ex is being difficult. If she catches wind of all this, she'll try to use it to hurt him, so you can't say anything to anyone."

Her eyes go wide again. "He's *married*? What kind of cul-de-sac cliché are you living in here, Moira?"

I shake my head. "It's not like that. She cheated on him, he left her. They were separated before any of this started. But they had a prenup, which means she's not getting anything from the divorce. Instead of admitting defeat, she's dragging it out."

"She sounds like a real prize," Gwen remarks. "So, you're his rebound? Would it be weird if I set him up with my friend after you're done with him? She just went through a drawn-out divorce herself, and she's finally ready to start dating again. She's got a cute kid. Does Griffin like kids?"

I turn back to frown at her. "He's not up for grabs. Why do people keep trying to auction him off like a coveted piece at an estate sale? Jesus."

"Because he's hot?" she suggests.

Of course, that's when Griff walks back in. "Thanks," he remarks dryly.

"Do you like kids?" Gwen asks, turning to look at him.

Since he clearly thinks she's referring to hers, he steps closer and looks down at Layla. "Sure, I do. Hey, little lady."

Layla smiles up at him. He starts to reach a finger out to her tiny hand, but he stops and looks to Gwen for approval. She grabs his hand, dramatically inspects it, then reaches into her purse for a bottle of hand sanitizer.

"Really?" he asks.

"Just to be safe," she states.

"I'm not diseased," I tell her, moving closer so I can smile at baby Layla. "Hello, beautiful."

Layla glances at me, but then she looks back up at Griff. He's properly sanitized now, so it's okay when Layla wraps her tiny hand around his finger and tugs it close. I'm hit with a brick wall of maternal warmth and I can't help drawing closer to him, leaning my head on his big, strong arm.

"Still feeling that baby fever?" he asks, lightly.

"Oh yeah," I tell him, nodding vehemently. "Reaching brain-boiling temperatures over here."

Gwen glances between us uncertainly. "Oh, dear. When does Sebastian get home? Maybe I should have you babysit later. I don't want to give you baby fever when your husband isn't here and your man candy is."

"I think he has to go back to work anyway," I tell her. "It'll just be me."

"How about this instead? Mr. Beef Cake here leaves you with all your eggs unfertilized, I stay here and you explain to me how all this works, and I'll run errands some other time?"

"God, Gwen, you can't just talk about the fertilization of my eggs in mixed company."

"She also called me a beef cake," Griff points out.

Gwen holds a hand up toward the ceiling and bows her head. "I'm doing God's work here. I will not be leaving you two unchaperoned. My brother-in-law will approve and he buys really good Christmas gifts."

I quirk an unimpressed eyebrow. "I pick out your Christmas gifts."

"And pay with his money."

I roll my eyes. "*Our* money."

"You have a prenup, too," she reminds me.

"We're business partners," Griff states. "I can fund the same Christmas gifts he can. You're allowed to like me."

Gwen leaps to conclusions at his wording. "See? Mr. Beef Cake wants to replace your husband. I'm staying until Seb gets back. Just try to get me out of here."

Griff shakes his head. "All right, I need to get back to work, anyhow." I lean away from his arm as he moves, so he rests a hand on my hip and attempts to get his finger away from Layla. She doesn't let go. "Can I have this?" he asks her.

She blinks at him and keeps his finger locked in her tiny little death grip.

Gwen untangles her baby's fingers, telling Layla, "We like Uncle Sebastian, you let go of that giant finger."

14

SEBASTIAN

As soon as I walk through the front door, I see Moira pacing, looking down at a tiny bundle of blankets in her arms. Since Moira did not have a baby when I left for work this morning, I look around for its mother.

My sister-in-law is sitting on the couch, popping grapes into her mouth and watching television. Her gaze brightens when she sees me. "The boss is home," she announces.

I smile faintly. I like Gwen. A little loud for my tastes, but she knows who's in charge. "Hello, Gwen. Are you staying for dinner?"

"I was staying for the free babysitting," she announces. "I adore Layla. Motherhood is beautiful and fulfilling and wonderful, but you know what no one tells you?"

"What's that?" I ask, though I'm not even mildly interested.

"It's exhausting and you don't get a break. Ever. One might think that since I have a husband, I might get a break, but one would be wrong." She lifts her eyebrows. "Side note, do you rent Griff out? And if you do, can you talk to Carl and convince him that letting his wife have a hot boyfriend who helps around the house is a good idea?"

A hot boyfriend who helps around the house?

I don't immediately understand, but then Griff comes back to Moira's side with a pink pacifier he must have just retrieved for her.

Aw, shit. Those two are going to get sucked into the "babies are cute, let's have one" vortex, aren't they?

Now that I'm here, Moira turns and hands the baby off to Griff. She beams at me and hastens over to throw her arms around my neck, leaning in to give me a lingering kiss. "There's my handsome husband. I've been missing you all day long."

I briefly kiss her lips before glancing past her and pointing out, "Seems like you have a lot of company."

"Mm-hmm," she agrees, running a hand down my chest. "But none of them are you."

My hands skim her sides until they settle on her hips, then I pull her in for a much less casual kiss. Her body melts against mine at the stab of my tongue, a faint sound of pleasure slipping out of her. I need to take her out. I need to spend some time with her.

I need to take her upstairs, strip off these clothes, and bury myself deep inside her.

Probably can't do that with her sister here, though.

Moira pulls back and smiles up at me tenderly, smoothing her hands down over my lapels. "How was your day, honey?"

"Not bad," I murmur. Then, raising my voice enough for Gwen to hear, I ask, "What is my favorite sister-in-law doing here?"

Gwen smiles and pushes up off the couch. "Your *only* sister-in-law is here playing chaperone. I had no idea you guys had a whole kinky love nest thing going on here. I thought I caught my sister being a desperate housewife, so being the dutiful sister-in-law that I am, I stayed here and made sure no funny business went on until you got home."

I shake my head, amused. "Well, much as I appreciate the loyalty, they're allowed all the 'funny business' they want. The more orgasms Moira can have in a day, the better that day is."

Gwen's shoulders sag and she sighs. "Why didn't I meet you first?"

Moira chokes on her laughter. "Back off my men, Gwen. Jesus."

Gwen pouts. "Being married with a new baby sucks. I don't get orgasms from even one man, let alone two. You guys are depressing me."

"Sounds like your husband is depressing," I remark.

"Compared to Mr. Give Her Orgasms, yeah. He can't even be bothered to come home at a decent time each night. After I've been parenting all day long on three hours of sleep. I don't have time to *eat*, and he can just go out after work and blow off steam. I'm lucky if I get a *shower* every day. You guys are so bad at marriage. How is she this happy to see you at the end of the day? Sometimes, when I'm getting up with Layla for the 18th time in a given night, I daydream about pouring scalding hot coffee over my husband's head while he sleeps. That's what marriage is supposed to be like. You guys are doing it wrong."

I smirk. "Well, my wife is happy to see me because I make sure she has plenty of time for sleep, showering, eating, and doing whatever else her heart desires. I also make sure she gets multiple orgasms each day. Sounds like Carl needs to step his shit up."

"I'm going to send him to you for husband lessons," she agrees.

I glance past the women at Griff, awkwardly cradling the

tiny baby against his chest. "How are you holding up back there, Griff? Need a break from baby duty?"

Moira grabs my arm, her eyes widening with urgency. "Please don't hold that baby. My maternal yearning is already off the charts; if I see you with a baby, too, I'll die."

I cock an eyebrow at her. "After everything your sister just said? That didn't put you off babies altogether?"

Moira blinks at me like I've just uttered the most ridiculous set of words she can imagine. "Have you *seen* how small her little hands and feet are? Heard the adorable noises she makes? She's wearing a onesie, Sebastian. Her legs are pudgy and adorable. She looks like an angel when she sleeps. Babies are majestic, and Layla is making me want one desperately."

"So you can be up all night and not have time to shower?"

Moira plants a hand on her hip and looks up at me expectantly. "Between you and Griff, if I can't find time to shower, then you should both be ashamed of yourselves. Besides, you rarely go out after work. You'll be home most evenings, and if you're not here, we'll make sure Griff is."

I can see she's picking up steam, and I need to shift her to a different track before she gets too carried away.

I lean in and tenderly brush my lips against hers. "I like to come home and spend my free time with *you*."

"Aww." Moira lights up, her eyes glinting with love as she grabs me and kisses me again.

Gwen sighs miserably, shaking her head as she goes over to Griff. "Give me my baby back before I stick my head in an oven."

"Yeah," Griff agrees, shifting the baby. "Being around them when you're in a shitty marriage is the most depressing thing in the world."

"I'm not in a shitty marriage," she mutters half-heartedly, like even she can't muster the energy to believe it.

Griff lifts an eyebrow, clearly unconvinced, but he hands her Layla. The baby fusses at first, but settles down once she realizes she's being handed off to her mom.

"There's my little buttercup," Gwen croons, kissing the baby's tiny forehead. "Did you like hanging out with Uncle Griff?"

Griff brightens. "I get uncle status?"

Gwen shrugs like she's not altogether confident, but the decision has been made. "The boss said it was okay, so I guess it's okay."

I smile and squeeze Moira closer, murmuring, "Have I mentioned I like your sister?"

Moira smiles up at me fondly, leaning into my side and wrapping her arm around my back. "She's a smart cookie."

Gwen spends a few minutes gathering up all her baby paraphernalia and saying her goodbyes. To be honest, I just want everyone out of my house so I can spend an evening with my wife. Since I've let Griff join us, I haven't had Moira to myself at all. I like having him around; it reminds me of how things were between us before I met Moira, when Griff and I lived together. But we do need time together alone, too.

Once Gwen leaves, Moira tells me she hasn't started dinner yet because she's been visiting with her sister and her niece.

"You don't have to," I tell her, snaking an arm around her waist and tugging her against me, chest to chest.

Her blue eyes twinkle at me. "I don't?"

"We're going out to dinner tonight."

"Just the two of us?"

I glance past her at Griff, scrolling through something on his phone with a scowl on his face. "You okay over there?"

He looks up, annoyance brushed liberally across his features. "Fantastic."

"Problem?"

"Lawyer bullshit. I'm never getting married again."

I smile faintly. "Well, yeah, bigamy's illegal, so at least until I'm dead, that's off the table. Ashley pulling some shit?"

Moira turns back to look at him. "Since you met with her?"

My eyebrows rise at this new nugget of information. "Since you *what*?"

"Don't worry about it; I've got it under control. I'll straighten this shit out tomorrow."

"I'm gonna need details on that, but not right now. Are you cool on your own tonight?" I ask Griff. "I'm gonna take Moira out."

He glances between us, then nods his head. "Sure. Go have fun."

I watch him for a moment. He still seems agitated, but I don't know if it's because of Ashley, or because I want Moira to myself for a bit. She insists she needs a shower before we go out, so I tell her to make it quick and hang back with Griff.

It's been a busy week. Apparently, I haven't kept a good enough eye on everything—got Griff out meeting his whore ex-wife, Moira yearning for babies, my time with my wife cut down to unacceptable levels.

I figured there would be an adjustment period. Personally, I hoped we could skip over all that shit, but I knew it was unlikely. I've been nothing but hospitable. I've done everything I could to make this easy on both of them.

They're both feelers, though, and feelers are a pain in the ass when things need to change. Griff's also more possessive than is ideal for this situation. I figure we should be able to get past it since Moira is mine in the first place, and if he wants her, that's the only way he gets her.

Thing is, I'm not sure if he *really* wants her, or he just wants what's mine. There could be some covertly competitive bullshit going on here. It may not be about her. It could be about me. If it is, he's not going to be satisfied no matter how fair we are. If it is, this isn't going to work. I'll share Moira with him, but if he starts to try to horn in and push me out, I'll knock the mother-fucker right back out.

It's probably not that. I tell myself it's not that, because I don't want it to be that. I want this to work. I want everyone I love to be happy and satisfied under my roof. No one making dramatic exits, no one hurting and torn apart by jealousy—all of us happy. My wife is capable of pulling it off. If Griff is here for the right reasons, we'll all be fine.

"What's up your ass today?" I ask him, while I wait for Moira to come back down.

"I don't want to tell you. You're a big enough pain in my ass when you're not telling me how right you are about everything."

I shrug, unable to summon even a hint of remorse. "Use your brain more often and you'll be right, too. What'd you do this time?"

"I met Ashley for lunch. Tried to, anyhow. She pissed me off and I left before we had a chance to order."

A faint smile tugs at my mouth. "That sounds about right."

"So she ran to her lawyer. Now she's requesting fucking court-ordered couples counseling."

A little bark of laughter shoots out of me. "Are you kidding me?"

"I wish. I need to call Carrie and tell her this is bullshit."

"Man, she is not letting you out of her clutches. You should just go talk to Donovan, put a hit on her ass, take care of it nice and simple."

Griff shoots me a narrowed look. "You're hilarious."

I lift my eyebrows, nodding. "Yeah, I was joking. Definitely joking." I miss a beat. "Unless you thought it sounded like a good idea."

He cracks a smile and shakes his head at me. "You're an asshole."

"Ah, but I got a smile out of you," I tell him, smacking his arm before standing and heading for the stairs. "She's taking forever. I'm gonna go tell her to get her little ass dressed before the restaurants close."

***

MOIRA SIGHS WITH CONTENTMENT, leaning into my side. My arm settles around her waist as we stroll through Rittenhouse square. It's a little chilly out tonight, but Moira loves to walk through here when we're nearby for dinner, and I don't like to deny Moira anything she loves.

I'm glad we came out tonight. I'm glad we spent some time alone together. Integrating Griff into our relationship is fine, but we still need our own time, too. Now that we've had it, everything feels calmer, like a peace I hadn't even admitted to losing has been restored.

I could enjoy doing just about anything as long as Moira came with me. I could walk through the fires of Hell, and as long as I had her nestled up against my side, I could look at it like a tropical vacation I didn't have to pay for.

Moira's thoughts must be in line with mine, because she suddenly tilts her head back and looks up at me. "I'm glad we did this."

I give her a little squeeze. "So am I."

"You always have the best ideas," she informs me.

"I do," I agree.

She grins and elbows me in the side. "You're so cocky."

"It's why you love me."

"One of many, many, many, many reasons." Peering up at me again, she asks, "Are you happy with how things are right now?"

"You mean with Griff?"

"I mean with everything. I've been trying to balance a new relationship and I haven't had as much time to devote to ours. I feel bad. Usually you get all my time and attention."

I smile, bringing her hand to my lips so I can brush a kiss across her knuckles. "And I am a greedy bastard."

"You are not," she says, dismissively. "You're shrewd, but you're generous."

"Only with my loved ones."

"I don't care about anyone else," she teases.

That's a lie, but I don't bother calling her on it.

Since I don't tease her back, she turns serious again. "I just want to make sure we don't get skipped over in any way because of the new developments. I don't ever want you to feel you're not getting enough of my time, and if you do, you need to tell me."

Given her sentiments are in line with my own, I have to acknowledge that even though I'm sharing her, our relationship is obviously top priority. That's sensible to me, but I don't know if it's going to work for Griff. He probably hopes things will be more equal. I guess I do too, because I don't want Moira to feel like Griff is a job, and I don't want Griff to feel like second best, but I can't force her to feel a way she doesn't, either.

"How are things going with you and Griff?"

She glances up at me, but she looks a touch hesitant. "How do you mean?"

"Just trying to get a read. How are you feeling about everything? Does he seem to be adjusting well?"

"I guess so. It's taking some time. We only just started looking at each other this way, so that relationship has quite a ways to go before we catch up. If we even catch up. I'm not sure if we're supposed to." She hesitates, then admits, "I'm a little worried about him feeling left out, but I don't know if I want him to have an equal place in my heart anyway. I can't even imagine that. You're my everything. You're king of my heart, no contest."

I crack a smile, but her words—however well-meaning—cause my worry to grow. "He'll be able to feel that, though. That's not fair to him. Are you holding back on purpose, or do you just not feel that way for him?"

She watches the brick path beneath our feet like it holds the answers. "I don't know. You know I love Griff, but sometimes he says things that make me feel like he's being competitive with you, and that's not okay with me. I try to reassure him, but I don't know how deeply it runs." Now she looks up at me, like she hates what she's saying as much as I probably hate hearing it. "I know you love Griff, I know he loves you, I just don't know if he's cut out for this."

"He just needs to feel secure in your affection. It's too soon to know whether or not he can hack it, but he needs to *feel* your love. That's the only way this stands any chance of working. If he feels like you're ready to quit on him, he'll feel insecure all the time. It'll all feed into inevitable failure. It's all right if this fails, we can't force it to work, but I don't want it to fail because you're worried about hurting my feelings. I don't want you to withhold from him to appease me. I don't need you to do that."

Still tentative, she asks, "So, what do you want me to do?"

"Keep doing what you're doing, but let go. Open up. Give it a real chance. Our love is secure. You and me are forever. Nothing can touch us. Loving Griff does not mean you love me any less. You're doing all this *for* me. You've got a big heart with plenty of room for both of us. Griff has plenty of good qualities. He's loyal as hell; he just needs to know he's got two feet on solid ground. We were both taught we had to look out for ourselves first, no one else was going to, so that's what he's doing right now. He needs to know he's safe with us. He needs to know we're not going to quit on him. As much as we can, we both need to commit to this. We can't get a read on whether or not it will work if we're half-assing it."

"But what if he tries to…?"

I shake my head. "Can't think that way. He'll feel it. Suspicion doesn't feel like love. He needs to feel your love. Let yourself fall for him, if you can."

She misses a step, then looks up at me warily. "You want me to fall in love with him? Like… the way I'm in love with you?"

"Sure," I say, nodding. "Wouldn't that be most enjoyable for everybody?"

"Not for you," she objects, frowning.

I love my wife, but sometimes it's tedious trying to explain shit like this to people. "It *is* best for me because that's how we're all happy. Being in love with him doesn't mean you're not in love with me anymore. You don't have to choose. You get both of us, so why not fall in love with each of us? Enjoy us both as much as you can. We each have different things to offer separately, and we'll have the best dynamic together if you have deep, legitimate feelings for both of us, not just me. Only being in love with me will breed resentment."

She doesn't answer. I give her a minute to process, but she still doesn't respond.

"I know I'm asking a lot of you," I tell her.

"It's just scary," she says. "I never expected to do any of this again. I have you."

I stop walking, so she does, too. I pull her in front of me, grabbing her hips and pulling her against me. She tilts her head back, her big blue eyes clouded over with conflict. I hate that. I know it's my fault. This wasn't her idea, it was mine. Because of *my* needs, she's already had to completely change her lifestyle. Now I'm asking her to take on a full-fledged relationship—with all the complexities that entails—alongside ours.

Her body may like when we're both paying attention to her, when we fuck her together and double up her pleasure, but this isn't just pleasurable—it's work. It's a risk. It's investing her own feelings in something that just might not work. I'm asking her to open herself up to heartache to keep someone around for me—and since she was brought up traditionally, this goes against her idea of normal to begin with. Moira's a little survivor so she adapts, but I don't think she realized this would be as complicated as it is. Letting Griff fuck her is easy. I almost wish he just needed to fuck her, because that's not risky. That could be uncomplicated fun, teaming up with my best friend to overload my wife with pleasure, using her together—I like all that. That's fucking fun.

Feelings are a lot less fun.

I've always known that myself, and now I'm foisting all the hard work off on Moira.

I'd shoulder it for her if I could, but Griff doesn't need me. He needs her.

15

MOIRA

It's late when we get home. I figured Griff might not be here since he knew Sebastian and I went out tonight. I thought maybe he'd go back to his own house and give us a night alone, but when we walk in the bedroom, he's on the left side of our bed.

I feel so many things—reluctance and concern, affection and sorrow.

I want to feel more of the good feelings like Sebastian wants, but I can't help worrying that my husband is wrong. I'm so deeply and profoundly attached to Sebastian. I know I managed to live many years without him, but to be honest, I'm not sure how anymore.

When I met Sebastian, it was like waking up one day and realizing you've been living your life as half a person. For every weakness I have, he has strength. For every pocket of uncertainty, he knows what to do. For every doubt that's ever crawled through my mind, Sebastian has confidence. It was literally as if

I had spent my whole life waiting for this partner—someone carved out precisely to fit me.

We were perfect together. Nauseatingly perfect, if you ask anyone who knows us.

When he needed me to add one more person to our family so he could keep him, I agreed. I have been abundantly cooperative.

But I guess Sebastian is right. I've opened my legs, but not my heart. In my heart, I've kept Griff firmly in a friend box.

I've been managing Griff, not opening up to him. I wanted him to open up to me, but I've held stuff back. I haven't stopped him when I felt him being competitive with Sebastian and told him it was a problem, and that I wanted him to stop.

I need to let him burrow deeper. I need to treat that relationship with all the care and investment I would a singular relationship if I didn't already have my other half.

I don't know how all this works. I'm not sure it'll go the way Sebastian expects it to, but I won't question my husband. The only way to see if he's right is to do as he says. If he's wrong and Griff becomes a problem, we'll deal with it. If it's too late and I've already developed deeper feelings for him, then I'll deal with the heartache.

Sebastian is my rock. As long as I have him, everything will ultimately be fine.

Griff is lying in bed, but he's awake, looking up at the screen of his phone. When we come in, he leans over and puts it on his bedside table, plugging it into the charger.

"Hey. Hope it's okay I'm here."

Sebastian doesn't respond immediately. I get the impression he's waiting for me to say something, but all the words stick in my mouth. Finally, Sebastian recovers with an easy, "Of course, Griff. You're always welcome here."

I glance down at the carpet. Sebastian's hands firmly grasp my shoulders, steadying me. He moves one hand to drag the zipper down my back. The sides of my dress sag and Sebastian pushes the sheath down, yanking it past my hips until my dress is on the ground.

I close my eyes as his lips brush the ball of my shoulder. He drags them a few inches to the right, then a few more. When he gets to the nape of my neck, he pauses and kisses me there. I exhale helplessly, goosebumps rising all over. His hand comes around the front of my body and he cups my breast through the thin fabric of my bra.

"Isn't she beautiful?" he murmurs, between kisses.

Griff's voice is low, gravelly. "Yeah, she is."

"We're lucky men," Sebastian remarks, pushing his hand down the front of my panties and cupping me.

I gasp, unprepared for the sudden sensation. It's never been a fantasy of mine to be watched, but I can't deny it's shamefully erotic to stand here on display while my husband plays with my pussy, Griff's hungry gaze drifting from him to me. He wants to play, too, but he's waiting to see if he's invited.

I know he will be. Sebastian doesn't want to play games tonight, he doesn't want to show Griff up; he wants him to be included. He wants me to fall for him. He wants me stripped bare and vulnerable, needing him, needing Griff. He wants me to let go. He wants a lot from me.

He'll give a lot back, though. They both will. I love the physical part of this arrangement. I'm a little less confident letting both of them inside my heart, but inside of my body is simple. It was only scary that first night, when I was worried it would hurt my relationship with Sebastian.

But it didn't. I pushed past the fear, moved outside of my

comfort zone, and now I'm overwhelmed with pleasure on a regular basis.

So maybe it will be the same with my heart. It's probably natural to be afraid, but just like when I let go of my fear before, maybe something great will come out of it.

Since Griff is watching, I reach down and grab Sebastian's wrist. He pauses and looks at me, awaiting an explanation.

"I want to go to Griff," I say softly.

Nodding, my husband withdraws his hand from my panties and tells me, "Go ahead."

It still makes me feel like I swallowed my heart to tell my husband I want to leave him and go to someone else, even if only in this moment, only across the room, but when I look at Griff and see the surprise on his face, I feel like it was the right thing to do. He needs to feel preferred every once in a while.

I smile softly as I approach. "Want to play with me, Griff?"

"I do," he murmurs, his gaze locked on me as I climb up on his lap and straddle him. His big hands move to my small waist, gently holding me in place. My breasts are still covered, but right in his face. I reach behind my back and unhook my bra, peeling off the scrap of fabric and dropping it on the bed beside us.

Griff's hungry gaze goes to my breasts and he pulls me closer, bending to take one of my nipples into his hot mouth. I can feel his cock straining against me so I grind against him. He groans against my breast, teasing the nipple with his tongue until I'm arching backward.

Sebastian walks up behind me. I can feel him standing at the edge of the bed, in front of Griff's legs. Just his presence creates tension in my loins, just the feeling of him standing behind me, watching me. His strength radiates off of him and seeps into me, melting me into a pool of need.

Behind me, Sebastian silently demands.

In front of me, Griff openly reveres.

My heart kicks up a couple of speeds. I'm drunk on the pair of them already, and I'm not even fully undressed.

Sebastian leans in, his hot breath triggering awareness even before his mouth lands. Then he begins kissing his way from my shoulder to my neck. When he gets to my hypersensitive neck, my brain shuts off and my body takes over. I arch my breasts against Griff's mouth while leaning my head back against Sebastian.

"I need you both," I murmur.

Sebastian's hand skates down my back. "That's right, sweetheart. You'll have us both." He straightens, then tells Griff, "Take off her panties."

Griff grabs my hips and flips me on my back. I gasp at the light impact. He's on top of me in a flash, dragging my panties down my legs.

"Spread your legs, Moira. Show Griff your pussy. See if he wants a taste."

Sebastian's words alone send shivers down my spine. I feel unspeakably naughty doing as he says, spreading my legs for Griff.

He looks at the apex of my thighs like Heaven awaits him there, then he bends to breach the gates. I throw my head back and close my eyes while Griff licks me where Sebastian touched me only moments earlier.

The bed creaks, and I open my eyes to see my beautiful husband joining me on the mattress. Even as tension builds within me while his best friend eats my pussy, the sight of my husband fills me up. I need him. I need his lips on mine, his skin pressed against me. I don't tell him with words, but he can see it in my eyes. I can tell by the way he smiles and leans down to brush his lips tenderly against mine.

I'm too desperate for tender, though. I grab the back of his head and crush his lips to mine, opening for him, needing more. Griff suddenly pushes two fingers inside me and jagged pleasure slices through me.

I cry out against Sebastian's mouth and hold him tighter. My husband's hand moves to cover the breast Griff lavished with attention. He gives it a gentle squeeze, kissing me leisurely, like he has all day to do it. It's so hard to concentrate with Griff's skilled tongue strumming my clit, my husband's deft fingers toying with my nipple while his mouth dominates mine. Pleasure fires on too many cylinders. I can't breathe. The whole world tilts on its axis, and Griff grabs my hips, holding me still when I try to get away.

"Oh, God. Oh, God." I break free from Sebastian's mouth, then latch back on desperately, needing his kisses, needing him to catch me. Griff sends me over the edge with his wonderful mouth. The bubble of pleasure bursts, and I cry out against my husband's perfect lips as ecstasy ripples through me.

"Mm, your pleasure tastes good," Sebastian murmurs roughly. Without waiting for me to put myself back together, he grabs my legs and shifts, dragging me sideways. I can't move, so I let him drag me, I let him spread my legs. I think nothing of his hand breaching my sensitive entrance, dipping deep and pulling from the well of my arousal.

I'm suddenly jolted into thinking, however, when I feel him draw that moisture out and spread it lower. My ass?

My stomach sinks. We don't make a habit of doing anal, but the only time he starts lubing me up is when he's going to take my ass. He must see the worry flit across my face, because he smiles and leans down to give me a reassuring kiss.

"Um… you want…?" I feel oddly shy asking about that with Griff here.

Griff's seen me naked, he's seen me get fucked, seen me suck Sebastian's dick, watched me suck his own dick—but we have not gone near my ass. When they fuck me at the same time, one takes my pussy, one takes my mouth.

"Griff, do you want her pussy or her ass?" Sebastian asks, pushing a finger into that tight, resistant hole.

Since this is uncharted territory, Griff looks a little unsure, too. He glances at me. "Does Moira *want* one of us to take her ass?"

Sebastian is dismissive. "Every hole on this body is ours to do with as we please."

Fuck, if that doesn't turn me on. I know my husband treasures me, but when he talks about my body like that… God, he sets me on fire with lust.

My greedy pussy is already starting to feel bereft without one of them inside me, especially with Sebastian saying things like that. I want to fuck something—someone's cock, someone's face, both of their cocks. I'm not completely comfortable with the idea, but that seems to be where Sebastian is heading with this.

Griff doesn't speak up quickly enough, so Sebastian decides for him. "All right, you take the front, I'll take the back."

"We're both going to be inside her at the same time?"

"Mm-hmm," Sebastian murmurs, reaching his free hand up to brush my hair back lovingly. "We're going to fill my beautiful little wife up with both our cocks. You'll like that, won't you, sweetheart?"

I can't quite manage words, but I nod my head.

Sebastian continues to caress me tenderly, while saying, "Yeah, you're my hungry little slut, aren't you?"

God, yes, I am.

"I need…" I stop just short of saying *you*, but fuck, do I need him. I need to be filled up. I need one of them inside me right now, battering the walls of my pussy, pounding into me until I'm bursting with pleasure.

Griff used Sebastian's playtime to finish getting undressed, so now he climbs on the bed, his heated gaze on mine. I'm writhing with need already. Sebastian is still playing with my ass, but seeing me in need, Griff reaches down and sinks a finger inside my pussy.

I moan with relief. "Oh, yes. Thank you."

Griff smiles, stealing a kiss and murmuring against my mouth. "What did I tell you about that?"

"Did you give her an order, Griff?" Sebastian asks, sounding impressed. "Good. If she disobeyed, make sure you punish her for it. Take her disobedience out on this pretty little pussy."

Griff meets my gaze and rolls his eyes at Sebastian. I crack a smile, but lose it almost as fast as their skilled hands send another spike of pleasure shooting through me.

"Lie down right here," Sebastian tells Griff. "She's going to ride you."

I'm horny enough to go along with it as Sebastian guides me, as my husband lowers me onto another man's cock and then tilts my body until I'm in just the position he wants me in. Even though it's foreign and strange, it's a little exhilarating, not being quite sure what comes next or how this works. Griff holds me close, offering comfort and stability, while my husband rams past the generous boundaries of my comfort zone, positioning himself behind me. The cock that I love so much breaches the wrong hole, and I tense.

"Relax," Griff coaches me, caressing my face with his big, rough hand.

That's easy for him to say; he's not about to be invaded by two huge dicks.

Sebastian pauses at Griff's reassurance and runs a hand down my back. "Relax, sweetheart. You're gonna like this."

There's no way he knows that, but he speaks with such confidence that I believe him. I take a breath and try to relax my body. Griff is already inside me, I only have to bear down and take one more cock.

My husband pushes his swollen head between my parted ass cheeks and I start to have second thoughts. Griff cuts them off, still caressing my face, but also drawing me in for a kiss. It's a gentle, tender kiss that gives me butterflies in my stomach. I want to ride him—*he's inside me, I want to feel him move*—but I have to wait for Sebastian.

Sebastian pushes into my ass and I let out a faint whimper against Griff's mouth. He holds me tighter like he wants to protect me, but my husband keeps pushing.

I squeeze my eyes shut and bury my face in Griff's shoulder. *Oh, fuck, that hurts.*

"Are you okay?" Griff murmurs.

"Yeah," I say breathlessly, holding onto his shoulders and glancing back at Sebastian.

"Fuck, you are tight," Sebastian says, reaching for my hair and grabbing a fistful. He tugs my head back while he withdraws, then eases inside me again.

I try to focus as he starts to give Griff directions, but once my body adjusts and they both start moving inside me, I can't concentrate on anything other than the new sensations.

My body has never been this full before. It's the strangest feeling already, but then thinking about it, about Griff and Sebastian both inside my body at the same time—it's dizzying. Griff is still checking on me, making sure I'm okay. Sebastian isn't. He knows my body can handle it, so he uses it for his pleasure.

The strangest—and most intoxicating—part of this, though, is how I have *absolutely* no control. I am powerless, the movements of my body dictated by the movements of theirs. They find a rhythm that works for them and I'm just along for the ride, sandwiched between them while they move in and out of my body in tandem, filling me with their cocks, running their hands all over me, grabbing, caressing, teasing. They do whatever they want to me with their lips and hands and cocks. I'm a receptacle for their desires. My body belongs to them—*I* belong to them. As if to emphasize their ownership over me, Sebastian turns my head sideways, claiming my lips while Griff thrusts up inside me so hard I can't keep from crying out.

The pleasure is beyond words. Beyond any feelings I've ever known before. Normally I feel like I'm building to an orgasm, but right now I feel like I live inside one. I can't breathe normally. Every stroke is so powerful. Griff and Sebastian seem to communicate without words, one speeding up while the other moves slower, pushing more deeply inside me, then switching paces. At one point they both pick up the pace and I feel like a fuckdoll, being bounced and used by these two strong men, chasing their pleasure inside my body.

It's incredible. It's intense. I have butterflies swarming my already too-full body. I'm floating in a pool of pure pleasure. They seem to accept that I have the hang of this now and they stop taking turns altogether—they both pound into me hard and deep. I lose my last shred of control and come apart, crying out as Griff drowns me in a sea of pleasure with his cock. Bless his girth, he hammers that big, beautiful cock into my G-spot until magic occurs. Only now the magic is happening and I have no control of anything, all I can do is cry out against Griff's chest while he continues to fuck me, while Sebastian buries himself inside me.

Oh, God, the orgasm won't end.

The friction of Griff's cock rubbing the same pleasure spot only seems to intensify it, the thrust of Sebastian's hips pushing me harder onto Griff's hard cock.

"Oh, God," I cry helplessly, lost to the pleasure.

And helpless, I am. The only thing I'm capable of right now is feeling, and I feel *everything*.

"Are you okay?" Griff asks again.

I nod, closing my eyes and letting them have their way with me.

Sebastian's hand tightens in my hair. "Ride his cock, baby. Ride it hard."

"I can't," I murmur. "I can't do anything." I try to obey. I try to grind my pussy but I give up. It's too difficult with both of them moving inside me at the same time.

"Do you like that?" Sebastian asks roughly.

He already knows the answer, but I tell him anyway. "I love it."

Their rhythm is perfect now. They thrust my body back and forth like they were born to. I take both of them like I was born to. I come again. And again. And again. I think they're separate orgasms, at least. I can't be entirely sure. I'm just a vessel of pleasure at this point. It all feels so good all the time.

Griff comes inside me first. I'm so relieved when he stops thrusting and I can collapse on top of him. He holds me in his arms while Sebastian continues to fuck me in the ass. I whimper and sigh; I bury my face in Griff's chest and start to touch myself. I'm exhausted, but I want to come with Sebastian.

I rub my clit while he fucks me, while I lie on top of Griff, and the pleasure expands inside me again. Sebastian wants it too, so he warns me, giving my body just enough time so I'm riding me climax as he explodes inside me.

I try to catch my breath. Sebastian pulls out of me and crawls on the bed beside us. My heart is still pounding. My husband grabs me around the waist and drags me off Griff, pulling me snugly back against his chest and kissing my shoulder.

This is his way of making sure I'm okay. He rarely asks, doesn't feel the need to, but he holds me now and that's all I need.

Griff rolls over on his side and scoots closer to me. I smile softly and reach out my hand to run it across his jaw. It's about all the strength I can muster right now. My body feels like Jell-o. Every ounce of strength has been fucked out of me. I want Griff closer, I want to be held by both of them, but I can't move.

"Come closer. I want you both to cuddle me."

Griff glances past me at Sebastian, perhaps for permission. Probably that. We're always looking to Sebastian to tell us what to do. I'm sure he likes that. I just hope Griff doesn't mind it.

That reminds me of all the work I need to do, and I don't have the mental capacity for all that right now. I just want the simple pleasure of having my two amazing men hold me close.

Griff must get whatever permission he needs because he slides closer and drapes his arm across my waist. His massive, muscular chest is so warm and comforting in front of me, while my husband's strong arms are locked around me from behind.

I close my eyes, feeling so safe and loved here between them.

I should probably feel filthy—filled with their cum, my body held between their hard, muscular bodies.

I don't, though. I feel treasured.

I know how much each of these men cares for me, I know how much they care for each other, and I love being the glue that holds them together.

16

GRIFF

I CAN FEEL A DIFFERENCE IN MOIRA TONIGHT. I DON'T know if it's because she had some time with Seb to recharge or because of what we just did to her, but she feels more open.

Even though she has granted me full access by all outward appearances, I couldn't shake the feeling I got on occasion that something was missing. Like I've spent my whole life longing for a home, and someone gave me the keys to a heartless model house—lovely to look at, but lacking in sincerity. It's a pretty set-up to show other people what can be theirs, but no one makes a home there.

I felt like an ungrateful bastard for feeling that way, though. Moira's been amazing. She's given me everything I asked for; she's there for me when I need her. She says all the right things at just the right time, but I didn't always feel like she meant them. I thought maybe it was me. Maybe it was because I was new to her, or maybe I just couldn't accept that she wants me. Maybe it's not enough that she wants me—I want more, but since she has to give to Seb too, I don't know how much more she has to give.

In this moment, I feel like I have what I didn't know I needed. There are no limits right now. No one is careful or tentative, no one worries about stepping on anyone else's toes. Seb holds her, I hold her, and Moira nuzzles her face against me like a contented kitten. Her beautiful face is so peaceful. I can't quite contain all the affection I feel for her and I can't keep from touching her. I don't have to, because she's mine.

She opens her eyes and looks up at me, looks through me, looks inside me. Her hand moves naturally to my face and she pulls me even closer, so my chest presses against her beautiful breasts. I can feel her needing me—and strangely I can feel just what she needs, so I dip my head and kiss her perfect lips. It's a soft kiss, gentle and undemanding. We're all satisfied, no one's chasing anything, we just need to be close.

"Tell me something," Moira says softly, still so close I can feel her breath on my face.

Anything.

I don't know if she's aware of how completely she owns me, so I don't say that. "Like what?"

"Something about your past. Something I don't know. Tell me about how you guys met."

"A cheerful story, then," Seb remarks lightly.

"You've each told me scraps, but I don't have the full picture. I want to know everything. Did you get along right away?"

I scoff, recalling the day I first walked into that house. Seb was already placed there and it was mayhem when I showed up. A four-year-old screamed at the top of her lungs; the dog had escaped out the front door. An overweight woman ran after the dog, calling out its name—Jasper, which I thought was an odd name for a dog—and glancing back at me.

I stood slouched next to the social worker with a trash bag full of my belongings slung over my shoulder. I decided in that moment to hate the placement. It was already a madhouse, but I felt annoyance more than disappointment. I'd given up hope for most of my placements a long time ago. No one wanted a 15-year-old boy who may or may not have mild to severe behavioral problems to complete their family. No one wanted them, but there were some houses that would tolerate us. I kept to myself so I was a little easier to place, but you could still feel the distrust upon meeting the new people whose house you had to live in.

I didn't blame them. I wasn't any more eager to stay there than they were to open the doors, but at least they got a pittance for it. I didn't like anyone paying for anything for me, so I tried to scrape up enough to take care of myself. Understandably, most of the families were fine with that.

Seb was the only calm one in the house that day. The mom was overwhelmed and embarrassed by the chaotic scene we walked into; an older teenage boy shot me an unfriendly look as he rummaged through the cupboards for a snack. Then there was this dark-haired guy around my age with intense blue eyes, sitting at the table, reading a well-worn paperback copy of *Franny and Zooey*. I knew that book wasn't on the summer reading list, so I assumed he must have been reading for pleasure.

For all the chaos going on around him, Seb was unaffected. For all the intensity you could see brewing in his oceanic eyes, he was completely composed. I think I envied him that control right away—I ran a little hotter than that, myself.

"You must be our new brother," he remarked, practiced disregard rolling off him in waves.

The feeling of being vaguely interested in him drained right out of me, and I flicked him a mean look. Before I could respond, though, the house mom willfully misinterpreted his sarcasm and went on to tell me of course, they were all family there, and they were so happy to meet me.

That damn sure hadn't been true, but she always cranked up the niceness when social workers came around; I picked up on that over the course of my time there.

Since I'm lost in my thoughts, I guess, Seb answers for me. "No, we did not."

I shake my head, floating between the past and present. "No. It was hectic when I arrived. A big, green farm house. They had a kid of their own, but they took in teens. There were three of us—me, Seb, and this vicious asshole named Arnie."

"Poor Arnie," she remarks. "That's not a great name."

"It fit. He was a belligerent douche. Liked to scare people."

"Strangely enough, had a hard time finding a house that wanted to keep him," Seb remarks lightly.

"He pulled a knife on Seb, that's how he got kicked out of ours."

Even though we're clearly here and fine, alarm fills Moira's face and she turns back to look at Seb. "What?"

He runs a calming hand down the curve of her side. "I was fine. Barely a scratch."

"Six stitches," I state, lifting an eyebrow.

"Any less than ten is just a scratch," he argues.

"Oh my God," she murmurs, grabbing Seb's hand and holding it steady on her side. "I hate Arnie."

"So did we," I tell her. "He's sort of what brought us together, though. He hated Seb. Hated how inscrutable he always was. He's grown into himself, obviously, and now even though he keeps a firm hand on everything, he's mostly healthy. Back then, though, he was still learning. He had all the emotional transparency of a brick wall. You couldn't get anything out of him. Nothing could shake him. For a certain kind of bully, he seemed like a challenge."

"Bully," Seb says dismissively, the word clearly distasteful on his tongue. "He was nothing. I had it under control. I was not *bullied*."

"Well, not for his lack of trying. You two were dangerous together. He kept pushing you; you refused to give him a response, so he pushed harder. I swear to God, he would've killed you, and with your last breath you would've laughed at him."

"I hate everything about this," Moira states. "I don't ever want either of you to have been in dangerous situations, even in the past. I'm going to find a way to time travel back and protect you both."

Seb shakes his head, smiling down at her fondly. "That's a sweet gesture, but having you there would have just been a headache for us." He glances up at me, lifting a dark eyebrow. "Imagine both of us trying to protect her while I'm trying to come off as unaffected and you're the gruff badass, both of us living every day fucking terrified she'd get hurt? No. That would've been terrible."

"Maybe I could have brokered peace," Moira suggests. "Failing that, I could have been sneaky. I could have recorded the asshole being an asshole and shown it to your caseworker or whoever."

Seb shakes his head. "I appreciate the sentiment, sweetheart, but it wouldn't have worked."

"Do you think you would've liked me back then?" she asks.

"Probably not," he answers, earning him a scowl. "You would've tried to peel back all the armor I had just equipped myself with and infect me with your love. I wasn't open to it back then. It took quite a few years before I leveled out. Learning to protect yourself against everything—there's a learning curve. There's no manual on how to do it right, so there's a lot of trial and error."

She drags his arm around her chest and snuggles it between us. "That makes me sad. I hate that you had hard lives. I hate that you ever felt the need to protect yourself. I hate everyone who has ever hurt either one of you. I'm glad you had each other, at least."

"We turned out all right," Seb assures her.

"I don't care," she insists. "I still want to wrap you both up in warm hugs and protect you forever."

Seb looks at me and rolls his eyes, but he's not fooling anyone—he loves it. Who wouldn't love someone being so nurturing and protective after a lifetime of having to look out for yourself?

"I'm so glad you walked into that coffee shop that day," she tells him. "I may have never met either one of you otherwise."

Seb nods his agreement, kissing the side of her face. "Then you'd have to settle for some basic asshole who wouldn't even fuck you with his best friend."

She shakes her head as if disgusted. "What a lackluster life I might have led. You're my hero."

He grins and she turns her head to kiss him. His hand is already snuggled up against her chest and wedged between us, but now he shifts it to cover her breast. He squeezes her smooth flesh and a soft moan slips out of her.

I love her body. Even after we both just fucked her into

oblivion, I bet it would only take a light warm-up to get her going again.

Sebastian's thoughts must be in line with mine because he rolls her over on her back and roughly kisses her breasts. Her eyes drift closed and she arches off the bed, tangling her fingers in his hair.

He pulls back, watching her writhe beneath him. Flicking a glance my way, he says, "You up for fucking her again, or should I take this round on my own?"

"Oh, I'm up for it."

He grins with approval. "Good."

After a night in heaven, I have to spend the next day in hell.

When I decided to file for divorce, I went in with the naïve assumption that the prenuptial agreement I had drawn up would make the process fairly simple. Especially because—while I had drawn up a generous agreement in the case of a faultless divorce—I included an infidelity clause that specified what would happen in the event of cheating. Of course, I would have to be able to *prove* she cheated, but since she's a moron who cheated in my club and there's footage, I can. Easily.

What makes it more difficult is that Ashley's a fucking lunatic and she's fighting back, hard. Since I wasn't a greedy asshole, I made certain provisions for Ashley when we got married so she knew I wasn't trying to railroad her. I've never liked the idea of an airtight prenup to begin with. I don't think a man should be able to steal years of a woman's life and then abandon her without any kind of reparations—unless it's warranted, like this. If she cheats, she doesn't get reparations.

Had I just fallen out of love with her, that would have been another thing entirely.

So now she's claiming I did. Now she's trying to get the prenup thrown out, crying alienation of affection, saying I cheated first, that I *drove* her to cheat, and she felt abandoned in our marriage. She's appealing to the courts for counseling, claiming our marriage can be saved and she's willing to do the work.

Obviously, I told my lawyer to tell her to fuck off, but now they're investigating the external factors surrounding the prenup, and I'm ready to lose my fucking mind.

Ashley texts me little fucking hearts and "I miss you" messages.

I want to text back and tell her where to shove her stupid fucking messages, but my lawyer has strictly forbidden me to engage. Since I seem to have made it all worse by meeting with her yesterday, I listen this time.

Then the fun part. Moira sent me a text while I was in the meeting. Given Carrie is also Seb's lawyer and Moira isn't the most common name, she connects the dots.

Our lawyer is discreet, but after seeing the warm look on my face when I open the message, she stops talking and stares at me.

I don't think about it until I put the phone down.

Her humorless gaze holds mine and she adds, "Not that I have to tell you this, obviously, but if you *are* seeing anyone right now, stop."

I frown at her. "Excuse me?"

"You aren't divorced yet. If Ashley can catch you with someone—especially someone you knew and spent time with while you were married—you are fucked."

"I'm fucked?" I reiterate, pointing at myself. "*She* cheats and if I start seeing someone while we're separated, *I'm* fucked?"

"You put an infidelity clause in your prenup, Griffin. Against *my* advisement, you decided to be a hero and make things equal. You're the one who fucked yourself in the event you ever cheated. Some kind of self-loathing bullshit? Misplaced chivalry? Whatever it was, I told you it was a bad idea, but you wanted things to be fair. Yes, Ashley cheating means she gets the shaft, but if you cheated first and she can prove it? You are *fucked*. Fucked hard, no lube."

My jaw locks and anger roils in my gut. "I *didn't* cheat. I never cheated."

"If it looks like you did, that doesn't really matter."

"This is bullshit. She cheated on me *years* ago."

Her eyebrows rise with interest. "Can you prove that?"

"No."

"Then it doesn't matter."

"Are you kidding me with this shit?"

Carrie crosses her arms, shaking her head. "I wish. I'm not. Adultery isn't enough to get an ordinary prenup thrown out, but you made yourself a perfect target. Personally, I don't see Ashley letting up. Seriously, your personal life is your own, but please, for the love of all that is holy, don't give her ammunition. You're a nice guy, you don't deserve to be taken for a ride by some money-grabbing opportunist, but you will. She'll take you for half of everything you've got—and considering you have a business partner in your ventures, I don't think you're the only one who's going to be pissed off about that."

I sigh, massaging my temples. This is the biggest load of shit I've heard thus far. All these hoops to jump through just because I make a good living. If I lived in a fucking trailer with

$10 in the bank, Ashley would be history already. "I fucking hate money."

"Well," she says brightly, "ignore my advice and you'll have a lot less of it. I guess that's your silver lining?"

"This was all Seb's dream, not mine. I never wanted this shit."

"We'll get this all taken care of as quickly as we can. If her lawyers can't turn up anything soon, then we're good. But I'm telling you now, she's hired a shark. He can find dirt on anybody, and I have a worrisome hunch you've been rolling around in the mud."

I shoot her a look of annoyance. I like Carrie because she's not a formal stick in the mud, but this isn't her business.

Well, I guess it could be. I obviously have not cheated on Ashley, but if she catches wind of anything between me and Moira...

Christ, I can't even think about that.

So, that's my fucking day.

I work late into the night, but when I leave, I don't go to Seb's house. For the first night since we got together, I go back to my cold, empty house. It's too fucking big. A lot of Ashley's shit is still here. The house is another complication in the divorce. The prenup protects all the assets I had when we *got* married, but I bought the house afterward.

I feel like a fucking idiot. I don't even give a fuck about the house. I'm ready to give it to her if it means she'll go the fuck away.

Seb texts me about an hour after I get home to see where I'm at. I tell him I'm not coming over tonight, that Carrie had nothing good to say, and I'm just going to stay home.

"Want some company?" he asks.

I don't answer. I go up to the master suite I fucking hate and take a shower. I lie in the bed I shared with Ashley and drink alone, scrolling through every text message she's sent me and glaring at them like she'll be able to feel it.

Seb shows up with a bottle of liquor, just in case I didn't have any on hand.

"What'd Carrie say?" he asks, without preamble.

"That I'm a fucking idiot."

Seb's eyebrows rise. "That does sound like Carrie."

I drop into a chair in my living room and watch as Seb takes a seat, leaning forward and pouring alcohol into a glass for himself. "What can we do?"

My irritable gaze lingers on the glass as he brings the strong liquor to his lips and takes a sip, but it's not him I'm mad at. It's not Carrie. It's not even Ashley.

It's me. I was trying to be nice and I put myself in a vulnerable position. No way I could have ever foreseen these recent events, no way I ever thought there was a chance I would do anything that could even be *technically* manipulated to look like cheating. That's why, in all my fucking idiocy, I made the agreement. Ashley was insulted that I wanted her to sign a prenup to begin with, so I wanted to show her I was decent, that I wasn't trying to fuck her over.

I was too fucking considerate. She actually cheated; she actually did something wrong. The honorable thing to do would be to accept that she fucked up her golden opportunity and retreat quietly. But no. Of course, that's not how it goes.

"Huh?" Seb prompts, since I haven't answered.

"I don't think we can do anything," I tell him. "Seems like all I can do now is wait."

"You'll be all right," Seb assures me, taking another sip, then balancing his drink on his thigh.

"I can't take Moira out. Not without you, at least. Not until the divorce goes through."

Unsurprised, he nods. "Well, I told you I didn't think you should do that from the start, but yeah. Ashley wants your blood and I'm not letting Moira get pulled into this bullshit. I've kept my nose out of it as best I can, but the minute Moira gets caught under the tires is the moment that ends. You play as nice as you want with Ashley; just keep my wife out of it."

"I wouldn't let her hurt Moira."

"Yeah, well, you didn't think you were gonna let her hurt you, either, but here we are. You try to be a nice guy, you try to be fair, and that's not how life works. Only the strongest survive—and the people under the protection of the strongest. People who play nice will always end up getting fucked, Griff. Now you know."

He's so fucking cynical sometimes. He's not altogether wrong, though. "Do you and Moira have a prenup?" I ask, out of curiosity.

"Of course we do," he replies, like he can't believe I'd ask such a stupid fucking question.

"And you didn't put a thing in it to protect her? We all know you protect your own interests, but what if you were the one who fucked her over?"

"I wouldn't," he says simply. "It's enough that I know that. I don't need to put it on paper and get the courts involved."

I shake my head, throwing back my own drink. "Yeah, well, Moira treats your word like fucking gospel; I'm not surprised she didn't push back. Ashley wasn't so agreeable. She was insulted I asked her to sign one in the first place. She wanted to know if I became an asshole like so many other men in the world, I would have to pay for it. I thought that was fair."

Seb is not impressed. "Yeah, well, that was your mistake. If you fell in love with someone else, you could have just *given* Ashley a pay-out. It didn't have to be in the paperwork."

"*I* wasn't worried it would happen, she was. Weirdly enough, I didn't think I had to worry about it. I'm sorry I tried to be a nice fucking guy."

"You should be," he states. "Nice guys finish last, Griff. We don't finish last."

I lean forward and put my empty glass down on the coffee table. "Yeah, well, it doesn't matter now, does it?"

"I'm sorry she's giving you such a hard time, I really am. Stupid bitch should be grateful you forgave her the first time."

"I'm not sure I did," I admit, shaking my head. "She said a lot of shit to me, but it wasn't all wrong. I never should've married her in the first place. I didn't do it for the right reasons. I didn't have the feelings for her I should've had."

"She didn't marry you for the right reasons, either," Seb points out. "Hardly matters now. All you can do is get the hell out of this thing and never make this kind of mistake again."

I have half a mind to tell him the rest of what Carrie said, about how if Ashley can get the prenup thrown out, that's going to have blowback on our business interests, too.

I don't, though. I don't want to give him another reason to tear me a new asshole. He may be inconvenienced and sympathetic about my situation now, but if Ashley's greed extends that far, if my bad decisions start to cost him, he's going to have a big fucking problem.

That's the last thing I want. I love Seb, I respect the hell out of him, but he'll play dirty if someone throws a sucker punch first. You may hit him once, but you best believe he'll win the fucking fight.

Ashley is used to pushing me around, but she's never dealt with Seb before—and she doesn't want to. He's worked entirely too hard to build his empire to let some gold digger take any of it away from him. He even has a prenup with Moira, and he loves the hell out of Moira. He doesn't give half a fuck about Ashley.

I don't even want to alert him to the possibility. It stresses me out just thinking about it.

I tell myself it won't come to that. He pours me another drink and hands it to me, smiling faintly, trusting me to take care of my own shit. I can do that. I can control this situation. I can deal with Ashley and get this matter resolved.

All I have to do is keep my distance from Moira. I can see her when Seb is home, of course, but overnight visits are probably out of the question for a little while.

We can be friends, we just can't be lovers—not in public, at least.

17

MOIRA

I LIE ON THE COUCH BETWEEN SEBASTIAN'S LEGS, enjoying the peace of this evening while he plays with my hair and responds to emails on his phone.

I love our life. I love this man. I love this pocket of peace, just the two of us.

It's been just the two of us a lot this week. Right on the heels of Sebastian nudging me to open up more with Griff, Griff stopped coming around as much. I guess there have been some complications with his divorce; Ashley's trying to stop it, and since Griff has no interest, she's trying to take as much with her as she possibly can.

Griff still comes over for dinner on nights he isn't working, but then he leaves. I haven't done more than kiss him since the night they double-teamed me.

As content as I am with my husband, I do miss Griff. I don't just miss him for me; I miss the casual interaction between Griff and Sebastian when we're all here in the evening. And, sure, I miss them both playing with me.

I've been getting lots of one-on-one time with my husband this week, but I can't help wondering if Griff is lonely. He should be here with us, not trapped in a big, lonely house full of memories that can only hurt him.

I twist back now and look up at the gorgeous man I married. He's dressed all in black today, his dress shirt unbuttoned at the top to show me a swatch of tanned skin. He's still wearing his black suit jacket, but that's unbuttoned, too.

His intense gaze is still on his phone, even though he must have felt me turn. Now he runs his hand over my shoulder and settles it on my back as I switch positions.

He still doesn't look at me.

I wrinkle up my nose, wanting his attention more since he isn't volunteering it.

I run my hand down his muscular chest and shoot him a devilish smile that goes unnoticed as I unbutton the next two buttons on his shirt. Now I know he's ignoring me to get a rise out of me.

"I know your game, Mr. St. Clair," I tell him, narrowing my eyes.

"I have no idea what you're talking about, Mrs. St. Clair," he says with feigned innocence.

I push my hand up under his shirt and run my hand over his pec, circling his nipple with my index finger and watching his face. Still ignoring me, damn him. I try harder, crawling up his body and trailing my lips along his collar bone, then kissing his neck. When I get near his ear, I murmur, "Your wife needs your attention."

"Then she should earn it," he states.

I narrow my eyes and bite down on his earlobe. "She's trying."

"She should try harder."

I want to be annoyed at him, but I fail. He knows just how to tease me and make me crazy. I was only checking on him when I turned—I was actually going to tell him he should invite Griff over since apparently I'm discouraged from texting him for the moment—but now he's pushing all my buttons and I want to shake him.

He may be able to ignore my kisses on his neck, but I know where he can't ignore them. Sliding lower, I open the rest of his shirt and kiss my way down his toned abdomen, my fingers unbuckling his belt.

"How's this?" I ask, peering up at him.

"Better," he says, like he could still take it or leave it.

I narrow my eyes at him and unbutton his pants, unzipping them and shoving my hand down the front. He still manages to keep his eyes trained on his phone, but I can see the corners of his mouth trying to tug up in a smile. He stifles it as fast as I see it, but then I wrap my fingers around his dick and stroke him. His gaze shifts to me.

"Little minx."

"*Your* little minx," I agree, watching his face for signs of pleasure. I see faint traces and I think I have his attention, but after a moment he goes back to his phone.

"Really?" I demand.

"Hey, if you're out of ideas..." He trails off, lifting his eyebrows.

"You're a wicked man," I inform him, yanking his pants down his hips. My blood stirs with desire when I see the bulge in his black boxer briefs. I run my hand over it, cupping him, then I tug those down, too.

His cock springs free and it feels like Christmas. I never get used to this man. I grasp his thick shaft and run my tongue along it from base to tip. I steal a glance up at him to see if I've won.

Now he's watching me. Now I have his attention.

I'm feeling lightly vengeful, so I toy with him, running my tongue over it but not taking him into my mouth. Then I stroke him with my hand and ask, "Do I have your attention now, Mr. St. Clair?"

"You do. What are you going to do with it?"

I narrow my eyes at him and release his cock, pulling away from his body and retreating to my own side of the couch. "Absolutely nothing," I say, with relish.

"Is that so?" he asks, blandly. "I disagree. I think you're going to come over here like a good little wife and wrap those beautiful lips around my cock."

"What could possibly make you think that?" I demand, lifting an eyebrow.

Now that I've adequately challenged my beloved husband, he finally tucks his phone away and crawls forward, grabbing a fistful of my hair. He drags my face back toward his lap and says simply, "Suck."

I still feel a little spunky, but more than that, I'm turned on. I really want him in my mouth, so when he guides my head there, I open up and take him.

"Mm, good girl," he says, tenderly rubbing my back as I suck him.

I'm dizzy with pleasure already. I get swept up in him, in his strong hand gathering my hair in a fist, guiding my head, in every sexy sound that comes from this man I'm so deeply in love with. I get spikes of pleasure myself, knowing I'm giving it to him.

I'm so wrapped up in him that it takes me a second to realize those couldn't possibly be his hands suddenly on my ass, or his fingers moving between my legs. I'm not wearing panties, so there's nothing in the way. A long finger sinks inside me and relief pours through me. So much that I pop off my husband's dick and turn to look back, lighting up when I see his ruggedly handsome face.

"Griff. I've missed you."

He smiles faintly and bends down to kiss me on the forehead. "I've missed you, too, believe me."

Now I don't have to miss anybody. Now I feel all the pieces fit together. Griff is home and Sebastian is pleased.

I bend to take my husband's cock into my mouth again, and Griff lifts my dress, positioning himself behind me. I hear a clink as he unbuckles his belt and drops his pants. He's still wearing a suit from work, so he only undresses enough to draw his cock out and shove it inside me.

It's perfect. Everything is perfect now that they're both home.

They fuck me on my sofa and I feel so happy afterward, not just from the pair of orgasms they gave me, but because I have them both here with me.

Since I'll get to cuddle my husband in bed tonight, I curl up with Griff on the couch and tenderly run my hand across his muscular chest.

"How have you been?" I ask.

"All right," he answers, trailing a finger up and down my arm. "I've had some issues with Ashley, so I haven't been able to come around."

I nod against his chest. "Sebastian told me. I'm sorry she's being a pain in the ass. I wish all this divorce crap was over with so you could stay with us again. I miss snuggling with you in bed."

That makes him smile. "Yeah?"

"Mm-hmm." I lean up and leave a few tender kisses along his neck. "You belong here with us, not at that big, dumb house all by yourself. I got used to having you both; now that you're not here, I've discovered I don't like it at all."

"I don't either. Bedtime is much less interesting without you two there to keep me company."

I beam up at him, then leave a flurry of kisses along his jawline. I think I'm happiest because he said "you two," meaning both of us and not just me. "Maybe you could stay tonight," I suggest. "You haven't been staying, so one night wouldn't be wrong, would it?"

Griff looks down at me with a small measure of regret, but I can tell he doesn't want to deny me. Leaning forward just slightly, he looks over at Sebastian. "What do you think? It has been a while."

With a casual shrug, Sebastian says, "Your call. If you're going to stay, put your car in the garage."

I take that as permission and run my hand along Griff's thigh. "So, you'll stay?"

"I'll stay," he agrees.

"Good," I say, before sighing contentedly and resting my head on his firm chest.

Sebastian pulls his phone out again and gets back to business. I only know it's business because now that his other partner is here, Sebastian starts talking about some idea he has for expansion, some retail space he wants to buy. I'm drowsy, and Griff trails his fingers up and down my arm while they talk. Before I know it, I drift off.

I stir when I'm jostled and open my eyes to find Griff carrying me up the stairs to the bedroom. I smile faintly and wrap my arms around his neck, nuzzling my face into his shoulder. "You didn't have to carry me."

"I wanted to."

"You're so strong," I murmur.

He chuckles and tells me to go back to sleep.

Once inside our bedroom, he deposits me gently in the center of the bed, then braces his weight on his knees and rolls me over onto my stomach. He tugs down the zipper on the back of my dress. It shouldn't feel so sensual, but it does. I'm half asleep and not completely with it, so having someone undress me feels unspeakably naughty.

I turn my head to look over at Sebastian and see him standing by the bedside, regarding me with tenderness as he tugs his dress shirt out of his slacks. Just the swatch of his toned, sexy stomach makes me want to crawl over there and lick him.

Griff grabs me by the bicep and rolls me over. He's only trying to help me out of my dress, but the moment of rough-ness sends desire curling through me. He peels my dress down over my arms and turns to discard it. As soon as he turns back, I climb up on my knees and lean in to kiss him. I'm wearing nothing more than a flimsy bra now, no panties. More often than not, if we're at home and I'm in a dress, Sebastian likes me to skip the panties in the interest of easy access.

Griff's rough hands skate down the smooth plane of my back as he kisses me, halting at the small of my back and pulling me against him. He's still fully dressed, the crisp fabric of his suit chafing my stomach, the buckle of his belt pressed against my pelvis. I want him again. I want them to wear me out before I fall back asleep.

I reach down between his legs to grab him and let him know what I want.

Then I hear my husband climb on the bed behind me. I feel him crawl across the bed and then his hands are on me. He gathers my hair and pushes it over my shoulder so he can place a kiss at the nape of my neck. I shiver at the touch of his lips against my skin.

"You know what I think she wants, Griff?" Sebastian murmurs, between the kisses he's dropping along my shoulder. "I think she wants both of us inside her again."

The memory of that night, of the intense pleasure, fills me with longing. I sigh against Griff's mouth, a little weaker at the thought of it. God, yes. I want that.

"Well, I'm not one to deny a lady what she wants," Griff states.

"Same here," Sebastian agrees, unhooking my bra.

"You're both upstanding gentlemen," I inform them. Griff grins down at me before cradling the back of my neck and kissing me.

Sebastian grabs my hips and pulls my ass back against him. I can already feel his hard cock demanding my attention, straining to get inside me. I need to feel Griff, too, so while he kisses me, I reach down and unbuckle his belt. I draw it off and go to discard it, but Sebastian snatches it out of my hands before I can.

A shiver of anticipation moves down my spine. I don't know what he's going to do with it, but I trust him implicitly.

He rubs one hand over my ass while I try to concentrate on unbuttoning Griff's pants, then his hands are gone. His body isn't pressed against my backside anymore. I bend slightly to pull down Griff's pants.

All of a sudden, there's a sharp sting as Sebastian whips Griff's belt against my bare ass. I cry out more in surprise than at the impact, but Griff misinterprets. In a sudden show of aggression, he yanks me away from Sebastian, grabbing the belt and ripping it away from my husband.

"You do that again, I'll fucking whip *you* with it."

"Whoa, whoa, whoa," I say, running a calming hand down Griff's chest and glancing at Sebastian to make sure he's not offended.

Sebastian smiles coolly, but his blue eyes flash. "You're welcome to try, but friends or not, that won't work out very well for you."

"No one is whipping anyone with anything," I state. "Well, *I'm* not entirely opposed to a little light spanking, but... none of this. I was totally okay with that, I was just surprised. The surprise is a good thing, not bad," I assure Griff. "I wasn't in pain, I was just..." Griff finally tears his glare away from Sebastian and looks at me. I smile faintly and run the back of my hand along his strong jaw. "I appreciate you wanting to protect me, but you never have to protect me from Sebastian."

Griff watches me for another moment, but he must not be entirely satisfied because he glares at Sebastian again. "I don't like that shit."

"Well, I do," Sebastian replies, a hint of challenge in his tone.

I feel like I've swallowed my heart. Since I'm the only peacekeeper, currently, I shift my body until I'm more or less draped across Griff's chest. I kiss his neck and let my hand move down to rub his cock until I feel some of the tension leave his body. "We all need to play nice," I murmur against his skin.

"Nice is not hitting one another," Griff states.

"He didn't hit me."

"Hitting with a belt is still hitting. That's too rough."

"Griff," I say, caressing and kissing with as much tenderness as I can pour out. "You know Sebastian would never hurt me. He was just playing."

Instead of letting me continue to soothe Griff's temper,

Sebastian grabs a fistful of my hair and yanks me back with more force than is typical. Cognizant of Griff's attention, I keep quiet, but dread moves through me. I have a bad feeling that Sebastian has a point to prove now, and he can only use me to do it. With little tenderness, watching Griff's face instead of me, he shoves my face toward his cock.

I peer up at him pleadingly, but he doesn't see it. Even tilting my head back that much pulls my hair since his grip is so tight. I don't want him to damage the progress we've made in a fit of anger, and I'm afraid he's going to. He can't take me from Griff because he's pissed and then expect him to feel secure. There's also the chance he's going to use me more violently than Griff can stomach watching, and they're going to end up in an all-out brawl.

I want to try to get Sebastian's attention to calm him now, but I'm afraid of coming off the wrong way to Griff. He's not as into my submissive side as Sebastian, so it could rub him the wrong way if I try to make amends for something Sebastian did.

Fuck.

All I can really do without causing any harm is stroke my husband's thick cock, then ease forward and take it into my mouth like a good girl.

Maybe he'll calm down on his own if I do a good enough job. Of course, sometimes Sebastian likes a good angry fuck—and we're rarely mad at one another, so he takes his ire where he can get it.

I don't need Griff attacking my husband, though.

I'm not enthusiastic enough so Sebastian shoves his cock to the back of my throat without warning. I gag around the intrusion, but he lets me pull back and take him slower. My heart kicks up, visualizing him holding Griff's gaze while I suck his cock. Ordinarily, Griff would be cool with it, but he's angry now, so I'm not sure.

I don't know why they can't just put their difference in kinks aside and fuck me. Then we'd all feel better about life.

My husband finally speaks as I move my mouth over him, working toward his pleasure. "You don't get to tell me how to fuck my wife, Griff."

"She's mine, too," Griff states, causing my speeding heart to sink. "You don't get to hurt what's mine."

"She wasn't hurt," Sebastian states. "She likes what I do to her. You go too easy on her. I have to keep her balanced out. Sometimes she likes the tender stuff. Sometimes she wants to be used. I know what my wife likes. I wouldn't do anything she didn't enjoy."

"Yeah?" Griff asks, not sounding the least bit threatened. "Why don't you tell me again how I'm not enough for her when I'm buried deep inside her pussy and she's coming all over my dick?"

I moan around Sebastian's cock, throbbing between my legs. I know Griff's words were aimed at Sebastian, not me, but fuck, I can still enjoy them.

Sebastian's tone warms slightly. "See? She liked that." He pets my back and I'm hit with relief. He's being rational, so he's probably not going to lock horns with Griff. I wasn't eager to try to stop that mess. "Don't worry so much about respecting her when you're fucking her," Sebastian advises. "She knows you respect her. She doesn't need to be convinced. Sometimes she wants you to fuck her like you don't."

Now he pulls back on my hair, yanking me off his cock and looking down at me. "What should we do to you tonight, beautiful?"

I'm so relieved, I can't keep it off my face. "Anything you want," I toss back coyly, glancing from Sebastian to Griff.

Sebastian gives me a light shove back on the bed and parts my legs, looking over at Griff. "Now, would you like to measure our dicks, or would you like to put your money where your mouth is and drive yours into my wife until she comes all over it?"

Thankfully for all of us, Griff chooses the second option.

18

GRIFF

I'm just getting out of the shower when Moira comes into the guest bathroom, face flushed, holding out my phone.

"I didn't mean to look," she says, grimacing.

I haven't even grabbed a towel yet, so I'm standing here ass naked when she runs in. Generally speaking, I like any morning I wake up and get to see Moira first thing, particularly in the bathroom during or after a shower, but right now instead of focusing on the drops of water sliding down my toned abdomen, she's avoiding looking at me altogether.

What the hell did she see on my phone? There shouldn't be anything that would cause her to react like that.

With a faint frown, I reach out and take it from her much smaller hand. As it transfers into my grasp, the screen lights up. I tap it one more time and it opens straight to a picture of a very naked Ashley splayed across a bed.

"Aw, Christ," I mutter, turning my own head for a second

before dragging the picture away. It shrinks and I see it's attached to a text message that reads "Thinking of you."

Instant dread. She's fucking haunting me. Why won't she just leave me alone and go away?

Well, that's a dumb question. There are a lot of reasons; all of them can be found in my bank account or the appraisal report of my fucking house.

Moira starts chattering nervously again. "I didn't mean to look. I didn't read your messages back and forth or anything, your phone lit up and it was right next to mine. Sebastian left early this morning so I thought it might be him, but it was obviously *your* phone, not mine. I wasn't snooping," she swears.

Smiling faintly, I put the phone down on the marble counter next to the sink. "I didn't think you were. Wouldn't matter if you did. I don't have anything to hide."

She doesn't respond, so she must not agree.

That's silly. I hook an arm around her waist and drag her against my body. "There's no back and forth to read. She sends me messages, I ignore them. Normally not messages like *that*. She must be getting desperate."

"She has very large breasts," Moira states.

"Mm-hmm," I murmur, reaching with my free hand for the comb on the counter and dragging it through my hair.

"I mean, I've seen them in clothing before, even a bathing suit, but somehow they look bigger without anything covering them. Like, whoa."

I smile faintly. "I told her not to get them that big. Maybe they're 'like, whoa' now, but according to the studies, they're going to be a real backache later on."

Moira's nose wrinkles up. "Do you like big breasts?"

"I like them Moira-sized," I inform her. "I just had a picture of a naked woman on my phone and I didn't even look at her boobs. That should answer your question about my preferences."

Still, she hesitates. Fidgets. Looks down at my bare nether regions. "We didn't really talk extensively about this, but you don't talk to other women, right? I mean, I know we're sharing, but we're sharing exclusively, right?"

"Absolutely."

She looks relieved. "Okay. I was just making sure."

I shake my head at my stingy little Moira. It's fine that I have to share her, but she's clearly not at all interested in sharing me.

I like that.

Not that I can even imagine needing to supplement her with someone else. Ashley had a pretty healthy sex drive at our peak, but Moira's is significantly more active. Beyond the rarest of occasions—vacations early in our relationship—Ashley and I would fuck a few nights a week. It dwindled down to once or twice a week, and then there were the times we went whole weeks without touching.

Whether because Seb trained her that way or it's just her natural inclination, Moira expects to be fucked every night— some days, twice.

Not that I'm complaining, obviously. I just thought I would get *less* sex sharing with another man, not *more*. Moira's sex drive was a very pleasant surprise.

"I'm sorry you had to see that," I tell her.

"Why don't you just block her number?" she suggests. "If you don't want to get messages from her, you don't have to."

That's true. Seb made the same suggestion. "I will once the divorce goes through. Until then, I hate to cut off her only way of reaching me. If I do, maybe she gets more desperate. Maybe she shows up on my doorstep. At the club." I shrug, putting the comb down and raking my fingers through to give my hair a good tousle. "I'd rather delete some text messages than see her face."

Moira slinks around to the front of me, wrapping her arms around my neck and gazing up at me in a way that makes my heart beat faster. "I like watching you get ready."

"Yeah?"

"Mm-hmm." She drags her lips along my neck, then lightly bites me.

My cock rises. She obviously feels it because her hand snakes down between my legs and she rubs until it's painfully hard, straining against her hand like a well-trained pet.

Then she drops to her knees, takes my cock into that sweet mouth of hers, and *really* gets my morning off to a good start.

Once my baser needs are taken care of, Moira hauls her cute little ass downstairs and starts making me breakfast. She really is a one stop shop, that Moira. I would have never believed someone could be so content living her life, but I'll be damned if she isn't convincing.

With her gone, I finally manage to get dressed. Even though it still makes me feel faintly guilty that she waits on me hand and foot, I'm eager to see what she's making me for breakfast. I like having breakfast with her either way, but since Seb is already gone this morning, I have her all to myself. That's nice sometimes.

I wonder what she'll do today. I have the morning clear, so I'm planning to stick around and find out. Technically, I should probably leave since I'm trying to behave until this legal shit is taken care of. My car is already stashed in the garage, though, so as long as no one comes over and we stay at the house, I should be fine to stay with Moira for a bit.

"Perfect timing," she announces, flashing me a smile over her shoulder as she plates our breakfast.

I watch her fondly as she puts my plate down, then takes her seat next to me. "Thank you, it looks delicious."

Moira gives me a light-hearted wink. "I aim to please."

"You certainly accomplish that," I assure her, grabbing my fork. "Were you like this before Seb?"

"Like what?" she asks, looking up curiously.

"As... um..." I pause, not entirely sure how to word it. "Sexual?"

"Oh." She flushes faintly, smiling and looking down at her plate of eggs. "No, not at all. I mean, I had sexual partners, but none as demanding as him. My first boyfriend had a healthy sexual appetite, but not on Sebastian's level. My second boyfriend had a slow libido, I guess, because we almost never had sex. Or, I guess it could have been because he was too busy cheating on me to fuck me," she adds, on a faint laugh. "Then after that dickweed was Sebastian, then you."

Somehow I'm still faintly surprised to hear myself on her list of lovers—ridiculous, given I pounded her into the sofa *and* the mattress last night, so clearly I've made the cut.

"So, four lovers total."

Moira nods, reaching for her orange juice and taking a sip. "That's right."

"No one-night-stands or anything in between?"

"Not really my style," she answers. "If I'm going to have a sexual relationship with someone, I want to be able to get comfortable with them and open up. To be honest, had I known I would end up with Sebastian, I would've just waited for him. I didn't think men like him existed in real life."

"He would've enjoyed corrupting you," I tell her, imagining her dressed up in lacy, virginal white, spread across his bed, waiting for him to pounce.

She nods, almost remorseful. "I would have enjoyed letting

him. Plus, I would have liked if you two were the only men who'd ever been inside me."

That shouldn't be so hot, but fuck, it is. Now I sort of wish that, too.

"You're the only two to find my G-spot, though," she says, brightly. "So maybe we can just say the first two don't count."

I can't help feeling a bit smug. "Lazy assholes. We'll definitely say they don't count."

Glancing across the table at me, she swallows a bite of her eggs and asks, "What about you?"

I grimace. "You don't really want a number, right?"

Seeming to reconsider, she grimaces. "No, probably not. More than four?"

I start to laugh, then shift it to a cough when she levels an annoyed look at me. "Yes, slightly more than four."

"How old were you the first time? That's probably a safe one."

"Fifteen."

"That's so young."

I shrug. Didn't seem young to me. "I think my fifteen and your fifteen were probably a lot different."

"That's true," she murmurs, a little sadly.

I lift my coffee and take a sip, regarding her newly solemn expression. I can tell it makes her sad to think about my childhood, and I hate for Moira to be sad. "No reason to look like that," I tell her, lightly.

"I just wish I could fix it. I know I can't take away the pain, but I wish I could've at least been there to help you guys through it."

I shake my head, dismissing the notion. "I didn't enjoy it at the time, but hardship forms a man. Maybe I come from rough beginnings, but I'd rather go through all I went through and come out a full-grown man than be coddled and grow up to be the cheating little bitch who couldn't even find your G-spot."

At that, Moira grins. "True. No one wants to be like him."

I shake my head. "He doesn't get to touch you anymore *and* he incurred your sister's wrath.

"Bad luck all around."

"Not luck," I disagree. "He made his own shitty choices and he paid for them. People who have it too easy in life don't have to grow. They can rest on their laurels. Men like me and Seb, we learned early to hustle and make our own way. Hell, if I lived a stable life, who knows what kind of asshole I would have grown up to be."

"I don't think you could have ever grown up to be an asshole," she puts in, loyally. "You're noble and sweet and good."

I don't see what she sees when I look in the mirror, that's for damn sure.

"That's funny," I tell her. "That's not how I see myself, but it is how I see you. Always have. I thought you must have had either the worst possible life, or a completely fucking magical life to come out the way you did."

Moira smiles faintly, watching her orange juice glass. "No in-between, huh?"

"None."

"Well, it wasn't magical," she informs me. "I can't say it was the worst, though. Yours was obviously worse than mine since you had no one."

I shrug one shoulder. "Not necessarily. Sometimes it can be worse to be stuck with the wrong people."

After a minute, she looks up at me. "Did you ever see the movie *Matilda*?"

"The girl who could move stuff with her mind, right? Liked to read a lot? Born to a family of morons? Yep, I saw it."

"Well, I wouldn't have said the family of morons part, but I related to her more than anyone when I was a little girl. We had an old VHS copy of it and I would hide out in the basement and watch it. That's actually why I started reading. No one in my family did, but I watched this movie with this little girl who didn't fit into her family either, who got pushed around and made fun of by the people who should be taking care of her, and I thought, 'hey, that's me.' So, Matilda didn't sit around feeling sorry for herself. She went out and discovered the world on her own. She found her own place since she didn't fit into the life she was dropped into." She smiles now. "I loved that."

"Did you follow in her footsteps?"

"Well, my path was a little less dramatic, but she started my journey. My house was always unpleasant and it made me feel depressed to be there, so as often as I could, I would go to the library after school. I would go on the computers there, peruse books and magazines. I expanded my own horizons. I learned about life outside of my own tiny window of experience. I learned to look at things from other points of view. I met new people—people more like me, sometimes. People completely different. It didn't matter. I read everything that caught my interest. I fell for roguish heroes, befriended young women facing troubles I would never encounter in my lifetime, read beautiful poetry written by the saddest women, went on boring fishing trips with fictional old men. My world grew and grew, and no one even knew. I could live hundreds of lives in the space of a year, and everyone thought I was just boring old Moira."

I reach across the table, catching her hand and twining our fingers together. "There's nothing boring about you."

Her eyes sparkle with mischief. "I know that, but it was my little secret."

"I'm in on it now," I inform her.

She grins. "That's okay. You and Sebastian are allowed to know every inch of me, just no one else."

It's strange, hearing Moira describe a self-imposed prison of her own. Hers was nothing like ours, but it was a prison all the same. I've been there; I recognize her description of the invisible bars. "Did you have many friends?"

Shrugging like it's insignificant, she says, "Not many. When I was young, I kept to myself. When I got older, the girls didn't like me. The guys did. That made the girls like me even less."

I nod my understanding. "It usually does."

"I always had Gwen," she offers. "Gwen didn't fit in either, but as you may have noticed, she's much more take-charge. Much more assertive. She was the lion and I was the lamb. I liked my peace and quiet. I avoided what I hated and surrounded myself with what I loved. Gwen fought tooth and nail and wore herself out. Our teen years were really hard for her. Lots of fighting, lots of tears. I tried to convince her of the virtues of pretending to roll over and play dead, but she didn't have it in her."

Since she's been dancing around it, I ask, "What were your parents like?"

It takes her a minute to come up with an apt response. "Comfortable, I guess. Not for me, but with themselves, even when maybe they shouldn't have been. You know how you said people who don't struggle don't have to experience growth? They just rest on their laurels? Well, my parents *did* have struggles, but they still never grew. They blamed everyone for everything instead of facing their own faults. I think you missed a crucial part. The struggle isn't enough to change people. If there's going to be any profound change, you have to accept responsibility. Otherwise you can fuck up your whole life and never learn a damn thing." She meets my gaze plainly. "That's what my parents were like."

Her words are so much softer than my worldview, than Seb's, but in a lot of ways, we believe the same things. It's strange how we traveled such different paths and wound up in the same place.

"Is that what drew you to Seb?"

She cocks an eyebrow, not quite understanding.

"I've never met a more accountable man," I state. "I've strived to be like that since I met him. I guess he shaped me a bit, in that way."

Running her finger over my thumb, she says, "I think if we're doing life right, we learn something from everyone who is important to us."

It was partially trying to be accountable that landed me in the hot water I'm currently in, actually. I haven't really talked to her about the problems popping up with my divorce, and I figure this isn't the right time.

Luckily, she answers the question I asked a moment ago and saves me from considering it further. "I don't think any one thing drew me to Sebastian, though. It was everything. His whole package. After spending my childhood fending for myself emotionally, I met this incredible, dominant man who gently wrested control from me and kept it in his pocket. He led me around like he already knew exactly where I wanted to go. It was a relief. He took so much pressure off me. He gave me the break I didn't even know I needed. I'm human, I didn't always make the best decisions, but he *did*. It was the strangest thing. He *always* makes the right call. I've never met someone and trusted them so quickly, but he was so capable, how could I not? It was like the entire world was his own personal yo-yo, and he wanted *me*."

The look on her face now is exactly why I call them newly-weds, even after years together. She's still so impressed by that lucky bastard; she gets hearts in her eyes just talking about him. I get it. He struck me as someone to watch as soon as we met, and he was little more than a kid, then. Now he's a man full-grown, and I can see why he impresses the hell out of his wife.

Moira goes on. "As for what first drew me to *you*…"

"Seb," I answer, since that's easy to guess.

But she shakes her head. "No, that wasn't it. That came after. First it was your strength. I could feel it. It rolls off of you in waves, the same way Sebastian's dominance rolls off him. You have the look and feel of a man who could walk through a natural disaster carrying a person over each shoulder and never miss a step. He controls everything, but you… you don't have to. You can survive anything. You're smart and strong and capable in your own right, but more than that, you're loyal. You could take on the world by yourself, but you choose to stick by Sebastian. You take care of your own. You love *each other*. You take care of one another. I love that." Her smile warms and she squeezes my hand. "I love *you*. I love you both. I'm the luckiest woman in the world."

A little smile tugs at the corners of my mouth. "Seb says that all the time, that he's the luckiest guy in the world."

"He is," she says, her tone teasing. "He has us, doesn't he? Now we're the luckiest threesome in the world."

19

MOIRA

GRIFF IS SUPPOSED TO STAY WITH ME UNTIL afternoon, but he gets called away to work and ends up leaving early. He promises he'll make it up to me later.

I walk him out to the garage, give him a kiss, and shut the garage door once he leaves.

We really need to get an extra garage door opener for him.

Griff helped me clean up after breakfast, so I have the afternoon free. Sebastian won't be home until dinner time, so I figure I'll do some yoga. I didn't go for my run this morning; snuggling in bed was more enjoyable. Good thing extra sex burns a few calories, because I've been majorly slacking since Griff joined our relationship.

Once I get into my workout clothes and braid my hair, I decide I may as well do a little extra work while I'm there. I grab my five-pound weights so I can warm up and do a little arm work before I start my yoga routine.

Only, the doorbell rings before I make it to my mat.

I wasn't expecting Gwen today. I almost think maybe Griff

left something, but Sebastian gave him a key and he knows the alarm code. He wouldn't ring the doorbell.

Glancing down at myself, I verify I am not fit for company. I'm wearing a stylish sports bra and thin athletic pants.

The doorbell rings again.

That's rather aggressive.

Unease crawls down my spine as I grab a sweater and head for the door. I tell myself there's no reason to feel this way—it's probably a delivery. Sebastian probably ordered something and forgot to tell me.

I unlock the door and pull it open.

My heart promptly drops into my stomach when I see none other than Ashley Halliwell standing in my doorway.

Well, this is awkward.

Last time I saw her, she was Griff's wife.

Last time I saw Griff, he was squeezing my ass and kissing me goodbye.

Yep, awkward.

I also know she's been causing some kind of trouble with the divorce, so I definitely should not talk to her. I can't bring myself to be rude, though. Part of me wants to. She cheated on Griff. I remember how he felt before Sebastian asked me to play seamstress and stitch him back up. I'm still not completely sure he's over what she did to him, but I know he's happy where he is now, so I can let it go as long as she leaves him alone going forward. I just want her to go away so we never have to see her again.

As if enjoying my discomfort, her fake smile widens with a hint of authenticity. "Hey, friend."

I look away uncomfortably, shifting my weight. "Hey, Ashley."

"Gonna invite me in?" she asks brightly.

I can feel my face heating up with embarrassment, but I shake my head. "I can't. Actually, now's not a good time. I, um… I was in the middle of doing something."

"My husband?" she shoots back, still smiling. "You're fucking him now, right? You're why he doesn't come home?"

Come home?

I want to remind her they don't live together, that he's trying his damndest to divorce her, that she *cheated on him* multiple times. But all those words get stuck in my throat. She's so full of confidence as she stands here like she has a legitimate bone to pick with me, like I'm the problem in her life and once she removes me, there will be no thorns left in her paw.

She needs to leave.

"This is inappropriate," I tell her. "I'm sorry, but I have to ask you to leave."

I go to shut the door, but she laughs, pushing against the door with her hand. "Oh, no, sweetie; I'm not going anywhere."

My heart accelerates. Even though I tell myself there's nothing she can do to hurt me, I don't feel confident in that assertion as she shoves my front door open and walks inside.

I fall back a couple steps, darting a desperate look toward the living room. I left my cell phone in there. I can't even call… I don't even know which one I call. Sebastian, because he's my husband? Griff, because Ashley is his problem?

Ashley slams my front door shut and looks around. She's been in my foyer many times so there's nothing new here, but she still looks around like she's seeing it for the first time.

"You have a beautiful house, you know that? What am I saying? Of course you know that. Gorgeous house, sexy as hell husband, life of leisure. You've got it made, don't you, Moira?"

"I'm a very lucky woman. You were, too," I remind her.

She turns back to face me, smiling benignly. "I will be again, don't you worry your pretty little head about it. Now, I realize it's going to be a little awkward, us being friends again after you've fucked my husband six ways to Sunday. He'll probably moon at you for a while and make it weird. I'm not excited about any of it, but it is what it is. You're his fantasy girl. You know how most husbands would want to fuck, say, Mila Kunis as their free pass? You're Griff's Mila Kunis, so I'm gonna forgive him for this one."

The very notion of her ever getting her claws back into Griff makes my skin crawl. He's not here and I know that won't happen, but I just want to grab him, snuggle him close, and protect him from her.

"You need to leave," I tell her again.

She ignores me, her heels clacking against marble as she walks in a slow circle around me. "The thing that really chaps my ass though, Moira, isn't that you're a homewrecking little slut, it's that you're a greedy little slut. You already have *everything*. You have the perfect life, the hotter husband, the *richer* husband—I don't for one split second buy that bullshit Sebastian feeds everyone about how he cuts everything down the middle between him and Griff. He's too fucking shrewd for that, and Griff is too fucking trusting to ever question him. That's beside the point. The point is, you already *had* the better hand— why did you have to take mine, too? Why do you need *both* of them? Is this a pity fuck? Griff was feeling down and Sebastian's just a hell of a friend, offered up his wife's pussy as a salve?"

"I've asked you to leave multiple times. I'm going to stop asking nicely—"

"Oh, boo hoo," she says, mockingly rubbing her eyes. She comes to a stop and stares me down. "Here's how this is going to go down, princess. You stop fucking my husband. He's never going to come back to me if your legs are open. Stop being a whore and stay the fuck out of my way so I can fix my marriage."

This is starting to piss me off. I don't like to be aggressive with people, but I sort of want to kick her in the face. "If you wanted to fix your marriage, Ashley, you had years to do it. You had a wonderful husband and you took him for granted. You're delusional if you think there's even a slim chance he'll get back together with you. You can send him all the nudes and clingy texts you want, he does *not* want you. That's not going to change, and it has nothing to do with me. It has to do with *you* cheating on him and hurting him. Fighting him tooth and nail like this is ridiculous. You don't love him. Not once have you accepted responsibility for hurting him, not once have you said a damn thing about *his* happiness or anything remotely related to love. The only person you care about is yourself. If you were the last woman on the planet, Griff still wouldn't want you."

She grins at me like I've just shown my hand, and I feel like I swallowed my heart. "How did you know what I've been texting him? Did he tell you? Did Saint Griff feel so guilty for looking at his own wife's vagina when he's clearly been burying himself deep in yours that he had to confess his sins?" She laughs. "He's such a good Catholic boy, isn't he? Well, you know, except for fucking his best friend's wife. That's not terribly virtuous, now, is it?"

I normally don't have a vicious side, but I'm sorely tempted to tell her he was too busy getting his big dick sucked to care about the picture she sent. I can't, since that would verify that I am sleeping with him, but I can't keep from offering up a sweet smile and at least telling her, "He didn't even look at the picture, Ashley. He deleted it and went back to eating breakfast with me and talking about life."

Her smile slips. I'm sure it's discomfiting, the reminder that our relationship isn't as shallow as theirs, isn't held up by childish games or boob jobs or fucking. Yes, we enjoy fucking each other, but that's not all we have. Griff and I had a friendship long before we ever touched one another intimately.

Ashley can't say the same thing. They were never really friends, not even once they were married. Their relationship always seemed more superficial, at least to me.

Her tone is less aggressive now as she reels herself in and talks more calmly. "You can't keep this up, Moira. Be practical. I don't entirely understand what the hell is going on here, but I do know Sebastian. He might be kinky enough to lease you out temporarily to ease Griff's pain, but he's not going to share you forever. The longer Griff fucks you, the more attached he'll get. Sebastian is smart enough to know that."

"You don't know my husband, Ashley. Don't pretend to."

"I've known your husband for years, sweetie. I think I've picked up a thing or two."

"If you had, you'd know better than to barge into my house and talk a bunch of shit to me. Now, get the fuck out before I call the police and file a restraining order against you. I'm feeling pretty threatened right now," I tell her, narrowing my eyes.

"You should," she tells me, smiling over her shoulder as she turns and heads for the door. Pausing with her hand on the handle, she informs me, "I'm going to drag your dirty laundry all over this fucking city, Moira. Everyone in Philly will know you're spreading your legs for Griff. Cheating on Sebastian. Oh, the things people will believe about you. Just wait. You're in for a treat."

My heart is in my throat, but I walk to the door and force myself to remain calm. "I would strongly advise against that. You've made your bed, Ashley. You had Griff. You lost him because you cheated on him. You got your just desserts. Walk away. You're young and beautiful; you'll find another bank account to milk."

Unaffected, she raises an eyebrow. "This is your only warning, sweetie. Stop fucking my husband, let him come back to me, and we can all get back to our regularly scheduled lives. He's not really your speed anyway. I know what you and Sebastian are into, and I know Griff isn't. This arrangement won't work, and when it fails—*after* the whole city knows what a dirty little slut you are—it'll tank their friendship. Griff thinks with his heart. You let him get in much deeper, he's not coming back out—not even when Sebastian tells him to. You're risking your own marriage to play this game. You're not ready for the big leagues. Do the smart thing. Get off Griff's dick and give him nowhere else to turn. Watch. He'll come home. I guarantee it."

I shake my head, astounded by how little she knows a man she spent so many years with. "You're wrong. And you're not welcome here, so don't come back."

"I'll give you the night to think it over. If Griff isn't home tomorrow after he gets off work, I poison the grape vine with sordid tales of how you single-handedly ruined my marriage. No woman in polite society will ever trust you again."

I stop in the doorway, but she's already through it and heading for her car. "That's bullshit and you know it. People will see this for what it is. No one will believe you."

"Stop collecting husbands and we won't have to find out," she calls back.

"You're horrible," I tell her. "You've done enough to that man. Let him be happy."

She turns back just so I can see her roll her eyes at me. "No."

I watch her drop into the car Griff bought her, the car she's still driving, and a claustrophobic feeling of helplessness steals over me.

I can't keep her from running her mouth, and while I told her no one would fall for her bullshit, I know better. Several of the women in our social circles already don't trust me, and I've never done a damn thing to warrant it. Their husbands are nice to me—their gray-haired, pot-bellied husbands. I'm married to Sebastian, for fuck's sake. My husband is sex in a suit; what use would I even have for the unimpressive louts they married? For that matter, what good is a man who goes sniffing around another woman anyway?

There's no logic to it, they're just threatened by me—my looks or my personality, perhaps the old-fashioned way I take care of my husband's needs and treat him like my king. I don't know if they're jealous of me or my relationship, perhaps just envious of the youth they no longer feel they possess. I *am* the youngest wife in our crowd. Most men of Sebastian's age aren't as established unless they're born into one of the right families, but Sebastian had a point to prove. When my husband has a point to prove, he'll move mountains to accomplish it.

That's why Ashley should keep her mouth shut.

She cost herself Griff's affection, and she knows it, she just doesn't want to let go of the bank account that comes with him. All she can do is try to terrorize him into giving in, and since she knows he's fond of me, she thinks she can use me to do it.

If she thinks I give a rat's ass what anyone thinks of my relationships, though, she's dead wrong.

We are all consenting adults. As long as we're happy and no one else is getting hurt, I don't see how it's anybody's place to take issue with our relationship—they will anyway, but they shouldn't. I don't care what they think about me. I care what they think about Sebastian. I care what is said to and about Sebastian.

I care because my husband, while wonderful, is not a man you embarrass. He may have patience for me and Griff because he loves us, but he doesn't have any for Ashley or the society set. If any of them make the mistake of mistreating me or laughing at him, my husband will feel compelled to punish them for it. He'll go to great—maybe even destructive—lengths to accomplish it if he has to.

Because of that, he's not the one I call.

I call Griff. I explain to him what happened. I tell him I'm not sure what to do.

The first thing he asks is also whether or not I told Sebastian.

"No."

"Good," he says, quickly. "Don't. Let me handle this."

20

GRIFF

$17, 177.31.

That's the amount in our joint checking account. Or, it was, before I made the decision to ditch Ashley. I made sure to call the bank three days prior and let them know I was withdrawing $17,000, then I made sure I waited until the money was in my hands before I kicked her cheating ass out of my house.

It's certainly not all my money. I keep my own separate account, too. Never could trust Ashley with all our money. I tried when we first got married. She went on an ill-timed shopping spree and our mortgage check bounced.

After that, I kept my shit separate but maintained a generous pillow in our joint account. That's the account from which all the bills were paid, the only account she knows about, and the only account of mine she still has access to. She bled it down to $2.13, but I couldn't give a fuck less about a couple hundred dollars.

Today I'm going to take her to the bank, put the larger chunk of money back in, and take my name off the account. It's hers.

She can have it. I'm going to give her the house, too. I just want her gone.

I can't fucking believe she confronted Moira. That was so far over the line, I don't even know how I'll be nice to her right now. I need to, though. I need to just shut her up and make her go away before things get any worse.

She opens the door of her hotel room, leans against the doorframe and grins at me. "There you are. I figured Moira would get you to answer me."

Leveling my stoniest expression at her, I state, "This is over. This is done."

Ashley holds up her hand, still laden with the wedding band and engagement ring I bought her. "No, sweetie. 'Til death do us part. It's not done."

"Don't fucking tempt me," I mutter.

Instead of believing my bluster, she shoots me a playful smile. "I'll let you choke me if you want to, but only if you put your dick in me first."

"I'd rather cut it off," I tell he bluntly.

"Ouch," she says, shooting me an exaggerated pout that I found cute once upon a time. Now it just annoys the fuck out of me.

I reach into my jacket pocket and hand her an envelope, thick with cash. Her eyes widen and her pout falls, revealing a more honest peek of her interest. "What's this?"

I shove the envelope into her hand and she immediately opens it, using her manicured pink fingernails to comb through the bills.

"Seventeen grand," I tell her. "I'm going to put it in an account for you so you have some money to get yourself started building a new life. You can keep your car and every material thing I've ever given you. You can keep the house and everything in it. I'll sign it over to you. All you have to do is sign the divorce papers."

Now she smiles, staring at me like I've brought her a bag of peanuts. "Are you fucking kidding me? What the hell am I supposed to do with $17,000, Griff? This is insulting. I thought you'd open with at least 25."

"Will 25,000 make you go away?" I ask. I won't be able to get that much cash out today, but I could damn sure write her a check. Hell, I could borrow the rest of the cash from Seb if that'll do it. He always has a decent chunk on hand.

"Fuck no," she says, laughing like I've just told the best joke of her life. "I just figured it was a good start. Oh, no, baby. I know what you're worth. I want what's rightfully mine. I want half."

"I just told you I'll give you the *whole* house. I don't give a fuck what you do with it. Sell it, take the money and get out of dodge. It doesn't matter to me."

Still, she shakes her head. "Not good enough. I've got you by the balls now, baby. Moira admitted she's fucking you. You may have taken your ring off, but your ass is still married. I hope her cunt was worth it, because you're going to pay dearly for it."

My skull feels like it's at risk of exploding. "You are the one who cheated on *me*, Ashley. You don't get to play that card. I would say I hope all the dicks *you* took were worth it, but you're a conniving bitch and you still have me over a fucking barrel. You're the one who causes all this shit, and you're still going to make out like a fucking bandit. There's no justice for me, but I don't care at this point; I just want you gone. I'm offering you our house and an envelope bursting with cash, and it's still not good enough for you."

With a sly grin, she runs a hand down my chest. "I don't have to settle, baby. I'm not mad you're fucking Moira. Oh, I'm not mad at all. I'm fucking ecstatic. Because guess what? That prenup is getting thrown out. When your sweet little girlfriend gets her subpoena and has to come clean about how she's taking your cock while you and I are still legally married? You're fucked—and not in the fun way."

I grab her wrist, twisting it and backing her into the room. She lets out a faint cry of surprise, but not pain.

Her sharp gaze takes in the fire in my eyes, the set of my shoulders. She can feel the anger coursing through me, and even though she's a conniving little cunt, she's not an idiot, either. She softens—pretends to, anyway—and subtly pushes her breasts toward me, trying to remind me I liked to fuck her once and if I'm about to get violent for the first time in our lives, she would like to be naked first.

Fucking women, man.

I kick the door shut behind me. Ashley's hot gaze remains on mine as I back her further into the room. "Do we need privacy, baby? I'm still open to fixing our marriage instead. We can stop this whole ugly divorce nonsense and spend the day making up."

"I would rather die than ever put my dick anywhere near your toxic snatch again."

Her eyebrows rise at my crassness. "Wow. That's a little harsh."

"No, that's the truth. I don't know what I was thinking to even start dating you, let alone marry you. What the fuck was I on?"

Everything even resembling softness melts away and she narrows her eyes at me, not appreciating the insult. "I'm a fucking catch. Don't fool yourself, Griff. You're bitter because you couldn't keep me satisfied and I had to go elsewhere to get the itch scratched. Apparently, it's a trend with you; now your dick is playing second fiddle to Sebastian's." Offering a snide smile, she adds, "Don't know why anyone who has a firm hold on his dick would even waste their time with yours. You're just a pity fuck to her, you know. Sebastian's little princess is out of your league. She only fucks you because he makes her."

"Shut the fuck up," I snap.

Her eyes dance, seeing she's drawn blood. "You know it's true, Griff. Moira doesn't like you that way. She'll do anything for Sebastian, though. Even *you*."

Her words sink into my worst insecurities and twist my stomach up in knots. My grip on her wrist tightens and I back her up a couple more steps, just to remind her I can. "I said, shut the fuck up."

Instead, she continues mockingly. "Poor, sad Griff. Maybe they've made it one of their little sex games. When you're not around and it's just the two of them, they probably compare notes and laugh at how inferior you are."

It shouldn't sting, but it's too close to private fears I've had at my lowest moments not to.

My phone vibrates in my pocket, distracting me for a blessed moment. I release Ashley's wrist and reach into my pocket.

I'm hoping it's Moira. I know she's not supposed to text me much right now, but I sure would like to hear from her.

It's not a text, and it's not from Moira. Sebastian is calling. Goddammit. Moira probably caved. I should have known she couldn't keep it from him for a measly fucking hour and let me handle things.

I ignore the call and slide my phone back into my pocket.

Taking the envelope of cash out of Ashley's hand, I tell her, "You're gonna wish you took this offer."

"You threatening me, Griff?"

"Nope. This is just the extent of what I'll give you. It's much more than you deserve."

"Oh, I don't think it is," she disagrees. "You're too much of a gentleman to make Moira talk about your personal matters." She smiles. "It's funny, isn't it? You look like a beast and act like a gentleman. Sebastian looks like a gentleman. Bet he fucks like a beast. I was always curious, you know. Maybe you should rethink this divorce and we can all become swingers. Between the two of you, I'm sure my attention can be held. Then you can fuck Moira anytime you feel like it, and I'll get something out of the deal, too."

"Seb wouldn't fuck you with someone else's dick," I tell her, shoving the envelope back into my jacket. "He thinks you're trash. I've come around to his way of looking at things."

Her gaze is fixed on where I just stuffed the envelope. Moving closer, she reaches out a hand, but I grab her wrist to keep her from touching me.

"That's good," she tells me. "Can you squeeze a little harder? I would *love* a bruise."

I release her wrist, my eyes narrowing on her smug face. "I'll give you the house and $25,000. That's it. That's my final offer. If you want to take it—"

She doesn't even let me finish. "I don't. But thanks for stopping by, baby. I'll have my people call your people."

When I leave Ashley's hotel room, I feel shittier than I have in a long time.

Seb calls again. I ignore him again.

I need to talk to Moira and find out what the fuck she told him.

I need to talk to Carrie. I need to find out how bad this is. Instead of calling Seb, I shoot him a text and ask him to cover my afternoon, tell him I need to meet with Carrie.

"Fine," he texts back. "Come over for dinner."

I'm sitting in my car, staring blankly out the windshield while I try to figure out just how fucked I am when I see Ashley come out, her long blond hair blowing in the violent wind as she heads for her car. Since she's more concerned about her hair getting fucked up than watching her surroundings, she doesn't look over here and notice me.

Where's she going?

I guess it's none of my business and I don't care, necessarily, but I am curious. So, when she starts up her car and pulls out, I find myself following her.

She heads to a seedy part of town and hits her turn signal to pull into a parking area that could be to one of three places. I can't pull in behind her—it's too small, she'd see me—so I coast to a stop at the red light just past it.

To my left is a shitty-looking club with a roll-down door. In front of it is a telephone plastered with flyers—some offering to buy your shitty houses, others advertising bands probably playing at this club, a lost dog, a missing teen. Tragedy, mediocrity, and excitement all on one telephone poll.

I know I'm going to miss seeing where she goes, but all I can do now is go around the block, come back, and check out what's in the buildings she parked near.

At least, that's my assumption. But when I drive around and come back, Ashley is still in the parking lot outside the club, closer to the street now. Some Jersey Shore-looking motherfucker stands there with his hands on her ass and his tongue jammed halfway down her throat.

I feel like I recognize him, but I can't exactly sit here and try to get a better look. Given Seb and I are owners of one of Philly's more popular clubs, obviously I know the competition.

This little shithole here isn't even that. No one is trying to decide whether they want to come to our club or this one.

I hang a right and pull into the first streetside spot available. I check both ways and jog back across the street toward the club.

There's chain-link fence around the parking area so I can't creep as close as I want, but there's a trash can and part of the building here to camouflage me a bit.

Now I get a better look, and I know who it is.

The Philly crime scene has been changing lately with a new player raking in most of the power, but there are still some little guys who think they're hot shit. Maybe guys Donovan hasn't got to yet, maybe guys so small he just doesn't give a fuck.

This little fucker attached to Ashley's mouth belongs to the "too little to matter" group. He owns this shitty little club and runs petty crime in this area, but I mean, so fucking petty that even I'm not impressed, and I'm no kind of criminal. He's a smalltime dealer, nothing to get excited about.

I don't even like dealing with Donovan, but unfortunately, when these bloodsuckers pop up and demand a tax, it's just easier to pay it. To my surprise, Seb didn't bat an eye at the situation. Maybe the way he saw it, we'd pay voluntarily, or Donovan would shake us down, and coming voluntarily built a better rapport.

Can't say it didn't work. While Donovan has a club of his own—bigger and more profitable than ours, go figure—he does pop into ours on occasion and talk to Seb like they're friends.

I fucking hate that.

Sometimes I worry about Seb, about his willingness to cross lines. He's a decisive guy, so when he has a problem, he doesn't waffle on it for too long. He looks at his situation, decides on a course, and does what benefits us.

I don't like him crossing paths more than he has to with terrible men who could invite him to go dark. I especially don't like it because right now Ashley thinks she can shake me down —and she won't shake *me* down without shaking *Seb* down.

Seb, he's not going to let someone like Ashley get the better of him. She might have this insignificant little fuck and think she's some sort of up-and-coming crime lord's bitch, but boy, is she mistaken.

When it comes to this stuff, Ashley doesn't know her ass from her elbow. This does give me a new perspective, though. She probably wants to take me to the cleaners so she and this little shit can rise up and become some kind of big deal.

God, I almost feel sorry for her. She doesn't know shit, and this little asshole has surely talked a big game. He's conned women out of their money before.

He finally pulls away and she grins at him. I can see the excitement on her face and it makes me feel bad again. I shouldn't. It's not exactly a noble aspiration, trying to be this little shit's moll, but Ashley's about as basic as they come. It probably sounds reasonable and exciting to her. Probably makes her feel pretty important.

She wasn't cut out for society—she didn't have the class— but since she's seen *Scarface* or some shit like that, she probably thinks she knows the score. She's been with a club-owner already, after all. Now she's found one that's younger and more exciting—an air of imagined danger, since he's fooled her into thinking he's hot shit.

What a dumbass.

I'd feel worse for her, except she's a major pain in *my* ass because she fell for this shit. I can't even try to talk to her and set her straight, because then she would know I followed her, plus she'd never believe me. She'd think I'm just trying to save my own hide.

They turn to head inside, no doubt so she can relay in person all the details of what just went down between us. My stomach sinks when I imagine this asshole's glee as she tells him I came with cash. Fuck, I shouldn't have done that. I showed weakness. I showed a willingness to negotiate. I thought I was only dealing with Ashley, not this little shit, so I went softer. I guess part of me still felt a little bad about the divorce.

I fucked up, and now I'm not sure how to fix it. I should have listened to Carrie. I should have listened to Seb. I should not have responded to her going after Moira.

Problem is, if I didn't, Seb would have—and he wouldn't be nice about it.

21

MOIRA

I feel terrible when Sebastian comes home this evening. He wanted to come home early, but he had to work late to deal with some of the stuff Griff didn't get to.

By the time he gets here, my poor husband looks exhausted and annoyed. He yanks his coat off and hangs it up, then storms into the kitchen, pulling at his tie. He looks dreadfully sexy when he's like this, but I want to relax him.

I just finished cutting tomatoes for dinner, so I make a quick stop to wash my hands. I made soup and I'm throwing together toasted sandwiches to go with it. Salads are all prepped and in the refrigerator, but I still have an abundance of nervous energy. I want everything to be all right, and I can't be sure it is until both men are in this house with me.

Sebastian drops into his chair and heaves a sigh. I immediately walk around the back, my hands moving to his strong shoulders and kneading. "I'm so happy you're finally home," I murmur, leaning in to softly kiss my way down his neck.

"Griff's not here yet, I see," he remarks. "Have you heard from him?"

"No, not since earlier. You?"

He shakes his head tersely. "He's avoiding me."

A ball of dread slowly sinks into my stomach, but I can't help asking, "You don't think he'd go back to her, right? I know he doesn't *want* to, I know he's happy with us, but you don't think he'd let her... blackmail him or anything, right?"

"Is there something she could blackmail him with?" he asks blandly. *Too* blandly. I think he's fishing.

"I don't know," I answer, since it's not exactly a lie.

Sebastian is quiet for a minute while I rub his shoulders. Finally, he says, "I'm going to put up a security camera on the front porch. I don't want you answering the door anymore before you check to see who's there."

I nod, even though he can't see me. "That's probably not a bad idea. I've grown to dislike the element of surprise."

"I need to know what she said to you," he states.

I fall silent. I know he expects an answer and he knows I'll give it to him, eventually, but my loyalty is torn.

Griff asked me not to talk to Sebastian about this until he took care of it, but then he went silent. Does that mean he doesn't have anything to report back, or is he just waiting until he gets home?

I'm quiet for long enough that my husband speaks a little more firmly, in case I need a reminder of his expectations. "Did you admit to sleeping with him?"

"No," I say quickly, since at least that much is true. "No, I didn't. It seemed like she knew anyway, but I never verified."

He nods. I think I did a good job until he bursts my bubble with a solemn, "It doesn't matter, then."

"Did I do something wrong?" I would hate to be responsible for making Griff's life harder.

"No. That she knew enough to show up on our doorstep is bad enough. The lawyer she hired has been known to play dirty, to send out bait and trap men if he needs to. Doesn't even need to trap Griff because I already gave him you. I should've waited. Didn't think about his stupid infidelity clause."

"Infidelity clause?"

"He had a good prenup, but he included this dumb fucking clause as a courtesy to her. If she cheated, she got nothing, so he made it even. If he cheated, it would nullify the prenup and he'd give her half of everything. It seemed safe at the time because he knew he wouldn't cheat."

"But he *didn't* cheat."

"I know that," Sebastian says patiently. "But now he's having sex with you, and since you two already had a close relationship prior to the split, the fact that you're intimate now matters. He's still not legally divorced, and Ashley is claiming you two had an affair first, and hers was in response. If she can prove he cheated before he can prove she did... we're both fucked."

My heart sinks. "You, too? Ashley can hurt you?"

He nods once, his head barely moving as he stares off at nothing. "Yeah. The little whore can fuck me, too, and I never touched her ass."

My hands still on his shoulders, then I move around to take a seat on his knee. "Well, what are we going to do? How badly can she hurt us?"

"I don't know," he tells me, settling his hands on my waist and peering up into my face. "I don't know what Griff is doing right now, but probably making things worse would be my guess."

"You should call him," I advise. "You should tell him to come over for dinner. We all need to get on the same page. If they're trying to say he cheated with me, does that mean I'll have to talk to the lawyers? Won't it go away once I tell them our relationship didn't turn physical until after he and Ashley were already separated? He had already kicked her out before that first night. I asked him."

Sebastian shakes his head. "I doubt it. Griff had feelings for you long before then; they'll just think you're lying. It doesn't matter, though; I'm not going to let anyone talk to you about this. They'll twist it all up. Twist *you* all up." Giving his head another firm shake, he says, "No, I won't let that happen."

I lean against him, running my fingers through his soft, dark locks. "So, what do we do?"

He's pensive, but he still manages a reassuring smile for me. "I'll figure it out."

22

SEBASTIAN

I GO UPSTAIRS ALONE AFTER DINNER AND FIND GRIFF lying on the bed, hands laced over his stomach, staring up at the ceiling. He came home shortly after I did, but he was quiet while we ate and came directly upstairs afterward, claiming he had a headache.

I hate seeing him like this. I hate every bit of this shit. I hate that the stupid little cunt he never should've got involved with in the first place is causing him all this trouble.

Griff's a good fucking guy. He didn't deserve to get his heart stomped on, he doesn't deserve to be dragged through the mud, and it pisses me off that it's happening.

I climb up on the bed in my spot, lacing my hands over my stomach and joining him in his ceiling inspection.

I don't even say anything at first. I don't think I have to. It's enough that I'm here. He knows I'm showing my support. He knows I'm here for him, whatever happens. Surely he knows as hard as I've worked over the years to get where I am, I'm not going to let some insignificant pain in the ass fuck it all up.

Right now, though, he's stuck feeling all this shit, so I want him to know he's not alone. He's never going to be alone again.

After a moment of companionable silence, I ask, "You okay?"

He nods, still watching the ceiling. "I was just thinking about our first place. Not the rental, but the place after that, the first one we bought." He turns his head to look at me, smiling faintly at the memory. "Remember that? The red brick row-house?"

"That piece of shit?" I offer back a faint smile of my own. "Of course. Who could forget it?"

"We had absolutely nothing then," he states, shaking his head. "Took us a year to save up enough to buy that place—we lived on those fucking bags of noodles, slept on twin mattresses, no box springs."

"I fucking hate twin mattresses," I state, turning my gaze back to the ceiling. "They always made me think of the group homes. Always made me feel inadequate. Remember that time I had Amanda Winters in my bed and she nearly fell off?"

Griff laughs. "I do remember that. I was in the same fucking room."

"I should've known then. It didn't bother me to fuck her in front of you. We should've just shared girls from the get-go. Fuck it. If they didn't like both of us, they weren't right for us, anyway."

"I wish we'd have met Moira a long time ago," he states.

"I met her about as early as I could. She was only 19 when we got together. One year earlier is about all I could've done. Despite the pair of you being sentimental, there's no reality where she could've stayed with us in that shitty row-house. She was just a kid then."

"Her childhood was shitty," he tells me, like I don't already know. "I know we couldn't have fucked her yet, but she still could've lived with us as a teenager. Done our laundry and cooked our fucking Ramen noodles. Our little unpaid housekeeper."

"I think they call those slaves," I remark, lightly.

"Nah, wife-in-training. You're into all that shit, right?"

"I'm into Moira having time to enjoy our life, if that's the shit you mean. I'm not sure she would've enjoyed that house quite as much as this one."

He waves me off. "Nah, she would've been fine. She could've stayed home and read her books while we were out hustling our asses off."

"We have plenty more years to look forward to with Moira, and none that require her living in squalor. It's better this way."

"It just doesn't feel right," he says, shaking his head. "After hearing about her childhood, it makes me feel bad. She's the one always wishing she could have met us sooner. Maybe it's more for her than us. Maybe we were always meant to be together. Our own little band of misfits—our own modified version of a family."

"It's not modified," I tell him, dismissing the notion that just because our family isn't like everyone else's, it's any less real. "We *are* a family. People may not think that when they see us, but fuck what people think."

"I'm not worried about that," he says. "I just wish we'd have found her sooner. We could've filled in each other's voids years ago instead of taking so goddamn long to come around to this."

I can't age Moira down to an unfuckable age in my head, so I can only envision her when I met her, leaving the coffee shop at the end of her shift and coming home to us instead of her apartment.

I understand Griff liking the idea of us all taking on the

world together, but I like that Moira didn't meet me until I made something of myself. I know she would've loved me just as much if she had met me when I had nothing to offer but my love, but I like taking care of her. "Can you imagine Moira trying to cook dinner every night on that twelve inches of counter space we had?"

He smiles imagining her in the shitty little house we started out in, but that doesn't make me smile. I hate the thought of her ever having to live like that—ever seeing *me* live like that. Doesn't matter that she'd be fine with it; *I* wouldn't.

"She'd stay with us if I cost us everything," Griff states. "Moira wouldn't leave us."

I don't know if he's assuring me, or fishing for assurances himself. I damn sure don't need them, so I guess it's probably the latter.

"Of course she wouldn't," I say. "Moira would still be ours if we had nothing else, but that's not going to happen. We've worked too hard to get here, Griff. I'm not going to let some little bitch take it all away from us."

Now he looks over at me, his gaze solemn. "I think I fucked us, Seb. She's messing around with Danny Long now. No doubt he's the one that put her up to all this—or at least fed into it. He's not going to let her go. I'm sure he doesn't give a fuck about her, but he knows we have deep pockets, and right now he has a hand to reach into them with."

I mull that over for a minute. "What did Carrie say?"

"That I fucked us. Hard, no lube, I believe is the way she put it."

"How much is it going to cost?"

"I don't know yet. A lot. Carrie said their next step..." He hesitates, so I know this won't be good. "They're going to make Moira come in and divulge the details. Supposedly so they can determine whether or not I spent any money on her, to see..." A bitter little laugh escapes him. "To see if I owe Ashley any financial reparations."

Quiet rage surges through my veins at that. "The fuck she will. No one's going to embarrass Moira."

"Carrie said she needs to be prepared. Ashley's already said she's going to subpoena her. She'll make this as hard as she can, Seb." He turns his head to look at me. "I'm so sorry."

I feel his gaze, but I don't meet it. I'm too angry, and I don't want him to think he's the one I'm pissed at. I know this isn't his fault. I mean, it is, but it's mine for ever letting this shit happen in the first place.

I should've been able to see all those years ago that he wanted Moira. I should've noted what a coincidence it was that he just so happened to meet "the one" right after I did—especially when Ashley damn sure didn't seem like "the one" to me.

This is my fault.

I should have taken this noble motherfucker under my wing a long time ago instead of letting him gallop around aimlessly on a white fucking steed and make a mess of everything. I should've brought him in a lot sooner, because Moira would never do anything like this. Moira would have always been loyal to us. Moira would have made us both happy.

She still will, it's just this Ashley headache I have to deal with first.

Over my dead body is anyone dragging my wife to a lawyer's office to deliver intimate details of our sex life. I'm not shy by any means, but I'm not going to let anyone humiliate her, and that's the motive behind this. She's not ashamed when she's in bed with both of us or living our life. It isn't sordid in practice.

But sitting there and reciting the raw details in front of people likely to judge her? That will make it seem worse than it is. It won't just incriminate Griff; it may make Moira feel like she's done something dirty and wrong.

I'm not about to let that happen.

Their days of making decisions without me are over. They both make terrible fucking decisions. They need me, or neither of them would ever have order in their lives.

Since Griff isn't in my head, he's not privy to any of this. He's just apologized and I'm quiet as the dead, so he goes on. "I'll bow out, if you want me to. I won't let them drag Moira in and question her. I'll just confess to everything so they won't have to. We can talk to Carrie in the morning and see how fast we could split up the business stuff. If it'll stick, we just separate everything. Even if I lose *my* half of everything—"

I interrupt, since everything he's saying is stupid. "No, Griff. That's not going to happen. That's not how we work. One of us doesn't abandon ship when the other is sinking."

He's quiet for a moment, then he states, "I tried to."

"I wasn't sinking," I point out.

"But I wouldn't have been there if you ever did. I tried to ditch you."

I'm dismissive because I have to be. Because it's what I need to believe, and I hope the bastard doesn't argue. "Eh, you were never going to leave. You just wanted to fuck my wife. Knew I needed some proper incentive. Well played, my friend."

I think he knows why I'm so dismissive about it. Normally, I'm a stickler for accountability; I would want him to own what he tried to do, but not this time.

Before Moira came into my life, Griff was the only person I knew had my back. The only person I could depend on to stick by my side, even if everyone else jumped ship. That's the reality I've known over half my life, and I need to believe it.

Griff needs Moira, Moira needs me, and I need Griff.

He doesn't have to, since I gave him an easy out, but now he tells me, "I'm really sorry for that, too. My head was a mess. I didn't mean any of it. I was just…."

I don't make him finish. I nod and murmur, "I know, Griff. It's all right. Water under the bridge."

"The water ever rises again, you never have to worry about me jumping," he states.

I turn my head to meet his gaze and offer a faint smile. "Same here."

"Good thing," he mutters. "I've got water up around my ears right now."

"I'm a strong swimmer. I'll get you out of this, don't worry. You need to stop trying to help, though. Stop talking to Ashley. Block her number. Don't see her again."

"I offered to let her keep the house today," he tells me.

I close my eyes briefly, massaging the bridge of my nose. "Remember when the lawyer and I both told you not to do that?"

"I know, but she came after Moira. I couldn't just do nothing. If I could throw some money at her—"

"If you throw money at the greedy cunt, she'll just ask for more. Jesus, Griff."

"I just want her to *go away*," he drawls. "I don't give a fuck if I have to pay. I just want her to leave all of us alone."

"She will, but not if you offer her money. Just let me handle this. I'm better at this stuff. You were married to her—you're too emotionally involved. Just back off and let me deal with it from here on out."

"You're gonna handle my divorce," he says skeptically.

I draw my phone out of my pocket. "I'm better at it."

After a few seconds, he says, "You're not texting her, are you?"

"Of course not. I have nothing to say to her that I want recorded." I push send and glance over at Griff, a crease marring my brow. "I feel like an asshole even asking this, but things didn't get physical when you went to see her today, right?"

He scowls at me. "Fuck no. Seriously? You think I'd have sex with her? I'm with Moira now."

"I was just making sure," I tell him. "No need to get defensive."

I already had Griff get tested to make sure his skanky wife didn't pass him anything, despite his assurances that they never fucked without a condom, but I can't be too careful with my Moira.

"There absolutely is a fucking need to get defensive," he disagrees, fully riled. "That's a bullshit thing to ask."

"I know her tricks," I remind him. "I know she's used sex to handle you before."

"Not when I had a better option at home," he states, still surly as hell. Then he looks up at the ceiling. "Or, not home, but you know what I mean."

"This is your home as much as it is mine." I miss a beat, then I tell him, "Ashley's damn sure not getting your house, but after this is all over with, you should sell it and move in here. You can have the guest room for yourself, but you can stay in here with us if you want. On occasion, you can have Moira alone in there—not frequently," I add, before he gets carried away with that offer. "But once in a great while. If we're going to be a family, we should all live under the same roof."

"I'd like that," Griff says. "That house is too fucking big to live in alone, anyhow."

I nod my agreement. "It's settled then. After I get rid of your wife, I get rid of your house."

"I think I can handle that part."

"A house won't try to manipulate you, so you might have better luck."

He shoots me a dry look. "She didn't manipulate me."

"She manipulated the *fuck* out of you."

"I don't want to talk about this anymore," he mutters, clearly getting annoyed with me.

I smile faintly. "We've talked about it enough. You don't have to worry about it anymore. Consider the matter resolved."

That should put him at ease—it certainly would Moira—but Griff questions me. "How exactly are you planning to resolve it?"

The bedroom door creaks open and Moira peeks her head in. She sees us on the bed, so she takes another step inside.

"Did you need something?" she asks.

I crook a finger for her to come closer. "We do."

"What do you need?"

"You."

23

MOIRA

My elegant husband waits on our bed, his gaze commanding me to undress so his mouth doesn't have to.

"I wasn't ready for bed yet," I murmur, kicking off my black kitten heels and reaching behind my neck to unfasten my necklace. "Griff owes me a movie," I remind them.

"We can all watch a movie after we're done fucking you," Sebastian informs me.

His words send shivers of desire through me. A faint strain of arousal already throbs between my legs, visions of both of them having me flashing through my mind.

It's a normal part of my reality these days, but it's no less intoxicating. My strong, gorgeous husband, Griff with his brute strength and rough hands—so big and blunt, yet he handles my body with such tender care.

I deposit my necklace on the dresser and reach back to unzip my skirt. "Am I the only one getting naked?" I ask, lifting a dark eyebrow since both of them are just lying there watching me.

The corners of Griff's mouth curve up. "We're enjoying the show first."

"Griff has had a rough day," Sebastian tells me. "I need you to make him feel better."

I drag my tiny black top off and drop it onto the floor as I approach the bed. "Well, what kind of wife would I be if I didn't drop everything and meet your needs?"

"A normal one?" Griff suggests.

I ignore him and climb up on the bed, straddling my husband's legs and running my hands along the muscular thighs I love so much. God, I love Sebastian's body.

Much more appropriately, my handsome husband grips my chin and tips my face up to look into his. Intense blue eyes meet mine, his handsome face wickedly stern. "The kind of wife that needs to be punished."

I lean down and flatten my body against his, tugging his dress shirt out of his slacks and unbuttoning it, holding his gaze all the while. "Well, as delicious as that sounds, here I am. What do good wives get?"

He smiles. "Whatever they want."

I pounce on him, climbing up his body and leaning in to kiss his sexy mouth. "I want you naked," I inform him.

"I can make that happen," he murmurs against my lips. His fingers skim the sides of my arms, then dip in to grab my hips. He flips me on my back and I let out a little squeal. Now he's on top of me, smirking. "You were getting a little too bossy there, sweetheart."

I sigh softly as he lifts my arms above my head, then skims his fingers down the undersides of my arms, causing gooseflesh to rise up everywhere. Now that he's planted me on my spot on the bed, Griff is right next to me. I reach my right hand out to give his arm a light caress.

"You okay, Griff?"

He nods, his gaze drifting from my face to my breasts, still covered by the strapless bra I wore today. The strapless ones never stay up very well, so I'm set to pop right out of it any second.

"He'll feel much better once he takes his aggressions out on you," Sebastian states.

My pussy throbs. I look up at Griff imploringly, letting my hand drift between his legs to rub the hard cock he hasn't released yet. I'm hungry for it, for him, and I'd like to coax him out of his comfort zone. If he has some aggressions to vent, I'm more than happy to help him out with that.

"Is that true, Griff?" I ask, holding his gaze. "Are you gonna take your aggressions out on me?"

I want him to say yes, to overcome this idea he has that I'm too precious to fuck roughly, but I can't tell if I'll get my way.

Maybe not tonight, but it's going to happen, dammit. One of these nights, I'll poke the bear until he can't hold back and he fucks me with all he's got.

I feel arousal pool between my legs at the mere thought of it and I shift, squeezing my thighs together.

"You can have her mouth tonight," Sebastian tells Griff.

I'm so happy to hear that. I want my husband inside me so badly. I know *he* won't hesitate to give me what I need, and I get to play with Griff, too.

"I have the best life," I inform them.

Sebastian grins down at me as he unbuttons his black slacks. "And we have the best wife."

Griff drags himself out of observation mode and comes to life, bending to kiss his way across my soft breasts.

I close my eyes as he pops a nipple into his mouth and begins to suck on it, sending bursts of pleasure all through my body. Then my husband gives my pussy some attention, sinking a finger inside me. Griff cradles my upper body in his arm and unhooks my bra, dragging it off and tossing it on the floor so he can lavish attention on my breasts without the obstruction.

It's so sexy when they both play with me at the same time.

Griff's voice is low and rough with need. "Tell me how much you want me, Moira."

My heart sinks and I wind my arms around him, holding him close. "I don't just want you, Griff." I lean in to kiss his neck. "I need you. I need to taste you. I need to feel you. I need to be taken by you."

I can feel my words soothing him. It's so much different from my relationship with Sebastian. I tell him I need him all the time, but I never feel like *he* needs it. Sebastian has more power in our relationship than I have, but with Griff, the power is mine. I can make his day in a minute, just by needing him with the same ferocity he needs me.

Sebastian strokes my pussy, thumbing circles around my clit. He doesn't say anything, but the pleasure he stokes feels like a direct reward. I've pleased him by pleasing Griff, and that makes me want to please him more.

I keep Griff close with one arm around him, but I let the other slide down to his firm ass. I give it a squeeze, then slide my hand around the front of him and go to work freeing his cock.

"Find something you like?" he murmurs against my breast.

My heartbeat thunders in my ear while I murmur close to his, "Please, Griff."

With one last searing kiss, he pops off my nipple and straightens, pushing my hand away and dragging down the zipper of his pants. "You want this, huh?"

"Yes," I tell him, eyeing up the bulge, letting him see how

greedy I am as he lowers his pants, then shoves down his boxer briefs. His cock is hard and ready for me. I twist and brace my weight on my elbow, grasping him with my other hand and stroking his hard length.

Sebastian pulls his fingers out of me and grabs my hips, turning me over the rest of the way so I'm on my belly.

Griff changes positions so I'm between his legs and I bend to take him in my mouth while Sebastian shoves two fingers into me and squeezes the globes of my ass.

Everything feels so good. Sebastian builds up my pleasure, thrusting his fingers in and out of me while I labor over his best friend's cock. Griff tenderly moves his fingers through my hair, emitting quiet, steady sounds of pleasure.

It gets harder and harder to concentrate on pleasuring Griff as Sebastian's skilled fingers travel the familiar path toward my pleasure. He's still only using his fingers, but Sebastian can get me off with any part of his body. Sometimes I think the man could *talk* me to an orgasm if he really set his mind to it.

It's hard to hold on when they hit my G-spot so relentlessly. I don't want to leave Griff hanging, but I have to pop off, my fingers digging into his muscular thighs. I cry out desperately as Sebastian pushes me closer and closer to the edge.

"Stop," Griff says, suddenly.

I don't think he's talking to me, but my heart obeys him. I look up, betrayal flashing across my features, and to my dismay, my husband listens!

"No," I object, looking back at Sebastian. "What are you doing?"

He watches Griff, cocking his head. Ordinarily Sebastian calls the shots, but he seems curious.

My husband further betrays me, pulling his fingers from my body altogether. I sag against the mattress rather dramatically, but *fuck*, why would you steal my orgasm right at the last second like that?

"I'm never having sex with either of you again," I threaten, despite the absolute lack of truth to that statement. "Never ever. I hope you both have good relationships with your hands."

Griff smirks, pushing me off his leg and climbing behind me. I should probably pay more attention to his movements, but I'm too sexually frustrated.

"Her mouth's not enough," Griff states. "Tonight her pussy's mine."

Relief drizzles through me at least knowing despite stealing my orgasm, now Griff is going to shove his long cock inside my pussy and fill the aching void.

Amusement is heavy in my husband's voice. "I don't know, she just swore she'd never fuck us again. Think she meant it?"

It's such a ridiculous notion, a burst of laughter shoots out of Griff.

"You're both assholes," I inform them, without moving from my crater of disappointment. "Somebody better fuck me or I'm going to finish the job myself."

"Go ahead," Sebastian says, apparently unthreatened. "We'll enjoy the show and still fuck you after."

"I'm not going to turn that down," Griff agrees.

"Nope. I'll make you both lie here with blue balls," I inform them. "I'll get myself off and then my pussy will be closed for business—and my ass and my mouth, before anyone gets any ideas."

"I guess now you know how to piss off Moira," Sebastian tells Griff. "Stop fucking her just before she comes."

"I'm gonna go find a third husband," I state. "One who will give me all the orgasms I want and never leave me—"

I don't get to finish my empty threat. I feel a large presence hovering over me, a cock poking me in the lower back, then a big, rough hand closes over my mouth.

Griff.

I don't know what he's doing, but a shiver of excitement flutters through me at this sudden burst of dominance.

His face burrows into my neck, then he nibbles on my ear lobe. His gravelly voice fills my ear. "I don't fucking think so, baby. You're all ours."

I tip my head back and easily get his hand off my mouth. It slides lower to my throat. "Why don't you show me, then?"

"Is that what you need?" he murmurs, before leaving a few hot kisses along the pale column of my neck.

I shiver and nod my head. "I need you to show me I'm yours, Griff. Fuck me like you own me, like this is your only chance to prove it."

His fingers dance along my neck one more time while he seems to consider, then his hand drifts away. I swallow, waiting to see what he'll do.

He grabs my shoulder and rolls me onto my back, pinning me beneath his powerful body. Excitement surges through me as he grabs my hands and wrenches them over my head.

Oh, god, yes.

"You keep these right here," he orders.

"Yes, sir," I murmur, watching him with interest.

His eyes narrow and I have to bite back a smile. He drags his hands down my sides, then grabs my thighs and parts them, positioning himself at my entrance. Sebastian got me ready for him so I'm already drenched. Now Griff's hips rock forward and his impressive cock sinks inside me. I exhale, my eyes rolling back as he fills me. Although I'm normally obedient, my left hand drifts to his shoulder so I can hold on.

As he pulls back and then drives deep inside me, Griff's

strong hand locks around my wrist. This time he pins it above my head with much more force. Fire in his eyes, he tells me, "I said keep these up here."

I hold his gaze, my heart kicking up a couple speeds. Some of that aggression I've been hearing about is painted all over his handsome face as he shoves inside me again and again. Instead of treating my body like the glass castle he was born to protect, he pounds into me now, storming the gates, fucking me like I'm the one who's been giving him so much grief and he's here to punish me for it.

It's fucking glorious. I try to move and he doesn't let me.

Now that he's let himself off his leash, he uses me violently, shoves me around like a rag doll, flips me over and buries himself inside me from behind. He grabs a fistful of hair and yanks until I cry out, then he fucks me even harder, taking instead of asking, possessing instead of worshipping.

They're the same thing to me. Even as roughly as he handles my body now, he takes care to position me just right so he can hit my G-spot. Every delicious stroke of his cock winds me tighter and tighter, pushes me closer and closer to the precipice.

I pant for him, my body pulled helplessly against his as he slams into me. One of his hands remains fisted in my hair, but the other does the greatest thing—it drifts down to my sensitive clit. I gasp, throwing my head back against his shoulder. He rubs it while he fucks me, while he pulls my hair.

I come so hard my vision goes spotty, but Griff holds on, keeps rubbing me, keeps fucking me. He's relentless. I'm exhausted. I'm spent. Until I'm not anymore. Until my toes start to curl and he drives me toward another impossible burst of pleasure. His fingers get me there first. My body feels so drained I try to get away from him, but he locks his arm around my neck and holds me in place. "Nope. You asked for it, now you're gonna keep fucking taking it until I'm done with you."

His words make me dizzy with desire, despite my exhaustion. He thrusts harder, deeper.

He owns me, just like I wanted.

Then he makes me come again, and it hits even harder than the first two times.

I can't think—I'm just pleasure in human form, clenching around his dick, crying out, trying to release some of the pleasure erupting inside of me to make it more manageable. He groans, shoves deep, and fills me with his cum.

I don't try to move. He collapses on the bed behind me and drags me over to face him. I guess since I'm not moving, he tips my chin up, pushing my mess of dark hair back out of my face to check on me.

"You okay?"

I smile up at him and use what little strength I have left in my body to roll up against him, smashing my breasts against his side, draping my arm across his torso and pressing a kiss against his chest. "Oh, yes," I assure him.

He offers a little smile back and strokes my hair. There's so much tenderness in his touch and I'm still coasting along on a sea of bliss, so I can't keep professions from tumbling right out of my mouth.

"I love you, Griff."

His hand stills for a moment and I hear him swallow. Then his fingers resume their path through my hair and he murmurs back, "I love you, Moira."

The bed creaks behind me as Sebastian sinks into his spot. I realize we completely left him out, and I roll over halfway to look at him. "I'm sorry, honey. Give me a minute to get feeling back in my arms and I'll get you off."

Sebastian smirks, shaking his head. "You're comfy. Don't worry about it. You can get me in the morning."

I reach back for his hand. He twines his fingers together with mine, but I need him closer. "Cuddle with me."

He scoots close, resting a hand on my hip and pressing his strong chest against my back. I can hear the steady rhythm of Griff's heartbeat beneath my head, and feel the heat rolling off my husband as he cradles my body from behind.

Now, everything is perfect.

24

GRIFF

I wake up to the unmistakable sounds of Moira getting fucked in the shower.

The door is cracked open; I can hear the steady spray of water, the slap of skin against skin. Moira cries out sharply at regular intervals. Sebastian says filthy fucking things to her.

My cock stirs with interest. Doing my best to ignore *them*, I stretch out on the pillow-top mattress and catch the lavender scent of Moira on the pillow next to mine. A helpless smile splits my face.

I'm fucking happy. I shouldn't be. My life is still in shambles, same as last night when I was miserable. Nothing's really changed, so I should still feel like a sorry bastard in a shitty situation, but how can I when I get to wake up like this?

All night Moira slept snuggled up against my side, content as a kitten wedged there between me and Seb.

I never dreamed we could both have this much. Sure, I've been riding Sebastian's coattails professionally for years, pouring money I didn't care about into his ideas, working toward his vision, but that wasn't personally fulfilling. None of that ever made me happy. That was for Seb. It was *his* dream to have financial success, to make a name for himself. He's the one who wanted all that stuff.

I wanted *this*. A family. A home. Something I could always count on, a safe place to call mine. I wanted to let in happiness, I just never felt comfortable enough to do it.

While I never consciously admitted it, being with Ashley never had the feel of permanence. I had settled into the idea that she was it for me—I married her, after all—but I never had this feeling of being where I'm meant to be. I found an abandoned building I could squat in for a time, but it never felt like it belonged to me.

Even sharing Moira, this does. I'm sharing her with my best friend in the world, the only permanent person I've ever had in my life.

It's not something I would have sought out myself, but now I think I almost prefer sharing with him to having something that's only mine. Maybe I failed to keep my own shoddy marriage afloat, but Seb can hold a ship steady through the most brutal of storms. Even if we eventually hit rougher waters, there's more stability with all three of us working to keep things steady. What could be better than the three of us taking on life as one cohesive unit?

Seb and Moira emerge from the bathroom together. That first night I felt like an interloper, but now I'm perfectly comfortable with it. It doesn't bother me that Moira's face is flushed, her expression a little dreamy, and I know it's because of what he was just doing to her.

Especially after Ashley cheated, I would've thought something like that would rankle, but it's entirely different; there's no deception here, no malice, no selfishness. No one is doing anything to hurt anyone else. Moira isn't just mine or his now, she's ours. We both love her, we both fuck her, and that's the way it is.

Absorbed in his own thoughts a world away from mine, Seb rakes his fingers through his damp hair and heads for the closet to get dressed. I want to know what's on his mind—especially since it's probably my shit—but Moira climbs up on the bed and steals my attention before I can ask.

"Good morning, handsome." She's wearing a fluffy bath robe instead of clothing this morning. I rarely see her without her hair and make-up done, but I like the intimacy of it. I lock an arm around her waist and drag her on top of me. She grins and leans in to give me a tender kiss.

"Good shower?" I murmur playfully.

"Could you hear us?"

I nod my head at the door to the adjoining master bathroom. "Door was open. Sounded like a fun shower."

"I'll probably have to take another one after I go for my run," she says, running her hands across my chest. "Feel free to join me."

Between her invitation and the sensation of her soft fingers against my skin, my head is suddenly flooded with images of fucking her in the shower, and my cock with a vehement desire to be buried deep inside her.

"I will definitely accept that invite," I tell her. "Provided I'm still here by then."

Seb steps out of the closet, buttoning up his dress shirt. Apparently he caught the tail end of that comment, because he says, "Today's your day off, isn't it?"

I glance at him as Moira climbs off me and goes over to help him with his tie. He certainly doesn't need help with it, but I get the impression it's part of their routine.

"It was supposed to be," I remark. "Since I flaked yesterday though, I figured I should probably work today."

Shaking his head, Seb meets my gaze. "Nah, you need a day off. Take it. Stay here with Moira. Relax. If you need to get any work done, just do it from here. I have a late meeting tonight anyway so I won't be home for dinner."

Apparently, this is the first Moira is hearing about it. "You won't?"

His attention shifts to her as she smoothes her hand down his shirtfront, over the perfect line of his tie. "You two are on your own. Modified date night," he offers, lightly.

"I can work with that," Moira says.

Since I'm planning to shower with Moira after her run, I just pull on a pair of sweats to go down for breakfast. Seb takes a seat and starts reading his paper while Moira makes the coffee.

"What can I do?" I ask Moira, leaning against the counter and watching her fiddle around at the coffee maker.

Flicking a surprised glance at me, she tells me, "You can cut the grapefruit in half, if you'd like."

I make a face at her since she knows I hate grapefruit. "You're not gonna make me eat it, are you?" I ask, reaching for the cutting board.

"No, I'll be nice to you. Though the health benefits—"

"I'm okay with dying a few weeks early if it means I never have to eat a grapefruit."

Moira shakes her head at me. "Your priorities are all out of order. It doesn't taste that bad."

"It's gross," I say, grabbing the fruit and slicing it in half.

"Thank you," she says sweetly, retrieving the halves and putting them on small plates. She drops one off on her end of the table and takes the other to Seb. He pauses in reading the paper for a kiss and a thank you, then she comes back to start on the rest of breakfast.

"What else?" I ask.

"I'm just making eggs, I don't really need help. You can get out the butter and jelly for the toast, if you'd like." Glancing back at the table, she tells Seb, "See? He helps me cook and everything."

Without looking up from his paper, Seb remarks, "Why do you think I got you a second husband? You're welcome."

"I can do dishes, too," I volunteer.

"And laundry?" Moira asks, with exaggerated gusto. "Best second husband ever."

"Knock yourself out," Seb tells me, but he can't help smirking. "You know you don't have to work so hard to impress her, right? She's already yours."

I roll my eyes at him. "Says you."

"I find you both exceptionally impressive," Moira states, preemptively cutting off any competition we could cook up. "I have the best of both worlds and I couldn't be happier. What about you guys? Both getting enough Moira time? Of course *I'm* satisfied; I have two men. If anyone ever needs more of me, you'll have to tell me."

"I get more of you than I ever got from a woman I *didn't* have to share," I state.

She wrinkles her nose up. "Yuck. Ashley's on my shit list."

"Mine, too," I offer, dryly.

Now Seb glances up from his paper. "I told Griff he should move in with us once we get everything settled."

Moira brightens. "I love that idea."

Once the food is cooked, we all sit down to breakfast together. It's so strange, sitting together like this every morning. I enjoy it, but it's not the kind of thing I've done since a couple of the try-hard foster homes I was shuffled in and out of.

Back then, whether because it was or I was just a self-defensive asshole, it always felt phony. The kind of thing people usually do as a family, only those people *weren't* my family. They were glorified innkeepers that I would have to move on from a few months later.

This isn't, though. For once in my life, I have permanence. For once in my life, I have a family of my own—traditional or not.

It's something I've thought about a time or two given Seb and I rarely use protection with Moira, but since we're doing this, I figure I might as well bring it up now. "I have a question about the future. Or, potentially the present, depending on the answer."

Seb infers by my delivery that this is going to be a serious thing, so he puts down his paper and meets my gaze. "What's that?"

"We both have sex with Moira."

"Correct."

"Neither of us consistently uses condoms. You never do. I have on occasion, but not on a regular basis. So... pregnancy? Is that something we should discuss?"

Moira replies quickly, before Seb has to. "I'm on the pill."

I glance at her, taking in her eagerness to resolve and file away this topic. I can't imagine Moira not wanting kids, so Seb must be the problem.

"Okay," I say, looking back at him. "So, we've got it covered now, but what about later?"

Seb sips his hot coffee, eyeing me over the brim. From the look on his face and the glance he cuts in Moira's direction, I gather he would have preferred I ask him about this without her present, but that's bullshit. She's more involved in this decision than either of us. She's the one who would be *carrying* a baby. So how the hell is that supposed to work?

"We're not looking to have kids just yet," he says, vaguely.

"But when we do. If we're planning to do this long-term, that's something to consider, right? How the hell are we supposed to do that? There's two of us and one of her. Do we take turns? You get first kid, I get second? Do we both just fuck her without protection and see whose sperm gets there first? Do we all even want kids? I want kids. I assume Moira wants kids. Obviously, I didn't think you were going to be involved in this part of my relationship, so I never thought to ask you about it."

"We'll have kids eventually," he assures me.

"But which one of us?"

"You know," Moira begins, in a tone I can tell means she thinks she's being helpful, "There's this HBO show called *Big Love* that we should totally watch. It's not our situation, obviously, and it's multiple wives instead of husbands, but they have kids. It is done. Obviously, the show is fictional, but... I think kids are pretty adaptable. Everyone's parents do something to make them ill-adjusted; at least our lack of convention is born from a place of love. Could be worse. And kids have multiple parental figures all the time. It's no different than if Seb and I got divorced and I married Griff, except there's no bitterness and we all live together as a happy, functioning family. I think it'll be fine. I think we can be completely functional in this arrangement with a baby—and it would be years before we even had to explain. Babies don't take inventory of their family members." Cutting a look at Seb to make sure he understands, she adds, "I still want babies. This does not change that."

"I realize that, honey," he replies dutifully, then cuts me another look of mild annoyance. "Thanks for this, Griff."

I shrug unapologetically. "It's an important thing to know."

"We can figure that out when it comes up."

"Moira, do you even want to have babies with me?" I ask her. Obviously Seb is the man she married, the man she planned her life out with. Even if I'm a welcome addition, something she has adjusted to and decided she could want, having kids together is another level of intimacy.

Reaching across the table, she places her hand over mine. "I think you'll be a wonderful father, Griff. I'm not sure how this works, I'd rather let Sebastian work out the details, but as long as it makes everyone happy...."

"When it's time," Sebastian adds more firmly. "Which is not right now. Moira's adjusting like a sport, but let's not leap ahead, hm? Give her time to adjust. Let the honeymoon period wind down first, for fuck's sake."

I shoot him a mild look of annoyance. "I'm not trying to leap ahead; I'm just trying to figure out how this works in the big picture."

"It works the way we need it to," he states. "I'm always looking at the big picture, but this stuff will come up when it comes up. It's too soon to worry about it now."

Bringing up babies at breakfast, it turns out, is a good way to get rid of Seb. He finishes his breakfast in record time, kisses Moira, and leaves for work.

It's weird as hell staying here with Moira after he leaves. I don't take a lot of time off in general—one day a week is good enough for me—and since things have been going so shitty with Ashley, even that has been too much. A day off just means time to think, time to stew, time I'm not busy and I can get lost down a rabbit hole of stress and aggravation.

Now days off are going to mean something different. It's foreign but peaceful the way Moira goes about her routine. I stay in the kitchen and talk to her while she cleans up after breakfast. When she's done with that, she gets out her sketchpad and oil pencils and draws for a bit.

I relax on the couch and catch up on a few emails while she works.

It's calm and uneventful and I can't wait for a hundred more days like this one.

Once she has drawn until she feels her food has digested, apparently, she gathers up her supplies and tells me, "I'm going to change into my workout clothes."

"You want company?"

Flashing me a smile, she says, "You just want to get laid, don't you? Come on up, I'll go a round before my run. Just don't wear me out so much that I can't finish. I've gotta get in two miles."

A burst of surprised laughter shoots out of me. "I meant did you want me to go running with you?"

"Oh!" Chuckling, she says, "Sorry, I'm in Sebastian mode. Sure, that would be great. He never runs with me. I asked him to once when we first started dating—I figured he clearly works out, right? Or he's just blessed with incredible genes. But he won't run."

I shake my head. "Nope. I will, though. Let me finish answering this question real fast and I'll be right up. I'm not saying no to the sex, if you're still offering," I call after her as she heads for the stairs.

"Wait until we get back and we can have shower sex," she calls back, her voice muffled as she heads for her bedroom.

It is a *damn* good day off.

25

SEBASTIAN

When Moira and I first started dating years ago, she surmised a certain truth about me early on.

"You're a man who does what needs doing, aren't you?" she asked one night, a look in her eyes like it impressed the hell out of her.

I'll be honest, I like impressing the hell out of Moira, but whether she liked it or she didn't, that answer would have been the same.

Yes.

I *am* a man who does what needs doing.

Doesn't matter if it's pretty or nice or fair. Doesn't even matter if it's what I *want* to do, in a lot of cases. I'm a realistic man. I know when to push my own agenda, and when to accept I can't change a thing doing it my way. I know that in order to survive, in order to rise, in order to thrive, sometimes you have to make certain adjustments.

Sometimes you have to do things you don't want to do,

learn to accept things that don't seem right, make compromises more naïve versions of you never thought you'd make.

In life, you will always end up surprising yourself—it's your call whether it's because you get further than you thought you would, or you end up a disappointment even to your own damn self.

Me, I've only ever entertained one option.

Whatever I had to do, whichever lines I had to smudge, I would never become that disappointment.

In the interest of success over ego, adapting to change over clinging stubbornly to what doesn't work, I have *become* a man who does what needs doing.

Every compromise comes at a cost, but so does being a pussy whose life falls apart because he's too caught up on his own fucking principles.

That's what I tell myself, sitting at this bar, sipping on this drink, waiting for Donovan to free up so he can give me a few minutes of his very expensive time.

A young woman in a tight red dress sidles up next to me, stealing not-so-subtle glances at me from time to time while I drink. She's on my left side and I know she checked my finger for a ring—clearly visible on the bar top here—but after a few minutes she still says, "Hey."

I glance at her, but I'm not in the mood to be nice tonight, so I don't respond.

Her daddy must not have loved her, 'cause she gets more interested.

"Strong, silent type, huh?" she teases, bravely bumping her arm against mine. She shifts and pushes her boobs closer, in case it somehow slipped my attention that she's attractive. "My name's Belinda, what's yours?"

Her voice is loud in my ear as she tries to talk over the fucking music.

I ignore her again.

"I know you can hear me," she says playfully.

Jesus, she is persistent. I hold up my hand to show her my ring, since ignoring the fuck out of her isn't making my point. "I'm married."

"Lucky lady," she says, though her tone is still flirty.

Wouldn't be so fucking lucky if I cared about another woman flirting with me at the bar, now, would she? I don't say that. I pull out my phone and check the time.

Come on, Donovan, hurry the fuck up.

"I'm really drunk," Belinda says so fucking loudly. She leans close. I know it's just an excuse to get closer to me, but at least she's not screaming in my fucking ear anymore. "Maybe drunk enough to make a bad decision. How about you don't even tell me your name?"

"Wasn't planning to."

"You're really hot," she tells me.

"I know," I deadpan.

She grins. "I like you."

"You need to work on your self-esteem, sweetheart," I tell her, tipping back my glass and finishing it off. I tap the bar top to the get the bartender's attention.

"Sweetheart?" she repeats, delighted.

I roll my eyes. Of course that's the only fucking part of that sentence she heard. The bartender approaches, and I tell him, "One more."

"Long day?" Belinda persists.

"Yep," I answer.

"What is it you do?"

The bartender makes quick work of getting me my drink. By

the time he slides it across the counter at me, Belinda accepts that I'm not going to answer her question.

Of course, if she hangs out in this club, that's probably not outside the norm. A lot of shady fucking people hang out here. The smart ones keep their mouth shut about what kind of business they're in.

"Can't tell me?" she asks, suddenly serious. "That's okay, I get it," she assures me, like I might be really worried. "But, like, if you do want to tell me, you can. I'm cool. I know the drill around here. Do you know Roscoe? We went out a couple times. We didn't fuck," she adds for some reason, like this might turn me off.

"Do you ever stop talking?"

Smiling slyly, she says, "When my mouth is otherwise occupied, I do."

"Are you a hooker?"

Her eyes widen. "No! Why would you think I'm a hooker?"

"You have about four inches of fabric on and you're throwing yourself at me even though I'm clearly not interested. Maybe you're a damaged individual, or maybe you're a hungry hooker."

Her jaw drops like she can't even believe what an asshole I am, but a firm hand on my shoulder stops me from having to respond to this little pain in the ass.

A tall, dark-haired man I've seen a few times stands behind me. He's probably never saved anyone from anything before, since his job is to do exactly the opposite, but I'm sure happy to see him.

"Donovan's ready to see you."

"Fucking finally," I mutter under my breath, grabbing my drink and spinning around on my bar stool. I hop off without sparing another glance at the hungry hooker.

"She's a pain in the ass, isn't she?" the man asks, mildly amused.

"Jesus Christ, yes. Like a dog with a fucking bone."

"Yeah, she's been around. Probably got excited thinking there was new meat on the table," he says, chuckling deeply.

I don't remark further as he leads me through the throng of people.

I see Donovan and his entourage tucked in a long black leather booth.

Donovan sits in the middle, his right arm draped across the narrow shoulders of some traditionally attractive redhead. I don't trouble myself to try to remember her name. Even if I could remember the name of the last girl he brought up, it would almost certainly not be this one. He changes women like he changes suits, and as a pair of women in short skirts pass by his line of sight, I can already see this one doesn't have much time left.

So does his flavor of the week. Appearing stressed, she turns suddenly and starts kissing his neck.

He pushes her away like an inanimate object and offers an amiable smile at me as I approach.

"Sebastian St. Clair—to what do I owe this great honor?"

He can't help mocking people, I swear to god. Ordinarily, I'm not a man who appreciates someone talking like that straight to my face, but ordinarily, I'm not a man who pays an "operating tax" to a rising kingpin, either; I adjust where I have to.

"Donovan," I offer, bowing my head once in acknowledgment.

Gesturing with his hand to the edge of the curved booth to his left, he tells me, "Have a seat."

I look at the spot, but it's not empty.

Or, it wasn't. As soon as the man seated there realizes where his boss is pointing, he swiftly gets up and finds somewhere else to sit.

Fuck, I like that.

I resist the pull, shake it off, and take a seat.

I have plenty. I have safety and stability—I'm not going to envy the power of a man like this.

"I must say, I was surprised to hear from you," Donovan tells me.

The first time this asshole sent his men in to shake me down, it pissed me off. You hear of shit like that, but you never expect to experience it first-hand.

Griff was mad as hell. Couldn't believe the gall of these guys, told me no way in hell were we going to pay it.

My pride agreed with him at first, but then I thought on it a little more.

It was one of those rare situations where I could not control the circumstances people were putting me in, I could only control my response to it. An old Irishman who owned a pub down the block had already told Donovan's men they could go fuck themselves before they ever saw a dime from him, and when he turned up with a busted up face, a shattered ankle, and a broken arm, everyone understood why. It sent a message to everyone else that no was not an acceptable response.

That wasn't why I decided to pay him, though.

I didn't make his men come back. I brought my tax right into the club myself—the last time I stepped foot in this fucking place—because I was going to control the situation.

I didn't give the money to the punk-ass kids who thought they were something, or even to his enforcer. No. I brought my envelope of money and hand-delivered it to the boss, because I wanted him to remember me. I wanted him to know my name and my face. I wanted him to know I was handing over my "protection" money because I wanted to open up a distant but amiable relationship with him, *not* because I'm cowering and bullied in my office, too afraid of a broken arm to tell him no, but reluctant to pay up, nonetheless.

You can't always control your circumstances, but you can *always* control the narrative. You just have to be able to control *yourself*, and I'm damn good at that.

Griff would never be sitting here in this club with this man. He would have been stubborn and resisted. If he did give in—not because Donovan hurt *him*, but because he went after his loved ones (the step after broken limbs, as the Irish barkeep's college-aged granddaughter found out soon after)—he would still be salty about it. He would still think of Donovan as scum, of himself as better, and instead of using a dark connection to his advantage, he would continue to fucking struggle.

Not me.

I'll lie down with dogs if I need to; I'm not afraid of a few fleas.

Now Donovan sits here and smiles at me like we're old pals. "What can I do for you, Sebastian?"

I flick a glance around the crowded club. The music is blaring, and even though we're close enough to talk, this is a matter of some delicacy and I don't really want to shout it from the rooftops.

Clearing my throat, I hunch forward and tell him, "I was hoping we could discuss this a little more privately."

He watches me for a moment, expression blank, eyes sharp. I understand his selectiveness in who he takes a private audience with—he's a man that a lot of other men would like to see dead, after all—but after a moment, he finally nods and sits forward.

"All right," he says. "Roscoe, come with us."

The dark-haired man who accompanied me over lifts a dark eyebrow. "Seriously? You want *Roscoe* in there with you over me?"

Donovan smiles, slapping the man on the shoulder. "Settle down, Sebastian's a friend. Aren't you, Sebastian?"

He must be seriously hurting for friends if he thinks I'm one of his, but naturally, I nod my head. Sure, I'll be the fucker's friend for the next fifteen minutes.

We walk past the private rooms lining the hall. I hear loud moans coming from inside a few of them, but I don't bat an eye. This isn't even a strip club so you wouldn't expect sleazy shit like this to be going on, but there's been plenty of speculation about his prostitution ring. That's probably what's going on in there.

"How's your wife, Sebastian?"

I tense just hearing him mention my wife, even if he doesn't know her name or what she looks like. I might not be opposed to the potential benefits of having an amiable relationship with him over a hostile one, but I still know he's a shady fucking snake, and I don't like him even thinking of Moira in a vague, conceptual way.

"The family's fine," I say, vaguely.

He opens an office door and steps inside first. I follow, and Roscoe comes in and closes the door behind me.

Donovan stops immediately and turns to face me. Doesn't offer me a seat, but I'm glad; I don't want to be here any longer than I have to. "Now, what's so urgent we needed to speak in private?"

"I have a bit of a situation," I tell him.

"You're paid through the end of the month, so I don't think we have any business right now."

"Yeah, well, I'm paying you for your protection, right?" I ask, nodding at him. "I'm in need of a little… protection."

He cocks his head curiously. "You are? Who's bothering you?"

"It's not—" I sigh, raking a hand through my hair. "It's not a business matter. It's personal. Someone's causing me problems. I've tried to handle it through more conventional channels, but she won't go away, and she's making my life harder than I want it to be."

With a knowing nod, he said, "I understand. Mistress?"

I frown. "No. It's Griff's wife, actually."

His eyebrows rise. "You're fucking your partner's wife? Damn, that *is* a tangled fucking web."

I want to smile at how backward he has all this, but the less I tell him about my home life, the better. "No, I'm not fucking her. Griff is trying to divorce her, but she's making it difficult. The long and short of it is, she's a real headache, and at this point we both just want her gone. Dealt with. Permanently."

"I see." His tone is solemn, but he doesn't seem unwilling to help. "You understand, of course, that a situation like this is not included in the protection I provide you?"

"Of course. I'll pay separately for this."

"All cash, all up front," he adds. "Once the deal is made, there's no backing out. You get cold feet, you don't get a refund."

"I understand all that. I'm not half-cocked, here. This is what needs to happen. I've made my peace with it, now I just want it done and over with."

Nodding once, he asks, "How soon do you need it done?"

"As soon as possible. I need it to look like an accident, though. Or a suicide. Just nothing obvious. Since she's been dragging out the divorce, Griff is the first person they're going to look to as a suspect if anything looks off."

"Of course," he says, like he's a professional and he understands. "I'll let you know when it's going down so you can make sure you both have alibis. Just in case you *were* fucking her, you'll want your ass covered, too."

"I *wasn't* fucking her."

"Look, a man shows up wanting a woman dead, ten out of ten times he was fucking her. I'm not your wife; you don't have to lie to me, Sebastian."

"I'm not..." I trail off, shaking my head. "I never fucked her. She's causing Griff problems, so that's a problem for me. I'm just a hell of a friend, all right?"

He watches me for a moment, debating whether or not to believe me. I don't know why it matters so much to him, but it seems like he doesn't like being lied to. I bet he's a paranoid motherfucker.

Finally, he must decide he believes me. "I like that. Good friends are hard to come by. I look out for my friends, too."

Griff's comment about Ashley fucking around with Danny Long comes to mind, but last I knew, he and Donovan weren't on good terms. That probably won't be an issue, but I figure I should tell him anyway. "His wife... well, no two ways about it, she's a whore. She's been sleeping around on Griff and Danny Long is one of the guys she's seeing now. I don't know—or want to know—your business, but in case you have any crossing paths, I thought I should mention that up front."

Shaking his head dismissively, he says, "Nah, he's nothing. I appreciate your honesty, though. I'll tell you what. I'm gonna do this job for you, and I'm gonna give you the friends and family discount," he tells me.

"Great. Is there a punch card I can get, too?"

He grins at me, but even his amusement is mildly threatening. "Buy the first nine hits, get your tenth free? No, but thanks for the suggestion. I'll see what I can do about that."

"What exactly *is* the friends and family discount?" I ask, in case that's a real thing and he's not just being a smartass.

"The friends and family discount means this: this is the first favor you've asked of me, right? So, I'm gonna cut the cost for you in half."

I know there's a catch, so I wait for it instead of responding.

Smiling faintly, he adds, "But then you'll owe me a favor. Now, could be you get lucky and I never need anything from you. Maybe you'll live happily ever after with your discounted hit and that'll be that. Or maybe you won't. Maybe I'll need something from you down the line, and no questions asked, you'll give it to me."

This makes me pretty fucking uncomfortable. Amiable or not, this is not a man I want to owe a favor.

Of course, this is a mere formality. Donovan is being pleasant enough right now, but I know what he's capable of. If Donovan needed a favor from me, he would demand it whether I owed him one or not.

So I nod my head once and say, "Of course. I'm always happy to help my friends in their time of need."

A dark smile claims his lips and he steps forward, clapping me on the back. "So am I, Sebastian. So am I."

26

MOIRA

Peace flows through my veins as Griff's big, rough fingers skate up and down my arm. I'm on the couch in front of him, sitting between his legs, and I swear, the man is trying to put me to sleep.

"You're not getting out of this movie," I say, leaning my head back to look up at him. "If I fall asleep, I'll just make you watch it tomorrow."

Smiling faintly, he bends to drop a brief kiss on my forehead. "I'm not trying to put you to sleep. I just like touching you."

"I like you touching me, too," I tell him, running a hand down his muscular thigh.

"Good, 'cause I'm gonna be doing a lot of it. I've got a lot of time to make up for."

I grab his hand, bringing it to my lips so I can place a kiss on the back of it. "We've got nothing but time. We'll get you all caught up, I promise."

Since it was his left hand I grabbed, his gaze drifts to his empty ring finger. Even though it clearly ended badly, then she dragged the remnants of their relationship over a bed of nails and made it even worse, I wonder if he feels any remorse over the ending of his marriage. He loved her once, so maybe it's still weird for him.

"How are you doing with all that?" I ask him, locking my fingers together with his, looking at our joined hands, at the difference in size. "I told you we could still talk about it if you needed to, and I meant it."

"I know you did," he says, evenly. "You ever get to the end of a relationship and, looking at the long and short of it, all you can think is, 'what the fuck was I thinking?'"

I crack a smile. "Yes. The minute man. The cheater Gwen wrote lipstick letters to."

"Yeah, well, basically it's a whole lot of that, plus I'm gonna have to pay for the privilege."

"Whatever we have to pay, it'll be worth it," I assure him, squeezing his hand. "We'll get you free of her clutches once and for all. Now you've got Sebastian to run things for you, and he would never let either one of us get into a mess like this."

At that, Griff rolls his eyes. "He's your husband, not mine."

I shrug innocently. "I mean, if you guys felt like getting affectionate…"

"Hey," he says, squeezing my side.

"I'm just saying, sharing is caring. A little kiss, a little caress. You love each other."

"And we both like to fuck women," he reminds me.

"You can totally fuck me after. I've had the mental image before, and it doesn't turn me off, I'll just say that."

Locking his arm around my neck, he tugs my head back and gives me an upside down kiss. "Don't make it weird."

"Fine," I concede, reaching behind his neck and drawing him

closer. Between kisses, I murmur, "You can just kiss me instead, how about that?"

"Now, *that* I can get behind."

I get lost in his kisses. His hand drifts to the column of my neck and my heart kicks up, remembering keenly how hot it was when he took me without holding back. I never want him to hold back again. I want him to own me. Maybe he was cautious before because Sebastian clearly owns my ass, but hell, they're partners in everything else, why not this?

Thinking about the way he pushed me down into the mattress gets me hot. I reach between his legs and rub him, enjoying the way he stiffens beneath my touch.

"Spread your legs," he says.

Without hesitation, my knees fall apart. I shudder with anticipation as his hand moves between my thighs and he presses his big palm against my pussy. My head drifts back against the wall of his chest. "Griff," I murmur, my voice already full of need.

His deep voice tinged with amusement, he kisses the shell of my ear and lightly traces my folds. "You need something, baby?"

My gaze jerks up as I see headlights through the window. Sebastian is home.

It crosses my mind that we should probably stop, but Griff's thoughts go in exactly the opposite direction and he pushes a finger inside me.

"We don't have time," I tell him.

"I'm in no hurry," he assures me.

I should be going to greet my husband, not lying here letting Griff stroke my pussy. Griff doesn't seem to agree, though; he keeps me pinned there with his skilled fingers inside me, with his kisses on my neck, his big hand groping my breast.

It's hard to argue with that logic.

A thrill shoots through me when I hear Sebastian drop his keys onto the end table in the foyer. I'm not entirely sure how he'll like walking into this—I don't know what kind of day he's had or what he needs from me right now. Assuming it isn't me spread on the couch letting Griff's fingers explore my body, he may be mildly annoyed.

I look up as he comes into view, wanting to see his face. As usual, he looks unaffected. Maybe a little tired. As soon as he sees us on the couch, his gaze drifts to my pussy, to Griff's fingers playing with me.

"Date night's going well, I see," he remarks casually, tugging his jacket off and hanging it across the chair in the corner. Then he prowls around to the front of the couch, dropping into the empty space on the other side, closest to my legs.

"How was work?" Griff asks casually, kneading my breast.

"Uneventful," Sebastian replies, unbuckling his belt and drawing it off.

"Get everything all caught up?" Griff asks, pushing a second finger into my body and drawing out a helpless moan.

"All taken care of," Sebastian says, tossing his belt on the floor and unzipping his slacks. "I'm glad to see you guys haven't sated all of your baser urges today; I am in dire need of a good fuck."

I can't help smiling, though my breath hitches as Griff thrusts his fingers deep and invites his thumb to the party, nudging my clit. "It's been so many hours since you last had me, hasn't it?"

"Two hours is too many," Sebastian states, lifting his hips and kicking his pants off. "Thirteen is approaching torture."

I feel the same way. Since I already had Griff once while he was at work, I should be less needy. Somehow I'm not. Sex with

Griff is great, but he's not Sebastian. It wouldn't matter if Griff spent the entire day fucking me while he was gone; I always crave my husband when he comes home. "Well, I'll be happy to work extra hard pleasing my husband," I assure him, watching as he gets up on his knees between my legs.

Grabbing onto my jaw, uncaring of Griff's arm reaching down my side, his fingers still inside me, my husband comes down on top of me. His blue eyes narrow and he says, "Damn right you will."

My heart soars, but before I can utter a word, his mouth claims mine and all my words escape. I lift my legs to wrap them around his hips, but Griff is still fingering me.

It's intoxicating, Griff still inside me in some way, my husband's hips smashing against me. The exhilaration of having them both on me like this ratchets up my arousal. Little helpless sounds slip out of me between kisses, then while Sebastian ravages my mouth, Griff starts kissing my neck.

Fireworks explode in too many sensitive areas and I can't take it anymore. I come already, crying out, riding Griff's hand, holding onto Sebastian, terrified he'll abandon my mouth.

Much of the strength leaves my body and I sag back against Griff. He withdraws his fingers from my body. I can feel his arousal pressing into my back as Sebastian pushes me even harder against Griff's muscular length. The raw physicality of these two men is too much to bear, but boy, am I up to trying.

"On the floor," Sebastian commands, tearing his mouth from mine.

My legs are still a little shaky, but I slide on the floor anyway. I sit back on my heels and peer up at him, awaiting further direction. Licking my lips, I watch intently as Sebastian strokes his cock. God, I love that perfect instrument. I inch forward, raising big, innocent eyes at him. "Want a little help with that?"

"I do."

That's all the direction I need. I crawl forward and climb between his legs, grabbing that much loved cock he's handling and close my own fingers around the base. I look up and hold his gaze as I open wide and take his head into my mouth, shallow at first, using my lips and enjoying the salty taste of him. God, I love the way he looks at me. He looks at me like I'm his everything, the very blood moving through his veins, the only reason he wakes up in the morning, the only person he could ever imagine going to sleep next to at night. He fills me up in every single way—and breaks me down in the playful, sexy ways we both enjoy.

Overcome with a burst of love, I lavish all that feeling on his cock. I'm already giving and giving, but he wants more. Shoving his fingers through my hair, he grabs a fistful and pushes more of himself into my throat. I struggle to take him all, not prepared for the push, but I meet my husband's greed with generosity. The more he takes, the more I want to give him.

His roaring desire always feeds mine. He consumes me, and I happily burn up with him every single night.

As I suck Sebastian, my gaze darts over to Griff. He's watching me, so his hot gaze lands on mine as soon as I look his way. While I've been pleasuring my husband, Griff must have been undressing; now he's naked as he strokes his big cock and gets it ready for me.

I moan around Sebastian's cock, throbbing with need. He grips my hair harder, uses my mouth more roughly.

"You can play with his cock soon," my husband assures me.

I massage his balls, taking him more eagerly in response.

A moment later, he yanks me off him and gives me a little push toward Griff. "His turn," Sebastian says.

I catch myself and crawl between Griff's legs. He's glaring over at Seb, probably for the push, so I grab his cock and steal his attention. I lick my way along his length, then hold his gaze while I run my tongue over his head, then take it deep in my mouth.

"Oh, fuck," he says, working his fingers into my hair so much more gently than Sebastian did. Reverently.

His tenderness makes my heart kick up a couple beats. I close my eyes and do my best to pay it back, stroking him, sucking him, worshiping every inch of his cock with my mouth.

I wouldn't stop, but Sebastian grabs my hair and pulls me off. He's in a rough mood tonight. I like it, but Griff doesn't, so I wish he would've saved it for when it's just us.

He drags me back and pushes me down on the floor.

"Hey, knock it the fuck off," Griff says.

"Don't start with me," Sebastian says.

"Griff," I say, my stomach fluttering with nerves. I reach a hand out to him like I want him, and even though he still tosses a look of annoyance at my husband, he joins me on the floor. I offer him a little smile and rub his side.

"Take her mouth," Sebastian directs, pushing my legs apart and climbing between them.

"Like this?" Griff asks, mildly surprised. "She's on her back. She'll have no control."

"I know," Sebastian states, like that's the point.

I let my hand drift down to Griff's thigh and I caress it, coaxing him nearer. Coaxing him to follow Sebastian's orders. "Take my mouth, Griff. Please."

Muttering a low oath, he stares at me for another moment before ultimately giving in and climbing on top of me. My brain works to keep up with my body and Seb's directions, but pinned down like this, my body is throwing off some mixed signals. Sebastian pins me down from time to time and I love it, but I've never been dominated like *this* before. I've never had two men pinning me to the ground, leaving me literally no control over anything. With Sebastian being in a weird mood and Griff quick to fight, though, I put my big girl panties on and brace a hand on one of the large, muscular thighs pinning me to my living room floor.

"Are you sure about this?" Griff asks.

Instead of answering, I reach for his cock and stroke it until he pushes it toward my mouth. I open my mouth for him in silent invitation.

"Don't take it easy on her," Sebastian says. "Make her take every fucking inch of you."

As if I'm not wet enough, he has to go and say a thing like that.

He's not going to start fucking me until Griff does, so I moan around Griff's cock, sucking the tip until the temptation is too much and he plunges forward. A litany of tiny moan-like sounds slip out of me, then my husband powers forth and buries his cock inside my pussy. I cry out and Griff tries to pause, but I grab his thigh, silently begging him not to.

Fuck me, Griff. Just fuck me.

Sebastian knows the score. There's nothing tentative about the force behind his thrusts, no reluctance as he buries his massive cock inside me again and again. I'm dizzy with pleasure, pinned helplessly and used as roughly as they want to use me.

Pleasure whips through me like a live wire, with the force of Sebastian's thrusts, the invasion of Griff's cock moving in and out of my throat. I don't know how I can bear this much pleasure, and then Griff starts playing with my tits. His blunt thumbs pinch my nipple and I groan.

"Oh, fuck," he says lowly, his baser instincts pushing him to thrust deeper, harder—to think of his pleasure instead of mine.

"You like this, sweetheart?" Sebastian asks.

I moan helplessly, sucking Griff's cock harder so he can groan my approval for me.

Sebastian chuckles lowly, pumping his hips forward and pounding into me again. "I'll take that as a yes. Good. Suck him harder. Get him off. I want him to pour his cum down your throat, sweetheart."

My fingers dig into Griff's thighs as he talks. I stroke Griff with my tongue, holding onto his thigh with one hand, grabbing his firm ass with the other and pulling him closer. I want to please my husband, I want to please Griff—it's a bonus that pleasing Griff pleases Sebastian.

"Fuck, Moira," Griff says, eyes closed as he runs his fingers through my hair. "Your mouth is pure magic, baby."

His words send a rush right through me. I climb higher and higher as he grips my head and gets lost in me, in the pleasure I bring him, cresting when he groans and empties himself down my throat, just like Sebastian told him to.

Griff climbs off and collapses on the floor beside me.

Now I can focus on my husband.

He wastes no time taking over as my sole user, the sole provider of my pleasure. He pushes my legs high and fucks me harder, having more freedom now to twist and move me however he wants. My heart feels so full as he hovers over me, his blue eyes boring into mine. I can't help reaching up a hand and caressing his beautiful jawline.

"I love you, Sebastian."

Sparing me a tender little smile, he assures me, "I love you, too. More than anything."

He fills me up with his love *and* his cock until I'm full to bursting. Until my pussy clenches around him and I cry out, clinging to his powerful body as he thrusts through my orgasm and growls through his own.

I'm weak as he comes down on top of me, but I wrap my arms and legs around him to keep him close. I bury my face in his shoulder and close my eyes, peppering his skin with soft little kisses, telling him without words how much I adore him. How happy he makes me. He already knows, but I'll never tire of expressing it.

Whatever put him in such a rough mood, I must have drained it out of him. Now he moves onto the floor beside me and wraps his arm around me, pulling me close.

"Damn," Griff finally says.

I grin. "Seconded."

"I'm glad you both enjoyed my production," Sebastian states, somewhat smugly.

"Best producer ever," I say, snuggling even closer.

For a few minutes, I lie there with Sebastian, but I don't want Griff to feel left out, so eventually I roll over so I'm on the ground between them.

Sated and boneless, I lie there and stare up at the vaulted ceiling. "Man, you guys really will go to any length to get out of watching Audrey Hepburn, won't you?"

Griff reaches over and gives my arm a little rub. "I'll give you a raincheck."

"We can watch it tomorrow night," Sebastian agrees. "We'll all be home. It'll be like old times."

"Except you're not allowed to hog Moira," Griff adds.

"I'm going to make steak and loaded baked potatoes for dinner," I inform them.

"As long as we have all the important stuff figured out," Griff remarks, wryly.

I turn my head to give him a playful glare. "Hey, I have to keep you beasts healthy and fed so you have the energy to keep up with my sexual appetites."

"And you do a wonderful job," Sebastian assures me.

"Thank you," I say. "At least someone appreciates me."

"Hey, now," Griff says, scowling. "I appreciate you."

"Which movie is this?" Sebastian asks, glancing at the television.

"*Charade*. It's good. If we ever get through it without having sex and missing half the movie, you guys will like it."

"Doubt it," Griff says.

"Plus, if it can't keep us from fucking you for an hour and a half, it can't be that good," Sebastian adds.

"Either way, though, it sounds like a damn good night," Griff surmises.

27

SEBASTIAN

CARRIE SITS ON THE EDGE OF HER DESK, HANDS clasped in her lap, staring us down.

Griff told me we needed to come in and talk to her today. Obviously, I know we don't, that I've already handled this situation, but since no one else can know that, I have to keep up appearances. Consequently, here I sit, burning time and money at this inane appointment.

I glance at the expensive watch on my wrist, subtly checking the time.

"Oh, I'm sorry," Carrie says, dramatically. "Are we boring you?"

Lifting my eyebrows as I glance up at her, I say, "Hey, it's not my divorce."

Cutting a look at Griff, then back at me, she says, "I maintain that I would prefer seeing Griff alone about his marriage, you alone about yours."

"I have no need to see you about my marriage," I inform her. "My marriage is fine. Glorious. The people writing cards for

Hallmark vomit thinking about how happy *my* marriage is. Only his needs to be dealt with."

Unmoved, she states, "There are things that need to be discussed that I can't say in front of you. Having both of you as clients... there could be a conflict of interest down the road, and I'm only going to be able to represent one of you."

Since she's tiptoeing around the elephant in the room, I call it out. "Is this because Griff is fucking Moira?"

My hardass lawyer's jaw gapes open and for the first time since I've met her, she looks as shocked as a schoolgirl. Her wide-eyed gaze jumps to Griff.

"He knows," Griff tells her. "It's not an affair. I told you I wasn't having an affair."

"I don't understand," she says slowly, her gaze shifting from Griff to me.

"We decided a marriage for each of us was too much work; we're just going to double team one and really knock it out of the park."

Griff smirks, shaking his head. "You shouldn't take such pleasure in this."

Eh, it's kind of fun to shock people. I don't care. "The point is, we can all stop dancing around like fucking ballerinas. I'm never going to need a divorce, especially not because of this. We're all on the same side here. I know you wanted Moira to come in, but she's not available today. I would prefer she not have to come in at all."

Struggling to keep up with what she's just learned, Carrie's brow furrows in thought and she sighs, pinching the bridge of her nose. "Well, hell, guys. I mean, your prenup's shot to shit. If you're sleeping with Moira, whether Seb knows or not, you violated your own damn clause."

I nod, ready to hurry this along. "All right, so what's next?"

"They'll find proof of the affair," she says. "People always think they're careful, but they always leave dirt somewhere."

"Wasn't an affair," I correct.

"It *looks* like an affair. Doesn't matter what it is. Fight to uphold the prenup, Moira gets called in."

"So the prenup gets thrown out," I say, firmly.

"I'm not sure you get it, Seb. You guys... You're both going to lose because of the way you split your business. This is not good."

"All right, so why don't we hold off another week," I tell her. "I'm going to talk to Moira—she's not available this week, anyway—and we'll figure out the financials. Let's just hold off. We'll take the weekend. Ashley's not pushing for the divorce anyway."

"She will be if she finds out about this," Carrie states. "Cha-ching. She'll sign those papers so fast your head will spin if she knows the prenup's tossed. Oh, Griff." She sighs, burying her face in her hands. "You won't even be able to afford me when this is over."

"He'll be fine," I say, rolling my eyes. "You're being dramatic."

Looking up and wagging her finger between us, she asks, "How does this work? Are you two...?"

"We're not here to fill up your spank bank, Carrie. Unless we get a discount for that," I add, half-jokingly.

"We're not pieces of meat," Griff agrees. "God."

I grin.

Carrie shakes her head at both of us. "Well, you assholes are in rare form. Men in your positions shouldn't—" She stops and snorts. "Your positions. Sorry."

"You're 12," I inform her.

Eyebrows rising, she says, "Not according to my present thoughts. I'm just saying. Who's the bottom?"

"He would obviously be the bottom," I state.

"What? Like hell I would," Griff replies.

"I sure as hell wouldn't. I don't have it in me to be a bottom."

"Maybe you'd have it in you if you let Griff be the top," Carrie fires back.

I roll my eyes. "Are we done here?"

"In all seriousness, if you ever do get divorced now, Moira's fucked. Of course, after Griff's divorce you guys are going to lose half your fucking money anyway, so I guess it doesn't matter."

Of course Griff climbs up on his white stallion and demands, "What do you mean, Moira's fucked?"

"Sebastian has the non-idiot version of an infidelity clause. Wife cheats, she gets nothing. Husband cheats, no penalty. If she's fucking you, she invalidated the generous terms we gave her. She doesn't get shit."

"This is irrelevant," I state.

"I don't like that," Griff says. "You should change that. That's not fair. She isn't cheating."

"We're not getting a fucking divorce," I state, beginning to lose my patience. "I'm not going to pay to change terms in a prenup that will never come up in a divorce I'm never going to file for. Jesus Christ. Are we done? I want to go home."

Griff and Carrie talk for a couple more minutes about shit that's never going to matter, but since I can't volunteer that information, I don't say anything. Might as well burn a few more minutes of billable time—this will all be over with soon enough, and we won't have to do this shit anymore.

After shaking hands and agreeing to meetings no one will need to have next week, Griff and I leave.

As we walk down the corridor outside Carrie's office, he tells me, "Well, that was weird."

I slap him on the back. "It's almost over. Hang in there, buddy."

He's quiet for a moment, then a little lower he mutters, "It's gonna be expensive."

"We'll make more money," I say, simply. "Actually, I wanted to talk to you about something that popped up on my radar. Remember that retail space I had my eye on? Price went down. We should drive by on the way home; I'll show it to you. I want to buy it while it's cheap. We can rent it out and make a killing."

Staring at me, he says, "Did you not hear Carrie? This isn't the time to expand, Seb. We're going to have to hustle our asses off to come out of this without losing what we've already got."

"We'll be fine," I tell him. "Even splitting half with Ashley, selling your house should turn a decent profit. Things have a way of working out."

Narrowing his eyes suspiciously, he demands, "Why aren't you stressing about this?"

"What do you mean?"

"You *know* what I mean. Money means too much to you; you shouldn't be this calm about potentially losing so much of it."

This is the annoying part. Donovan assured me he'd get this taken care of quickly, but he hasn't let me know a specific day yet, and I wish he would. Until the little bitch is dealt with, I have to pretend to be worried about her enough to allay suspicions, and I don't fucking feel like it. My life is damn near perfect right now. I've got everything, Griff's got everything, and Moira's got everything. Everyone I love is happy, and I want to enjoy it.

But no. I have to fake it like this loose end is going to unravel my life instead of get snipped off like all greedy fucking loose ends should.

Since I can't say that to Griff, I just smile at him. "Just looking forward to that steak Moira's making us for dinner, I guess."

"No one's this cheerful because of some meat," Griff states.

Laughter shoots out of me as I press the elevator button. "Tell that to Moira."

I START to get stressed when Monday rolls around and I still haven't heard from Donovan.

My stress levels rise on Wednesday when Ashley's lawyer scores big.

The waiter from the date Griff took Moira on is willing to testify for Ashley. Given the way Griff's head hangs when he hears the news, that must be really bad.

"We're fucked," he said, staring at the ground.

But we're not supposed to be fucked. I paid good fucking money—even with that supposed discount—to make sure we weren't fucked. I always keep a large store of cash in the house in case of emergency, and right now, I'm cleaned out. Gave every last wrapper full of cash to Donovan, trusting he would handle this.

It was absolutely worth the investment if the problem went away, but if the hitman I hired doesn't deliver, I can't exactly call the Better Business Bureau about it.

So, yeah.

Maybe we are fucked.

The worst part is, Griff told Moira. I wouldn't have told Moira until and unless the fucking bank took our house, but Friday I come home from work to Moira sitting at the table, all upset.

"Why didn't you tell me?" she demands.

Glaring mildly at Griff seated beside her, I answer, "Because there's nothing to tell. Not yet. We're still figuring things out. We don't know how bad it is, and even if it's the absolute worst... I'll figure something out."

Shaking her head, she stares at the table top. "We shouldn't have done this. We should have waited. We should have let the paperwork go through first—"

Before she can say anything else Griff can latch onto with his goddamn insecurities, I cut her off. "Hey, no. No. Stop that. This is why I didn't tell you. There's no problem, okay? Not yet. We did what we needed to do."

Her eyes, so full of concern, flash to mine. "And now you could lose everything."

I reach across the table and cover her hand with mine. "Not everything," I tell her, firmly. "The most important things I have can't be taken from me. From any of us," I add, glancing pointedly at Griff. "We all have each other, and we're all going to be fine."

Despite my assurances, she says, "Maybe we should sell the house. If we sell ours and he sells his, we can use the money to keep your businesses going. We can move into a smaller place. We don't need all this room. We all sleep together anyway—hell, we can move to a one bedroom for now."

"Moira." I meet her gaze and hold it, draining the franticness out of her. I need her calming presence. I already have to deal with Griff being touchy about shit, I need Moira to be steady and trust me.

Fucking Griff.

Staring her down calms her considerably. Even though as far as she knows, the facts do not back me up, I manage to convey to her that I have things under control.

Or, I think so, until she says, "I could get a job."

"All right." I keep her hand and stand, pulling her to her feet. She doesn't know where I'm going with this, so she hesitates. I pick her up and drape her little ass over my shoulder as she squeals.

"Sebastian! What are you doing?"

"Come on," I tell Griff, nodding as I head for the bedroom.

"Are we done talking about this?" he asks tentatively, standing and following me nonetheless.

"Yep."

After we've worn my wife out and she sleeps nestled against Griff, I stare at her naked back and let the doubts creep in.

If Donovan doesn't come through, the money he took me for is the least of my problems. Tens of thousands of dollars can be made up, but without that prenup, Griff's toast. Obviously, she can't touch my house, but Moira's right; we would have to sell ours. We'd need the money.

Our first house flashes through my mind, even though we wouldn't move to a shithole. It's not like we'd be completely broke, and we would build things back up, but all those years, all that effort... everything just ripped away from us... it's bullshit.

It makes me fucking sad. I logged all those hours and worked as hard as I did then so I wouldn't have to now. Now I have Moira and Griff and we can be a family; I don't want to spend 18 hours of every day gone.

I'm tempted to go see Donovan again, but he told me not to. Conveniently, he told me that until the job is done, I shouldn't come around.

Helplessness is not a feeling I'm accustomed to anymore. Once upon a time, I felt that way, and I vowed never to let it happen again. That claustrophobic fucking feeling.

There's nothing worse than powerlessness.

Moira shifts in her sleep. I'm feeling a little selfish so instead of letting her remain asleep, I give her hip a little squeeze and let my hand drift forward, placing the flat of my palm against her abdomen and lightly rubbing.

Her dark hair tickles my face as she turns to look at me over her shoulder. "You're still awake?" she whispers.

I shrug.

Her husband senses on high alert, she eases off Griff and rolls over to face me. Her pretty face is relaxed and calm, none of this stress weighing on her mind. Exactly how I want it.

Not wanting to stress her out, I let it go myself. I reach for her and drag her close, tucking her beneath my chin. Her sweet little body snuggled up against mine, her lips pressed lovingly against my chest as she kisses away whatever worries must be keeping me awake, I'm cognizant of this being what really matters. Hell, even Griff lying there on the other side of my bed, happy for once in his fucking life.

We have all we need.

I *want* my stuff, my businesses, the empire I've poured countless years of my life into building, but all I *need* is right here in this bed.

No one can touch this.

28

GRIFF

THE PHONE IS STILL PRESSED TO MY EAR, A SHRILL voice lobbing obscenities at me, but I can't quite process any of it.

This can't be real.

This can't be true.

Ashley's hysterical sister isn't making any sense at this point, but between the lines of hurled insults, casual accusations, and muffled sobs, one statement rings clear, reverberates off the walls of my mind.

Ashley is dead.

Last night while Moira's sister visited us, while I played with her baby and Moira snuggled close... Ashley decided to end her life.

That doesn't make sense.

There are a lot of things I know about the woman I spent years married to, and there's one truth I would stake my fucking life on.

Ashley is too vain to put a gun in her mouth and shoot a

hole through the back of her head. The amount of pain she would have to be in to even *consider* it...

There is no fucking possibility. If Ashley wanted to kill herself, she'd use pills. Not only because there's a good chance she would fail and just get a fuck load of sympathy and attention out of it, but because it's more dignified and glamorous than blowing a motherfucking hole in her head.

I can't even imagine it. My stomach feels sick. I don't *like* Ashley at this point, let alone love her, but I didn't want her dead. Sure, in moments of anger I might have thought that, but...

Fuck.

"You did this!" her sister suddenly screams, drawing me out of my thoughts. I wince and pull the phone away from my ear.

"I didn't do anything," I state. "Look, I'm sorry to hear this, Sara. Obviously. This is... Jesus. But this is not my fault."

"Yes, it is! You took everything from her! You divorced her—left her for another woman!"

This is an impressive revisionist history, but since the woman is clearly mourning and in pain, I don't bother setting her straight.

"Look, I'm at work. I have to go. When you've had a chance to calm down, call me and we'll talk about..." I want to say 'funeral arrangements' but the words get stuck on my tongue.

Funeral arrangements? I can't be talking about funeral arrangements. Ashley's a year shy of thirty fucking years old. I can't be planning her funeral.

Visions of white roses spring to mind, clustered around a casket. I don't know what she'd want to be buried in. Can there even be an open casket?

My stomach rolls over.

"Sara, I can't do this. I have to... I have to go."

She vents a few more muffled, obscenity-laced insults at me before I give up and disconnect the call.

I can't breathe right and I need to get out of this office.

Shoving my phone in my pocket, I push up out of my seat and make a beeline out of the building. I tug at my tie, trying to pull air into my lungs.

A cold burst of winter air hits me, reminding me I left my jacket inside. I'm outside in a thin dress shirt, my sleeves rolled up to the elbow, and somehow I still feel hot under the collar.

Dead.

Ashley is dead.

The words keep playing and replaying in my head. No matter how hard I struggle against them, no matter how impossible they feel, there has to be some truth to it. This can't just be a mistake. You can't *think* someone is dead and go so far as to notify people and then it turns out to be a mistake.

No, this is *permanent.*

The woman I married is dead, and the circumstances are fishy as fuck.

I don't even think Ashley would know how to fire a gun. I lived with her for years; I would know if she ever went to lessons. She would've made me buy her some pink, rhinestone-encrusted fucking thing so she could go to a range once and get bored.

I should have asked what kind of gun was used.

Why would I think to fucking ask that? Sara probably wouldn't even know. I don't even know where it happened. Couldn't have been our house; I took her key.

Holy fuck.

Nothing about this feels right. Ashley would never in a million years go quietly. She would need a complete fucking lobotomy for any of this to add up. Even if she somehow overcame her self-obsession enough to decide to end her life—and she was *not* in that headspace last time I saw her, which wasn't long ago—she would call me first. I'm the one who resisted her tricks and pissed her off, so she would have reached out to me. Not for any nice reason, of course, but to punish me. She might've emotionally blackmailed me with threats of hurting herself, or maybe sent some well thought-out, heartfelt text, backhandedly explaining all the ways I made her miserable, all the reasons it's my fault she has come to this—without using that verbiage, of course.

Dread moves through me at the thought of it, but it's perhaps worse that she can't do any of that shit to me ever again.

Because that means she's gone—not just from my life, but from the world.

Was she dead when Gwen left late last night and Seb and I took Moira up to bed? Was Ashley dead when I was buried balls deep inside Moira, getting off on her moans, the feel of her body, the visual of Seb right across from me fucking her mouth?

Before that? Was she dead when Moira shuttled her baby niece between me and Seb, bursting with maternal love? When baby Layla played with my face and slobbered all over me? When I slipped away to clean the baby drool off and Moira subtly followed, pushed me in the bathroom, and made out with me for a few minutes? She winked at me and slipped back out to attend to her sister and niece, but fuck, I felt good.

Everything felt good, and now I know this was happening.

I need to talk to Seb. I need to tell him. He's gonna fucking flip. I mean, he won't be torn up about it—not like he was married to her, and with all the trouble she's been causing lately, the bastard might even be relieved to...

My thoughts slow to a crawl.

Now, *he* might be persuaded to put a gun in someone's mouth. I can't picture him pulling the trigger because I love the fucking guy, and that's just not a thing you can picture someone you love doing...

No, it couldn't have—he wouldn't *do* that. That's too far. Seb's not a fucking murderer, what am I thinking? Plus, he was at the house with us. He's the one who told Moira to invite her sister over for dinner, and he was there with us all night visiting. Gwen didn't leave until late, and he was right there at the front door seeing her off.

No, of course Seb didn't have anything to do with it. I can't believe that thought even crossed my mind.

Overwhelmed with a need to see him, to tell him about this, to see that he's shocked, too, I pat my pocket for my keys. Finding them, I head straight for my car. My jacket's still in the office, but who fucking cares?

I fire up the engine, back out of my spot, and peel out of the parking lot. I break several traffic laws along the way, but I can't drive fast enough.

Thankfully, there aren't many people on the road today, but Seb's across town so it still takes forever to get to him.

I could've called, given him a heads up, but I didn't bother.

Since I didn't bother, I shouldn't be too shocked when I get to where he's supposed to be and he's already left. The curly-haired girl who watches his every move when he's around—major infatuation there, but she's just a kid, so it's nothing to worry about—told me he was meeting with his Realtor over at the retail space he told me about.

The fucking retail space? How the hell is he meeting at the retail space not just without me, but without telling me? It wouldn't be a big deal any other time, but right now, he knows we don't have the money to buy it. He knows our finances are tied up and looking dire given the Ashley situation.

Irrational anger surges through my veins when I pull up and see him standing inside the building, hands shoved into the pockets of his long, stylish jacket, talking to the Realtor. I park up front so he spots me immediately; a wary look passes across his face.

He should look fucking wary. I kill the engine and get out, slamming the car door behind me and heading inside. Since Seb watches all this, as soon as I swing open the door and let myself inside, he tells the woman, "Give us a minute."

I've obviously met with her before and she knows I'm his partner, so she glances between us uncertainly, then nods and click-clacks into the next space over to give us some privacy.

Seb's gaze drifts up and around, and I know immediately the motherfucker is checking for any potentially working cameras.

Goddammit.

"Did you do this?"

His voice level, his face vaguely annoyed, Seb asks, "What are you talking about?"

"I think you know what I'm talking about, Seb. What are you doing here? I told you we had to hold off on this place. You know we can't afford to buy it right now."

"I had to come," he tells me. "I know you wanted to wait, but there's another buyer sniffing around and this place is too good a deal. If we wait around, we'll lose it. Obviously, I would've looped you in before I did anything official, but—"

I don't let him finish bullshitting me. I'm not in the mood for it right now. "But you *knew* we didn't have the fucking money!"

Passing a hand over his mouth and caressing his strong jaw, he regards me like he's appraising an angry pet, determining whether to throw it a bone or slip it some tranquilizer pills in a piece of lunch meat to keep it from attacking.

"Why don't I finish up here?" he finally suggests. "We can go somewhere and talk."

"About what?" I ask, lowly. "What do we need to talk about, Seb?"

"Whatever has you upset," he says, evenly. "Let me just tell Elsa I'll call her tomorrow."

I'm still restless as hell, but I wait for my best friend to go handle fucking business while I stand here with a dead wife—and he might've been the one to kill her.

This is a fucking disaster.

People can't just do shit like this and get away with it. What am I supposed to do if he gets caught?

I'm getting ahead of myself. I still want to believe he didn't do this, but I know there's a darkness lurking beneath Seb's well-assembled exterior, a scrappy willingness to do whatever he has to do to save himself.

As a kid he always had to fight, and he never really stopped, he just upgraded his arsenal. Maybe he doesn't have to come to blows with the house bully or build an emotional force field around himself anymore, but what if he felt like he needed to protect me and Moira? Ashley did come to the house. Moira was going to have to admit to our arrangement and we were going to be outed publicly—and not on our own terms, but in a way that made the whole thing seem sordid and wrong.

Seb has been like a brother to me, and I know the man well. I know his heart and soul, and I know he's loyal as hell, but I also know he shuts off that heart to anyone he feels has turned on him, abandoned him, left him out in the cold.

If Moira hadn't stopped me leaving, *I* would've felt the arctic chill of his indifference.

So how easy would it be for him to look at Ashley— someone he never had a single strong feeling for—not as a person, but as a problem he needed to solve? Lately she's been presenting herself like his enemy, and Seb wasn't a great enemy to have when he had nothing, but now?

I think of the cash I know he keeps at his house. Large sums, larger sums than any rational, fiscally responsible person would keep hidden away. The money could be invested instead, but he liked to have rainy day money around that he wouldn't have to go to a bank to get.

The kind of money there'd be no paper trail to because it's cash, and he's had it stashed for so long that whatever paper trail may have once existed has been blown away by the winds of time.

Intense, oceanic eyes regard me once more as Seb walks back into the space I'm occupying. His hands are still shoved into the pockets of his charcoal gray jacket. Without a word he nods ahead of him to the door, letting me know we're leaving.

It occurs to me for the first time in all our years together, maybe I shouldn't feel as safe with him as I do. His love runs deep, but what if it ever stops? My favorite part of last night flashes to mind again, Moira stealing those few minutes in the bathroom with me.

What if I ever became one of Seb's problems? If he can discard people as easily as that, like so much dead weight, just because they're in his way... what happens if someday I'm the one in his way?

Instead of going to his car, he slides into the passenger seat of mine and shuts the door, enclosing us in this chilly fucking pocket of privacy.

I look over at my best friend in the world, the man I've built my whole life with, and I don't know what he's capable of.

"What's on your mind, Griff?" he asks me, his tone still that of a man in charge.

"A lot of fucking things, Seb," I answer honestly.

"Can you be more specific?" he asks, patiently.

I can, but I don't know how. How do you ask someone the things I need to ask him? How do you look a man in the face and ask if he's capable of murder? Even if he didn't pull the trigger, if he had a hand in things, this is his doing.

My stomach rolls over again. I feel like I'm gonna lose the lunch I didn't even fucking eat, but I take a deep breath and try to keep it together.

He should be thrown by the way I'm acting right now, but he's not. He should have questions. His brow should be furrowed in concern as he tries to figure out what the hell is wrong with me.

The fact that he doesn't feels damning. It just makes my stomach hurt worse.

My throat feels thick and I honestly don't want to ask him a damn thing, but I need to. "What would you do for Moira?" I ask him.

It's a clumsy question without context, but he understands and answers without hesitation, "Anything."

That's exactly what I expected him to say, so I nod my head. Then I force myself to meet his gaze and ask, "What would you do for *me*?"

He holds my gaze, searching for the right answer, but after missing no more than a beat, he repeats, "Anything."

My stomach sinks with a whole assortment of fucking feelings.

On some level, a sick level, that's reassuring. I know he means it. I don't doubt the look on his face or the inflection of the word. Seb would do anything for me. Hell, he already has.

When I tried to leave him, he opened his life up to me and shared his beloved *wife* with me, for fuck's sake. He's already proven he would do anything for me.

But this?

I never asked for this.

I want to look at his face when I tell him, but I don't have the stomach for it right now. Staring at the wedding ring on his left hand instead, I tell him, "Ashley's dead."

I think he understands there's no point in putting on a dramatic show of surprise, because I wouldn't believe it at this point.

"Damn."

That's it. Damn.

At least he says it in the way people do when something unfortunate happens, and not with the sarcastic inflection of someone who couldn't give less of a fuck, but it doesn't matter what he says or how he says it.

He did it.

Somehow, he did this.

After a moment, he adds, "Are you okay?"

"Am I okay?" I repeat with surprising calm for someone sitting in a car with a fucking murderer. "You know the husband's always the first suspect, right? If anyone else concludes—as I already did, in the last 20 minutes—that Ashley wouldn't have shot herself to death even if she *did* commit suicide, which I also consider very unlikely... I'm her husband. Not just her husband, but her husband who was trying like hell to divorce her, whose prenup wasn't going to stand up in court, who was set to lose half of everything... Jesus Christ, Seb, do you know how guilty I look?"

As I look at him, a different sliver of suspicion slices through me.

What if he *does* know that? What if he planned on it? He seems to like sharing Moira with me, but what if he realized he doesn't and he needs me out of the way now?

I search his impenetrable face for some sign of menace, some sinister flicker in his blue eyes, but nothing turns up.

Of course nothing turns up.

Fuck, I'm paranoid.

Well, maybe paranoid is the wrong word. Maybe I'm justified in worrying about this shit, if he's guilty of what it looks like he's guilty of.

"You'll be fine," he assures me. "When did it happen?"

I cut him a 'come on' look.

"Last night?" he questions, even though it feels like he already knows. "You have a solid alibi for last night. Gwen and Layla came over for dinner, Moira and I were there with you. We even took pictures with the baby. Each and every one of us could attest, with evidence to support our claims, that you could not have possibly killed Ashley because you spent the whole night with us."

"Gwen is Moira's sister," I remind him. "Since I'm fucking Moira, it'd be easy to say maybe she'd lie for me. And the time-stamps on iPhone pictures can be manipulated, all you have to do is go into settings and manually change the time before you snap the pictures."

"Perhaps," he allows. "But after Ashley showed up at our house, unhinged and attacking my wife, I felt she might be a danger to us, so I put up surveillance cameras. The recordings are time stamped and cannot be manipulated; they can verify our story."

"Our story," I repeat, a bit cynically.

"Let's not be naïve; if there's an investigation, yes, you need a story. As you said, you're the husband. There may not even be an investigation, though. If it's ruled a suicide, that's that."

"Please, this fucking reeks of foul play, Seb."

Placing a hand I know he means to be reassuring on my shoulder, he gives it a squeeze and tells me, "Relax. I'm not going to let anything happen to you."

I shrug his hand off, glaring at him. "You can't fucking control everything."

Sounding unconvinced, he murmurs, "Well, we'll see. I'm sorry you're upset, but this isn't worth getting pissed off at me over."

"Don't tell me how to feel," I mutter.

"I told you I would handle it and I did," he says, firmly. "It's over now. We can all move on with our lives. We can live our life with no obstacles in our way. Ashley wanted to suck you dry, Griff, and for what? You never did a goddamn thing to her. She was a shitty person."

"That's *not* your call to make. You can't play god like that, Seb. You're not judge, jury, and executioner."

"I didn't execute anyone," he says mildly. "I had dinner with my wife, my best friend, and my sister-in-law; I spent the evening playing with my niece."

"She was my *wife*, Sebastian."

"She was a leech," he replies dismissively. "You wanted free of her and now you are. I know you love to wallow in your unhappiness, Griff, and by all means, if that's what you need to do, fine, but I'm not going to play the bad guy here."

A little laugh of disbelief shoots out of me. "*Play* the bad guy? I don't know, Seb, I think you took it a step beyond play-ing. I think you owned the fuck out of that role."

"All right." His patience clearly at an end, he pulls the latch and pushes the car door open. "I'm going back to the office. I'll tell Moira the news. I think it'll go down easier coming from me. I'll see you at home for dinner?"

I don't answer. I stare out the front windshield and wait for him to leave.

Now he hesitates, ducking his head back into the car and saying, "Griff?"

I turn my head to look at him.

"Don't do anything foolish," he says, simply.

29

SEBASTIAN

It's a long, stressful day after I leave Griff.

The hours seem to stretch on forever and I'm not sure what to do with them. I pour myself into work as a distraction, but I beg off early and head home to Moira anyway.

In a sense, I'm glad I got home before Griff. I want a chance to tell Moira about Ashley. Between Griff and the stress of the day, my emotional stores have also been depleted. Moira fills them up as soon as I get home, greeting me with her warm blue eyes so full of love. A weight is pushed right off my broad shoulders as Moira secures her arms around my neck and leans in for a lingering kiss.

I lock my arms around her waist a little tighter than usual and bury my face in her neck, inhaling her scent.

She hugs me and kisses me, holds me close; for what must be the millionth time, I'm so grateful to have her to come home to.

Not knowing where Griff is, though, there's still a weight on me. I didn't think he'd figure it out, and if he did, I definitely didn't think he'd figure it out so fast. Since he knows I have an alibi, he must also know I had help, and if he knows that, he can guess whose help I had. Knowing that, he *has* to be smart enough not to go to the cops.

I could see the doubts in his eyes, though. That stung a little. I did all this *for* him, and he looked at me like he didn't trust me. After all I've done, after all I've given him, he still found a reason to doubt me.

Asshole.

Moira's brow furrows and she kneads my shoulders, still securely in my arms, her chest flush with mine. "What's wrong, honey?"

"There's something I need to tell you, and I'm not sure how," I begin.

Her face etched with worry, she asks, "Something bad? Where's Griff? Is he okay?"

"Yeah, no," I say quickly, shaking my head. "Griff's...." Actually, I guess Griff isn't okay. I got a little defensive earlier and I probably shouldn't have, but he was pissing me off. I don't even know exactly how to help him through this. My instinct is to offer up Moira, to remind him what he has now that Ashley's out of the way. I could use her to help him through it, but now I'm a little worried what he might say to her.

I didn't even want Griff to know I had a hand in this, but I damn sure don't want Moira to find out.

I don't make a habit of keeping secrets from my wife, but this is one truth she doesn't need to know. This was an isolated incident, a one-time solution to a very big problem. Regrettably, this was the only end Ashley left me with. Griff tried to pay her off, and she wasn't even willing to take that. She had no right to ruin my life, but because of her blatant greed, she would have. She would have settled for nothing less than total destruction, and our money would have gone straight into Danny Long's pocket.

That asshole wouldn't bat an eye at what I'd done, so I'll be damned if I do. I'm not going to let Griff's Boy Scout bullshit get under my skin.

So I did a bad thing.

People do bad things all the time.

Pushing my fingers through Moira's carefully styled curls, I smile tenderly and lean in to brush my lips across hers.

She must understand I need to get lost in her for a while, because even though I just told her I had news, even though I only started telling it then stopped, she lets me haul her little ass upstairs and fuck my frustrations out.

Afterward, as she lies in my embrace, her hand resting over my heart, all I can think is, I love her *so fucking much*. I won't lose her, not for anything.

Not even for Griff.

Maybe Moira is the only person in the world I can count on. Maybe Griff would rather hold onto his principles and wallow alone in his unhappiness than get over it and have a life with me.

He's the reason we were in this mess to begin with. He's the one who couldn't just tell me years ago he wanted my fucking girl; instead he went out and made a mess. Created all his own problems, writing legal documents with his fucking heart instead of his head, marrying someone when she wasn't even the woman he wanted...

Griff got us into a shitty situation, and I got us out of it.

Now all our heads are above water, and he wants to bitch about the life raft I employed.

Well, not to be a consequentialist, but yes; in this scenario, the end justified the means.

THANKFULLY, Griff comes home.

He's a little drunk and a little ornery, but he shows up. That has to be a good sign.

I broke the news to Moira about Ashley's "suicide" while we were upstairs in bed together, so as soon as he comes through the door, my big-hearted wife fills up with sympathy. She throws herself at him, wrapping him up in her loving arms; he holds onto her like she's all he has left in the world.

It hurts a little.

I hear her whisper, "I'm so sorry, Griff."

Tension knots my shoulders as I await his response, but he doesn't say anything back. He just holds her.

Moira fusses over him now that he's here, lavishing affection and attention on him, asking if he's all right—just generally trying to ferret out what he needs so she can give it to him.

He doesn't talk much. He's so fucking dramatic. It's not like he had any love left for the fucking woman; he wanted her gone nearly as badly as I did, he just doesn't have the balls to make it happen.

He's starting to piss me off, but when he finally cuts a cold look my way, I see just as much anger reflected back at me.

Ignoring the strain would be a Herculean effort, so Moira picks up on it. She doesn't know what to do with it, though, so she does her best to pretend there isn't a tight rope of tension between the two of us as she ambles across it.

She takes Griff's hand and brings him into the living room. She sits him down on the couch and he takes the end furthest from me, like I'm a disease he's afraid of catching.

When she sits down and snuggles up against his side,

resting her head on his shoulder, it takes every ounce of self-control I have not to reach over and yank her over to me.

If Griff wants to be an asshole, maybe I should remind him who the *king* fucking asshole is in this relationship. I've given him everything, and I can take it away just as fucking easily.

Before I can respond in anger, Moira's gentle hand claims mine and she tugs me close. She wants me with her, too. Since something is clearly wrong with us, she must want to snuggle out our aggression.

It doesn't take any added incentive for me to cuddle my wife, though. Fuck Griff and his shitty mood. Resting my hand on her hip, I move up behind her. With her head on his shoulder, her neck is exposed to me, so I leave a trail of kisses there. When she sighs with pleasure, Griff's jaw locks with annoyance.

I smirk. That's fun.

I want to fuck with him some more, so I reach a hand down inside her dress and cup her breast as I kiss her. Even if Moira knew he was definitely mad at me, she wouldn't hold back from me, so just like she would if we were all on good terms like we should be, she responds. Griff has to feel her writhe on his body under my ministrations, and where most nights it would be fine, maybe even hot, right now it makes him mad.

Before long, his body is so taut with anger that I wonder if he wants to hit me. It's almost like old times, before I shared her with him, if he felt anger at me over it back then. Maybe I'm not using words to remind him how much I mean to Moira, but I'm using something much harder to ignore—a visual. I'm no fool. I know he's probably considered telling Moira what an evil bastard I am today, turning on me, taking her and running. Even if only for a minute, if only in a fit of anger, I know Griff. I know how he works. I know he has that pain in the ass white knight streak.

I don't.

And Moira likes that I don't. She doesn't need me to be a white knight—she likes me just the way I am.

Moira's breasts are bare now, her dress pushed down. I can keep pushing Griff, or I can offer an olive branch.

"Care for a taste?" I ask him, nodding toward her breasts.

He looks over at me through narrowed eyes. I cock an eyebrow and bend to take her left nipple into my mouth. Moira's head drifts back against the couch and she reaches for Griff, giving him the last nudge he needs.

Glaring at me in frustration, he nonetheless joins me in feasting on my wife's breasts. I feel victorious as Moira holds us both close, one hand in his hair, one in mine; she brings us together, even if only temporarily.

Since I've been rubbing in how much she wants me, he leaves her breast after a moment and shoves me off her, swinging his thigh across her body and straddling her. A little breathless, she looks up at him uncertainly, then he gives her a searing kiss he surely hopes I'll hate.

I don't, though. It's hot. I like to see him dominate her; he doesn't do enough of it. He's only doing it now because he's pissed at me, and the only weapon we can use against each other right now is Moira's body.

That gives me hope. He's angry, but he's still playing within a set of rules. He's still respecting limits. Maybe he thinks he can annoy me by angrily fucking what's mine, by showing me my wife wants him, too, but he's not crossing the line. He's not bringing the ugly truth into my house and poisoning my wife with it.

Not yet, at least.

Instead, he pushes my wife down on the couch and frees his

cock. He watches me instead of her while he pins her down and shoves his cock into her mouth.

I smile.

His eyes narrow and he thrusts harder.

I like that even more.

It's hilarious that this is how he thinks he's going to piss me off. I'd be more pissed, more afraid, if he didn't want to touch her. If it seemed like he was pulling away and I was losing my hold on him.

I'm not. All the evidence is right here on the couch, in the tension in his body, in the sounds my wife makes as she takes every generous inch of him. And then afterward when she's sucked him dry and he comes back down, when he realizes he's using her as a weapon so he pulls her close and snuggles her, kissing and caressing her, trying to make it up to her.

He doesn't need to; Moira's perfectly content. He's still not used to her, though. Despite all the evidence that should have shattered it, there's still a part of him that refuses to let go of his image of her as his Madonna.

After snuggling for a little while, Moira tilts her head up and looks at him. "Are you hungry? I can warm up some dinner."

Griff shakes his head, looking down at her with so much tenderness, I almost feel like an intruder. "I just want to hold you."

Moira smiles softly and leans up to kiss him, then she settles back into his embrace and gives him exactly what he needs.

GRIFF GOES UPSTAIRS to take a shower, so I get my wife back for a little while. She curls up beside me and rests her head on my shoulder.

I think she's waiting for me to turn on the television, but I don't want to watch anything. I don't even want the background noise. I want to know the perfect way to explain to Moira that I need her to handle Griff, remind him the chain of command, and oh, by the way, he might try to convince her I killed Ashley —or at least contracted her death.

Turns out I don't have to bring it up; Moira does.

"That's so awful about Ashley," she says, shaking her head.

"Yes," I murmur, not bothering to muster much fake sorrow.

By the end, Moira didn't like her either, but she still feels bad. "Poor Griff. I can only imagine what he must be feeling."

"I think he'll need you tonight," I tell her.

"I figured."

"Maybe you alone," I specify. "Tonight might be a good night to spend in the guest room with him. In case he needs to talk to you and he doesn't want to do it in front of me."

"He could talk in front of you," she says, a touch dismissively. "I'd rather sleep with both of you in our bed. That could be just as good for him."

"He's in a precarious place right now, so we'll see what he wants. I think he'd rather have you alone. And if he does, I need you to know something."

"All right," she says, easily.

"I'm not sure what he'll say to you. Obviously, Ashley's death is a shock to us all, but he seems to be having difficulty accepting it. Accepting how it happened."

I watch confusion darken her pretty face. I'm only telling her partial truths and they don't entirely make sense. Since she has a brain, she notices, but she trusts me enough to accept if I'm not telling her, I have a good reason. I don't want to abuse that trust, I just want to protect her. Running the back of my hand along her jaw, I search for a concise way to explain without raising any alarms.

"Griff knows Ashley has been coming after us, trying to hurt you, trying to take what belongs to us. He knows she wanted to hurt our family, and he knows I'm not a man who stands by and lets someone get away with that. It seems like his inability to accept her suicide together with that... he's concocted this idea that perhaps I was involved."

Her eyes widen slightly, but she remains relaxed in my arms. She doesn't move an inch, still holds my gaze, still accepts and enjoys my touch.

Warmth rushes over me. Griff may be wavering, but Moira doesn't doubt me.

"He thinks you were involved in Ashley's death?" she asks, apprehensively.

"I don't know if he really thinks that, but the idea has crossed his mind. His head is a mess today, that's all. But, if that's where his head is, he might say something to you, and I wanted you to be prepared."

"I don't think he would say something like that to me."

"He might." I stop caressing her jaw and cradle it in my hand instead, pulling her into my chest.

Still, Moira argues. "He may feel like lashing out because he's in pain, but he won't try to hurt you, Sebastian. He loves you."

"He loves *you*," I state.

"*And* you," she insists, frowning.

"I know, but... he's having trouble remembering that right now. In any case, I need you to be prepared for the worst. It's difficult enough with Griff waffling on me today; I can't have him getting in your head, too."

Scowling, Moira pulls out of my embrace just long enough

to climb up on her knees. Now she leans in, now hers is the hand cradling my face.

Her ordinarily soft blue eyes flare with passion. Her tone is firm and unyielding as she swears, "That will *never* happen. Never. There's nothing anyone could ever say to take me away from you."

I've always been confident in that, almost to the point of arrogance, but her words make me feel better, nonetheless.

Instead of telling her that, I smile tenderly. "I know."

"You better," she says playfully, running her hand down my chest. "I'm yours forever, Mr. St. Clair. There's no getting rid of me."

I draw her face close and brush my lips across hers. "Good. What's the point of life if I don't have you?"

Nuzzling her face into my neck, she assures me, "You will never have to find out."

30

GRIFF

Given the accusations I leveled at Seb today, the last thing I expect is for Moira to scamper into the guest room after I go to bed alone.

I didn't want to sleep in that bed with him tonight. I wasn't sure how much sleep I would get, anyhow. My guilt over Ashley's death still hangs heavily on my mind, but when Moira creeps in and approaches my bedside in a skimpy, see-through scrap of fabric, I welcome the distraction.

"Want some company?" she asks, bouncing slightly on the balls of her feet.

My gaze drops to her breasts as she does, the way they bounce as she moves. I just got off a couple hours ago, but my dick still responds. If it ever stops responding to her perfect fucking body, I'll just assume I'm dead.

Pulling back the blanket, I pat the empty side of the bed. "Always room for you."

With a little smile, she climbs in beside me and snuggles right up against my side. "I guess Sebastian was right."

Just hearing her say his name causes me to tense. "About what?" I ask, a little too harshly.

Watching me closely, she says, "He didn't think you'd want to sleep together in our bed tonight. I figured you wouldn't want to be alone." Shrugging, she says lightly, "Good thing we didn't put any money on it."

"I'm not alone," I point out. "I have you."

"You're not alone because you have *us*," she corrects, immediately. "Both of us. I'm the only one in this bed right now, but make no mistake, you have *us*. Why are you pushing him away?"

"I'm not," I mutter, since she clearly does not approve. "I just needed some space from him tonight."

"He wants to be there for you, too, you know," she offers, her tone a bit softer.

I roll my eyes. "Sure, *now* he does."

"He's been there for you all along, Griff. Sebastian has been doing everything he could to help you sort this mess out. I understand you're upset, but I don't understand why you're taking it all out on him. That's not fair."

"You think that because you don't know everything."

"I know he loves you. I know he wants what's best for you, for all three of us, and whatever you think he's done to hurt you, I am *sure* that was not his intention. Occasionally, he steamrolls over feelings without noticing, but it doesn't happen a lot. He doesn't mean to do it. I'm sure he's sorry, even if he hasn't said so."

Even though I've done the same damn thing many times before, it irks me that she's making excuses for him. He can *literally* get away with murder, and still he has Moira fooled into admiring the hell out of him.

"Don't you ever get tired of his shit?" I demand. "Don't you

ever feel like telling him to just fuck off? He oversteps boundaries all the fucking time and we just deal with it, so he takes a
little more. He doesn't give a fuck about what anyone else
wants."

Her brow furrows as she either processes my frustrations or
tries to formulate a response to them. Finally, she says, "I'm not
sure that's a fair take away, but... Personally, no, I don't get sick
of his shit. Sebastian fits me like a glove, perfectly designed and
stitched together to accommodate my every bend, every nook. I
think I'm very blessed in that. I'm not sure most people ever
find that. It's okay if you don't feel the same way. He doesn't
need the same things from you he gets from me. We all have
different needs, and together, I think we meet all of them.
Right?"

"He can't just take over the running of my life," I tell her.
"Sharing you, moving in here, doing all this... it only works for
me if there are *some* boundaries. If he at least *consults* me before
he makes big fucking decisions about my life."

She rubs my chest with casual tenderness. "Then talk to him
about it. Or I can, if you don't want to. Sebastian is a reasonable
man, but he's not a mind reader. This is like any other relationship, Griff. If something is troubling you, we have to communicate or we can't fix it."

I can't help scoffing. "How can you, of all people, say that?
He controls every aspect of your life. I asked you if you wanted
to have a baby with me, and you told me it was up to him.
Come on, Moira."

"Because that's what we like," she states, looking at me like
I must be oblivious not to see that. "Sebastian likes to have
control, and I love to give it to him. Yes, he makes the big decisions—because I trust him to. I get so much out of it, I would
hate for things to be any other way. An intimacy runs between

us that's so intense, so much more fulfilling, so much more *important* to me than weighing in on every little mundane thing. I don't *need* that. I'm secure with myself and very happy with my decision to let him deal with the heavy lifting. He always does what's right for us, so I don't need to. Sebastian is a wonderful, capable man. He's strong and smart, and he *loves* us. He wants to protect us. Sometimes... sometimes obstacles get in the way, and it takes a ruthless leader to make the hard call. I don't want to make the hard calls. Do you?"

I cock my head, frowning at her toward the end of that little speech. "Do you know?"

"Know what?" she asks innocently.

I watch her for a moment, searching for some indication of what's going on inside that pretty little head of hers, but she gives me nothing. A canvas of pleasantness.

For the first time, I wonder if I haven't underestimated sweet little Moira. She's so mild-mannered in her habits, so sweet in her disposition, soft spoken and unapologetically domestic. She's a nurturer who cooks and practices yoga. She reads books and doodles pictures of snowflakes for pleasure, for Christ's sake. Sure, some of the things she likes sexually are pretty fucked up, but I assumed she liked what Seb taught her to like, despite her insistence that her likes were her own.

Is Moira just kinky, or is there a hint of darkness in her I've missed? Just how much has Seb corrupted her?

"Is there anything he could do to make you stop loving him?" I ask her.

Her answer is immediate and firm, though her tone remains pleasant—like a schoolteacher reprimanding a pupil who stepped out of line. "No."

"Nothing?"

"Nothing," she verifies.

"What if he cheated?"

Her confidence is unwavering. "He wouldn't."

"What if he hurt someone?"

She hesitates. "Did he hurt you?"

"No, I'm just... hypothetically."

Raising her hand and gesturing individually to the four walls surrounding us, she says, "The people inside this house are my top priority. Was he protecting one of them? If he was, then it's unfortunate that happened, but I trust he did what he felt was right."

"What if he *killed* someone?"

Her gaze shifts to my chest. I'm not sure if I've upset her, but I know I've at least annoyed her.

When her gaze returns to mine, her eyes are clearer, her face more open, but I can't shake the feeling she closed some part of herself off. She moves her body closer, sliding one smooth leg between mine.

My stupid dick falls right into her trap, hardening almost instantly. Then she touches it and I'm gone. Her soft hand grips me and she brushes her sweet lips against mine. Her teeth come down lightly on my bottom lip and she tugs.

My heartbeat kicks up, my stomach tightens with need, and suddenly the only important thing in the world is getting inside Moira.

"I love you, Griff," she says, dragging her lips along my jawline. "I just want to make you happy. I just want all of us to be happy *together*."

"I want that, too," I say, struggling to focus with her fingers working magic between my legs.

"Good." Her blue eyes twinkle with approval. "That makes me so happy. I want us to be a family." Leaning lower, pressing the soft mounds of her breasts against my chest, she says, "I *do* want you to put a baby in me, Griff."

My caveman instincts flare up. I reach for her neck, yanking her down so I can kiss her some more. "Yeah?" I murmur.

"Yes," she says, one hand still working my dick, one running up and down my neck. "Someday, when it's time. But we'll never get there if you and Sebastian can't play nicely together. I adore you both. You love each other. People in relationships fight, and that's okay, but please don't let stupid shit come between us. You know Sebastian can't cope with that. He needs to know we're always in his corner, even when we fight."

That pulls me halfway out of the lust fog she has me shrouded in. "Stupid shit? You think I'm overreacting? Blowing shit out of proportion? You think Ashley, the vainest woman either of us has ever met, shot a hole through the back of her skull?"

Running a calming hand up my chest and across my bicep, she leans in and places a series of kisses on my pecs. "Of course I don't think your feelings are unwarranted. You feel however you feel— with me. If you're in pain, feel it. If you're angry, feel it. If you need to vent it, please do. I don't want you to live a lie or hold anything back. But you're gonna have to let this one go, Griff. Ashley was poison. She was horrible to you while you were married, and even worse when you split up. She tried to hurt each and every one of us after destroying her own marriage. I absolutely feel for you, and if there's some part of you that still loves or misses or mourns her, I completely get that. I support you no matter what. I want to be there for you. But we need to agree that Ashley was a troubled woman who got involved with some bad people, and if anything sinister happened to her, it was her own doing—not Sebastian's."

"Even if it's a lie?" I challenge, boldly.

Her lips curve upward, but there's not much humor there. "Especially if it's a lie."

My stomach drops with her words, but then she lavishes more attention on my dick, grinding against me and moaning into my mouth until all sense of logic flees.

Seb's sweet little wife turns my brain right off, and by the time she's done fucking me, I'm too tired and satisfied to think about anything but the feel of her warm body nestled against my side as she sleeps.

31

MOIRA

I HUM A LITTLE TUNE FROM THE MUSICAL *ANNIE* AS I reach into the refrigerator and gather the ingredients I need to make breakfast. I spread them all out across the granite surface, swaying over to the cupboard and grabbing my trusty chopping board.

If Griff were up, he would help me chop the vegetables. I like doing it myself, but I enjoy doing it with his help, too.

I don't think I would take pleasure in Sebastian helping, even if he offered. They have very different roles for me, and while I love and appreciate Griff for every noble thing that he is, I don't want my husband to be like him. I love Sebastian exactly the way he is.

As I grab the knife and start to chop, I feel the powerful presence of my husband come up behind me. I feel him like a physical force, and even in this kitchen preparing breakfast with all of our clothing on, our bodies not even touching, he intoxicates me. The part of me that craves him every moment of every day comes alive and wordlessly beckons him nearer.

He answers the call, his heat intensifying as he stops a mere inch from my back. Whether it's more alive in him this morning, or just my imagination because of the things Griff and I discussed last night, I feel his edge of danger more keenly today. Strangely, it makes me feel safer.

"Tomorrow, huh?" he murmurs, referencing the song I was just humming. Normally, he lets me cook in peace, but I know he was a little tense about my spending the night with Griff last night, so he probably needs to check in. There's nothing tentative in him, though, so he doesn't test the waters like a normal man. He locks an arm around my waist and pulls me close. "Will tomorrow be a better day?"

I lean back against him, soaking up his presence. "I hope so. Tomorrow I plan to wake up naked between my two favorite men, and that's a hell of a way to start the day."

"Oh yeah?" he asks with interest. "You talked to him, then?"

I nod, bringing my knife down on the white head of cauliflower. "Yep. I've got a handle on everything. Don't worry, honey. He just needs a little time. He'll be fine."

"Mm, you're the best wife a man could ever hope for." Sebastian leans in and kisses my cheek appreciatively. The scent of him—his innate smell, the spice of his aftershave—fills me with longing. Food be damned, I drop the knife and push back the board, turning in his arms.

Sebastian was the most handsome man I had ever seen when we first met, and as I got to know the incredible man that he is, my attraction to him only intensified.

I don't know if it's because I spent a night away from him for the first time since we first moved in together, but he's never looked sexier to me than he does right now. The unapologetically confident curve of his perfect lips, the tender sense of ownership in his gorgeous blue eyes as he looks at me, the way his black suit jacket falls, the way his muted blue shirt hugs his muscular body—everything about this man is my picture of perfection.

He's not wearing a tie today. My hand drifts along his chest where it should hang. A pang of regret shoots through me as I realize I wasn't there to tie it for him this morning, so he must not have bothered putting one on.

God, I missed him. One night and I feel like I've been away for a week.

My hands creep up over those sexy shoulders and wind around his neck. Gazing up at the man I'll always feel lucky to call mine, I inform him, "I've decided nights away from you should be reserved for very infrequent, special occasions. Death of a loved one, birthday—end of list."

Sebastian smirks. "Missed me, huh?"

"So much," I murmur, pulling myself up to kiss him.

Part gratitude and probably partially because he missed me in his bed, his touch is greedy and aggressive this morning. He grabs my ass and pulls me against him. He's hard, and excitement shoots through my veins like a bullet train.

"Get a room."

I gasp, pulling back, as Griff's voice suddenly rings out from across the room.

I didn't think he was awake yet. I crept out of bed to shower, get dressed, and come make breakfast for Sebastian, but we were going to let Griff sleep in since he had such a hard day yesterday. I hope he didn't hear what I just said.

Offering up a warm smile, I say, "Good morning, handsome."

Instead of letting me go now that Griff is in here, Sebastian leans in and starts kissing my neck. Given how pissy it made Griff last night, I watch him.

He flicks a glance our way, his gaze lingering for a few seconds, but he proceeds to the cabinet above the coffee maker and grabs himself a mug.

As much as I enjoy my husband's affection, I know he's just testing Griff's reaction right now. That should make me enjoy it less, but nope.

Eventually, he concludes Griff is in a better place today and he gives me one last kiss on the lips before heading to the table and leaving me to finish breakfast.

Now that Sebastian isn't all over me, Griff drifts closer, taking a sip of his coffee and looking at the veggies on the counter. "Need any help?"

I shake my head as I finish chopping up the cauliflower and start on the broccoli. "Nope, I'm okay. Thank you, though." I miss a beat. "How'd you sleep?"

"Much better than I expected to," he answers. "Thanks for keeping me company."

He comes in for a brief kiss of his own now. "Of course." Then, flashing him a hopeful smile, I add, "I hope you'll come back to bed tonight, though. I'm greedy. I want both of my big, strong men in bed with me."

He rolls his eyes, but nods his head. "I'll come back to the bedroom."

We don't talk as I finish up the broccoli and move on to slice up a couple of potatoes.

Griff lingers by me like he'd rather stand over here than go sit with Sebastian.

I know he'll get over it. I know it's inevitable they'll lock horn sometimes—they always locked horns *sometimes*, and that was before they occupied all the same spaces. Now they're going to work together, live together, and sleep with me together.

Now that selling his house is less complicated, I hope they'll hurry that along. I like having Griff here, but I want it to feel permanent. I want him to make this his home, not shuttle his belongings between places—especially now that the other house is tarnished by what has happened to Ashley.

God, I don't think he's been back there since before, unless he went last night. I don't want to make him go alone.

Flipping the veggies in the pan, I take a step back and drift closer until I'm standing next to Griff. He's shirtless, wearing just a pair of sweatpants this morning. He looks damn good in just sweatpants.

"Have you gone back to the house yet?"

His gaze darkening, he looks down at his coffee cup and shakes his head.

"I'll go with you, if you want," I offer.

"I don't want to go there at all," he says.

Flicking a glance at Sebastian, I consider pointing out Sebastian could go instead, then he wouldn't have to. Given what he said last night, though, I doubt he'll take that route, even if it is easiest. He's such a stubborn brute sometimes.

Struck by a peculiar sting of fondness, I smile softly and lean my head on his shoulder. He's surprised by the contact, but he puts his coffee down so he can gently grab my waist and tug me around front, pulling me close.

"Good morning," he adds more tenderly. "I forgot to say that."

I lean in and hover above his lips for a moment before kissing the corner of his mouth. "Good morning right back."

"You snuck out of bed like a ninja."

I grin. "I had breakfast to make."

"Seb might've starved," he mockingly agrees.

I nod solemnly. "He probably would have."

Rolling his eyes, Griff says, "He wouldn't starve. The man can pour cereal into a bowl, can't he?"

"I've never appraised his cereal dumping skills, but it's just easier to assume the answer is no and feed him myself."

Sebastian pipes in from the table, proving he's eavesdropping. "I also don't eat cereal for breakfast. I'm above the 'cereal for breakfast' age."

"I don't think there's a cut-off," Griff states. "I've had cereal for breakfast lots of times as an adult."

"Yes, well, you didn't have Moira."

I nod my head in agreement. "I prefer a hot breakfast to start the day. With cereal, I'm always hungry again in an hour."

Unconvinced, Griff tells me, "Cereal one morning wouldn't have killed him—and hey, if it did, karma."

I scowl. "Hey, now."

Griff lifts his eyebrows, shrugging, but apparently not sorry he said it. "I'm just saying."

"You wanna say that a little louder—and to *me* instead of my wife?" Sebastian replies.

Placing a stabilizing hand on Griff's chest, I steal his attention before he can turn around and start fighting. "Come on, guys. Play nice. For me?" Since Sebastian requires no convincing, I flash my puppy dog eyes at Griff.

Sighing heavily, he said, "That's not fair."

"It's so fair."

"I shouldn't have to play nice. *He's* the one who doesn't play nice."

Smoothing my hands down over his muscular biceps, I tell him, "Yes, but we already knew that, so we can't really be surprised. Besides, he's been fair plenty of other times. Remember when he decided to let us fuck each other on the regular? Super nice."

"That was nice," Griff grudgingly admits.

"Uh-huh," I agree, grabbing his hands and planting them on my waist. "And now you get all the Moira time you want. A mean best friend wouldn't have agreed to that."

"I'm not saying he never has good ideas."

"His good ideas far outweigh his bad ones," I point out.

"Yeah, but his bad ones are murder. Do *I* get a free pass to kill someone and you'll still love me?"

I hear Sebastian's cup hit the table with far more force than it should and look up to see my husband standing.

Aw, shit.

His brow is furrowed, his jaw set. His blazing blue eyes are narrowed.

I attempt subtlety as I move in front of Griff, holding my hand out to intercept my husband's passions. "Honey—"

Sebastian interrupts, glaring at Griff. "You don't say shit like that to my wife. I'm done with this. I'm done with the sulking."

I place my second hand on Sebastian's chest and step closer, trying to ease him back.

It fails hard because Griff just comes closer from my other side. "What are you gonna do about it, then, huh? Kill me?"

"Griff," I snap, shooting a look of disapproval over my shoulder at him.

Instead of helping me keep things civil, my husband replies with menacing calm, "That depends; are you in my way?"

"He's kidding," I tell Griff.

"No, he fucking is not," Griff shoots back. "He killed Ashley."

Sebastian reaches past me to grab Griff by the throat, but I catch his arm and remain in his way. "Stop it. Please."

"You're an ungrateful bastard," Sebastian tells Griff. "I wish you'd left."

Gasping at the cruelty of that blow, I say, "You do not." I look back at Griff to reassure him. "You know he didn't mean that."

"I don't know anything anymore," Griff states, holding Sebastian's gaze and shaking his head.

"I do *everything* for you, and all you do is fucking bitch about it," Sebastian fires back. "You were falling apart at the seams. You were miserable. She was taking everything from you—from *us*. Everything we spent our whole goddamn lives building. Maybe you'll let people roll over you, Griff, but that's not how I work."

"No, because you're the one who does the rolling," he fires back. "Everything is your call. We open the businesses you want, buy the spaces you want, live where you want—I didn't even want to stay in Philly, but you didn't want to leave. Did I make a mess? Yeah, I made a fucking mess, but it was *my* mess. When you said you'd handle it, I thought you meant with lawyers, not with a fucking bullet in her skull!"

"Shut the fuck up," Sebastian says, shoving me back to get at him. "Stop fucking saying that. You think you're going to poison Moira against me? You think she'll believe you over me?"

"Stop it!" I call out, finally raising my voice.

Both men look at me, faintly surprised. I'm not generally noisy outside the bedroom, but *fuck*. They're still on either side of me, vibrating with barely restrained rage.

"Okay," I say, lowering my voice to a more civilized level. "There are a few elephants in this kitchen today. I wanted to just pretend they were part of the décor, but that doesn't seem to be working. You two have to stop attacking one another. Sebastian, you don't have to worry about Griff turning me on you. I told you, that isn't possible. He doesn't want to, anyway.

He loves you and you love him. You two are not opponents, you're partners, and it's time you remember that. We all lose with you on opposite ends. Now, you two got me into this fucking situation, and you're not going to turn on each other over some other woman. Are you?" I glance back at Griff, eyebrows rising expectantly.

Griff scowls, not appreciating my wording. "That's not fair."

"It is fair. You both love me, right? You both love each other? You both wanted this relationship?" Pointing to Griff, I say, "You emotionally blackmailed your best friend with abandonment issues into sharing his wife or losing you." I point to Sebastian. "You made me do this in the first place. Now I'm in it, I like it, and I'm attached—you two aren't going to fuck it up over a dead gold digger. Now, I'm sorry to say that, Griff, I know she was your wife, but she's not anymore. If you both love and want me so much, stop fighting over another fucking woman."

"We aren't fighting over—you make it sound... He *killed* someone."

"I don't care," I state.

At least now I have Sebastian's attention. He cocks his head, as if surprised.

"Now, let's put this behind us," I suggest. "Griff made a mess; Sebastian may have gone a little far in fixing it. Everybody feels badly about it, but it's done and over with. Going forward, Griff doesn't want you to make all his decisions for him. He wants to be consulted. He wants to feel that his input is respected and he has control over his life. In return, Griff is going to stop holding Ashley over your head like a golden ticket, because I'm the only person he could possibly be trying to influence, and I'm only going to say this one more time: I don't care. This is my family. Two days ago, my family was in trouble and now we're all free to be together. I say, we make the most of that freedom and get back to enjoying one another. That's reasonable, isn't it? Can we all agree to that?"

"I guess," Griff grumbles.

Sebastian just watches me. I take that as agreement.

"Okay, good," I say brightly. "Now, unless you both want your breakfast burned, stop trying to rip one another's throats out and let me finish cooking."

I keep one hand at each of their chests for a few seconds, then take a tentative step back. When they don't lunge at one another, I slowly lower my hands and take a few more steps back.

"Are we good?" I ask them, glancing between them like tigers running loose at the zoo.

"I can let it go if he can," Sebastian states, arms crossed over his chest.

"I guess, as long as he's not going to keep doing shit like this," Griff mutters.

"Do you have more wives I need to get rid of?" Sebastian asks dryly.

Griff cuts him a dry, unamused look. "I get the situation, but it was still a shitty fucking thing to do."

"I didn't say it wasn't," Sebastian agrees.

"And you should have told me what you were planning," Griff adds.

"Didn't want to get you involved. Plus, I knew you'd never go along with it."

I grimace. It was a stronger argument without that second half, but at least he's being honest, I guess.

"I can't feel good about this," Griff tells him.

"You don't need to feel good about it. That's why I took the burden onto my shoulders—so you wouldn't have to feel anything about it except relief."

I don't want to interrupt, but I have to duck between them to retrieve my scrambled egg mixture to pour over the other food in the skillet. "Don't mind me."

"Part of me does feel relieved," Griff admits. "But that just makes me feel worse."

Sebastian shrugs. "Wasn't your doing; no need to feel bad."

I dump the eggs in and set aside the bowl, grabbing my spatula.

"I'm sorry I said I wish you'd left," Sebastian says, surprising me. My husband is not a big apologizer.

Griff is dismissive. "I knew you didn't mean it. I'm sorry I told Moira things I shouldn't have."

I glance back over my shoulder to see how that one lands. Sebastian's gaze lingers on me, his lips tipped up at the corners. "That's all right. I kind of like knowing she loves me anyway."

Sparing him a little smile and a private wink, I remind him, "Like I said at the church, for better or worse. Now, why don't you two hug it out?"

Griff rolls his eyes. "We don't need to hug it out."

"Your new wife disagrees. Wives are always right." I gesture between them. "Go on, I'm waiting."

Griff still isn't all the way on board, but Sebastian doesn't wait. He grabs Griff and gives him a hug. My insides get all mushy and warm. Seb winks at me and smiles.

Yep, it's official.

I'm the luckiest woman in the world.

EPILOGUE
GRIFF

"You look so handsome."

I stand near the double doors of the crowded ballroom, like I'm ready to flee at any given moment. Moira stands before me in a dark blue ball gown, the cut of her dress drawing my poor, helpless eyes straight to her cleavage as she fixes my bowtie.

"There, perfect," she says, smoothing her hands across my chest and down my arms.

"I feel dumb wearing a tux," I tell her.

Eyebrows rising, she looks me over, making no attempt to hide her appreciation. "Well, you do not *look* dumb, if that's any consolation."

Putting my hands on her narrow waist, I draw her closer. "I'm tired of talking to these people. I want this thing to be over. I want to take you home and get you out of this dress."

"You and me both. I wish we could go home, cuddle up on the couch with Sebastian, and watch *Sabrina*."

"That is not where I thought you were going with that."

"You guys owe me a movie. You always owe me a movie.

Every single time I turn on a movie I like, you team up and distract me with sex. It's not fair. I never get to watch anything I like."

I cock an eyebrow. She's right, we do that, but half the time I think she picks the movie just because she knows we will. "I've never heard any complaints."

With a sly smile, she says, "I didn't say I had any."

"Then let's bail and do that instead."

"Nope. I've invested way too much time and effort into this benefit to beg off early. Come on, let's go find Sebastian while we have a chance," she says, grabbing my hand and dragging me across the ballroom.

Tonight we are attending—and hosting—a gala that Moira herself came up with and put together—the Better Tomorrow Ball, an annual gala in honor of Ashley Halliwell. It's kind of egregious, exalting Ashley's death given the circumstances, but Moira saw a chance to do good in the world in Ashley's name, and she went for it.

Even though I never really liked this kind of thing to begin with, I've gotta admit, Moira did a hell of a job. The ballroom is decorated beautifully, and the event is just about at capacity. Circular tables with elegant floral centerpieces fill the space around the dance floor, every single one bringing in thousands of dollars for suicide prevention programs. There's even a scholarship in Ashley's name given out to some high school senior who survived her own battle with depression and went on to have "better tomorrows."

It feels a little morbid to me, but it makes Moira feel better about what Seb did. That's what I tell myself, anyhow.

Either way, it's for a good cause. Not a cause that has a damn thing to do with Ashley, but I guess that doesn't matter.

Our table is right in front of the dance floor, way too close to the live music. Seb is sitting there now, looking profoundly bored until he sees Moira hauling me across the room. His expression lightens and he pushes back his chair to stand.

"Done socializing for the moment?" Seb asks.

"Hey, I'm the hostess, I can't just ignore everybody," she states.

"I disagree. You've done your part; now let them get drunk on champagne and make fools of themselves on the dance floor."

"I wish people would stop mentioning her," I say. "I never liked these things to begin with, but when they come with a dollop of guilt..." Regarding Seb, I ask, "You don't feel weird about being here?"

"Why should I?" he asks. "I poured plenty of money into sponsoring this damned event."

"Damned is right," I mutter. "We're all going to Hell."

"Well, if we do, we'll see Ashley again; we can tell her all about her party," Seb says easily.

"That's horrible," I state. "You're horrible."

As if innocent, he says, "What? She'd love it. Have you heard how nicely everyone is talking about her tonight? Nobody liked her that much when she was alive."

I hold up a hand and shake my head. "Just... stop talking."

Interceding, Moira goes straight into Seb's arms to draw his attention away. She wraps her arms around his neck and gazes up at him like he's the only man in the room. I'm not bothered by it, since just a few minutes ago she was looking at me the same way. "You're a real Prince Charming, you know that?"

He smirks at her. "Prince Charming isn't your type."

"True," she allows. "Still, I wouldn't say no if a certain dashing gentleman asked me to dance."

"You must be waiting for someone else, then, 'cause I don't

ask." Resting his hand possessively on Moira's hip, Seb glances over at me. "We'll be back."

I nod, dropping into my seat. "You kids have fun."

Moira's hand brushes my shoulder as she walks past. "Don't worry; I'll save the next dance for you."

She drags a little smile out of me. "Lucky me," I call before she gets too far away.

I say it like I'm joking, but she knows I mean it. Seb and I are the luckiest bastards around, no contest.

Moira looks back at me with a playfully narrowed gaze before Seb leads her out on the dance floor. I turn in my chair to watch them. I don't know why I do. It's not like I can't see her in his arms any day of the week—usually in fewer clothes. Usually right up close, where I can touch and kiss her, too; where Seb and I can team up to make her dizzy with pleasure, turn her to putty in either of our hands.

My mind is wandering to places it shouldn't when I'm in a ballroom full of people, so I turn back around and grab my drink, tipping it back, shifting to accommodate the slight bulge in my pants. Just a couple more hours.

Suddenly, a brunette woman in a long black gown comes up to my table, offering me a little smile. "You guys sure know how it's done, don't you?" she remarks.

Since I've never seen her before and I damn sure don't know what she's talking about, I raise a questioning eyebrow. "Excuse me?"

She indicates our table, which should seat eight. We bought out the table just for the three of us. "You must really like your space."

"Bad table manners. Didn't want to embarrass ourselves."

Grinning, she drops into the empty seat beside mine. "You're Griffin Halliwell, right?"

I don't know why she knows me, since I sure don't recognize her. "Yep, that's me."

Her smile dims and she nods. "I just wanted to stop over and say how sorry I am for your loss. I think it's beautiful that you're doing all this in tribute to your wife. You must have really loved her."

That drains the humor right out of me.

Noticing that, she grimaces. "Sorry. I didn't mean to... I'm sure tonight sucks enough, and there I go—"

I raise a hand to stop her, shaking my head. "You're fine. Thanks."

She's still sitting here and I don't really know what to say, so I grab my glass and take another drink. Her eyes go straight to my left hand, to the wedding band on my finger. "You still wear your ring," she remarks.

I look at my hand, now that she mentions it. "Uh, no. I mean, yeah, I wear a ring, but it's not..."

It would be complicated to explain to someone who *wasn't* sitting here offering me condolences at my dead wife's benefit, but I can't even begin to explain it under these circumstances. Normally, people see the ring, but know just enough not to ask about it.

"I think it's sweet," she says, somehow mistaking my hesitation for something else.

"I'm not in mourning. It's not like that."

For some reason, she slightly brightens.

Everything I say somehow comes off as positive to her, so I just stop talking. I feel like I'm digging myself a hole—probably my own guilty conscience, but it's still uncomfortable.

"Do you dance?" she asks.

"What?"

Nodding her head toward the floor, she says, "I think they're about to play another slow one. I mean, if you think it would be weird, I understand, but if not...."

I didn't see that coming at all, so I'm sitting here dumbstruck when Moira comes back and leans down behind me, wrapping her arms around my neck and leaning close. My new friend's eyes widen at the clear show of affection/ownership.

"Am I interrupting?" Moira asks.

"Not at all," I assure her, placing my hand over hers.

The newcomer's gaze drops to Moira's hand beneath mine, to her wedding band that matches mine. She can't see Seb's hand as he walks around to his seat, but if she could she'd see he has the exact same one. Even without knowing that, she's wildly confused.

"Sorry," I tell her, pushing back from the table and putting a hand on Moira's waist. "This dance is spoken for."

Moira doesn't say anything when we're standing there, but as I haul her away, she says, "All your dances are spoken for, mister, not just this one."

I grin at her possessiveness. "You're allowed to have two lovers, but I'm not allowed to dance with another woman?"

"Absolutely," she says with a vehement nod.

I smile down at her as I pull her close on the dance floor. "You're the only one I want to dance with, anyhow."

Her blue eyes sparkle with warmth as she secures her arms around my neck and sways with me. "Good."

I hold Moira close as the song goes on, breathe her in when she rests her head against my shoulder and sighs. I love when she does that. I love when I can feel her contentment rolling off of her in waves.

This is my home. Not the house we all live in together or the bed where we fall asleep each night.

This. This is where I want to live, in moments like these.

With Moira pressed against me, the smell of her, the taste of her…

Well, hell, I can't taste her right now, can I?

Gently lifting her chin until she pulls back, I lean down and fix that. I taste her lips and she opens for me so readily. Even here, in this crowd full of people, her hunger for me bleeds out of her in soft little sighs, in the way her heart rate kicks up. Her teeth catch my bottom lip and I growl low in my throat, yanking her hips against mine.

"Keep that up, baby, I'll haul your little ass right out of this ballroom."

Grinning as she lingers close, she teases, "Is that supposed to be a threat?"

"Nope," I murmur, leaning in to nibble on her ear. "It's a promise."

Her head drifts forward and sags against my shoulder. "Stop tempting me. You know we can't leave. Between you and Seb, I swear to God, you make it impossible for a girl to get a night out with clothes on."

"You prefer a night in with clothes off," I point out.

"I *do*," she agrees, strongly. "Why do we ever leave the house? We should stop doing that. There's nothing for us out here."

As if to emphasize her point, I catch an older woman watching us, her mouth pursed in disapproval.

After a few months of keeping things quiet about our relationship, Sebastian decided it was time to take it public. He wanted to control the narrative, he said. Didn't want people thinking me and Moira were doing anything we shouldn't. Moira, of course, was fine with whatever he wanted, but I was a little more worried about it.

Ultimately, though, I wanted to be able to take Moira out

from time to time, and I wanted to be able to kiss and touch her the same way he could. I didn't want anyone thinking anything bad about Moira either, so I came around to it.

Most people who found out where surprised. Some didn't care; a couple thought it was interesting; some thought it was weird, and a few became irrationally outraged by our situation. The woman glaring daggers at Moira's back right now is one of them. On impulse, I run my hand protectively down her back, like I can fend off her bitter disapproval. Of course, I can't. The judgmental old broad hones in on the wedding band I wear to symbolize my commitment to our relationship, and her lip curls up in disgust.

Keeping my hand on Moira's back protectively, I close my hand but for my middle finger. The old biddy gasps, her gaze jumping to mine, and I give her my most charming smile as I flip her off.

Mind your business, lady.

She huffs and storms off the dance floor like I've ruined her night.

Oh well. She sure hasn't ruined mine. I still get to hold the most beautiful woman in the room and call her mine. I get to build a life and a family with my two best friends. Somehow all three of us were lucky enough to find each other; this perfect mix of cast-offs the world didn't have a proper place for. We made a place.

A lot of people look at us and see something bizarre, something sordid, maybe something sad. They look at us and think we share because we have to.

We don't *have* to share; we *get* to.

NOTES AND ACKNOWLEDGEMENTS

I hope you enjoyed the story of Sebastian, Griff, and Moira! If you enjoyed *Stitches* and feel like shouting about it, a review would be much-appreciated! :)

If you're new to my books and you enjoyed this one, make sure you check out my Morelli family series! I wrote this book (Sebastian, in particular) after completing that one; I was trying to come down from my Morelli hangover and transition into my next project. If you like your love interests with a touch of darkness, Mateo Morelli has it in spades.

That series isn't a ménage romance. (There are some excessively hot ménage fantasy deleted scenes in the last book, though, which is sort of what inspired me to write a full-length ménage love story.) The journey the Morelli family takes you on is ten kinds of crazy, and lots of sexy fun. It gets a little darker than this one, though, so if you have dark romance triggers, it may not be a great fit. If you don't, run and grab *Accidental Witness* so you can #meetthemorellis!

Accidental Witness (Morelli Family, #1)
Amazon: http://amzn.to/2hUyVk2
Amazon UK: My Book
Amazon CA: My Book
Amazon AU: My Book

If you're looking for the Sam Mariano club house, I have a reader group on Facebook you could join. :)

Sam Mariano's general reader group

Special thank you to the people who helped me make this book what it is: Jennifer Curtis, alpha reader extraordinaire. Now you have plenty of Sebastian to enjoy! Ginger, Krista, and Sara—thank you for your input and your eagle eyes, helping me iron out those pesky wrinkles!

As always, thank you to the wonderful ARC readers and bloggers who help spread the word! You guys are the greatest!

Thank you for reading!

- Sam Mariano

ALSO BY SAM MARIANO

Contemporary romance standalones

Untouchable (bully romance)

The Boy on the Bridge (second chance bully romance)

The Imperfections (forbidden romance)

Descent (dark billionaire romance)

How the Hitman Stole Christmas (unconventional, a pinch of mafia)

Mistletoe Kisses (student-teacher romance novella)

Coming-of-age, contemporary bully duet

Because of You

After You

Forbidden, taboo romance

Irreparable Duet

If you're a **series reader**, be sure to check out her super binge-able Morelli family series! It's dark and twisty mafia romance, and the first book is *Accidental Witness*

ABOUT THE AUTHOR

Sam Mariano loves to write edgy, twisty love stories with complicated characters you're left thinking about long after you turn the last page. Her favorite thing about indie publishing is the ability to play by your own rules!

If she isn't reading one of the thousands of books on her to-read list, writing her next book, or playing with her lovely daughter... actually, that's about all she has time for these days.

Feel free to find Sam on Facebook, Goodreads, TikTok, or her blog—she loves hearing from readers! She's also available on Instagram @sammarianobooks, and you can sign up for her totally-not-spammy newsletter HERE

If you have the time and inclination to leave a review, however short or long, she would greatly appreciate it! :)

Printed by Amazon Italia Logistica S.r.l.
Torrazza Piemonte (TO), Italy

56691794R00208